I0788188

Also by Amanda Casey

Ocean Apothecary Series
Blue Mermaid Memories
Blue Reflections
Tidal Ancestry
Ocean Origins

Witches & Demons Series
A Demon's Book of Shadows
A Witch's Forbidden Bloom

Join Amanda's newsletter to receive a free novella!
amandacaseybooks.com

Ocean Origins

Book Three of the Ocean Apothecary Series

Written & Illustrated by
Amanda Casey

To my readers.
Thank you for swimming to the stars with me.

CONTENT WARNING

This book contains situations and themes that include blood and violence, language, explicit sexual intimacy, death, ptsd, and hallucinations.

CONTENTS

PROLOGUE
Moon Goddess

Damien's feet were startlingly warm, given the fact that he stood in freezing, ankle-deep water. Moments before, he'd seen Amy, and a stag with a starlit crown that silhouetted a giant mountain.

After seeing Amy, Maria had appeared. His ghostly wife from his past had walked with him along the beach, stating that someone wanted to speak with him.

When he'd asked who the individual was, she had replied, "*The moon goddess you've spent the past ten years painting.*"

He stood before a giant moonlit temple that looked like something from a different time. The stone exterior was illuminated by the moon, which cast the markings he assumed were hieroglyphics in silver light. A tall, rectangular door sat at the temple's center.

His feet shifted in the sand at the base of the staircase that led toward the dark door. Something about the setting felt unnatural—an illusion, even. The scent of spice and humidity drifted on the warm breeze, stirring his senses. Maybe all of this bizarre imagery was from a bad shot of whiskey. One of his cousins had absolutely slipped some extra shots of alcohol into his drink. While it wasn't uncommon for his family to play pranks at the annual Malloch Christmas gathering, he'd never been this loopy for so long.

Prior to seeing Amy, the stag, and now this strange temple, he'd been hunting with his daughter for fairies that afternoon, before a storm blew in. A dull ache struck his chest. That memory bled through him like he was reliving it. He had no fight in him to make it disappear. He had one choice—to relive that memory and grieve it. He knew what had happened shortly after he'd experienced it.

Sophie had been next to him. Her little fingers were interwoven in his hand. She refused to let go of him, rooting her bare feet into the sandy beach they had scoured in Scotland.

"Daddy, the fae live down in there," she said, pointing to where now loomed the ominous moonlit temple. Silver light draped over the giant stone structure, illuminating an image he was very familiar with.

His moonlit signature—what he'd spent the past decade signing his paintings with—decorated the entire structure. The image glowed silvery blue, the spiral shimmering brighter than the moonlit reflection below it.

He squeezed his fingers into his palm, remembering what it felt like to have his daughter's small hand there. Grief did strange, unpredictable things to one's emotions and sense of reality at times.

He walked toward the temple, ascending the steps. A few torches lined the hallway, illuminating the space. More of the moonlit hieroglyphics decorated the stones. Voices echoed off the walls, the words spoken in a different tongue.

"Alcyone."

"Merope."

"Electra."

"*Celaaaaaaeeeeeeennnnoooooooo...*"

The last one sent a shiver up his spine. The voice was more like a war horn crying out into the night.

He kept walking, the sounds building inside of him. The voices harmonized in an impossible way. The words and tones created colors, painting an image for him. He stopped as the moonlight flooding through a window illuminated a tall ghostly figure. Flowing robes of light clung to her body, offsetting her from the other blurry figures.

The light in her eyes was beyond anything he'd seen before. Her skin was as white as her hair. She towered over him, holding her hands at her sides as a pair of luminous wings arched over him.

Damien took a step back, startled by just how large she was. "Who are you?"

"I am the moon goddess who created the symbol you have spent the past decade painting. My name is Isis."

Damien shook his head. Sure, he'd signed his paintings with the lunar symbol, but he most certainly hadn't been painting a moon goddess. Not that he believed, however.

Isis's hand rose, fingers beckoning in a come-hither motion. "Son of Ewan, walk forward."

Damien squinted into her impossible light. "I don't know who you are speaking of. Who is Ewan?"

Isis's fingers came to his forehead, and a light pulsed through him. A bright, searing light that illuminated the sky, blackening the stars. An image flashed before him.

First came an ocean as wide as the horizon.

Then came the first cry of his daughter.

Then, the last hug he gave Maria before she and Sophie left in the car.

Emptiness settled upon him. He remembered his art studio where he'd spent a decade alone, painting through the night, wishing the moon would offer him some kind of guidance for the loneliness that had settled deep into his soul. He'd been painting the day he first saw Selia at the Celtic Sea. He'd seen a blue light dancing on her that day, one that seemed to heal him. She'd brought light back into his life in ways he never believed to be possible.

Tears burned the corners of his eyes, bringing him to his knees. He stared up at Isis, blinded by her incredible beauty. "What do you want with me?"

Isis lowered her wings, allowing moonlight to flood over Damien's body. His eyelids became heavy, and they closed.

"You will go to retrieve something of great importance to Selia, an item that I have long intended for her to inherit. My temple is where you will find its origin."

PART I
INHERITANCE

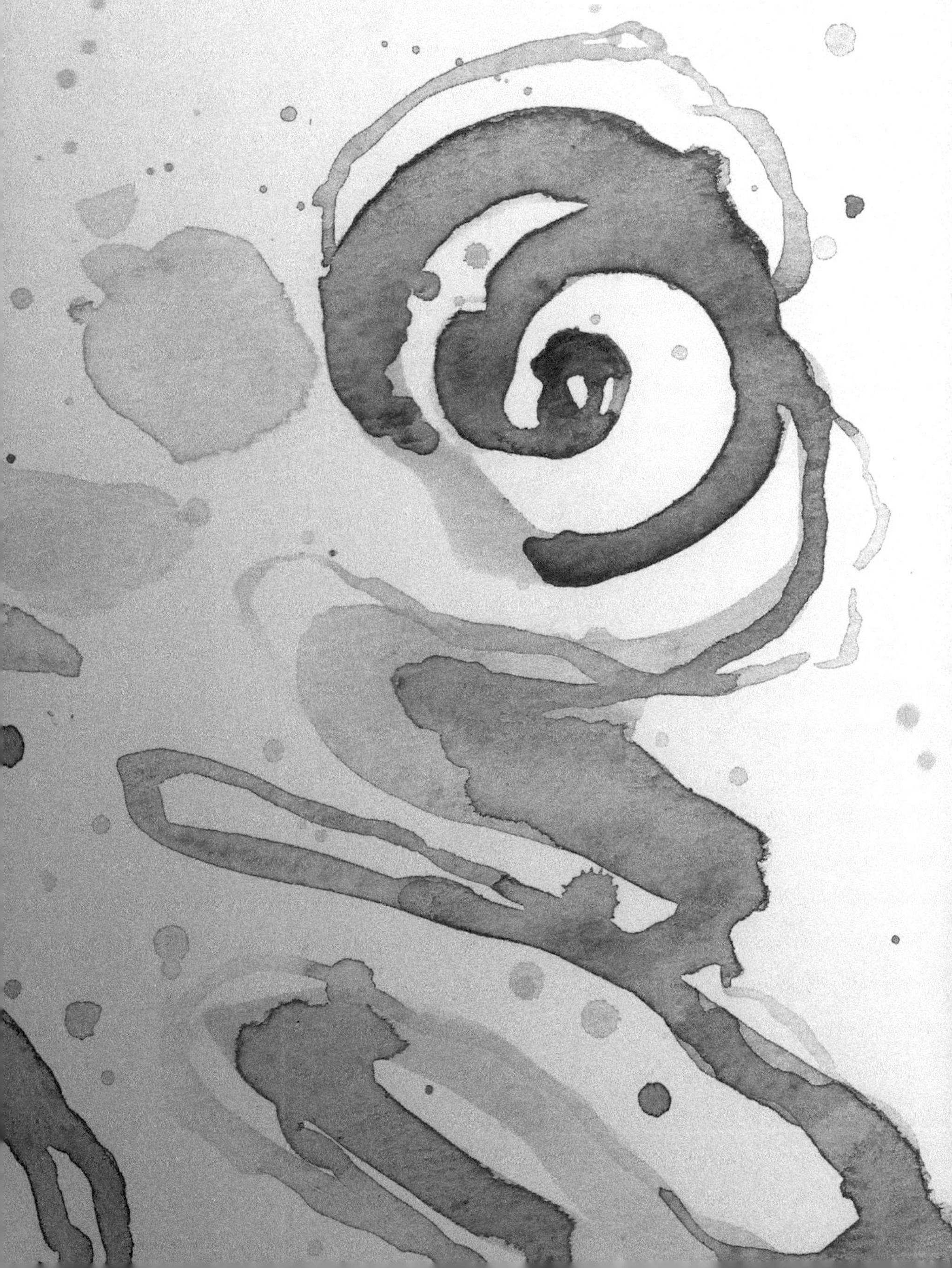

I
EGYPT
Damien

"Human, wake up."

Water splashed Damien in the face, surging into his mouth and nose. He coughed, blinking into the light. He lay on a hard, soggy surface. The movement of water sloshed around him, forcing him upright.

He was propped onto an algae-coated rock, facing the sea. A few boats drifted in and out of the water. The puttering sound of engines and voices echoed around him. Children tossed stones into the water, then ran off laughing.

He hoisted himself up, squinting into the sunlight. Where the heck was he? He patted his soggy jeans. No wallet. He was all wet and had an awful splitting headache. He needed to dry off, which shouldn't take long according to the temperature of wherever he'd ended up. The air was hot, almost too difficult to breathe. This place was nothing like Scotland. Where was this horrible wasteland?

He blinked a few times. He had to be imagining things. Were the blurry triangles dancing in the mirage the *Pyramids*?

"You are in Cairo, Egypt," a voice rumbled like thunder into his head.

He jumped from the rock, sloshing through the water toward land. "Who was that?"

A low, growling rumble followed, echoing out across the water. *"I'm Celaeno's storm dragon."*

Damien tilted his head to the side. Water must have gotten into his ears. No way had the thunderous voice replied to his question.

A *storm dragon*? What was that?

He hopped from one rock to the next, hoping to ground himself. *Celaeno* was one of the names he remembered echoing in the temple in the dream.

"*Celaeno is an ancestral salt mother.*"

Damien didn't care about the names he'd heard, or the ancestral mother of the sea. The only mother he wanted to get back to was the one who was about to give birth to his baby.

He hopped onto the beach. His shoes squelched with every step he took. A wave sloshed toward him, gripping his ankle and stopping him.

"*Stay close to the river. Isis has requested an important task of you.*"

Try as he might, Damien couldn't free himself from the watery restraint clinging to his ankle. He spun on his heel, facing the water. "What does Isis want with me?"

"*Isis has given you your task. You must retrieve what she has requested from her temple—an item that she wants Selia to inherit. One does not ignore the request of a moon goddess.*"

Damien steadied himself as the water released him. He squinted into the bright light that reflected off the water. Here he was, being told by a storm dragon to retrieve some inheritance for Selia from an Egyptian temple?

He was definitely losing his mind.

He spun on his heel, searching for the storm dragon who kept pestering him. A cloud of water vapor hovered over the river, which he assumed was the dragon's source. "What is your name?"

"*Balfour is what the Order calls me.*"

Damien blinked into the light. Why did that name sound so familiar? And why did his head hurt just thinking about it? "I don't know how the hell you brought me here, but I'm going home to find Selia."

The water thrashed, splashing him. "*I won't let you see her until you do what Isis has requested of you. The only humans she would trust to retrieve Selia's inheritance are the Sons of Atlantean Kings.*"

"Son of *what*? I have no idea what that means."

"*You don't need to. You only need to do as you are told.*"

"What are you going to do to stop me?" Damien ground out, the hot, dry air burning his nostrils.

"*I don't know, drag you out into the Mediterranean Sea and leave you for dead?*"

Damien ground his jaw. The sooner he did what this storm dragon named Balfour told him, the sooner he could see Selia. With no wallet and no phone, it was impossible for him to get a hold of her.

The name *Balfour* suddenly lit up in his mind. He remembered the towering man inside of the Rusty Selkie months ago who wore a black biker jacket with a dragon snaking up between his massive shoulders.

Balfour was the giant, grizzly man who was Alexandra's henchman.

"Balfour? You're a *dragon*?" Damien stammered.

"*Yes, now get moving. I've never been one for small talk.*"

"Where is Alex?"

"*Alex is dead.*"

Damien's stomach hollowed. "I don't understand, how did she die?"

"*If you don't listen to me, the selkie who killed Alex could harm Selia.*"

Damien swallowed. A selkie had murdered Alex? "Fine. Take me to this temple."

"*We must travel up the Nile,*" Balfour's voice thundered again. Low and icy, the sound made Damien's ears ache. "*Return to the water. It's best not to keep Isis waiting.*"

Damien returned to the Nile, stopping where the sand met the brown water. Like a serpent, the water coiled around his legs.

2

ZAKAI

Selia

Wind, rain, and thunder rattled the high windows in Selia's room. She sat in a large fabric chair, her fingers thumbing over one of Damien's paintbrushes. She'd found his brush, along with his frozen watercolor set, on the beach when she washed out of Masika's tidal cavern almost two months ago.

She gazed out the window, watching snowflakes flutter down from the sky. The past few weeks had been the emptiest she'd felt in her life. Days blended into weeks for the time she'd spent locked behind the sterile walls of the mental institution.

Gwen discovered her the morning after the winter solstice gathering standing drenched and nearly naked on the beach, screaming at the sea. She'd screamed about Sika, the local selkie, murdering an Iridescent, along with a storm dragon who had tried to form a tidal bond with her over three thousand years ago. Thinking about Balfour only made her angry. She had tried multiple times to connect with him, only to have silence follow. She wondered if he had given up on the tidal bond they were supposed to create together.

After Gwen found her with lacerations on her arms and chest, it was assumed she'd tried to take her life. In the eyes of Damien's family, Selia was insane. Gwen, thus emitted her into Scotland's leading mental institution in Edinburgh for her own safety.

Selia shifted in her chair. No matter what position she found herself in, she could never become comfortable. Without Damien, her own grasp on reality seemed to slip away. She was alone, and pregnant with his baby.

Her hand began to tremble on the arm wrest. Her skin was doing that strange thing again. Even if her engagement ring hadn't been confiscated, she wouldn't be able to wear it, anyway.

She wiggled her fingers, watching as the chair and floor became visible through her skin. The physical world seemed to fall away as her hand became transparent. This new ability, whatever it was, had something to do with her salt aura.

Masika had done the same thing, appearing and disappearing as she pleased, manipulating her form to terrorize Selia. She wondered if their fight in the cavern had somehow infected her with the salt venom.

She grabbed a magazine from her bedside table. The one good thing about being locked up in solitary confinement, was the fact that she was allowed time to do plenty of reading. She'd been obsessing over baby names. While thumbing through a magazine one day, she'd stumbled across popular baby names originating from Egypt. The name Naunet translated to *mysterious goddess of the ocean.* Masika, too, had a meaning, *born during the rain.*

Tap, tap, tap.

Selia straightened herself in her chair, finding a fuzzy brown face with ink-drop eyes peering through the icy window. Perched atop the windowsill was a familiar fae bat.

Selia stood from her chair and opened the window, allowing Peppercorn inside. Peppercorn fluttered in, her wings flitting past her ear as she hovered in front of her.

"Settle down," Selia said, holding her arm out for Peppercorn to perch upon.

Peppercorn flitted down to her arm, landing. She swung herself forward, dropping so that she hung from her sweater. Clipped in her foot was a tiny roll of parchment. Pixie had since started using the bat as a messenger. The parchment was no bigger than what you would find in a fortune cookie, fastened to her ankle with a rubber band.

Selia worked her fingers over the rubber band, tugging it off her little foot.

Peppercorn crawled her way up Selia's arm, perching atop her shoulder. She buried her fuzzy face into her hair, nuzzling her ear as Selia unfolded the note.

The texture of the paper was different from anything Pixie had sent her. It was thick and coarse, reminding her of papyrus. She read over the note, finding a simple message inside.

```
Meet by South window.
This is about Alex, and your inheritance.
```

Selia's breathing stopped. Alex had been engulfed by the inferno of Masika's venomous rage, murdered before her very eyes. Who was asking her to meet with them?

And what was this *inheritance* mentioned?

Knock, knock, knock.

Peppercorn jumped from Selia's shoulder and took off out the window as the door opened.

A nurse poked her head inside. "Selia? You have visitation hours."

Selia stayed a few paces between the nurse who escorted her down the hall.

The nurse stopped so abruptly, that Selia almost ran into her. "You have one hour."

Selia nodded, dipping into the room. She was allowed inside the common area where other patients socialized. She found a seat close to the door, facing the south-most window the note mentioned. Most of the patients were quiet, busying themselves with board games, cards, or reading.

Peppercorn usually didn't show herself, as she knew it caused some of the patients distressed. But her tiny brown body went flitting back and forth across the window.

The lights in the room blinked, the faded. Nobody seemed to notice, but Selia. Her salt nodes began to ring with the gentle buzz of electricity.

Another woman manifested in the corner of the room, standing by the window where Peppercorn was busy doing somersaults in the wind. She wore long light grey robes that tapered down to her legs. Her arms were clasped behind her back. She was tall and slender, her white hair tied back into two braids that draped over her shoulders. Whether or not her ears were pointed, she couldn't tell, as the tips were concealed by her hair.

Her eyes swept the room. Selia knew from the colors glinting in them that the woman wasn't only a nymph, she was an Iridescent.

She snapped her fingers just like Alex had done many times before, and the room faded away. "Now we can discuss your inheritance," she said, her voice echoing in the void of shadows that consumed the sitting room.

"Who are you?" Selia asked.

The Iridescent held up her hand, signaling for her not to stand. "My name is Zakai. I am Alexandra's superior and a representative for Gaia's Codex."

Selia vaguely remembered Alex mentioning a document Naunet was in charge of inscribing: a document the Order had some duty to preserving and protecting. "Does Gaia's Codex have something to do with storm scrolls?"

Zakai nodded, sending a few strands of her white hair into her eyes. "Yes. Among many other duties the midwife of the sea performed, creating storm scrolls documenting the bonds between sea nymphs and storm dragons was one of her primary responsibilities."

"Do you have any idea where Balfour is? I've tried calling out to him, but he never responds."

"He is currently with Damien. The two are working to recover your inheritance."

Selia's heart trembled. She'd wondered why Damien hadn't tried to call, or visit her. The last memories she had of him juxtaposed between reality, and hallucination. He'd passed out at the winter solstice gathering, and she'd last seen him unconscious in a hospital bed.

Then, Alex had shown up to help her pick up where she left off developing her salt trancing talents.

"Alex only started the process in helping you to further develop your talents," Zakai's thoughts entered Selia's mind, apparently reading her own thoughts too.

"Is that what you are here to do?"

"Your inheritance will shed new light on what you are truly capable of, Blind Moon." Zakai's eyes narrowed hawk-like onto her. "What are the last memories that you have of the midwife of the sea?"

Selia closed her eyes, thinking back to what she had seen in the tidal cavern. Alex and Balfour had brought her to the giant tidal stones in order for her to see a discussion between Naunet and Alex regarding blue minca and storm dragons. "I can see her face. I can hear her crying." Her breath shuddered as she reopened her eyes. "Then, there is nothing but darkness."

Zakai reached into her robes, retrieving another item. "That darkness is what your inheritance will hopefully remedy."

"Is Naunet alive?"

"Naunet's whereabouts are unknown, even by the Order. It is assumed, however, that she is still alive."

Selia's stomach pitted. Would Masika attempt to find her older sister?

"*Not after what you did to her,*" Zakai entered her mind again. She reached out, offering Selia the item she had withdrawn from her robes. "Tell me if you can read this."

Selia took the item from Zakai. An oblong stone with a chalky texture settled into her palm. "Why are you giving me a salt trancing talisman?"

"You've seen this symbol many times at this point, but never have you attempted to understand its origin."

Selia squinted at Zakai. "I don't understand what you mean. I know how salt trancing talismans are made—they are created when a sea nymph gathers salt chrysalises from a male minca moth, and presents them to a storm dragon. If he chooses to bond with her, they transform into talismans."

Zakai's mouth twisted. "History does not always tell the full story of origin." Her hand closed Selia's fingers over the stone. "Now, tell me what you see."

Selia closed her eyes. Maybe this was Zakai's strange attempt at teaching her yet another bizarre salt trancing ritual. Blue light flashed in her periphery. The sea manifested before her. But the sea she saw was not multi-colored—brilliant streaks of pigment danced across paper.

Selia reopened her eyes. "Damien's watercolor paintings are what I see."

The corners of Zakai's eyes creased into a smile. "I think you are ready."

"Ready for what?"

"Use the talisman to discover Balfour's original name."

"His name isn't Balfour?"

Zakai shook her head. "The Order named Celaeno's storm dragon Balfour after Atlantis sank. If you summon him with his true name, he cannot ignore you. You must call him by his true name if he is to return Damien and your inheritance to you."

Zakai folded her arms beneath her robes like Alex had done so many times before. Her white braids trembled. With a flash of light, the shadows evaporated, returning Selia to the room. The salt trancing talisman in her palm pulsed a brilliant ultramarine blue.

3
NEPHTHYS

Amy

The earth smelled of dampness and salt down in the deep, dark corridors of wherever Amy had gone. Her mother, Amphitrite, strode ahead, her long green robes trailing along the ground, collecting the curling ends of sea grasses that grew along the stone path.

Moments ago, Amy had been atop the sacred mountain in the snowy ruins of an ancient temple, bleeding somewhere between the past and present. The seven ancestral salt mothers had gathered around Masika's spirit, chanting *minca* as they mourned her.

Amy had blinked, and the seven ancestral salt mothers, including Celaeno, disappeared, leaving her to follow her own mother down the dark path. Stone walls surrounded them, enclosing like a tomb on either side.

"Mother, wait," Amy said as she slowed her steps. Her fingers ached from the cold that didn't belong to Winter Forest. "What happened to the ancestral salt mothers? To Masika?"

Her mother kept walking, her long red hair swaying behind her.

Amy took off in a jog as she struggled to keep up with her powerful strides. She couldn't shake the cold, no matter how much she shivered, or wrapped her cloak around her. The starlit crown of the mighty Errindoor began to fade in her memory. The scent of woodsmoke and Ewan's blood still filled her nose. The animal hide clothing Ewan had given her was now frayed and sunken as though time had weathered it.

Amy's footsteps slowed as the chamber narrowed. "Mother, where are we?"

Amphitrite ducked as the ceiling dipped, making walking more difficult. "The temple we are in is connected to Poseidon's crown. That is all I can tell you about our whereabouts."

Poseidon's crown. Amy had heard of the term before, yet her memory of what it was and what purpose it served failed her. All she knew was that after Atlantis sank, Poseidon's crown broke apart, scattering the many storm dragon territories that once held the Abyss together.

She focused on the stone walls lining the path she and her mother strode upon. Hard, shiny textures clung to the damp surface. The cavern was rich with species of coral she had never seen before. Amy stretched her fingers toward one of the corals, curious about their bizarre purple and red color.

"Don't touch those," her mother said, her voice filling the cavern. She paused in her step, turning to face Amy with an outstretched hand.

Amy met her mother's warm gaze. Even when she was a child and her mother was upset with her, the green of her eyes always brought whimsical warmth in an unsettling way. "Why?"

A long red lock of curly hair unfolded over her shoulder. "There are many unidentified species of coral living within the crown, many of which are venomous."

Amy pulled her fingers away from the wall. The last thing she wanted to do was think about anything that was venomous. Her stomach had twisted itself into a fury of knots regarding what happened between her and Masika. She could still taste the bitterness of the past. A dull ache constantly filled her chest.

"What will happen to Masika's spirit?" Amy asked, remembering how she had discovered her atop the sacred mountain, surrounded by the ancestral salt mothers.

Amphitrite's green eyes darkened. "Her spirit is now in the hands of the Egyptian goddess of death."

Amy chewed the inside of her cheek. Her mother kept her answers brief, and short, as though someone might be listening to her speak. The Egyptian goddess of life was Isis, and her temple had been where Naunet had worked. She knew little about Isis's sister, other than that her name was Nephthys.

"My daughter's spirit would not have been in his situation, had it not been for your daughter's careless obsession with the past," a female voice hissed from the dark.

Shadows tendrilled before them, serpent-like in form. Coiling and folding at the base of a woman's feet, they dispersed across the path like an onyx fog. Dark fabric clung to her narrow body, covering her legs and torso. Porcelain white skin shone upon her chest and arms. High angular cheekbones complimented her prominent lips and strong, straight nose. Her eyes were as dark as the water that glistened on either side of the path. Amy recognized the sea nymph's cold glare. Pherusa had the same stunning, dark beauty as both of her daughters.

Amy's stomach twisted. Her aunt Pherusa always had a way with words, most of which were not warm. A condescending tone always followed her assumptions and accusations. Sometimes Amy wondered how she was related to her mother.

Amphitrite took a step toward her sister. "I know you must be worried about Masika. But she, like my own daughter, has always had a rebellious spirit. Maybe it is time that she learned to deal with the consequences of her actions."

A smirk tugged at the corners of Pherusa's thin wine-red lips. "Be grateful that your daughter is not a salt daughter of Celaeno. You do not know rebelliousness until you have raised one of your own," Pherusa scolded, her eyes landing on Amy once again. A shimmer of rage filled them. She held out her hand, and one of the coiling shadows tendrilled toward her, the evaporated.

Turning on her heel, she took off into the dark chamber. Amphitrite followed her shadowy sister.

Amy's feet remained rooted on the ground. She didn't want to think about seeing Masika again. Having Pherusa stare her down was enough to convince her that she blamed her for Masika's current situation.

Water dripping from the invisible ceiling convinced Amy to follow her mother and her aunt into the darker chambers of Poseidon's crown. Their footsteps echoed off the walls. More shadows coalesced in the chamber as she rounded the corner.

Amy spotted her mother and aunt, both standing at the edge of a giant pool. They appeared so different from each other, with her mother's rich red curls, and

Pherusa's straight black hair. Instead of approaching them, Amy decided to stay back and watch the event unfold.

Another much larger figure stood at the center of the pool, their wrists and arms forming wave-like movements. The individual's back faced them. Long black wing-like structures arched from their shoulders, curving up atop their head. The figure was the goddess of death, Nephthys.

Nephthys maneuvered around a pedestal at the center of the pool. Another figure sat before her.

Pherusa's daughter sat beneath Nephthys, her attention focused toward the water surging into the cavern. Masika's eyes had no pupils, just empty voids that matched the same inky black color of the water.

Pherusa knelt before Nephthys, her head bowed. "Nephthys, goddess of the dead, I beg of you to help me recover the spirit of my second-born daughter."

Nephthys held her hands over her head, tugging down the tendrilling shadows from her onyx wings. They fell around Masika in sheets, until she was swallowed by them completely. The goddess of death turned to face Pherusa, one of her sharp eyebrows arching into her dark bangs. "The fate of your daughter's spirit is not for me to decide. The Chamber of Salt contains other spirits who in turn, are allowed to share their opinions about displaced sea nymph souls other than I."

A whimper escaped Pherusa as Amy's mother set her hand on her shoulder. "Please, Naunet refuses to speak with me. She ran away after the plague of salt venom broke out. Masika is the only daughter I have left to truly call my own."

Nephthys's gaze settled onto Pherusa, liquid fire and ash stirring behind her eyes. "Why don't we consult with Naunet's scribe?"

4
THE TEMPLE OF ISIS
Damien

Damien's head throbbed so fiercely, he thought he was either suffering from a concussion, or the worst hangover of his life. He'd spent what felt like hours drifting in a strange, water-filled passage that had no end in sight. Apparently, storm dragons could not only take on a human or a dragon form, but they had the ability to manipulate water in ways that didn't seem natural.

A solid surface he assumed was Balfour's body sat beneath him, shimmering with silver and purple iridescence. Every time Damien asked Balfour what the passage was, the storm dragon gave a growl that rumbled and cracked in his mind. Balfour's thunderous protests became so deafening, that he finally gave up.

As the water cocoon enveloped him, the droning sound of the liquid began to put him into a lucid state of mind. His thoughts drifted to Selia.

How was she doing? And how was their baby? And who was this selkie that killed Alex? Did that mean that Selia was also in danger?

How his body ached just thinking about them. He still had no idea how much time had passed since the winter solstice gathering, and him waking. The sooner he got on with this business Balfour wanted him to contend with in the temple, the quicker he could hopefully get back to her.

Finally, the river seemed to change. The liquid passage Damien was encased in evaporated, revealing the light of day. While the sun dipped on the horizon, the air was still scorching hot. Groves of papyrus lined the river, which gracefully thinned into a shimmering orange and yellow surface.

The spray thickened, stirring Damien out of his lackadaisical state of being. The river became smooth, the texture calm and silky. A few boats cluttered the water. An island appeared dead-set within the river.

Membranous fins enveloped Damien as his journey up the Nile finally came to an end.

"*This is where you can jump,*" Balfour grumbled, his voice just as haughty and annoyed as Damien felt.

Damien jumped onto the riverbank, his heels sinking as he straightened himself.

In a cloud of mist, the man he remembered from the Rusty Selkie manifested. Instead of wearing a black biker jacket and combat boots, Balfour wore loose linen clothing that made his large, wide body look even bigger. His dark, unruly hair was tied back into a ponytail. His black facial hair concealed his expression. Onyx eyes reflected something both liquid and ancient.

"*You are human. You must eat,*" Balfour grumbled into his head. While his tone was low, it was harsh enough to make Damien's headache worse. But he couldn't ignore the fact that his stomach felt like it was about to cave in.

He dug his hand into his pocket, finding his wallet. No use trying to use European currency here in Africa. Besides, his money was soggy. "Do you have any suggestions?"

Balfour turned on his heel. "*Walk with me.*"

Damien followed the storm dragon, eager to see this temple he'd brought him to.

A gust of wind tore through a food vendor, making a young boy curse in a foreign language as he tore after an umbrella that went fling into the air.

A clump of tin foil and a water bottle fell at Damien's feet.

"*This is the best I can do,*" Balfour said. "*Bon Appetit.*"

Damien grabbed the water bottle first and chugged it down. Next, he unraveled the tinfoil bundle of whatever Egyptians fed their tourists. The food smelled edible, but didn't look it. He chewed the leathery meat, barely able to convince his mouth to salivate. He rolled his last bite around with his tongue and swallowed. "Where are we now?"

"*Philae, the current name for Isis's temple,*" Balfour replied, his giant bare feet shifting in the sand as he walked.

A group of tourists gathered around the outside of the temple.

"*This is your chance. Act like you're part of the tour,*" Balfour said, grabbing his shoulder and shoving him toward the flock of tourists. "*The moment you step inside, I will disappear from your thoughts.*"

"Why?"

"*Storm dragons are not allowed to speak while in the presence of the Codex's guardian.*"

A shiver rippled up Damien's spine. It was the first time he'd heard Balfour's voice sound somewhat, timid. Dare he say, *afraid*?

He ducked behind a group of elderly women who were busy fanning their faces with their pamphlets.

"*Hold it,*" Balfour said.

Damien felt a tug on his shoulder, forcing him to a halt. "*I'm going to miss my group if I don't hurry up.*"

Balfour held out his giant hand and unraveled his fingers. Sitting at the center of his palm was a scroll. "*Take this. It will help you find the item Isis has requested you to retrieve. The guardian of the Codex is very protective of the midwife of the sea. If he does come after you, don't hold your breath.*"

"Who is coming after me? And the midwife of *what*?" Damien stammered, taking the scroll.

Balfour's voice receded, diminishing to a whisper. "*Make sure you avoid the shadows.*"

In a fit of mist, Balfour evaporated. Damien spun on his heel, scroll in hand. He didn't even know what he was looking for. All Isis said was that he would find answers about the origin of the item in her temple.

Origin of *what*? Why should he even care about this item Isis wanted him to retrieve? And why couldn't she, a goddess of her own temple, do so? Why was he being asked to accomplish this task if all he had done was sign his paintings with a moonlit signature?

All he wanted was to get back to Selia.

Damien walked into the temple, which was flooded with just as many tourists as there were outside. He took out the scroll Balfour had given him and unraveled the gritty parchment. Written in black ink was a simple statement: **To summon an architect, you must state the origin of your intention. The god of shadows often speaks in riddles. If he presents a riddle to you, do not attempt to answer it.**

Damien squinted. An *architect*? What was that? Was this architect also the god of shadows?

He glanced around the temple. No way was he going to try and summon something called an architect with this many people around him. He walked over to the corner, shifting sideways as a group of nuns walked by.

A moth fluttered above, drifting silently over the tourists flooding the temple. Should he follow it and branch off from the tour? The moth had a slight blue glow to it.

He blinked. A group of young women stood along the far wall. Were they sea nymphs, or humans? And why did the look transparent?

One of the women turned to face him. She smiled, and his heart warmed. The blue in her eyes matched the same blue hovering in her aura.

"Selia..."

He stopped. The young woman vanished. He had to be imaging things. How could he be seeing Selia here, of all places?

As the moth fluttered from the corner of the temple toward the dark, Damien's stomach hollowed. The air felt heavier, like it held its own gravity. Didn't Balfour say something about avoiding the shadows?

His mouth became parched. Something heavy fell atop his shoulders and began to compress him. His knees buckled and he fell to the ground, unable to fight the weight forcing him into submission.

"Bow to me, human."

This voice was much huskier than Balfour. It was wide and consuming, spreading out into his head and destroying any thoughts that tried to fight it.

"Show yourself!" Damien barked. Not a good idea.

The gravity moved toward is neck, buckling his spine. *"Asking the creator of Gaia's Codex to show himself is not wise."*

Damien buckled over as the voice seemed to crawl through his body. The sensation felt like his chest was compressing and expanding at the same time—what a horrible way to die. If he didn't act now, this dark entity called an *architect* was going to kill him.

"What business do you have in Isis's temple?" it growled thunderously.

Damien's mind blanked. Why the hell was he here? What had Isis wanted him to retrieve?

"Who sent you?" it demanded, this time with skull-shattering force.

"A storm dragon," Damien mustered as his body crippled further to the ground.

Dry laughter echoed in his mind. *"My descendants send a human in their place? How weak have Poseidon's sons become?"*

The shadow retreated, leaving Damien to catch his breath. Hot, dry air whipped around him. Was this thing *scenting* him?

"The only reason I haven't killed you is due to the fact I can smell Naunet's moon daughter on you." The shadow shifted, releasing Damien's neck.

Damien coughed, struggling to gather enough of his voice to answer his question. "What is your name? How do you know Selia?"

"The great Erebéus, sea nymphs used to call me. How much my purpose has been forgotten in history. As for Selia, I highly doubt she has any remaining memories of me." The shadows thickened, tendriling toward Damien's arms. *"Isis sent you, didn't she?"*

"Yes, Isis sent me to retrieve Selia's inheritance."

The air shifted, churning and forming, changing from hot to cold in an instant. *"Inheritance?"*

"Yes, that's what Isis instructed of me."

The shadows tendrilled, forcing their way towards Damien's chest. He closed his eyes as the gravity on his body began to compress. *"Be warned. The item Isis has requested can only be in your possession temporarily. All things borrowed from the Codex must return to my shadows, eventually."*

The shadows released him. He gasped, sucking in the dry air as the pressure in his chest subsided.

Erebéus was gone.

Damien shoved his hand into his pocket, pulling out the item.

A crystal?

He held the crystal up to the light—a crystal that shimmered like starlight.

5

BALFOUR'S MESSAGE

Selia

The moment Selia returned to her room, she rushed over to her bed and sat down, eager to try and contact the storm dragon who stopped responding to her months ago. There were so many questions she still wanted answered that Zakai hadn't even touched on.

Where had Amy gone? Was Masika's spirit still somewhere, alive? What was the status of the tidal bond she and Balfour were supposed to create together?

Most importantly, was Damien all right?

Peppercorn swooped into the air, seeming to sense Selia's excitement. Selia had forgotten that she'd left the window open a crack for her to dip inside.

Heart pounding, she retrieved the salt trancing talisman from her pocket. How was she supposed to use the symbol to retrieve Balfour's original name?

She held the talisman up to Peppercorn, whose tiny head hadn't stopped swiveling. "What do you think?"

Peppercorn crawled over Selia's bed to where she set the talisman, working her little wings until she was inches away from it. "*Shreeeeeeek!*"

"Okay, I obviously don't speak fae bat," Selia protested.

The talisman began to glow blue. The symbol at the center flickered. Only a few months ago, she'd discovered the box of storm scrolls, fragments of Naunet's work Alex had confirmed originated from Gaia's Codex. She still knew so little about Naunet's role as midwife of the sea, remembering only small details of her life.

She remembered her smile. Her dark, liquid eyes, and how they seemed to drink in the Nile. Shame pitted in her stomach. How horrible it was to forget such a loving individual who'd been her mother figure, before a horrible plague swept through Egypt.

Selia grabbed the talisman, holding it upright. The symbol flashed again, this time changing form. Was the talisman trying to communicate with her? If so, how could she make sense of the strange symbols morphing across the surface?

She closed her eyes, remembering how Zakai had instructed her to read the symbol moments before. Once again, a vision of the sea unfolded out of her periphery, flooding like water into a visionary painting.

"Beeelllleeerrrooooooooo."

Selia jolted as a thunderous sound echoed past her salt nodes.

What if the word was a name? It started with the B, and it sounded similar to Balfour. But she highly doubted that she would be able to pronounce it correctly.

She ran the statement in her head over again, focusing on the ebb and flow of the waves that took the word and morphed it.

"Beeelllleerooooophhhooooonnnnn."

As the word elongated, so did the sea in Selia's vision. Soon, waves were crashing, thundering past one another as a storm manifested.

"Shreeeeeeeek!"

Selia opened her eyes, finding that Peppercorn was fluttering around the room. Pieces of plaster fell from the ceiling. The windows shook with a new ferocity that didn't come from rain or thunder.

The light began to tremble on the table.

Selia shot up from her bed and threw her arms out.

Earthquake!

"Why have you summoned me by my original name?" Balfour's thick, stormy voice came crashing into her head like a tidal wave.

"Shame on you for not speaking with me for so long!" Selia yelled, but her voice didn't sound very powerful spoken. She'd forgotten how much more powerful speaking with your pulse sounded. *"Bellerophon is a mouthful. I'd rather stick with Balfour, it's much easier to say."*

The lamp stopped shaking and the screaming outside her room died away. *"What was that all about?"*

"Tell Zakai that giving away a storm dragon's true name without him knowing has been known to summon earthquakes."

Selia had read in one of her magazines in her room, that Poseidon was the god not only of seas and storms, but of horses, and earthquakes. *"Where are you, and what are you doing?"*

"I'm trying to bring Damien to you, but he must retrieve something Naunet wanted you to have from the Temple of Isis first."

A spasm shot through Selia's core. Another shooting pain clawed up her back, this time reaching around the front. Her legs were suddenly damp and hot.

No.

It was *two months* before her due date.

This couldn't be happening.

Her water broke...

6

MAERA

Amy

With the ebony shadows of her wings finally dispersed, Nephthys stood before Amy's mother and her aunt. Pherusa hadn't stopped glaring at the goddess of death.

Amy's stomach made an unruly noise. Why did Nephthys suggest speaking with Naunet's scribe?

Nephthys walked to where Masika sat on the altar and stood behind her. She picked up a blue vase and held it in front of her chest. Liquid sloshed down the sides, dripping onto Masika's head. The liquid crashed over her like a wave, seafoam cascading down her in thick indigo sheets.

A basin lay before them, shadows pouring out of it. As the blue liquid fell from Masika's body into the basin, Nephthys reached into the vase. She withdrew a small item Amy instantly recognized—a salt trancing talisman.

Nephthys held the talisman over the basin. The water shimmered and frothed, liquid indigo blending with the shadows. She dropped the talisman. As it fell toward the basin, time seemed to slow. When the talisman struck the water, ripples cascaded across the surface.

"Maera, I summon you to the the Chamber of Salt," Nephthys said, her voice taking the ripples and turning them into waves. The basin became a storm of seafoam, blue, and shadow, spiraling up into a shimmering liquid display.

Minca moths flooded into the chamber, their wings grazing past Amy's face as they fluttered near the pool. Another sea nymph emerged from the shimmering mist their movements created. She wore a long silver dress that matched the color of the moth's wings. Her incredible blue eyes settled upon Nephthys. "Nephthys, what is it that you request of me?"

Nephthys's dark eyes flickered with the light of the queen's silver wings. She poured the liquid from the vase into the pool. "I have come into the possession of the spirit of one of Celaeno's salt daughters—Naunet's younger sister."

Maera's eyes drifted to Masika, who remained still beneath Nephthys. "Masika? *How*?"

"Celaeno's moon daughter has rendered her to this state by bonding with one of Poseidon's sons," Nephthys replied.

Maera approached Masika, reaching her hand toward her face.

Pherusa lunged. "Don't touch her," she spat.

Amphitrite grabbed Pherusa's shoulder, tugging her back.

Maera faced the goddess of death. "If their bond did form, this means that Celaeno's moon daughter will soon be looking to retrieve her inheritance."

"Retrieving her inheritance will not be easy. Selia will first need to bypass the god of shadows who now guards it in my sister's temple," Nephthys replied. "Erebéus's shadows have always possessed a special kind of manipulative magic."

"He is not the only individual who has a connection with the shadows," Maera said as she glanced at Masika once again. "The origin of sea nymphs lives alongside both storm dragons and their ancestors. The fate of Masika's spirit is not for me to decide. My suggestion would be to speak with your sister about how to proceed with her soul."

Nephthys threw out her arms, spilling shadows from her fingers. They coiled at Maera's feet, dissipating around her. "You know that Isis hasn't been seen since Erebéus banished her from her temple. And even if I could speak with her, she and I have long had different opinions on how to handle displaced souls."

Maera folded her arms in front of her, facing the water that spilled out of the basin into the sea. "Then turn Masika's soul over to the plague victims. Have those who suffered from salt venom decide her fate."

Pherusa took a step toward Maera, her long black hair swaying behind her. "When I find Naunet, I will make sure she knows that her loyal scribe betrayed her younger sister."

"Naunet will never return to you, not after how you treated her in Egypt," Maera replied, a sneer lingering on her lips.

Pherusa's icy glare ignited into liquid fire. With a flick of Pherusa's wrist, Indigo liquid erupted from the basin. A wave of thick, salty water broke into the air, sloshing over Maera.

As the water rained down in thick coiling sheets, her shadow serpents attacked. Maera didn't flinch as one of the serpents coiled around her neck.

"Stop this at once!" Nephthys roared, her voice shredding the ends of Pherusa's cloak.

In a violent eruption of seafoam and shadows, Pherusa fell backward, landing on the ground.

Amphitrite rushed to her side, dropping next to her.

Nephthys held up her hand. "You are hereby banished from this temple!"

Pherusa threw out her hand, "Wait! I beg of you. Please. What must I do to save the soul of my second-born?"

"There is another way to save Masika's spirit," Maera said, taking a stance between Pherusa and the goddess of death. "But your sister, Amphitrite, along with her Ocean Apothecary, must be in agreement."

Amy stepped toward her mother out of instinct. What did this scribe of Naunet want with her mother's Ocean Apothecary?

7
SKYWARD

Damien

Damien staggered out of the temple, dragging his feet as he tried to regain his composure. Erebéus's heavy voice still echoed in his mind, threatening to crush him.

Balfour stood outside the temple, his thick arms crossed in front of his chest. His eyes had storms brewing inside of them that reminded Damien of home. *"What did Erebéus say?"*

Thick tendriling shadows crowed Damien's mind just thinking about the entity's name. He staggered down the stairs, stopping in front of the storm dragon. "He said the only reason he didn't kill me, was because he smelled Naunet's moon daughter on me."

"It sounds as though he cooperated. He must have given you the item Isis requested," Balfour replied, almost joyfully. He held out his massive hand. *"Show it to me."*

Damien kept the crystal concealed in his pocket. "I want to know why you sent me into Isis's temple, and not yourself. He mentioned something about Poseidon's sons becoming weak."

Balfour's dark eyes flashed with a mixture of anger, and fear. *"Storm dragons are descendants of the great architects. My father, Poseidon, did not get along well with Erebéus when he ruled the great city of Atlantis."*

Damien shook his head. "Your father is *Poseidon*? The god of the sea?"

Balfour's expression thickened. *"The history of my ancestors is told differently in human mythology."*

"But architects, I've never heard of them before. If Erebéus is your architect ancestor, then what's the difference between storm dragons and architects?"

"My kind originate from the sea, and his are from the cosmos. You could say our origins are both from separate oceans, only mine is ruled by storms, and his is ruled by the stars."

"Are there other architects, or is he the only one?"

"Erebéus is the last architect who remains awake. His loyalty to Gaia's daughters was rewarded long ago by Gaia. She gave him a special task—creating Gaia's Codex."

Damien pondered the "He also mentioned that what is borrowed from the Codex must eventually return to his shadows. What is this Codex he mentioned?"

"The Codex documents the bonds between architects and his dragon descendants with Gaia's nymph daughters. These bonds are what shape and sculpt the planet. Everything from mountains, to weather patterns, to how life evolves and changes is shaped according to the bonds documented within the Codex."

"Does this Codex include information on fae creatures?"

"Of course. Life first emerged from the plant and animal fae kingdoms, which Gaia's nymph daughters have always been very close to." He held out his giant hand again. *"Show me the inheritance Isis has requested of you."*

Damien fumbled the crystal in his pocket. "Why should I show you what he gave me?"

"Because the sooner you do, the sooner I can get you to your fiancé. She just told me that she's about to have your baby."

Damien's mouth dropped open. "What? Two months early?"

Balfour cocked his head sideways.

"Here, take it," Damien said, tossing Balfour the crystal. "I need to get to Selia, now."

Balfour grabbed the crystal, holding it up to the light. He took great care to inspect each of its seven shimmering sides.

"Well? Don't just stand there, turn into a dragon and take me to her!"

As Balfour's giant hand curled around the crystal, membranous fins manifested around his sides. In a fury of wind and fog, Damien was hurled skyward.

8

A NEW STAR

Selia

Selia's fingers gripped so tightly onto the salt trancing talisman, that stone turned to dust. The remains of what had once been a symbol was quickly pulverized by her squeezing the talisman in response to her violent contractions.

"*Why are you breathing so heavily? I can feel a spike in your pulse,*" Balfour's voice boomed into Selia's head.

Selia staggered over to her bedside table and pressed the button to summon a caretaker into her room. She winced as another contraction rippled through her body. "*I'm going to have my baby!*"

A gust of rushing wind ripped out a reply. "*Keep breathing. Damien should be arriving any moment. Tell the little tyke not to storm out of you just yet.*"

"Like I can possibly do that!" Selia replied, clutching anything that she could dig her fingers into just to distract herself from the pain shooting through her in agonizing rhythmic motions.

"*Yes you can. Just suck in a breath and hold it until—*"

"*Bellerophon!*"

The room shook with another thundering tremor.

The door flew open as one of the attendants entered. "Do you have an emergency?"

"My baby is coming, now!" She fell back onto the bed. This baby was coming with force of a tsunami.

The attendant grabbed the phone from the wall and dialed. "We have a labor in room eighteen. Get a nurse up here, now."

Selia stared up at the ceiling, where stars had started to form.

"Focus on your breathing. Just think of the gentle ebb and flow of the tides," Balfour thundered into her thoughts.

Selia wanted to grab Balfour by his scaly lips and clamp his fat mouth shut. The last thing she wanted to think about was anything to do with the tides. Right now, she was at the mercy of them, and the great round moon of a belly trying to sway her into an early birth.

The door opened, and a very wet man stormed inside. He staggered into the room, his wet hair dripping in front of his face as he stopped at her side. "Oh my God, Selia…"

Selia's contractions seized, but only for a moment. She struggled to recognize the man's voice as he fell beside her. "Damien? Is that you?"

Damien dropped to his knees, falling to the side of the bed. Her grabbed her hand and began kissing her forehead.

"Sir, you can't come in here like this, especially not sopping wet," a female voice carried from the other side of the bed.

"Oh, good heavens, give them a moment!" another woman responded who entered the room. She took up a spot at Selia's legs. "You need to start pushing."

Selia blanked. How on earth was she going to push with this much pain rippling over her? She wanted to squeeze Damien's face, just to make sure he was the *real* thing, and not some hallucination. The last time she'd physically touched him felt like eons ago.

Damien's hand gripped hers. His touch wasn't a hallucination, it was *real*. While his skin was cold to the touch, his affection and strength was present. His scent of fresh rain and some distant spice washed over Selia that reminded her of Egypt.

"Please tell me it's really you," she whispered as another contraction erupted through her body.

Damien squeezed her hand in his warm one. "I'm here, love. I'm never leaving your side."

Selia cried out as another contraction ripped through her.

"Breathe!" Balfour's thunderous voice echoed through them both.

Damien's face blurred as her labor intensified.

"Squeeze my hand as hard as you need to," he said, "I'm here to take it all away from you."

"Listen to him. He's better at this than I..."

Selia tried to focus on Damien's strength as Balfour's boisterous voice echoed in her ears. When she felt like she might pass out, everything went quiet.

The most perfect, beautiful sound in the world rang in her ears, a melody unlike anything she'd heard before. A tiny, intricate being emerged from her body, setting the world, and the sea, and any care she had other than this moment aside.

9

THE PLAGUE VICTIMS

Amy

The ground shook beneath Amy's feet as she approached her mother. Something else lurked within the Chamber of Salt. A violent *hissss* filled her salt nodes, rattling her senses.

"Amy, look at me," Amphitrite said as her emerald eyes darkened. "No matter what happens, you must not hold your breath. The victims of the plague will not hold back."

Amy jolted. *Plague victims?*

Maera returned her attention to the blue waves cascading out of the basin. Water surged into the room, sloshing at Amy's feet as the waves gained momentum. Amy backed against the wall, floundering away from the water.

Her mother remained before her, taking a stance as the waves surged and frothed. Amphitrite was a sea goddess, and she was not easily deterred by floods or violent onslaughts of water.

Maera held her hands at her sides and summoned something up from the sea. "Even the brightest stars in the sky find their origin in the darkest waters of the ocean."

Minca moths dove into the sea, their sharp wings slicing through the water. The second they struck the sea, blue light erupted, pulsing like starlight through the cavern. While water frothed and poured out of the basin, Nephthys withdrew into the shadows, her long, extended hands disappearing.

A jagged structure manifested before them. Was it coral? A giant crown-shaped form branched as far as Amy could see. The water thrashed violently. Lumpy forms unfolded out of the seafoam unnaturally. Elbows and arms jostled against one another, fingers gripping the jagged structure as it rose out of the sea.

"What are they?" Amy asked, terrified at the scene.

Amphitrite withdrew from the surging waves, falling back to Amy's side. "They are sirens—victims of the salt venom plague. All are salt daughters of Celaeno. Neither dead, nor living."

"Do they have bodies, or are they spirits?" Amy asked, wondering how something could be neither alive nor dead. They appeared to have bodies. Then again, so had Masika in the past.

"They are exactly what they need to be," a voice said from the altar.

Masika was no longer sitting, but standing. Her hair thrashed out on either side of her face as the waves cascaded around her.

"Masika, come with me," Pherusa said. "I won't allow the victims to take you."

Masika threw out her hands, sending a black wall of water toward her mother. Pherusa was knocked back by the wave as it broke over her.

Maera caught Pherusa as she was forced back by the ebony water.

Pherusa threw herself forward, her dark hair whipping over her shoulders. Black strands stuck to her face as she threw herself into a fist of hysteria. "Masika, wait! Please. Your soul has no place to go."

Amy shuddered as Masika's dark eyes flicked up toward her. "Amphitrite's daughter gave me exactly what I needed from the past to make sure that I will find Naunet. When I do, I will ensure that she surrenders to the salt venom."

She ducked as the wave exploded over her head. She coughed as salt water flooded into her mouth and nose. Staggering over the sodden stones, she elbowed her way out of the pool she'd fallen into.

Something was approaching her. A deformed figure climbed out of the water, its arms and body folding unnaturally.

One of the sirens had found her...

Amy backed away as the siren crawled toward her. "No, stop!" she cried, lunging for the water.

As she plunged into the sea, the grey bodies of the sirens coiled around her. Bony hands and limbs thrashed in the sea as she struggled to free herself from becoming caught.

Blue light pulsed in the water below.

A crystal floated before her.

Amy reached for the crystal, her fingers cramping as it illuminated the water.

A hand clasped her own, tugging her into the brilliant blue light that illuminated the sea like a star.

10
FATHERHOOD

Damien

Damien's heart hadn't stopped thundering. A very delicate being lay bundled in Selia's arms. He stood next to the bed, his opportunity to steady his pulse long gone. The need to breathe had suddenly escaped him.

He could stand here forever, not caring in the slightest about where he was, or what he needed to do from this moment forward.

Selia's eyes drifted up to him, complete happiness swimming in them. "Damien. Look at her..."

Damien's knees buckled, and he collapsed before mother and daughter. This couldn't be real. One look into his daughter's tiny, perfect, scrunched up face left him helpless.

"*Is everything all right? Is the baby healthy*?" Balfour's voice echoed through his head.

A shuddering reply escaped him. "*She's absolutely perfect...*"

A nurse emerged into the room. "Even though she's two months early, she's very large, comparable to the size of a full term baby. She is beyond healthy. And look at those freckles!"

"Hi, sweetheart," he whispered down to her.

"Do you have a name picked out for her?" the nurse asked them both.

He glanced down at Selia, who was just as beautiful as his daughter. "I was waiting for you to make that decision."

Selia grabbed his hand. "She's not my baby, she's *our* baby! Right now, she's daddy's little girl," she said, lifting her toward him.

Damien took his daughter into his arms. His stomach swelled. Looking into her face, naming her didn't seem possible. Even without a name, this tiny little being was beyond perfect. Her body was so fragile tucked against him.

He'd felt this love before. He'd known what it felt like to hold such an innocent, loving being in his arms, all before the sea took her away from him. He held her close, unable to think beyond this moment.

How perfect was this tiny little being, with freckles on her tiny face that made him think of stars.

PART 2
ORIGIN STORIES

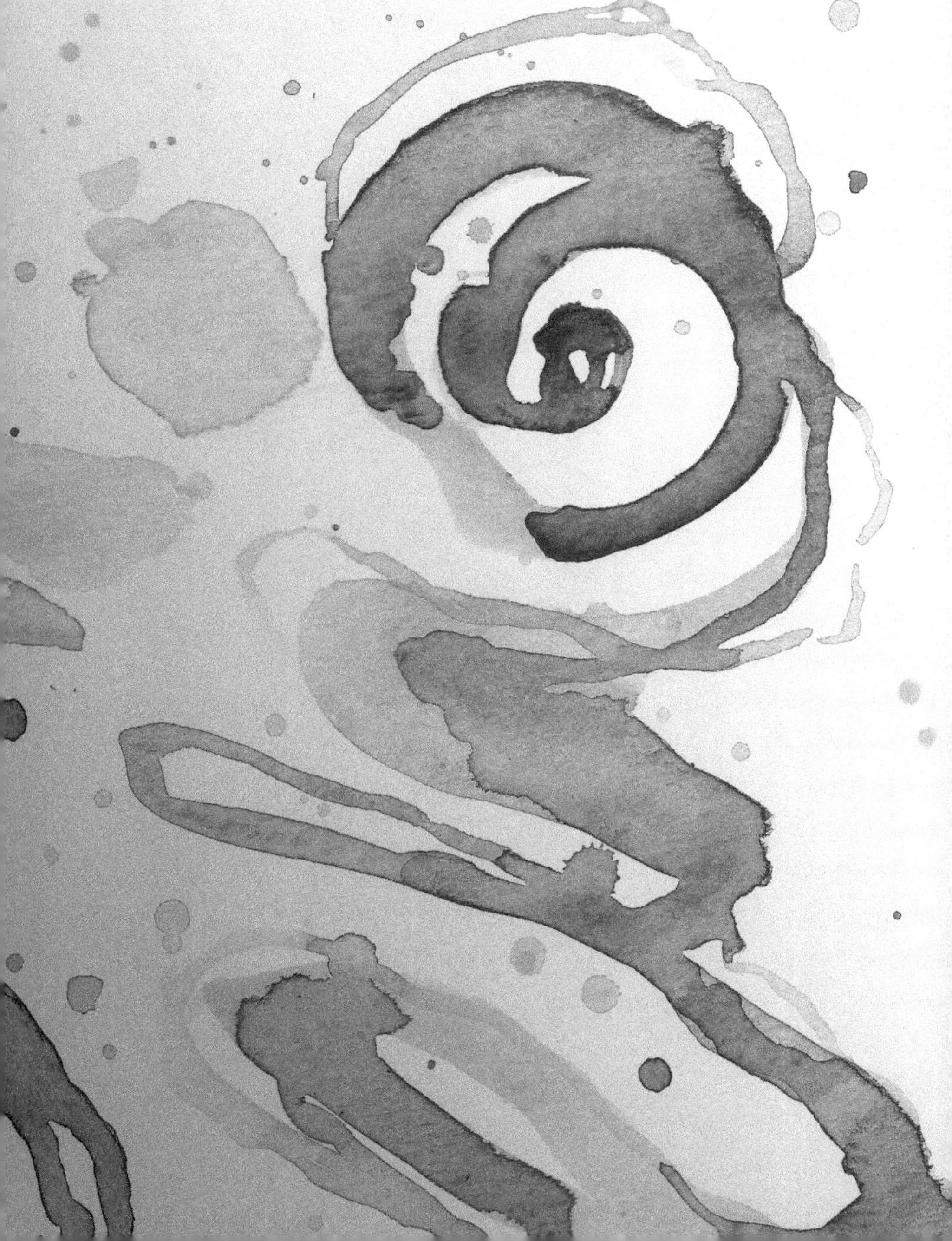

II
THE PAST MEETS THE PRESENT
Selia

The two new parents fell into a rocky rhythm over the next few weeks. Selia wasn't allowed to leave the mental institution until she passed a test that deemed her sane. Not only did Damien refuse to leave, he insisted the facility move them into a larger room, where all three of them could live, complete with a baby crib.

Selia sat in their new bedroom, cradling their still nameless daughter in her arms as she drifted in and out of sleep. She bundled her into her blanket and set her down into her crib. She kept the baby monitor on, in case she awoke. When she emerged in the center room, she spotted Damien hunched over his sketch pad.

He sat by the window, his expression etched with something raw and vulnerable. At times, Selia thought she was observing a complete stranger. Damien had been through this journey before.

"What are you working on?" she asked as she approached him.

Damien held up his journal, revealing the sketch he'd made. A temple sat next to a river with moonlight dancing across the waters surface. "Something that I hope will help us give her a name."

"What is this beautiful place?" Selia asked.

"A temple I visited."

"You visited the Temple of Isis?"

He stared at her, bewilderment morphing his expression. "How did you know the name of this temple?"

"I have childhood memories of being there." She lowered herself into his lap, taking his hand into hers. "There is so much I've learned about my past over the last few months that I need to share with you."

He set his journal aside. "I didn't know if you thought I might be insane when I told you what I experienced with Balfour."

"I take it you know who he is now?"

"What, the fact that he was the bloke in the biker jacket who punched me when I got too drunk at the Rusty Selkie?"

She laughed, wrapping her arms around him. "Not to mention that he's also a storm dragon?"

He shifted beneath her as he chuckled. "Yeah, that sort of blew my mind. I thought for sure I was going insane when I learned that he's also one of Poseidon's sons."

A laugh escaped her as she settled into his embrace. "It can't be any more insane than being in an mental institution together."

He took her hand into his, a smile parting his lips, which quickly turned into a frown. "It all started with these dreams, or memories, I can't really say what they were. Things were blurring together to the point I couldn't make sense of them."

"Well, you *were* in a coma," Selia replied. "I can only imagine that being unconscious for so long could have an impact on your sense of reality."

A lump in his throat moved. "I had this vision where I saw a stag atop this giant starlit mountain. Amy was there, then she was gone." He swallowed. "Then, I was down on the beach, where I saw my deceased wife."

His gaze trailed away as a shudder ran up his body.

She set her hand on his arm. "You saw *Maria*?"

His gaze returned to her. His eyes were glassy and unfocused. "Yes. I still don't know what to make of it."

"What happened? Did she talk to you?"

He blew out his cheeks. "She stated that I needed to meet with the moon goddess I'd spent the past decade painting."

"Was this moon goddess, Isis?"

"Yes. In this vision, Isis told me to retrieve your inheritance from her temple. Then, I woke up. I was wet and hot and completely miserable. Balfour had taken me all the way from Scotland, to Egypt."

Selia jumped, thinking back to the inheritance Zakai had mentioned. "Well? Where is this inheritance? You retrieved it from the temple, right?"

"Not after I had an encounter with this giant shadowy thing called an architect that wanted to kill me. Balfour said he was some ancient ancestor of his, and a creator of Gaia's Codex."

"Did this architect have a name?"

"Balfour called him Erebéus." He grabbed his throat. "Erebéus said the only reason he gave me your inheritance was because he smelled Naunet's moon daughter on me."

Selia's body went numb.

Naunet...

Hearing her name aloud sent shivers up her spine.

Damien lowered his hand away from his neck. "Anyway, I gave the crystal to Balfour, and I haven't seen him since he brought me to you."

"My inheritance is a crystal?"

He nodded. "I have no idea what it's used for. Balfour wouldn't tell me."

Selia's thoughts about her inheritance were overrun with memories of the midwife of the sea. She remembered her kind eyes, and stunning dark beauty. "I can tell you who Naunet is. She served in Egypt as the midwife of the sea. She was in charge of facilitating salt births, the primary way sea nymphs reproduce."

Damien's brow furrowed. "*Salt* births?"

Selia nodded. "Most sea nymphs reproduce using the ancestral salts. There are seven salt ancestries total."

Damien grabbed his journal and flipped the page. "Okay, I'm going to draw this. Can you name all seven of the salt ancestries for me?"

"Sure. The seven ancestral salts are Maia, Alcyone, Asterope, Celaeno, Taygete, Electra, and Merope. Combined, they form something called the Abyss, which is the ancestral mother, or womb from which the ancestral salts originate."

He jotted down seven different circles, labeling each with the names as she described them. Then he drew a giant circle around them all and labeled it *Abyss*.

"Naunet found me in the Nile river, and raised me in Egypt. She was the sea nymph who named me Selia, meaning Blind Moon."

Damien's mouth dropped open. "What? Selia, this is huge. You found your mother?"

"Naunet did not give birth to me, she *found* me."

Damien squinted at her. "Then, who is your actual mother?"

Selia gazed into his hazel eyes and grabbed his pen. "My mother is the sea. Celaeno is where my salt ancestry originates from. Celaeno is also where the problems started." She crossed out the word *Celaeno*, and drew a moth above it. "Right around the time of my birth, Celaeno gave birth to a fae minca moth queen who introduced a toxin into the sea. Do you remember the mystery bottle Amy had, the one called selkie salt skin?"

"Vaguely."

"Well, the selkie salt skin has a different name. Salt venom was born from the fae queen's blood, and introduced into the sea. It brought a plague into Egypt, where it wiped out all salt daughters with Celaeno's ancestry."

Damien glanced from his diagram of the Abyss, then back to her. "How were you not infected like the others by this salt venom?"

"Balfour took me to the Abyss to protect me."

"I don't understand. Is the Abyss a place, or an entity?"

"Both. The ancestral salt mothers can manifest as spirits, but they are housed in the sea." Guilt struck her gut as visions of the plague victims Masika shared with her flooded her memory. "Do you remember the folktale about Sika the selkie in Montrose?"

"Yes, I do."

"Sika was short for Masika, who is Naunet's younger sister. She was the one speaking to me through the journal I found in your sister's bookstore."

Damien gripped her tightly. "I knew I had a bad feeling about that journal. So glad that Peppercorn shredded it."

"But shredding it didn't get rid of Masika's spirit. She continued to haunt me, threatening me to do as she told until—"

"Masika is no longer a threat. It is vital that you both focus on your inheritance."

Selia jumped at Zakai's sudden voice.

The Iridescent appeared by the window, her colorful eyes flashing in the dim light of the room.

Balfour too, emerged by the window. Mist tendrilled around his broad outline, offsetting him against Zakai's luminous presence. His deep-set eyes were completely cast in shadow. "*Where is the tiny nameless one?*"

"She's sleeping," Selia said. She had yet to introduce their daughter to either of them. She faced Zakai. "Damien, this is Zakai. She took Alex's place after she—"

"—Balfour told me that Alex died," Damien interrupted her." But I still don't know the story of how it happened."

Zakai approached Selia, stopping at her side. "Alex's death is not what you need to be focusing on right now." She turned to face Selia, withdrawing an item from her robes. "This is what Damien retrieved from the Temple of Isis. Take it."

A hard, lopsided crystal landed in Selia's palm. It was both cool and warm to the touch, depending on which surface her skin came into contact with. The texture was also not uniform. It shimmered in some places, and was dull in others. Liquid light seemed to refract through its colorful sides.

She held the crystal in her hand, tilting it from side-to-side as light reflected off it's seven-pointed structure. "What is this?"

Zakai dipped her chin, making a few short pieces of her spiky hair fall in front of her eyes. "It is one of three crystalline fragments of the original star of the sea. The crystal dates back to Atlantis. It houses special powers, all of which have belonged to prior midwives of the sea."

"What kind of powers?" Selia asked, instantly thinking of Naunet.

Zakai's mouth twitched. "Powers that Naunet abandoned over three thousand years ago. The powers the midwife of the sea borrows from Isis and Nephthys—the powers of life, and death."

"In other words, a cycle of reincarnation?" Damien asked.

Zakai nodded "That cycle was greatly impacted when plague broke out. The reincarnation cycle was disrupted for Celaeno's salt daughters."

"Where did the plague victims go?" Selia asked.

"With so many deaths associated with the plague, and no place within the Abyss for them to return to, these souls lost themselves to the ocean. For thousands of years, they have relied on the protection of Poseidon's crown."

"What in the world is *Poseidon's crown*?" Damien asked, his brow drawing up.

"It is the coral structure in the sea where the plague victims have found refuge." Zakai replied.

Selia squinted at the crystal. "I see someone with flaming red hair and emerald green eyes."

"Who is it?" Damien asked.

Selia held the crystal up to the light. "It looks like Amy, no." She squinted again. "There are *two* of her. Two sea nymphs with vivid green eyes and brilliant red hair."

"You must be seeing the sea nymph who fragmented the crystal," Zakai said. "Amy?"

"No, her mother, the true goddess of the sea, Amphitrite."

"But I thought Amy *was* Amphitrite."

"Her mother named her after her, but Amy refuses to go by her mother's name," Zakai replied, her eyes locking on to the crystal. "Can you see where they are?"

"Maybe," Selia said. "There's a lot of water, and…" electrical sparks erupted out of the crystal. "Wow, is that a dragon?"

An electrical burst jolted Selia's hand.

She threw the crystal down, where it landed on the ground with a clatter. "I've never seen so many storm dragons before."

Balfour shook his head. "*My brothers love to put on a stormy show whenever they appear.*"

Selia glanced up at Balfour. "You have *brothers*?"

"*Too many,*" Balfour grumbled.

"Why are they all of a sudden appearing?" Selia asked.

The baby monitor went off.

Selia walked toward the bedroom.

Zakai grabbed the crystal from the ground and made a motion to follow her.

"Hold it," Damien said, grabbing Zakai's arm before she could venture into the bedroom. "I have some questions for Alex's friend before we make any decisions about Selia's inheritance."

Zakai backed away from the door. "Fine, but only if Balfour is allowed to accompany me." She glanced up at the storm dragon. "I'm sure he will have details to share about the crown of his father."

12

AMPHITRITE'S APOTHECARY

Amy

The taste of something bitter filled Amy's mouth. She opened her eyes, startled by her blurry surroundings. Colors drifted in and out of her periphery—oranges, and yellows, followed by an incredibly vivid green.

The sirens—where had they gone? She could still see their blackish-grey bodies, their hollow eyes, and gaping mouths. There had also been a vibrant blue crystal floating in the water. The light it put off still clung to the back of her eyelids like stars. She blinked a few times, trying to dull the light that seemed to linger.

"Keep drinking. The sirens cannot touch you, I promise," a woman said, her voice stirring Amy's memory on some primal level.

A woman with red hair and a prominent dusting of star-shaped freckles sat across from her. She wore a dark green dress, the color too deep to be emerald like her eyes. "I was wondering when you would come to. Amy, my dear, you have never had me this worried before."

Amy's mouth went dry. This had to be a dream. She was no longer in the Chamber of Salt, battling for her life as waves of sea water and sirens surged toward her.

Her mother sat across from where Amy sat in a giant chair, one that nearly swallowed her. A tea set sat on a table between them, complete with two cups that mimicked the shape of seashells.

Amphitrite grabbed one of the teacups and poured herself a cup of hot water. Steam billowed between them as the liquid sloshed into her cup. "Had I not found your body in the North Sea floating amongst sea ice, you would not have survived."

Amy glanced down at what she was wearing—a green linen dress that matched her mother's lace one. Her arms were a deathly pale color, her freckles dull and lifeless. "How long has it been since you discovered my body?"

"It has been almost a month since you stepped into the past," her mother replied, setting the cup of scolding hot water between them. "You were always my one and only rebellious daughter, but never have I seen you take such drastic steps for those you love."

Memories of the past from Winter Forest flashed through Amy's memory. Masika trying to kill her. Ewan dying atop the sacred mountain. She'd loved *both*, and failed to obtain either one. What had going to the past really accomplished?

Amy glanced down at her tea, overcome with the new reality. She gazed around the room once again, finding the light streaming through the window cold and grey. The sky was overcast, making the room dull. The space oddly reminded her of Pixie's Bat Blitz coffee shop. Shelves lined the wall, each cluttered with herbs and spices. A giant map hung from the wall—a map of an island that wasn't Scotland. "Where am I?"

"I brought you to Ireland, hoping to revive you," her mother replied as she tipped the spout of the teapot, refiling Amy's cup. "You have been in and out of consciousness for over a month. The salt trance you put yourself into was deep enough to put you into a slumber you would not have awoken from." Hot water poured over the cup, almost burning Amy's hand. "Had I not found you when I did, you might not have survived."

Her mother's hand trembled as she set the teapot down on the table. Remorse, and even a glimmer of anger, shimmered in her liquid eyes.

Amy blinked, avoiding her mother's gaze. "What is in this tea that helped you to revive me?" She tilted the cup to her lips, tasting the bitter liquid.

"Seaweed that only grows in the shallow seas of the Emerald Isle. I'm quite fond of infusing what humans call mermaid hair in many of the teas that I drink."

Amy nearly spit out the tea, realizing what she was drinking. She gazed at the liquid, finding something else floating at the bottom. The mystery particles, whatever they were, shimmered and sparkled.

A hollow sensation filled her stomach. This had to be a dream. Amy hadn't seen her mother in so long. And here they were, sharing tea together?

She set the teacup down, locking her eyes with her mother's. "Why," she croaked, emotion suddenly clouding her voice.

Amphitrite's brow furrowed. "Why what?"

Amy's hands clenched into fists. "Why did you never come searching for me?"

Amphitrite straightened herself. "I've been here, watching over you. Have you never wondered who was sending you bottles in little silk pouches full of salt extract ingredients?"

"I don't understand. Your Ocean Apothecary sank with Atlantis. That's the last memory I have of you, before a giant wave swept over land and…"

Her mother's face blurred as waves of emotion came surging forth. Fear. Anger. Abandonment.

The Abyss had taken her…*hadn't it*?

While her body numbed, a hot, burning ember ignited inside of Amy's gut. That ember told her to get up and run as far as she could in any direction, as long as she eventually met the ocean.

Amphitrite reached out, grabbing Amy's arm. "Please stay. I know how upset you must feel right now. Thousands of years between us. You were so young when I left you to grow into a woman alone in Egypt."

"I've tried to bury that time in my life," Amy said, her voice withering into a whisper. "It brought be great pain every time I thought of losing you, and not knowing what happened to you after the great city sank."

Her mother's eyes reddened, misting with emotion. She gathered her into her trembling arms. "Amy, how sick I have become, not having you know that I have been here all along."

Amy fell into her embrace, not knowing what to say, or think, or feel. All she could do was focus on the sobs escaping her.

Tears dolloped down her face as she fell into a rhythm with her mother's sobbing. This wasn't a memory. Her mother was here, *crying* with her. The distance time had settled between them seemed to pour from every direction, undoing her from the inside out.

She sat back down in her chair, spent from crying. Her mother's blurry form trembled in front of her. "Was being in the Chamber of Salt all a dream?

Amphitrite's misted eyes refocused as she sat next to her teary-eyed daughter. "What you saw was very real. What do you remember?"

Amy swallowed, thinking back to the strange, dreamlike encounter. "I saw Pherusa, and Masika. Then, Nephthys summoned another sea nymph into the cavern, one I don't have memories of. Was her name Maera?"

Amphitrite nodded. "Maera served as Naunet's scribe in the Temple of Isis before she too, became a victim of the plague. When she died, however, something strange happened to her spirit. She became trapped Temple of the Three Origins."

Amy's heart leapt. "This temple, has it also be called the Temple of Salt, Storms, and Starlight?"

Amphitrite's eyes shimmered. "Yes. This temple dates back to kingdoms that predate Atlantis. The Chamber of Salt is the newest of the three origins, one that is owned by sea nymphs. There was not one single temple, but many that made up the many regions of the old kingdom. These kingdoms were ruled by storm dragons and their ancestors."

Amy's body heated at the memory of what she and Ewan had done atop the sacred mountain. They made passionate love to one another in the ruins of a temple that had once been part of the old kingdom. "How did Maera become trapped in this temple?"

"She must have done something to disrupt one of the three origins, which I am assuming you remember?"

"The three origins represent the afterlives for sea nymphs, storm dragons, and—" she shivered as shadows crept into her mind. "What is the name of the last one?"

"The ancestors of storm dragons—the great architects."

Gooseflesh ripped across Amy's arms at the mention of an architect. They were ancient cosmic beings who Gaia created for one purpose only—to serve her nymph daughters. When Amy was young, she only knew of one architect who remained. He lived as a shadow in Isis's temple. She used to shiver whenever Naunet mentioned is name. "Maera mentioned his name earlier, is it Erebéus?"

"Yes, Erebéus is the last architect remaining. He guards the Temple of the Three Origins, allowing Maera to leave the temple temporarily. And he, like Pherusa, is also trying to find where Naunet might have gone."

"It sounds like he's had the same luck finding her as Masika," Amy said, bitterness thickening her tone.

Amphitrite's gaze darkened. "Naunet does not want to be found. The last record the Order has of her was that she had been spotted in the Orient. But that was centuries ago. She has been missing ever since the plague of salt venom."

Amy set her cup of tea down. "Nephthys mentioned that Erebéus banished Isis from her temple. Do you have any idea why?"

"It has to deal with protecting a starlit treasure from the sea he felt that Isis could not protect—the same treasure that I have recruited Maera's help in attempting to find."

"So you and Maera are working together?"

"Maera and I have been working to restore this treasure so that we can remedy the issue with the plague victims. If we cannot restore the Abyss, the souls of plague victims will vanish."

"Meaning that they will disappear, forever?" Amy asked.

"Yes. If we do not find a way to remedy the Abyss, all salt daughters of Celaeno who died during the plague will perish."

Amy stomach rolled with anticipation. Masika was also a victim of the plague. Did that meant that she too, would vanish? "How have you and Maera decided to restore this treasure? And did you say something about starlight?"

Amphitrite's emerald eyes shimmered. "My daughter, you have added a unique element to the situation by venturing to the past." She reached into her robes and withdrew a small silk pouch. She undid the twine and poured the contents out. A silvery blue item no bigger than her palm tumbled onto the table.

Amy squinted at the item she remembered floating before her as the sirens swarmed. Its powerful light helped her to escape. But here on the table, it looked so different. Little flecks of light drifted like liquid behind the crystalline surface. "Is that a storm dragon scale?"

"You tell me."

Amy grabbed the item, tipping her fingernail against the keeled edge that ran the length of the silvery surface. "Didn't Poseidon's sons disappeared into the Abyss after the plague of salt venom broke out? I remember visiting Naunet in Egypt, where she expressed her confusion about their disappearance."

Her mother shook her head. "Balfour's six older brothers were put into an icy slumber by me. After Atlantis sank, they became violent with one another about how to handle the territories within their father's crown." Her green eyes flickered. "A recent event involving forces of the moon and one of Poseidon's sons has stirred them from their slumber. As I'm sure you remember, time back then was much colder. Ice and snow dominated the landscape up north three thousand years ago."

Amy swallowed, trying to forget Ewan's handsome face. "I remember so little from Atlantis and Egypt, let alone Winter Forest."

"But you remember *him*, don't you? The lead huntsman of the Sgàthan clan?"

Amy glanced at her mother. "How do you know about Ewan?"

Amphitrite's eyes closed. She sucked in a breath, and exhaled slowly. "I can see him in your salt aura. I can smell the woodsmoke and the cold winter air as it blows through you. I can feel the love you have for him, and the love he has for you."

Amy's heart thundered. "You are mistaken. Ewan is dead, lost to the past. You are speaking as though that love is somehow in the present."

Amphitrite opened her eyes, both of which were twinkling. "When you went to the past, Masika tried to destroy a storm dragon scale that Ewan held dear to himself. The scale was passed down to him by his father, who inherited it from his ancestral kings in Atlantis. He believed the dragon scale belonged to Poseidon."

"Masika *did* destroy it," Amy concluded, remembering the fiery rage that erupted out of the flames. "I remember it bursting into a thousand pieces as she became angry with me."

Her mother took the dragon scale form her. "Look closer, and tell me what you see. Memories we have of who we love always find a way to return to us one day."

Amy squinted at what she assumed was a storm dragon scale. Memories of Errindoor's giant starlit antlers framed by the sacred mountain flashed in her mind's eye.

13
CRYSTAL FRAGMENTS

Damien

Damien kept his sight on the Iridescent who had no business coming into their life. Something about Zakai was off. He didn't like the fact that any time he tried to ask a question about Alex, or something about the Order, she cut him off. He especially didn't like that she had some kind of say over Balfour, who while in her presence, became silent. It wasn't like the grumbly storm dragon to be so quiet.

There was no sane reason to trust her. The last time a member of Gaia's Order walked into Selia's life, it was to threaten her. While Selia tended to their daughter, he did the common thing to do when one had guests, unexpected or not—he prepared tea. It was the proper Scottish thing to do, even if he didn't want the extra company.

Zakai remained standing in the middle room, gazing into the crystal fragment she identified as a piece of the star of the sea. Balfour sat at the table not far from where Damien stood, watching the tea kettle on the stove.

"*How does one do this*?" Balfour asked as he tapped the kettle with one of his massive fingers.

"You've never had tea and biscuits before?" Damien replied.

"*No.*"

Damien folded his arms across his chest. "I can tell you that watching a kettle doesn't make it boil any faster." Steam might as well be bursting out of his ears with the frustration he felt. Zakai needed to leave. The Order had no business bursting into their life with what was sure to be another threat of some kind.

Finally, after what felt like hours, the kettle began to scream. Damien grabbed the tea set and biscuits and set them on the table. He poured hot water and dunked tea bags into the cups, which both Balfour and Zakai sat in front of.

Balfour dunked his biscuit into the tea, his massive sausage-sized fingers causing the hot water to pour out. He winced, then stuffed the soggy biscuit into his beard, tossing it into his invisible mouth.

Zakai set the crystal at the center of the table and dabbed up Balfour's spilled tea with a napkin. She grabbed the pot of hot water and prepared him a new cup. "Just wait and let it steep this time."

Balfour let out a sigh.

Damien refused to take a seat. He glared at the crystal, wanting to launch it out the window.

Zakai prepared his cup as well, her fingers gripping the handle of the teapot. "I'll make an extra cup for Selia."

"Selia won't be joining us until I have some questions of my own answered," Damien grumbled back.

Zakai folded her hands on the table, the colorful sheen in her eyes darkening. "Ask away."

Damien pulled out his sketchbook and held it in front of him. "What in the world is this?"

Zakai squinted at his drawing. "It appears to be a badly sketched image of the Abyss."

He shook the book. "Selia just got done explaining to me that she has something called a *salt ancestry*?"

"Sea nymphs originate from the sea, specifically the ancestral salts."

He slapped his journal down. Oh, right. So the baby we had together, she was what, produced by *salt*?"

Zakai tapped her fingers together. "I see you are confused about some things."

"Confused is an understatement."

"What other questions can I help to answer?"

Damien scoffed. "I don't know, why don't we start with the giant storm dragon sitting next to you who has never eaten tea and biscuits before?"

Balfour slouched, defeated by Damien's words.

Zakai's eyes shimmered. "All right, let's discuss Balfour."

Damien flipped his book to a sketch he'd created months ago. "You see this place? You see *him*? Almost a year ago, he punched me in the head at a pub called the Rusty Selkie. Then he turns out to be one of Poseidon's sons? He's a freaking storm dragon? How is that sane?"

Zakai clasped her fingers together. "Storm dragons have been around for much longer than Atlantis. The same goes for the fae."

Damien threw his hands up. "Don't even get me started with the fae. They're supposed to be invisible beings who want to remain unseen, not disguised as incredibly annoying common-day animal species."

Balfour and Zakai exchanged curious glances.

Damien set his elbows onto the table, knocking his cup of tea to the side. "Look, I grew up in Scotland, a land where fairy tales were piratically born. I have an aunt who raised my sister and I, who to this day, believes that her garden is haunted by fae creatures she calls Vixen Sprites. But even I know that if I shared the stories with my aunt that Selia and I have endured over the past few months, she would deem me as crazy."

Zakai sipped on her tea, then set her cup back down. "Are you preparing to share those stories with us?"

Damien kept flipping through his sketch pad. "I have the notes the Order threatened Selia with. I kept the one she found when Alexandra broke into her office at the Louvre and stole her salt trancing talisman." He probed his finger onto the note. "Explain how sending Selia and I on some crazy adventure to track down a fae treasure made any sense. And I'm not taking *Selia is Celaeno's moon daughter* for an answer."

Balfour grumbled what could have been a chuckle.

Damien pinched the brow of his nose. "The fact that storm boy here brought me half-way across the sea to retrieve a crystal from an Egyptian temple, where some ominous dark shadow tried to *kill* me?"

Zakai sipped her tea, setting the cup gingerly back onto the table. "Balfour's ancestor has never been the nicest shadow to contend with."

Damien leaned forward. "Before you uproot my family and embark on some quest to do who knows what, I need some answers, *now*. Why did you send me into that temple to retrieve some crystal inheritance? And why should Selia and I even care about it?"

Zakai's eyes narrowed. "Selia is Celano's moon daughter. Regardless of what you think, she has an obligation to the work that Naunet abandoned with the Codex when she left her role as the midwife of the sea in Egypt."

Damien slammed his fist down. "Selia has an obligation to *nothing*. The only individual she has an obligation to right now is our daughter. Before you go spilling what kind of obligations you think my fiancé has to *who* or *what*, I need to know the name of the selkie who killed Alex."

Zakai shot Balfour a dissatisfied glance, "You let this slip, didn't you?"

Balfour sighed. "*He wouldn't stop asking me questions, and I needed to get him to Isis's temple.*"

"Alex was killed by Naunet's younger sister, Masika," Zakai confirmed. "She was the selkie haunting the town of Montrose. Her spirit is cursed by a toxin born of fae blood called salt venom."

Damien's thoughts traveled to the journal Selia had become fiercely obsessed with. "Well, where is this Masika? Could she try and hurt Selia?"

"*Not while I am with her,*" Balfour cut in. "*My attempt at forming a storm bond with the Blind Moon was done to protect her.*"

Damien squinted at the storm dragon. The words *protect* and *bond* floated through his brain, not making any sense at all.

"This is not a matter of asking," Zakai interjected. "This is a duty to her ancestors. Selia's actions could eventually impact the health of your little one."

Damien set both of his hands onto the table, lowering himself to Zakai's level. "You have threatened my family and I for the last time. You and your shit show Order can get the fuck out of here, now."

"*Zakai is not the one to be angry with,*" Balfour said, grabbing Damien's hand and instantly dwarfing it. "*I am the one who looped Selia into this mess, when I attempted to form a storm bond with her.*"

Damien made a double take. He glanced at Zakai, who took another sip of her tea, then looked back to the storm dragon who said something about a *storm bond*. "What the heck is a storm bond?"

Balfour released his hand. "*Historically, storm dragons formed bonds with sea nymphs in order to keep the ancestral salts healthy.*"

"Balfour formed a *tidal* bond, specifically," Zakai chimed in. "This storm bond falls under a different class of bonds called origin bonds, those that form between a natural element such as water, and a celestial body."

"What are we talking about, the sun and the moon?" Damien asked.

"And the stars," Zakai added. "Balfour attempted to form a tidal bond with Selia to protect her from Masika. In doing so, he has awoken his brothers from an icy slumber Amphitrite put them into long ago. When they awaken, they will pick up where they left off thousands of years ago in their attempts to find the crown of their father."

"What is this actual crown? Is it a physical item?"

"*No,*" Balfour answered. "*Poseidon's crown is an ancient storm dragon territory, one that combines all dragon territories within the Abyss. His crown is connected to the Great Storm, or all past territories formed between both storm dragon lineages.*"

Damien's cheeks and neck heated so fiercely, he thought he might explode. "That's it. I'm not listening to any more crazy talk about some crown of Poseidon, or some star of the sea, or a tidal bond. Get out." When he stood, his hand knocked the crystal flying. It spun on the table, eventually coming to a stop. When it did, blue light pulsed out of it.

"We know who the crystal showed to Selia," Zakai said, propping her hands onto the table and clasping them. "I'm curious to know. Who do you see, Damien Malloch?"

Damien stared at the crystal, squinting as the blue light intensified. A woman with brown hair appeared, with equally brown eyes. Only the brown eyes he remembered of her flashed a brilliantly blinding blue.

He withdrew from the table, his back slamming into the wall. It *couldn't* be her. Not after all this time.

"Nobody," he stammered. "Now, as I said, you and Balfour take your crystal and get the heck out of our life."

Zakai's eyes flickered. "I think she was someone very close to you. The star of the sea shows the sea nymph souls that we are bound to, either in the past, present, or future."

Damien's body had gone numb.

Zakai propped her elbows onto the table and folded her fingers together. "Maera's work to preserve the crown has come back to haunt you."

He turned to face Zakai, anger rising through him. "Did you just say *Maera*?"

Balfour shot Zakai a wary glance as though he was bracing for something.

Zakai nodded, not taking her fierce gaze off him. "Maera is Maria's true name. When she lived with you, she took on the name Maria, as it sounded similar."

Damien's throat closed. "Are you trying to tell me that my deceased wife was as sea nymph?"

Balfour glanced at Zakai, who remained silent.

Damien's legs felt like they were about to collapse beneath him. His knees buckled as he sat back down. He slammed his fists onto the table. "You are crazy. Maria is *dead*. She and my daughter are buried in Scotland."

Zakai's mouth twitched. "Her body was buried, yes. But her spirit still lives on. Maera is a very powerful sea nymph, one who like Selia, also has a salt ancestry that originates from Celaeno, the Dark One."

Damien swallowed. "What are you saying? That she's just going to haunt me until she gets what she wants? What *does* she want?"

"Damien?" Selia said from behind him, panic in her voice. "Something is wrong with the baby."

Damien tore out of the room. "Show me what's wrong."

"I was feeding her, and then she just fell asleep in my arms, and—"

Damien darted into the room before Selia could finish her statement. His daughter was in her crib, bundled in her blanket. Her eyes were closed and she was unresponsive.

"I can't get her to wake," Selia stammered. "Why is she glowing? Why am *I* glowing?"

Blue light emanated out of them both.

Zakai lingered in the doorway.

"Hey, I didn't say you could come back here," Damien growled back at her.

Balfour stepped into the room. "*Let her explain.*"

Zakai walked over to the crib, and held the crystal over their daughter. "When a sea nymph gives birth to her first daughter, she forms an umbilical connection with her. This connection is a bond between a mother and a daughter's salt aura."

"What in the world is a salt aura?" Damien asked.

Zakai dropped the crystal between them. It levitated, hovering toward Selia's chest, before it began to drift toward their infant. As the crystal traveled between mother and daughter, a glowing blue line manifested.

The light pulsed between them, until the crystal finally sank down into the crib next to her.

She started to cry.

Selia reached down, picking her up. "Thank goodness..." She brought her across the room.

Damien rounded on Zakai. "This crystal can make my daughter's salt aura healthy?"

"Not only healthy, but it is vital for her development."

"What do we need to do to obtain the other fragments?"

"Show us your artwork, specifically the moonlit paintings you created after Maria left you," Zakai answered.

Damien swallowed. The only reason he would even dream of revisiting that painful time in his life, would only be for his daughter. "If I cooperate and show you my artwork, then you must both promise me something."

"*We will do as you ask,*" Balfour thundered into his mind.

Damien glanced over his shoulder, then returned his gaze back to the storm dragon and the Iridescent. "Promise me that you won't tell Selia about Maera."

Zakai nodded. "Balfour and I will not say a word about Maera to Celaeno's moon daughter." She glanced sideways at the storm dragon. "Right?"

Balfour nodded, lightning flashing in his dark eyes. "*Maera will be kept our secret.*"

14

LITTLE ORIGIN

Selia

The next day came bathed in golden light. Since Selia learned about the umbilical connection between her and her daughter's salt aura, a name had burst into her head. Did sea nymph infants give their mothers their names? If so, why did this name seem so...*odd*?

Selia didn't even know what the name meant, but it wouldn't leave her. She wanted to run it by Damien, but he was still sleeping. She sat up in the bed, blinking in the first rays of daylight as they bled into the room. Damien sat passed out in the chair next to the crib with his arm draped over the edge.

A large shadow descended over the window. Even though the skies were mostly clear, thunder followed. "*Come outside. I need you to meet someone.*"

Selia dressed herself and made her way into the courtyard. The air was damp and cool as mist rolled over the hedges.

Balfour stood beneath one of the trees. He was gazing at a bird bath, where a few finches swooped in and out of the water. Peppercorn accompanied them, a few of her bat pups still spiraling above her. They were getting so large, nearly the size of their mother.

Balfour turned, his facial hair patchy in spots. He looked haggard, his hair sticking out at awkward angles.

Selia approached him. "Who did you want me to meet?"

"*She's on her way.*"

"Okay, well. That gives me time to discuss something about the baby. Her name, specifically."

"She still doesn't have a name yet? What's wrong with you and Damien? Wasn't she born over a month ago?"

"Hey, I'm new at this, all right? Besides, I'm glad I didn't name her yet, not after the crazy stormy dream I experienced last night."

Balfour lowered his gaze. *"I specialize in translating the language of storms. I'm listening."*

Selia closed her eyes, attempting to re-imagine what she'd experienced. "It started as this great wind that just blew through me. Then, it turned into thunder, and lightning."

"Was it raining, or was there snow?"

"It was a mixture of both."

Balfour made a thunderous noise. *"What did it sound like?"*

"It sounds like this. Nyyysssssaaaaaa."

Balfour held out his wide palm. *"Try it again."*

Wind tunneled off his hand, taking her spoken word and channeled it through the stormy elements.

Selia's salt nodes thrummed with the sheer force of the aquatic melody that erupted from his fingertips. "It's music?"

"It's a melody of storms—a language only storm dragons can speak."

Selia's hands were vibrating. "It's absolutely beautiful. What does it mean?"

Balfour lowered his hand, his thick brow furrowing. *"If I had to translate that melody, I would say it means beginning, or new from the sea."*

"In other words, Nyssa means *origin*?"

Balfour's eyes glinted. *"Yes, or origin of the ocean."*

"Okay, why are we all talking about origins of the ocean?" a female voice said from behind the grove of trees.

Selia turned, finding another individual admiring her from a distance. The hedges shifted as she approached. Everything about her screamed *nymph*, but Selia didn't see her as a nymph who came from the sea. She had an earthy air about her, with golds and greens and browns shimmering in what could be an aura.

"If it isn't Selia, the Blind Moon!" she said, her voice high and cheerful. She stopped a few paces before them, a sly grin turning up her impish features.

Selia squinted at the newcomer. "Why do you sound so familiar?"

The nymph laughed. "You've been my bestie for a while now." She reached into one of her cargo pockets and tugged out her phone. "I'm sure you have been missing my texts about how my Siamese cat likes go guzzle down leftover Chinese food?"

Selia's mouth dropped open. "*Deidra?*"

"In the flesh!"

Deidra wasn't dressed anything like Alex or Zakai. No long, dramatic robes flowed at her sides. She looked more like a park ranger with her khaki cargo pants, olive green shirt, and long blond hair tied back into a wavy braid. Her skin was honey brown. A dusting of freckles lined her nose and cheeks. Her eyes were cat-like. The centers had flecks of green around them, surrounded with golds that screamed *woodland meadow* in the midst of summer.

Deidra closed the space between them, lowering the duffle bag slung onto her shoulder to the ground. "I promise I didn't mean to ghost you like I did with my texts. Alex ordered me to stop sending them as soon as she discovered that you opened the vault."

"Wait, you worked for Alex?"

Deidra glanced at Balfour, who rolled his massive eyes. "Hey, don't you waggle your fins at me, storm boy. You try playing the part of the dumb blond dryad who's supposed to convince a sea nymph with no memories of her past to go on a wild goose chase to Scotland to find a fae treasure with a rambunctious little fae hermit crab who tried to sabotage the entire journey."

Selia couldn't help herself as she was thrown into a laughing fit. "I think Henrietta gave the Order a run for its money."

"That annoying little crab gave me quite the headache with all of her escapades," Balfour grumbled in agreement.

Selia's sides stopped trembling. "What was your relationship with Alex?"

Deidra's green eyes flickered, emotion swelling in them. "Alexandra was the Iridescent I reported to. Her mission was to prevent you from finding and opening the vault, as she knew Masika was using it to try and find you."

Selia's laughter died at the thought of Masika. "I owe my life to the effort Alex put into protecting me from Masika."

A low grumble filled her head. *"Not to mention your loyal storm dragon."*

"Speaking of Masika, do you have any idea what happened to her?" Selia asked.

"She got what she deserved," Balfour grumbled, taking a step toward Selia. *"Right now, we need to focus on your inheritance."*

"Easy, I was getting to it," Deidra grumbled at him, jabbing her thumb in his direction. "Are storm dragons always this cantankerous?"

Selia sighed. "I don't know. I've only ever met one."

Balfour lowered himself onto the stone bench next to the bird bath. He crossed his giant arms in front of his chest, where a couple of finches jumped from the water and promptly perched on his shoulders. *"Leave it to a dryad to spend all morning chatting instead of getting any work done."*

Deidra shrugged. "Anyway, neither Alex or I expected you to get whisked off your feet by a handsome watercolor artist like Damien. Speaking of which, I'm assuming he's with the baby?"

"Yes. They're both still sleeping."

"Good. Because like Balfour so kindly reminded me, Zakai ordered me to share some top-secret news to share with you regarding your inheritance. But before I do that." She bent down to the duffel bag and unzipped it. "I come bearing gifts!"

Selia watched as Deidra rummaged through the duffel, and tugged out a beautiful dress. "I figured that aquamarine might be a favorite color of yours. Do you like it?"

"Is this for me?" Selia asked.

"Of course!" Deidra replied as she handed Selia the dress. "I got you some other items for you and your daughter."

"I've never owned a dress so beautiful in my life," Selia said as she held it up to her body. The fabric was light and wispy, something she'd only imagined Amy would wear.

"I also brought some items for Jo, but I'll save save those for later." Deidra plopped down onto the stone bench next to the bird bath.

Selia sat next to her and tucked the dress back into the duffel. From what she could tell, dryads didn't have salt nodes behind their ears, but Deidra did have some odd-looking freckles on her wrists.

Deidra glanced sideways at her. "I'm sure you have so many questions about your past, even after remembering what you have about your childhood in Egypt."

A low growl from Balfour sent the finches scattering away from him. "*Inheritance.*"

"Hey, Selia deserves to know how her choice with her inheritance is going to impact a whole lot of shebang in the ocean. She needs to understand what it has to do with Amy's mother."

Balfour let out a long, thunderous sigh. "*Please, get on with it then. We cannot waste time on the past right now. The crown of my father is waiting for her decision.*"

Deidra reached into one of her cargo pockets and pulled out an item. It looked like a wonky green stick, with little root fibers sticking out of it. "You've never seen a dryad practice root reading, have you?"

"I've never seen a dryad, other than you," Selia replied.

Deidra grinned impishly. "Sea nymphs play with salt. I play with soil. It's time to show you what the art of root reading is capable of." She tossed the root onto the ground and began rubbing her hands together.

The tree behind her began to tremble. A holographic image of the ocean burst out of the root in golden light. What appeared to be coral came rising out of the water.

Two giant women manifested atop the coral shaped like a crown. They stood next to each other, facing apart. One was bright white, the other was cloaked in shadows. Both had wing-like auras that branched over one another.

"Who are these figures?" Selia asked.

"The goddesses of life and death. Isis, and her sister, Nephthys. Together, they created the star of the sea in an effort to help Amphitrite's sister, Pherusa, who served as the midwife of the sea in Atlantis. Long story short, the bond between Pherusa, and the architect, Erebéus, was weak, making her duties difficult to perform. Pherusa got super pissed when the goddesses stepped in without consulting with her first, so she tried to get Poseidon to bond with her to get even with them."

"I'm guessing that didn't work out?"

"Nope. Poseidon was a sea god of a storm dragon. And he only had his eyes set on Pherusa's sister." The goddesses disappeared. A beautiful sea nymph with long red hair and emerald eyes emerged. A dusting of star-shaped freckles covered her face.

"Amy's mother, Amphitrite," Selia added.

Deidra nodded. "That's when the god of shadows, Erebéus, came into play. As Poseidon's ancestor, he didn't want to cross bonds between himself, and his storm dragon descendants with the midwife of the sea."

"Why not?"

"Bonds that cross between architects and storm dragons have been know to cause mass extinctions on the planet," Deidra replied. "So Erebéus approached Amphitrite, requesting that she fragment the star of the sea into three parts. Pherusa never wanted the help of the crystal to begin with, so Amphitrite did as requested. She gave two crystal fragments to the goddesses who created it."

"What about the third fragment?"

"Erebéus insisted that Amphitrite take it. But she was afraid of the crystal's power. She also didn't want it to contaminate the salt crystals in her Ocean Apothecary. The last record the Order has of Amphitrite's crystal fragment dates back to Atlantis. It hasn't been seen since the city sank."

"What did Nephthys do with her fragment?"

"She hid it somewhere that not even her sister Isis could find."

Selia squinted at Balfour. "If Isis had one of the fragments, then why did Damien have to confront Erebéus when Isis asked him to retrieve it?"

"Retrieve what?"

Selia turned. Her heart warmed as Damien emerged in the courtyard, holding their daughter.

15

THE STAR OF THE SEA

Amy

As the image of Errindoor's starlit antlers faded from her mind, Amy squinted once again at the dragon scale. It shimmered differently on one side. A small crystalline item was embedded in the scale's lumpy surface.

She blinked, suddenly blinded. "Is something hidden inside of it?"

"A fragment from the star of the sea," her mother added, whimsy dancing in her tone.

"A star of the *what*?" Amy asked.

Amphitrite tilted the scale to the side, making the crystal shimmer. "The star of the sea contains all seven of the ancestral salts in its composition."

"Wait, all seven ancestral salts are inside of this crystal?" Amy asked, momentarily blinded by it again.

"Prior to the Abyss, all seven salt ancestries were combined as one. Our origin all stems from the same source, the same crystalline stars like this one."

"What is the crystal made of?"

Amphitrite's green eyes caught the crystal's reflection. "The star of the sea was created by Isis and Nephthys from the starlit corals."

"Where can you find these corals?"

"During Atlantis, the starlit corals were the primary ingredients in my Ocean Apothecary. But today, they can only be found in what remains of the ancient storm dragon territories within Poseidon's crown."

"Why did Isis and Nephthys create the crystal? What is its purpose? Does it hold some kind of power?"

Amphitrite's freckles darkened as she lowered the scale and the crystal embedded inside. "Do you know what makes a sea nymph the midwife of the sea? Do you know what gave both Pherusa and Naunet their power?"

Amy shivered as she thought. "Why do I feel like Erebéus was involved?"

"Bonding with an architect transforms a sea nymph, making her the midwife of the sea. The bond creates an everlasting power of fostering salt-born fertility. But with this power comes certain tasks and responsibilities as I'm sure you remember seeing with Naunet. You were too young to remember the struggles my sister had in Atlantis."

"You're right, I don't remember much from Atlantis. What did Pherusa struggle with?"

"Erebéus and Pherusa never got along. Because their bond was weak to begin with, her task of collecting and sorting the ancestral salts suffered. Salt pregnancies began to decline. Isis and Nephthys noticed her struggles, so they created the star of the sea to help where their bond suffered."

"In other words, the crystal was created to help reinforce their bond?"

Amphitrite nodded. "Pherusa became embarrassed, claiming that she didn't need the help of the goddesses, or the architect she became to hate. She believed that she could convince one of Erebéus's descendants to bond with her instead."

"Poseidon?"

"Yes, Poseidon, the great storm dragon god of the sea. When Erebéus discovered what Pherusa was attempting to do, he came to me. He knew that I possessed the same starlit corals in my Ocean Apothecary that Isis and Nephthys used to create the crystal. He asked me to fragment the star of the sea in case Poseidon did choose to bond with her."

"Did they ever form a bond?"

"No. Poseidon never bonded with my sister." Amphitrite shifted in her chair as her expression became rigid. "As you might remember, Poseidon had eyes," her voice shook as she spoke, "he had eyes, for me."

Amy's cheeks heated. Watching her mother become so flustered over an encounter with the kingly storm dragon was new to her. "Did Poseidon attempt to bond with you instead?"

"He did. So many times, that I lost count," Amphitrite replied, her face reddening. "He wanted me to reign along side him. He wanted me to be his queen—his sea goddess."

"He loved you, didn't he? He wanted more than just to form a storm bond with you."

Amphitrite drew in a slow breath, exhaling as she continued, "I was aware of Poseidon's feelings for me early on. And I knew that while sea nymphs and storm dragons could form romantic bonds with one another, they often led to passionate outbursts of unpredictable weather. I did not want to risk creating storms with him that could result in harming the sea life I was so invested in protecting."

Amy flushed for her mother's sake. She could only imagine what those *storms* she mentioned were insinuating. "Back to the star of the sea, did you fragment it like Erebéus requested?"

"I did. Pherusa did not argue with me. Eager to prove that she did not need the crystal's assistance, she welcomed me fragmenting it. Erebéus requested that I fragment it into three parts. I gave both Isis and Nephthys their own fragments, as they were the original creators. Erebéus insisted that I keep the third fragment for myself as I was the one to fragment it."

"What did you do with your crystal fragment?"

"I was afraid of the crystal's power. It had been formed with magic by the goddesses of life and death. I didn't want it to contaminate the starlit corals I had in my Ocean Apothecary. So I asked Poseidon if he could do me a favor, and hide the crystal inside the scale of one one of his sons. The human Atlantean kings at the time adorned their crowns with shimmering storm dragon scales."

Amy's breath caught. "The crystal was worn on the crown of Atlantean kings?"

Amphitrite nodded. "The crystal and its crown was passed down from king to king, until eventually, the great city fell. Only then was the scale recovered by Ewan's father, who eventually passed it along to him." She turned the crystal over, making it shimmer. "Every winter, Ewan followed the mighty fae king up into the mountains so that he could witness what?"

"Errindoor—the giant king, shed his antlers, or his crown," Amy answered.

Amphitrite's freckles brightened. "Isn't it fascinating how history repeats it-self?"

Amy gawked at the scale in her mother's hand. "Even though you fragmented the crystal for her, your sister must have still been incredibly jealous of you."

"Pherusa was beyond jealous. She blamed me for Poseidon's refusal to bond with her. After Atlantis sank, I refused to follow her to Egypt. I wanted to give her and her daughters the ability to recover after her failure to reign as a successful midwife of the sea in Atlantis."

Amy glanced around the shop, spotting jars of bath salts, dried herbs, and the occasional bottle of seashells. The little bit of clarity her mother had given her only clouded her mind with a thick emotional fog. "You disappeared, because of Pherusa's jealousy?"

Amphitrite's gaze softened. "I removed myself because I did not want to harm the relationship between Pherusa and her own daughter."

Amy's stomach pitted. While she wanted her mother's concern for her sister to make her feel better, it didn't. Why did she have to put Pherusa's concern for her daughters over their own relationship?

She choked back the emotion, not allowing it to cloud her list of unanswered questions. "And now you want *me* to help you?" Her words sounded harsher than she wanted them to.

"Amy, you have always been my crystal child. I remember when Poseidon was handing out rain and wind bonds like candy to youthful sea nymphs. Yours, however, transformed into the form of a crystal, did it not?"

Amy glanced at the crystal in her mother's palm. One of her earliest childhood memories consisted of her reaching into a pool she remembered containing Al-cyone's brilliant red salt crystals. The crystals put off light that shone in the same fiery color of her mother's hair. She would have fallen into the water, had her mother not been there to grab her. "Yes, my storm bond is crystal. Why does it matter to you?"

Her mother beamed. "What matters is that I have my daughter here to reclaim what I lost when the great city sank. What remains of my Ocean Apothecary is located within the temple. I cannot access the starlit corals if the issue with

Celaeno's salt daughters is not remedied first. The star of the sea must be mended in the same place in which it was created by Isis and Nephthys."

Amy saw the plea in her mother's eyes as jar upon jar of salt crystals reflected in their emerald depths. The samples seemed *dead* compared to the magic she remembered her possessing in Atlantis. "Does that mean we must return to the Chamber of Salt?"

"You and I must return to the Temple of the Three Origins. The chamber of Salt will be our entry point, which is located in the heart of Poseidon's crown."

Amy swallowed. "Are you telling me that I first need to help you obtain the other two crystal fragments?"

"No. The other fragments are well on their way to reuniting with one another. Maera is working to recover the fragment Nephthys had, and Celaeno's moon daughter is in the process of obtaining the other from Erebéus as he currently resides in the Temple of Isis."

Amy's mouth opened and closed. "You mean, *Selia*?"

"Selia is vital to ensuring the star of the sea is mended. Before Isis left her temple, she told Erebéus that the only individual who could ever inherit the fragment in her absence would be Celaeno's moon daughter."

Amy's thoughts were riddled with the grotesque grey bodies of the sirens again. Not only did the fate of the plague victims rely on restoring the star of the sea, but so did what remained of her mother's Ocean Apothecary.

Was she willing to risk her own life to help the souls of the plague victims?

16

LEAVING SCOTLAND

Damien

Damien emerged in the courtyard, transfixed by the glowing tree. Golden daylight beamed through the clouds, illuminating the branches unnaturally. Three individuals were present. Balfour had both of his arms crossed across his front, where he stood next to Selia.

Damien didn't recognize the third individual. A long blond braid swung against her back. She wore black combat boots, an olive green shirt, and khaki cargo pants.

His daughter let out a squeal in his arms.

When the newcomer turned to face him, she clapped both of her hands against her cheeks. "Oh my goodness, she's *soooooo* cute!"

Selia walked over to where Damien stopped, setting her hand on his shoulder. "Damien, this is Deidra."

Damien blinked a few times, trying to run that name through his brain. Why did it sound so familiar?

"I'm Selia's dryad friend, the one who was always sending her confusing text messages?"

"I vaguely remember. Why are you visiting?"

Deidra's yellow eyes narrowed onto him, which felt a bit unsettling. "I'm sure Selia will be sharing with you what I just shared about her inheritance." She waved her hand over her head. "Three is a crowd, four adults and a cute little baby is a party."

Golden light bloomed over their heads, ballooning around them.

"There," Deidra started. "Now nobody can eavesdrop on our top-secret discussion."

His daughter began to squirm in his arms, so Selia took her and walked over to where Deidra sat. "Would you like to hold her?"

Deidra held up her hands. "Oh, no. I will *look* at babies, but I do not *hold* them."

"*What is wrong with you?*" Balfour cooed, suddenly standing and towering over both of the nymphs. His head bumped into the golden light barrier Deidra had created, sending golden sparks raining down on them. "*I want to meet your daughter.*"

Pudgy hands reached for the sparks as another squeal of delight erupted. Balfour took their tiny daughter into his massive arms, where she nearly disappeared. She wouldn't stop reaching for his beard, grabbing handfuls of wiry ebony mass, and tugging it on it.

Balfour didn't flinch. His eyes became deep liquid pools as he soaked in their infant. "*You've stolen my heart, Little Origin,*" he thundered like an afternoon storm into Damien's mind.

Damien's chest swelled at the sight. Never had he seen Selia look so proud. This was just the beginning of their beautiful life. "Little Origin, huh? Is that a nickname?"

Selia beamed. "Damien, I think we have a name for her. I had this crazy dream last night, and it just blew through me," she turned to Balfour. "Tell him what you said the name meant in storm dragon?"

Balfour wasn't listening. He was too fixated on their daughter, who was blowing a snot bubble out of her nose.

Selia grabbed Damien's arm. "Anyway, Balfour said the name Nyssa means *origin*, or *new beginning*. What do you think?"

He grabbed Selia, kissing her forehead. "If that's the name you want for our daughter, then so be it."

Balfour rocked Nyssa in his beefy arms. "*I'm a stoooorrmmm draaaaagoooon,*" he grumbled, his voice rumbling like distant thunder. "*My father made hurricanes and tsunamis. But I devour them when I'm hungry.*"

Nyssa exploded into a fit of giggling.

Deidra laughed so hard, her eyes teared up. "Okay. Well. I'm glad that Balfour can get one of us laughing hysterically."

Selia grabbed Damien's arm. "Deidra works with Zakai. She just got done with telling me why the star of the sea was created, as well as who fragmented it."

Damien shot the dryad a wary glance. "Has Deidra mentioned anything about the cursed selkie who killed Alex?"

Selia squinted at him. "Who told you about that?"

"Zakai did last night," Damien confirmed. "She also told me that Balfour tried to form a tidal bond with you to protect you from Masika."

Selia glanced up at her protective storm dragon as he rocked their baby in his massive arms. "Is this true? You tried to form a tidal bond to protect me from her?"

"*Not without repercussions, however,*" he grumbled. "*Me attempting to form a tidal bond has caused my brothers to wake from their icy slumber. They will soon be regrouping to find the crown of my father.*"

Selia glanced at Damien. "Amphitrite fragmented the crystal into three parts. We have one. The problem is that Amphitrite lost hers, and Nephthys hid her fragment in a place that not even Isis could find. Do you think if we found Amphitrite, she could answer what she did with her fragment?"

"*Only if you want to deal with the stormy personalities of my brothers,*" Balfour grumbled.

"It sounds to me like nobody knows what is really going on, and the Order wants us to go running off into another quest that leads to nothing but confusion," Damien grunted just as grumpily as Balfour sounded.

Selia shot him an applaud look.

Damien returned it with a frustrated one. "Look, I'm not doing a thing until we know where Zakai is. I need to talk with her about some things that she still hasn't answered about this confusing crystal inheritance."

"Zakai will be along shortly," Deidra replied. "She informed me that I needed to share some additional history with you regarding Selia's inheritance."

A bright golden light zipped overhead, taking a strand of Deidra's blond hair with it. She let out a big sigh. "Apparently I'm not the only one volunteering to give you a history lesson."

"Oh, who do we have here?" Selia asked as the vibrant golden-winged creature hovered above them. It's body was thin and long. It zipped between Selia, then Deidra, then landed momentarily on Balfour's nose. His eyes crossed as the creature shook a set of four shimmering wings, then took off in one quick motion.

"I named him Zipper, because he likes to zip into discussions and situations unannounced," Deidra said, her yellow eyes darting through the air after the insect's incredibly swift movements.

"I'm guessing this is another fae creature?" Damien asked.

Deidra pinched her brow. "And an incredibly nosy one at that."

Zipper hovered over Damien's head. "Let's have a count on how many fae creatures we've met so far. A fae hermit crab, a bat, and now, a *dragonfly*?"

Deidra smiled. "There are more fae creatures disguising themselves along current-day species than you might realize. And you haven't even met an extinct one yet."

"I don't think I really want to," Damien said, suddenly thinking about dinosaurs. Dealing with a storm dragon was already ancient enough.

Deidra shook her head. "No, Zipper, you are getting ahead of yourself. We aren't flying anywhere. I haven't gotten to those details just yet."

Zipper flitted between her and Balfour, zipping in a fury that set his golden wings ablaze.

"Can you talk to him?" Selia asked.

"Interpret his messages is more like it. You would be amazed at how much I learned about the migratory routes of fae species like bats and insects over the past few months. They have incredible instincts when it comes to navigating dangerous situations, especially when it comes to storms."

Another creature swooped in front of them.

"Speaking of bats. Who is this?" Deidra asked.

Schreeeeeech!

"Peppercorn, be nice," Selia scolded the little bat as she circled, then dove to perch on Deidra's shoulder.

"Are you a fruit eater, or an eater of insects?" Deidra asked, holding up a finger to her face.

"Careful, she'll bite your nose if she gets the opportunity," Damien warned.

Peppercorn's furry little head swiveled in Zipper's direction as he darted above their heads.

"Okay, well. My dragonfly is not breakfast. Can we agree with that?"

Peppercorn's ears flicked back and forth as Deidra chatted with her.

"What? Did you say that Zakai has already left for the Celtic Sea? Why? I haven't even performed my root reading yet."

"Root reading? Is that similar to salt trancing?" Damien asked.

Deidra made a curious look. "I was planning to show you more about the origin story of the star of the sea. Root reading is the art form us dryads practice to tap into those ancient histories."

"Zakai kept saying that Selia needs to pick up where Naunet left off with her work in Gaia's Codex. Where is this Codex kept, anyway?" Damien asked.

"Gaia's Codex is kept in the same place the star of the sea was created, the Temple of the Three Origins."

"Do you have any idea what the three origins are?" Damien asked.

"We already know *one* of the three origins," Selia cut in. "The Abyss pertains to the ancestral salts and the life cycle of sea nymphs."

"What could the other two be?" Damien asked.

"No idea. But knowing what the other two origins are could possibly help me figure out how to use my inheritance." Selia glanced at Deidra. "Does the Order know how to access this temple?"

"Only certain individuals are allowed to enter it. Goddesses, and prior midwives of the sea," Deidra replied.

"Then we should be trying to find one of these goddesses or midwives of the sea. What about Isis?" Selia asked.

"Not long after Naunet took up her reign as the midwife of the sea, Erebéus forced Isis out of her temple. She hasn't been seen, nor has she had any contact with her sister goddess, Nephthys. And Naunet hasn't been seen since she abandoned her work in the Codex."

"What about Pherusa? Could she give us information on the temple?" Selia asked.

Deidra shook her head. "I don't think you would want to run into Naunet's mother. Everything I've heard about her is pretty nasty to put it lightly."

While Zipper continued to flutter frantically between the two, Damien's hair stood on end. Why would Zakai just take off for his art studio and not tell him?

He took Selia's hand. "Can I talk with you for a moment?"

Selia followed him away from the tree, where Deidra and Balfour watched them curiously. Peppercorn followed, flitting down and landing on Selia's shoulder.

Damien turned his back to the group, focusing on Selia, and Peppercorn's disappearing body as she buried herself beneath her hair. "I know where Zakai went. Last night, while you were with the baby, I talked with her. The Order is trying to gather information on Poseidon's crown, which she believes my artwork could help with."

Selia's eyes went wide. "I always knew your artwork was special. Do you have any idea what she wants to use your artwork for?"

Damien ground his jaw. There were other haunting things from his past that he had yet to tell Selia about, specifically about Maera's work with the crown. "No, I don't. But I think we need to follow her. She might know where Amphitrite is. I think we need to find her because she fragmented your inheritance. We both know that this star of the sea can help remedy this issue between you and Nyssa's salt auras."

"Then what are we waiting for? We need to get to your art studio, now." She brushed past him and walked up to Balfour, who was nodding off. She shook his arm. "Wake up. You're taking us to the Celtic Sea."

Balfour jostled awake. "*I'm what?*"

Selia grabbed a sleeping Nyssa and the crystal from his arms. "We are going to Damien's art studio."

Zipper flitted overhead, his wings shimmering with excitement.

"Oh, I guess we *are* flying, then. At least *you* are," Deidra said, glancing up at the fae dragonfly.

Balfour folded his arms in front of his chest. *"Gather your belongings. I'll be waiting here."*

The two parents headed back inside of the building to gather everything they might need for the journey ahead. Deidra followed, standing in the hallway as they packed, including the items Deidra had gifted them.

Selia finished shoving supplies into her bag, then swaddled Nyssa to her front. "How are we escaping? They won't let me leave the facility until I show I'm not mental."

Deidra laughed. "The people who run this place are mental." She led the way down the hallway. Selia and Damien followed. As they walked down the hall, Deidra held out her hand, casting light over all four of them. Sunlight branched form her fingers, along with a flew flowers that blew up into the air. The people they passed in the hall didn't give them a second-glance.

"Why are we stopping at the front desk?" Selia asked.

"We're wiping the log that you were ever in this insane place. I might have hooked you up with a social security number back in the day, and I can just as quickly erase it. Also, I think you are missing a piece of jewelery that they confiscated." She shifted her hand. "You two head back outside where Balfour is waiting."

Deidra kept walking toward the lobby, her curtain of glowing sunlight branching over them like an umbrella as they turned the other way.

Cool, crisp air drifted past Damien's face. Balfour was waiting outside, his body morphing in and out of mist-like form. The membranous edges of his tail coiled around the fountain.

"Hurry up," he grumbled.

Damien walked with Selia up to the thickening fog. Bluish-black scales appeared from behind the water vapor.

"Climb on just like last time. And don't grip my scales so hard, you're going to chafe them."

Selia went up first, positioning herself on the onyx surface of Balfour's back.

Damien followed, making sure that Selia was firmly situated on Balfour's lumpy spine. He positioned himself behind Selia, gripping the scales with his feet as he wrapped his arms around her.

"What about Deidra?" Selia asked.

Deidra appeared in the courtyard. She gazed up at them as mist began to conceal Balfour's fins. "A dryad has her own ways of transporting from one landmass to another, but first." She walked over to where Balfour was busy transforming into a dragon. "Here, catch!"

Selia caught her cell phone and set it into her pocket.

Damien caught the second smaller item that flew toward him. "I was wondering where this went," he said as she handed Selia her engagement ring.

The moment she set it onto her ring finger electric sparks jolted out of the stone. "Thank you so much, Deidra," she called down to the dryad, who made her way over to the tree at the center of the courtyard.

She beamed, waving her hand. "See you at Damien's art studio!"

Damien shifted back as muscles and scales contracted beneath him. Balfour's long membranous fins expand, launching them up into the air. They flew higher, leaving Scotland below, with nothing but steel-grey ocean before them.

"*Keep your arms and legs tucked against me. The jet stream can become very turbulent at times.*"

A large fin branched out of Balfour's neck, shielding them from the elements.

"I will never joke about storm dragons not being able to fly again," Selia said as she tucked Nyssa close to her. "This is incredible."

As open ocean surrounded them, the clouds they were climbing into began to move upward.

"Something is wrong." Damien dug his heel into Balfour's side. "Hey..."

"*Hmmmmmm?*"

"Why are we dipping out of the clouds?"

"*Sorry, I nodded off.*"

"You fell asleep *midair*?"

"*I'm so jealous of your daughter right now and how she can just drift off like that.*"

"How about we don't fall asleep while we're flying hundreds of feet up in the air over open ocean?" Damien scolded.

"Hey...I've been awake while my brothers slept for the past three thousand years. I'm long overdue for a nap."

17
RETURN TO THE LOUVRE
Selia

Dark storm clouds rolled before Balfour's thick purple fins as they journeyed south. Selia remained tucked behind the membranous fin that jutted out from the back of Balfour's head, shielding his three passengers from the wind and cold. She never would have imagined that traveling on a storm dragon could be so comfortable. Nyssa slept as soundly as she could, not making peep as they continued on their journey.

Peppercorn remained tucked beneath her hair, shielding herself from the wind. The stormy atmosphere only mirrored how Selia felt. If her inheritance wasn't whole, could she really use it to help her daughter's salt aura develop properly?

"Wow, this is magnificent," Damien said as he stood up behind her.

"*Stay seated at all times, or you will be ripped out to sea by the jet stream,*" Balfour grumbled in his most studious fashion.

"What are you now, a flight attendant?" Damien stammered as he sat back down.

Balfour chuckled. "*You have yet to feel the turbulence generated by a storm dragon.*"

At Balfour's grumbly reply, his body pitched to the left.

"How long until we arrive at Damien's studio?" Selia asked.

"*At least another hour. I'm not feeling like spreading my fins too much. Quite frankly, I'm exhausted.*"

Selia closed her eyes, ready for a nap. Balfour's movements were soothing, like laying on a water bed.

Lightning ripped across the sky, followed by an aggressive roll of thunder. Electricity crackled, sending sparks jumping between the scales that shimmered right above their heads.

A low, thunderous voice echoed in the clouds.

Nyssa began to fuss.

"What was that?" Selia stammered.

"*Another storm dragon,*" Balfour grumbled back.

Rain fell in thick sheets around them, carrying the electrical sparks closer as water dribbled down Balfour's protective fins. Selia tucked Nyssa to her core, shielding her from the onslaught of elements.

Damien repositioned himself behind Selia, gripping her tight.

"*It's too dangerous to go over open water. We must go inland.*"

He pitched to the side, nearly sending Selia and Damien off his back. "Hey! Don't do that!"

"*That wasn't my fault,*" Balfour grumbled back, his giant body shuddering once again with the turbulence. "*Stop trying to fly up my nose.*"

"What's trying to fly up your nose?" Selia yelled.

A shimmering yellow fleck went darting above her.

"Zipper is here!" she yelled, watching Deidra's dragonfly maneuver without a problem.

"*He keeps getting in the way,*" Balfour thundered aggressively.

"Why don't you follow him? I think he's trying to tell you something," Selia replied.

"*Are you telling me follow a dragonfly's directions on how to navigate stormy weather?*"

"Just do it. Deidra said that they know all kinds of secrets about escaping dangerous situations when it comes to storms."

Another thunderous grumble followed as Balfour pitched to the left, taking off after Zipper's shimmering golden wings.

Selia could have sworn she heard the word *brother* rip through the thunder.

As they drifted inland, the thunderstorms lessened, and the skies became less treacherous. The weather was far less violent inland than it was over the sea. Clouds rolled beneath them as the countryside emerged.

"Look up there," Damien said from behind.

The countryside blended with towns, until the Eiffel Tower came into view.

Selia's stomach filled with butterflies as the City of Lights manifested beneath them. "That little bug is taking us to *Paris*?"

"You told me to follow him. Now, hold tight. Landing is going to be very inter-esting."

Balfour's membranous fins cocooned around them, then retracted as scales and backbone became small enough for him to fit beneath the buildings. Torrents of rain fell from the sky with Balfour's descent as he tucked himself down into an alleyway. The shudder of his body told Selia he'd made contact with the earth.

Damien slid down his side first, and Balfour dipped himself low to the ground to help Selia with her dismount.

Zipper flitted before her, his golden wings shimmering as he took off down the alleyway. "I guess we follow," Selia said, glancing back at Balfour, who was struggling.

"You go ahead and follow the Glitter Wing. I'll catch up."

Selia was glad they made an impromptu pit stop. Nyssa needed to be fed and changed. She and Damien regrouped as they trudged down the street toward the iconic symbol of the museum—the giant glass pyramid.

It had been almost a year since she had been back to the museum. She wondered if it was even worth stopping by her office, where Alex had broken into it to steal a salt trancing talisman so long ago. Did Dr. O'Connor still work here? She still remembered the stale smell of cigars anytime he bound through the hallway on his shiny leather shoes.

Memories began to flood her—memories of Damien coming to meet her after their brief encounter at the Celtic Sea. She remembered how the water droplets from the fountain settled upon his eyelashes when he'd retrieved the bottle of selkie salt skin she'd dropped into the water. She almost wished the fountain would have swallowed the substance she later learned Amy had renamed from salt venom.

Zipper's golden wings flit in front of them. Together, they entered the museum.

Speaking of stale cigars. The pungent aroma lingered in the hall.

"Is that your old boss?" Damien asked.

"It is," Selia replied. She tightened the swaddle around Nyssa, bracing herself for what was sure to be an awkward reunion.

Dr. O'Connor swiveled on the balls of his feet like he always did when he spotted something entertaining. His shiny bald head caught the dim light of the room. "Miss Fontaine? Is that you?"

Her old boss practically leapt across the floor, skidding to a halt before her. "Oh my word, it *is* you." His eyes dropped to her engagement ring. "You've been married? And have a baby?"

Nostalgia swept over her.

Nyssa let out a squeal.

Damien thrust out his hand, which Dr. O'Connor took. "So glad to see you again."

Dr. O'Connor shook Damien's hand fiercely. "My lad, you have no idea how good this makes me feel, seeing that Selia has left this dusty old museum behind to start a family?"

Damien beamed. "I'm the lucky one."

Dr. O'Connor released Damien's hand, turning to face Selia again. "I tried calling you, but alas, you never replied. I thought you had up and quit after someone broke into your office. I had to fill your position. I hope you understand."

The smell of rotten eggs erupted between them.

"Oh, somebody has a stinky diaper," Damien said as he grabbed Nyssa. "You two catch up while I change her."

Selia handed Damien her bag, which he took and walked away. "Who is the new employee?"

"She's out for lunch. If she comes back, I will introduce you, all right? Would you like to see your office, for old time's sake?"

"Sure, why not." Selia walked with Dr. O'Connor down the hallway, passing visitors as they went.

"What brings you back to the museum?" Dr. O'Connor asked as he bobbed along side her.

She glanced over her shoulder. There was still no sign of Balfour.

Slowing her pace, she matched her step with her old boss. "I wanted to apologize for never following up with you after I left so spontaneously," she lied.

Dr. O'Connor waved his hand. "I knew you had been unhappy with your job for a very long time. Seeing that someone broke into your office seemed like the last straw. It didn't take long before I found someone who not only worked in a museum before, but like you, had a profound interest in the sea. She spent a great deal of her life working as a marine biologist."

"Dr. O'Connor, when do you need me to report to our afternoon meeting?"

Selia's hair stood on end as the voice of a woman prickled against her ears. She turned, finding a woman standing next to an Egyptian statue. She had warm brown eyes, and equally brown hair. Her clothing was plain, yet intricate. Blue seashell accents lined the hem of her skirt and blouse.

Who was she? And why did her aura scream *sea nymph*?

"Hello," she reached out to shake Selia's hand. "My name is Maera."

"Hi Maera, I'm Selia." She took Maera's hand, which was incredibly warm. "I hear that you filled my position?"

Maera nodded. "For the past decade, I have worked at the British Museum. When I discovered a positioned opened up in Egyptian Antiquities at the Louvre? I couldn't help myself."

Selia's pocket began to glow once she made contact with her.

Maera released her hand. "I hope you don't mind about how I redecorated your office."

Dr. O'Connor bounced on the balls of his feet. "Maera, would you give Selia a tour of her old work space? I need to prepare for our afternoon meeting."

"Of course," Maera said, making a motion toward the door.

Dr. O'Connor gave Selia a friendly pat on the back. "I'm so sorry to run like this, but you know where to find me if you need me." He turned on his heel and took off down the hallway.

Selia followed Maera into her old office. Her salt nodes flushed. The room *smelled* like the sea. She glanced around the space that used to be stuffed full of artifact catalogs and filing cabinets. Judging by the decorations, Maera had a profound love of the ocean. Shelves were lined in jars of what appeared to be real coral samples. Seashells and pieces of driftwood were intermingled with Egyptian artifacts.

A shadow drifted in the corner of her eye, where it disappeared by a cardboard box stowed on top of the shelf.

Selia's stomach hollowed.

The box had been mailed to her a decade ago by Damien's deceased wife, Maria. It had originally contained a salt trancing talisman.

"Why did you keep this?" Selia asked, remembering the drawing Damien's daughter, Sophie, had made on the box.

"I didn't want to throw that out. It seemed too personal." Maera ran her fingers over the dog-eared cardboard. "What do you think this drawing is? A fairy?"

Selia's mouth had gone dry. "How about a moth?"

Maera smiled, her high cheekbones cutting against the brown bookshelves behind her. "I guess it could be. There are still so many marine species out there in the sea that we have so little knowledge of."

Selia blinked. She swore that a shadow drifted between Maera and the box. "Dr. O'Connor raved about your credentials. He said you worked at the British Museum, and that you had also worked as a marine biologist?"

Maera nodded. "Yes. I've always been fascinated with the sea."

"What did you study as a marine biologist?"

"Coral, and the reproductive cycles of marine life." Her eyes dipped to Selia's pocket, where she kept her crystal fragment. "I find that some of the greatest truths about marine discovery exist just beneath the surface of the water. These truths are like stars, only becoming visible in complete darkness."

The phone on the desk lit up. Maera pressed the red button, and Dr. O'Connor's voice blared through the speaker. "Our meeting starts in five minutes! Don't be late!"

"I'll be there shortly," Maera replied as she disconnected the phone. "It was so nice to meet you, Miss Selia. If you will excuse me, I have a meeting to attend. You know how pressing Dr. O'Connor can be."

The two left the office, and Maera locked the door.

Selia watched her walk down the hallway, disappearing behind the visitors that flooded the museum.

Something unsettling ached in her gut. She wandered back through the hallway, disoriented by her encounter with Maera. Why did it feel like she had met her before? Something about her didn't seem human. Was she also a sea nymph?

18

LACHLAN

Amy

Amy's gaze hadn't wavered from the dragon scale with the crystal fragment embedded in its center. "You mentioned that this scale belonged to one of Poseidon's sons. Which son of his does it belong to?"

Amphitrite smiled. "The storm dragon you are going to find. His name is Mestor." She held out her hand, and a seashell bobbed from the sleeve of her dress into her palm. A creature with ink-drop eyes and bright blue claws shuffled back and forth, seemingly excited about the adventure ahead.

"Really? A *hermit crab*?" Amy asked, slightly annoyed at her mother's choice of marine life. She'd gotten so sick of Henrietta's escapades, that she was not likely to befriend one of the annoying crustaceans ever again.

The crab climbed from her mother's arm onto her wrist. "This is not just any hermit crab, it's one of the rare blue crabs who used to live in Atlantis."

Amy bit her bottom lip. Maybe this crab would give Henrietta a run for her money, who knew. "I know that we need to re-enter the temple through the Chamber of Salt. How do you propose that we find Poseidon's crown?" As her new companion settled onto her shoulder, emotion struck her. "And why do I feel like we are saying goodbye?"

"I'm not letting you out of my sight. As long as she is with you, so am I." She placed Mestor's scale into a small velvet pouch, then handed it to her. "This scale is what you will use to summon Mestor when the time is right. He will be the one to help us navigate the waters of the sea to find his father's crown."

Amy's stomach hollowed as the crab burrowed itself into her hair. "How will I know *where* to find him?"

"Little Blue will help you."

She and her mother embraced. Why did it feel like they were parting again?

The two left the shop, walking out onto the sidewalk.

Amphitrite faced her. "I will meet you when you find Mestor. I cannot tell you exactly when, but it will be as soon as the tides come in."

Amy nodded, her vision suddenly blurry.

"Oh, and one other thing," her mother said as she rummaged through her pockets. "Galway is full of fishermen. If you do find one you fancy, don't be afraid to give him a sample of this tea." She handed Amy another silk pouch. "You never know when his boat might come in handy."

Amy took the pouch and stuffed it into her robes along with the dragon scale.

Her mother kissed her on the cheek, the bundled her cloak up around her neck. "Amy, you have always been my star of the sea. Don't ever forget that."

Amy blinked, trying hard to prevent the tears from forming. Her mother was such a beautiful force of nature, even in the way she said goodbye.

Amphitrite, goddess of the sea, departed. A few women with red hair walked down the cobblestone street. Amy's heart thundered as her beautiful redheaded mother merged behind them and disappeared, blending in with the other people of Ireland.

Numbness settled into her body. She had the fragment of the star of the sea, a storm dragon scale that belonged to Balfour's eldest brother, and a new fae creature who was supposed to help her find him. She'd been on many spontaneous journeys in her life. But this was the first one that involved her mother's Ocean Apothecary.

Amy took off through town. It was late on a Friday afternoon, and people in Galway took to the streets, eager to start their evening with friends and family. A boatyard came into view. Fleets of fishing boats were docked along the peer, bobbing in the low tide. One of the boats caught her eye—the *Sea Dragon*. Little

Blue snapped her claw toward the boat's direction. She must have agreed with her.

Amy scoped out the boat, curious about the name. An odd aroma wafted from inside its cramped quarters. Her nose filled with the scent of firewood and leather.

She hopped onto the boat deck and ducked inside. Her first impression was that the boat belonged to a caveman, not a fisherman. A deer skull with a full wrack of antlers hung on the far wall. A Scottish flag hung beneath the skull. Flints and leather items covered a table.

Amy's breathing stopped. She had to leave this boat. It reminded her too much of Ewan, and the heart of his frozen forest.

She turned to leave, finding a stocky man standing in the doorway.

He propped his hands onto his hips, his face concealed by the shadows cast inside the cramped opening.

"I was just leaving," Amy stammered.

"Sure you were," he said, jumping into the space. "I'm not used to women just welcoming themselves onto my boat, unless I invite them aboard."

His face emerged out of the shadows, and Amy made a double-take. His hair was a gorgeous chestnut brown, wavy in texture. Unruly locks tapered behind his ears, framed by wide cheekbones and a strong bridged nose. His deep-set eyes were a glorious hazel, with deep shades of viridian that reminded her of a forest.

Amy swallowed. Not just any forest—*his* forest—the winter wonderland that existed in Scotland over three thousand years ago. Only Ewan's eyes had that kind of green, the kind that became dangerously deep at a moment's notice.

He kept his hands planted firmly on his hips, not extending one for her to shake. "Oi. My name is Lachlan. And you are?"

"Amy," she replied. Even his sound held a similar tone to the giant huntsman. She scanned the room, finding a small table cluttered with a variety of framed photographs. "Who do we have here?"

"Photos of my nieces and nephews. My family is massive. I have thirty-nine aunts, uncles, and cousins. You can imagine how many children I need to keep tabs on for Christmas presents every year."

A fuzzy warm sensation filled her stomach. "What about this one? Why is this little girl all by herself?" Amy asked, noting how her picture frame had a piece of leather wrapped around its base. The decoration set the photograph off from the others.

Lachlan's face hardened. "That's Sophie, my cousin's little girl. Damien lost her and his wife over a decade ago in a car accident."

Amy's body went cold. Lachlan was related to *Damien Malloch*?

He grabbed a small leather pouch off the table and stuffed it into his pocket. "Why don't I offer you a drink?"

"*Mother, I hope I'm not getting in over my head,*" Amy thought.

Little Blue gave a swift pinch of her claw, which Amy assumed was her mother's approval.

Amy walked alongside Lachlan as he escorted her to the pub. While he wasn't the tallest man, his stride was long and powerful. Amy found herself struggling to keep up with his pace. Finally, he slowed, grabbing a door handle to the pub. He hesitated before opening it. "Do me a favor, and don't tell any of the blokes in this pub what you saw on my boat."

"What did I see?" Amy asked.

Lachlan's big hand clenched around the door handle. "Not an Irish flag hanging on my wall."

"You don't want them to know that you're Scottish?"

"Aye, the only Scotsman in this pub. Everyone here in this pub is *proud* Irish. I've convinced them that I am, too. I come to this port quite often."

Lachlan tugged the door open and ushered Amy into the pub. Fiddles and fifes were already blaring as the evening hour settled in.

He made a motion with his hand to the far corner. "Go on over to the bar, I'll by you a drink."

Amy nudged her way between the other customers, finding one open seat. A grizzle-toothed sailor swing his head her way. "Yer no Galway girl."

"A what?"

"You looook Irish though. Red hair, and greeeeen eyes." The one tooth sticking out of his lower jaw jiggled. "What do you saaaaaay that I buyyyyy you a driiii-ink?"

Lachlan set his hand on Amy's lower back. "Let's go over here." He escorted her away from the rowdy pub customers, settling by a table that wasnthankfully free.

"This place is hopping, and it's not even Friday night," he said. "Wait here. What do you want?"

"Guinness?" Amy replied. She didn't like beer that much. But they were in Ireland, and the dark brew was the drink of choice.

He winked, beaming at her. "I'll make it a double."

Amy sank down onto one of the stools at the table meant for two. The pub was full of couples flirting with one another. As she watched Lachlan bustle his way up to the pub, her heart escaped to Winter Forest.

Seeing the liveliness of the people here made her reflect on the conversation she'd had moments before with her mother. Sea nymph souls returned to the Abyss when they died. Where human souls went, however, was still a mystery. Where did Ewan's spirit go? After being killed atop the sacred mountain, she felt like he deserved another life somewhere, minus the brutality from his fellow huntsmen.

But the cycle of life and death was not hers to control. That choice lay in the hands of Isis and Nephthys, at least for sea nymphs.

"We'll find the treasure before the end of the month!" a man jeered over the crowd.

Amy swung her head in the direction of the table where Lachlan was standing. He held two pints of Guinness in his hands as he spoke to one of them. He spotted her and made his way over to her table.

He set the drinks down in front of Amy and took a seat across from her.

"What kind of treasure are your friends discussing?" she asked.

Lachlan dug out the leather pouch he'd stuffed into his pocket. "Will you excuse me for one moment? I need to set these haughty blokes straight."

As Lachlan sauntered over to his friends, Amy stared at the frothy beverages on the table. She retrieved the bag her mother had given her, undid the top, then sprinkled some of the mystery contents into his drink.

The Guinness frothed, turning the foam head from tan, to green.

Lachlan returned and flopped down in front of her. "It's not Saint Patty's day yet. I wonder why they gave me a special pint? And why it just now turned seaweed green?"

Amy smirked. How she had missed her mother's quirks. "Maybe you're just special."

Lachlan gripped his pint with one large hand. "I agree with the bloke at the bar about you. You definitely aren't from Galway, are you, my Sea Star?"

Amy flustered. "What did you call me?"

His blue eyes narrowed. "Your freckles, they look like stars. And you were on my boat, so you obviously love the sea. I figured the two fit together."

Fury heated Amy's cheeks. "If you can give me a nickname, then I can give you one, too."

"Oh? What's that? Super stud muffin—"

"—how about smelly shrimp boy?"

Lachlan's brow furrowed. "Well, that's not very nice sounding."

"It wasn't intended to be."

While Lachlan's face twisted at her insult, Amy began planning her escape. He'd already seen through her too quickly.

He took a swig of his drink in quick recovery. "What brings a pretty lass such as yourself into town, other than trying to steal something off my boat?"

"Come on, Lachlan! We aren't going to hold your place all night!" a man yelled from the table.

She sipped on her beer. "I didn't take anything. And it looks like your buddies are waiting."

He shook his hand. "They can wait. They all live for gambling."

"What are you gambling over?"

He took a swig of his beer, then propped both of his elbows on the table. "I'll tell you a secret. I'm not gambling money. Tonight, I'm gambling this." He tipped the bag over, spilling a silver, oval-shaped item onto the table.

Amy nearly spilled her beer.

Lachlan grabbed the item, holding it in front of her. "What do you think it is?"

"A dragon scale," she whispered.

His eyes went wide. "Wow, you are the first person who has *ever* agreed with me on that."

"Where did you find it?"

"It got caught in my fishing net a couple of months ago. I've shown it to some folks, but nobody can identify what it is or what sea creature it might have originated from." He held it up to the light. "I know one thing—it's got to come right from the treasure itself—Poseidon's crown."

Now it was Amy's turn to have her mouth drop open. These blokes were discussing Poseidon's crown?

Lachlan's cheeks dimpled. "Do you know anything about the crown? They're all placing bets that it was lost somewhere in the Bermuda Triangle."

She sipped on her beer some more, completely bewildered at their discussion. "I have heard of the crown, yet I do not have any knowledge on its whereabouts."

His eyes shimmered like warm embers from a hearth. "I think the crown is hiding close by the Celtic Sea. I think it's somewhere right under our noses. It's probably guarded by selkies."

More drunken laughter erupted from the table.

Lachlan shook his head. "You probably think I'm some crazy fisherman."

"No, I don't," Amy replied. "I think you have some insight about the crown that not many people today have."

"I'm willing to bet that they are wrong, and we are right," he said, tucking the dragon scale back into his bag. "Now, my Sea Star, if you'll excuse me. I have a gambling bet to win."

Amy smiled. This was her chance to head south to the Celtic Sea. She also had a storm dragon scale, one that looked nearly identical to the one Lachlan had. Did they both belong to the son of Poseidon named Mestor?

19
BALFOUR'S MEMORY
Damien

The heavy weight of a massive hand fell onto Damien's shoulder. "*Where is Selia?*"

"She went back to her office to chat with her old boss, why?"

"*I didn't see her there,*" Balfour grumbled out a reply.

Damien's stomach hollowed. The two took off, repeating their steps. She'd only been gone a few moments.

Electrical sparks erupted from Balfour's heaving shoulders, making his beard stand on end. As he rounded the corner, shadows tendrilled at the base of the Egyptian statue Selia was staring at.

Balfour practically flew across the room toward her, snatching away the crystal from Selia's hand.

"Hey, what are you doing?" Selia stammered, trying to grab the crystal back from him.

Balfour glared at the Egyptian statue. "*Do not allow your inheritance anywhere near the goddess of death.*"

Damien read the display tag on the statue's bottom:

Nephthys: Twin sister of Isis, and the Egyptian goddess of death.

Damien glanced at Selia, who looked just as taken aback by Balfour's sudden fear of a statue. "Hey, is everything okay?"

Balfour wouldn't look at him. He ground his jaw, making his profile ridged.

Nyssa reached out, grabbing for his beard. Sparks flew from his face, throwing her into a maniacal giggle.

More sparks jumped from Balfour's body, jolting off Nephthys's statue. Museum visitors began to shoot them wary glances.

Damien grabbed Balfour's arm. "Hey, why are you reacting this way?"

Balfour grabbed his beard, and an explosion of electrical sparks jolted through his hair. Nyssa squealed with delight as Balfour stormed, quite literally, out of the museum, leaving a trail of electrical mist in his wake.

"Well, that was rather unexpected," Selia said. "Wow, I've never seen him this upset. He's always been pretty calm and collected."

Damien and Selia took off in the same direction he'd seen Balfour roam. He passed a few shops he remembered visiting a little less than a year ago when he'd first come to Paris to visit Selia.

Balfour's giant body was slumped over in a chair behind a hedge of roses that grew at the edge of a bistro.

He handed Selia Nyssa. "Here. Take the baby. I'll go talk to him."

"Should I say something?"

"No. I just think he needs some guy time. At least that's the vibe I'm getting from him." Damien approached Balfour, stopping at the empty chair across from him. "Can I sit for a moment?"

A thunderous growl rumbled out of him. "*If you must.*"

Damien grabbed the chair and tugged it out. He flopped down in front of the grumpy storm dragon. "Selia and I shared wine together at this very bistro almost a year ago. I'll buy you a drink."

"*I'm going to need more than one.*"

Damien smiled. At least Balfour was talking to him. He flagged down a waiter, who made his way to their table.

"What can I get you two?" the waiter asked.

"Paris has better wine than it does beer," Damien suggested.

Balfour eyed the menu as he spoke aloud, "Three pints of ale for me. He'll have one glass of the overpriced grape juice."

The waiter left, leaving Damien to contend with a stubborn dragon who had an apparent taste for ale. While he didn't consider himself a wine connoisseur, Paris had always been a great place to expand his palette.

"Look, I don't know about all the details of what happened back in the museum, but I know that you reacted to seeing that statue. Did something happen that you need to tell Selia and I about?"

A thunderous growl sent Balfour's beard frizzling into a tizzy. The waiter returned with their drinks, spun on his heel and promptly left, leaving the three pints of ale and Damien's glass of wine on their table.

Damien braced himself. Maybe it was best that he let Balfour decompress a bit before he dove into the details of his stormy tantrum.

Balfour grabbed his pint and guzzled down the booze until it frothed over his beard. A giant belch erupted, rumbling like thunder. "*Have you ever had a disagreement with one of your siblings?*"

"I have one, and she's about as crazy as they get. You know she was the one to admit Selia into a mental institution, right? My beautiful, pregnant fiancé had to live in a place meant for crazy folks for over a month?"

Balfour downed another swig of his ale.

Damien took his first sip of wine, relishing in the burn it gave his throat. He took a second sip, then set the glass down on the table. "I still don't know how I'm going to confront Gwen when I see her next."

Balfour downed another swig, his throat bulging as he knocked off his first pint and grabbed the second. "*Try having a disagreement with one of your brothers over the death of your father.*"

Damien's body tensed. "That statue made you think about the death of Poseidon?"

Balfour held his second pint to his lips. "*Mestor and I almost brought on a second ice age with all of our bickering over our father's sudden death. Storm dragon arguments result in triton currents. These currents generate the weather patterns on the planet. When one of them gets too violent, so do the storms that we generate.*"

"So you and Mestor had some big stormy argument. I've had yelling matches with Gwen before."

"*This is not mere yelling. It's tail and scale-ripping your fins off rage because you can't control your temper kind of roar.*" His hand put a dent into the metal mug, sloshing his ale down the side.

"Tell me what happened. Spell it out for me like I'm a child, like you would to Little Origin."

Fear glinted in the ebony depths of Balfour's eyes, a look Damien was not used to seeing in him. "I have a memory of Nephthys, one that makes me ill to remember. The memory consists of her visiting my father's temple in Atlantis." He took a massive sip of his ale, his hand trembling as he drank. "*I was the one to find my father dead on the throne. The last individual I remember seeing with him, was Nephthys. But I cannot prove that she had anything to do with him dying.*"

Damien slammed his fist onto the table. "I don't care what other's might think. Do *you* believe that she killed him?"

A belch parted Balfour's lips before he spoke. "*I can't say that Nephthys killed my father. But I know in my bones that she had something to do with his death. What? I don't know. But I know that she did something to enable it.*" He turned back to his ale. "*Our argument over the death of our father lasted for years, until one day, I became so sick, that I couldn't fight with Mestor any longer. I abandoned my territory within the Abyss, the territory I had worked so hard to protect. The ancestral salts that gave birth to the toxic fae queen, and those of which The Blind Moon was born from.*"

"Celeano?"

"*Yes, the Dark One,*" Balfour admitted as he belched again.

Damien's heart thundered as he watched Balfour suffer. "Is there anything you and Mestor could do to prove how your father died? Is there nothing that could give you a real answer?"

Balfour grabbed his third pint and brought it to his lips. With three large gulps, he finished it. He set the mug down and wiped the frothy beverage away from his beard with the back of his hand. "*There is but one hope in the sea for Poseidon's sons—it is to find the ancient storm dragon territories locked with his crown. Its remains will tell the truth about our father's death. The only reason the crown wasn't destroyed was due to the fact that Amphitrite put Mestor and my five other brothers into an icy slumber.*"

"Amphitrite, as in Amy's mother?"

Balfour nodded. "*If it weren't for Amphitrite's Ocean Apothecary, Mestor might have destroyed half of the seas by now.*"

Damien pondered the thought. Sure, Gwen had a dragon-like personality at times, but nothing compared to what Balfour had dealt with.

"*You don't need a storm dragon to help you any longer. It's probably best that you go on to the Celtic Sea without me,*" Balfour grunted.

Damien sloshed the wine down his front. "What do you mean, we don't need you? Selia and I and our baby do!" He glanced over his shoulder, finding that Selia was bobbing Nyssa up and down, waving at them both. "If the crown could reveal how your father died, what do we need to do to help you find it?"

Balfour sighed. "*Finding it would require that all of Poseidon's sons work together. It would take a miracle to make that happen. I never should have put Selia and you in this situation. It is only a matter of time before my brothers awaken from their slumber and begin questioning the bond I formed with her.*"

"Why did you choose the tidal bond, and not another one? I assume there are other storm bonds you could have chosen?"

"*I could not risk Masika harming her. She has long been corrupted by the salt venom.*"

"Do you regret choosing that bond?"

"*No, I do not. The tides were necessary to save Selia's life. I had to take her deep into the sea to escape the inferno Masika set into the cavern. Salt venom is very flammable, and Alex suffered the consequences.*" He tipped his mug. "*The tide is only seen at the surface, but it holds its power deep within the ocean. It churns the sea floor, blending and mixing the darkest waters of the ocean not even the stars can see.*"

Damien pondered Balfour's poetic words. "You and Alex both looked out for Selia, haven't you? You were both like stars, looking down on her after she left Egypt?"

Balfour dipped his chin. "*I would die for Celaeno's moon daughter. She was born from the very salt pod I used to protect. You do not know how much pain it caused me in abandoning it.*"

"I don't think Selia understands how lucky she is, having a storm dragon like you at her side."

Balfour looked up, a storm glinting in his dark eyes. "*As Zakai mentioned, the bond I chose for Selia originates from the celestial bodies. In the case of the tidal bond, it is the moon. I am devoted not only to her, but to you and your family, Damien Malloch. Forever, and always.*"

Damien swallowed down his wine, emotion suddenly gripping his throat more than the burn of the alcohol. "What do I need to do to make sure that the tides turn in our favor? How can I help you find your brothers and in turn, find your father's crown?"

Balfour chuckled darkly. "*You don't need to do anything. You just need to be the father Little Origin deserves.*"

Damien gazed at Balfour, feeling completely put out. He wanted to do something special for him. He wanted to repay him somehow. "Look, you helped Selia to name our daughter. If anything, I want you to be Nyssa's godfather."

Balfour's usually dark eyes flashed with white as his pupils dilated. "*You want me to be your daughter's guard dragon?*"

"Is that same thing as a godfather?"

"*It's a life-long guardian. At least that's how sea nymphs in Atlantis used to describe it. There is a ritual involved. All primary individuals in the family unity must be present.*"

"I'll have you tell Selia if you agree or not. Then you can tell us what that ritual is, all right?"

Balfour gazed down into his mug. "*It will also give you both some time to consider if you would like to reconsider or not. My family can be crazy at times.*"

Damien chuckled. "If there is anyone who has a crazy family, it's me. I don't have any brothers, but I do have a crazy dragon-obsessed sister, and thirty-nine some odd aunts, uncles and cousins, all of who are proud Scottish. When was the last time you saw this brother of yours?"

"*Over three thousand years ago. Mestor and I are opposites. He's the oldest, and I'm the youngest.*"

Golden sparks caught Damien's attention from behind the roses as Zipper flit between the flowers. "Now, the real question is, did that little dragonfly have this planned from the beginning?"

"*We might not have wings, but storm dragons used to be the true rulers of the skies, not those tiny fae pests who dominate everything.*"

Damien raised his glass to Balfour. "I've never been fond of that bat anyway. I think we can both agree on that."

"*That Glitter Wing is not my favorite.*"

"Do you have nicknames for all fae creatures?"

"*Just the ones who fly.*"

"What do you call Peppercorn's kind?"

"*Depends on what they eat. Bats who feast on insects, Flapper Wings. The ones who like fruit, Sticky Wings.*"

"And you call our daughter *Little Origin*?"

"*The name is—hic—fitting for her, and Selia—hic—adored it.*"

Damien's heart warmed. He was starting to grow fond of the strange quirks of Balfour, and just how much he cared about Selia and their daughter. "I'll buy you another round, but only under one circumstance."

Balfour's massive brow furrowed. "*Name it.*"

"You give Selia back that crystal. It's the only thing that has kept our daughter quiet, and I'd like to spend some time with Selia to reconnect after we've been apart for far too long, got it?"

Balfour handed the crystal to Damien. "*Deal. Hic—And you must not say a word to—hic—the Blind Moon about my—hic—brother, got it?*"

Damien clinked his glass against Balfour's pint. "As long as you promise not to storm out on us again."

20
RAINSTORMS

Selia

By the time Damien finished talking with Balfour, the day was more than half gone. As soon as Balfour returned the crystal to Selia, he took off into the sky, and all of Paris was blanketed with a low-hanging fog.

Balfour was quite literally summoning a storm with his snores, leaving Selia and Damien only one option—they needed to retire for the evening. They checked into a hotel for the night. They they took turns showering while the other watched the baby.

Selia nursed Nyssa, who once again, responded to the presence of the crystal. Her phone chimed. Deidra had texted her.

> Okay. Where the heck are U guys? Zakai and I literally arrived at Damien's studio hours ago…an update would be nice…

Selia didn't feel like telling Deidra all of the details of her day. She was exhausted and needed some food and sleep. So did Nyssa and Damien.

> Balfour is currently too intoxicated to fly.

> What? Storm dragons can get drunk?

> Apparently. We hit some bad weather on our way south, so we took a detour to Paris. Damien and I need to sleep. It's been one heck of a day.

As the evening wore on, more rain fell upon Paris. Balfour's thunderous snores echoed above them. Damien left the hotel in search of food, leaving Selia to tidy up for the evening.

As soon as she changed into her sleepwear, which consisted of an over sized blouse and panties, she put Nyssa down to sleep. Her hand, once again, became transparent. She walked to the window, startled by her sudden change in appearance. Her torso and legs also changed as she started to levitate off the ground.

Selia's feet dangled below her as she tried to find something to ground herself with. How many more of these strange salt aura episodes was she going to experience? Did they get worse post birth?

If so, how could she get them under control without feeling like she was going to rip out of her skin at any moment?

The door opened. Damien walked into the room, "Selia, where are—"

"—I'm up here," she interrupted him.

He staggered backwards, nearly dropping the takeout. He set the boxes on the table and grabbed a chair. "I'm coming up there."

"Careful, you'll fall," she argued.

"Don't care," he huffed, setting one foot onto the bookshelf next to the table. The rickety thing wobbled under his weight. "There, now we're even," he said, dimples appearing.

Selia hovered before him, wishing that her weightless, ghost-like experience would somehow end.

Damien's shoulders began to tremble. His mouth broke open as a chuckle escaped him.

"How are you laughing right now? What if I float out the window?"

Damien's chuckles rumbled louder, matching the volume of the distant thunder.

"Shhhhhhhh! You'll wake the baby," she scolded him.

"No I won't. Thunder puts her to sleep, see?"

They both glanced down at Nyssa, who was blissfully unaware of her parents argument above.

He held out his hands, which Selia was able to grab. "Remember the time I came to Paris to find you, and you dropped that little bottle in the fountain? I thought it was perfume. Boy, was I wrong. Never in a million years would I think that what was inside would lead us to where we are now."

"Why are you being so nostalgic?"

"Because I'd rather risk breaking my neck up here than be alone at my art studio. Chasing the blue light I'd seen in your aura that day was the best decision I ever made."

Selia fell into his arms as they embraced. "I don't know what's happening to me."

"I don't either, but I promise we will figure it out," Damien said, comfortingly. He grabbed her around the center, lowering her down to the chair.

She folded into his lap, wrapping her arms around his neck as he sat onto the chair. "I'm starved, can we please eat?"

Damien brushed his face past her neck, grazing her ear with his lips. "Not until I've tasted you first."

Selia's body heated at his suggestion. It had been *months* since they'd shared any intimacy together.

She kissed his lips, loving every flick of his tongue against hers. "Love, it feels like ages since I've actually *kissed* you. I don't want to rush this, I want to savor it."

"Then let's savor it together," he whispered back. His hands dipped under her blouse as she removed it. He grabbed his shirt and tore it over his head. She straddled him on the chair, his lap hardening as they continued to kiss one another.

Damien's teeth raked across her neck, tracing a scorching line down to her chest. He nipped and kissed the top of each breast. "Selia, you have no idea how much I've been craving you." He gripped for the clasp of her bra.

"I'd prefer to keep my bra on, for reasons," she said, feeling vulnerable. She was a new mom, and that brought all kinds of changes to parts of her body that Damien had always explored.

"I want to look at you, *all* of you," he said, not skipping a beat. "Having a baby just means that there are new parts of you to love."

His words, along with his hands, made quick work of the clasp. Her hair became tangled in their heated moment, so she reached behind and undid the fabric.

Her breasts fell onto his chest. She jolted at the awkwardness of their skin-on-skin contact.

"Do you know how absolutely fucking beautiful you are?" he said, looking her in the eye.

"I don't think I've ever heard you curse like that before," she replied as she wrapped her arms around his neck and grabbed a handful of his thick, tousled hair.

His cheeks dimpled. "I'm yours, my moon goddess."

Selia gripped onto him as he stood up from the chair. She clasped her legs around his center as he took her to the bed. She released her legs, standing before he could drag her into the sheets.

"Am I being too aggressive?" he asked, hesitating.

"No," she giggled, setting her hands onto his heaving chest. "But you still have your clothes on."

She grabbed his belt and tugged. His pants dropped to the ground, taking his boxers with them. Seeing him naked, his beautiful combination of softness and strength, made her body ache.

She walked around him, tracing her finger along his shoulder. She kissed him, biting and flicking her tongue along his broad shoulders and back.

"So fucking beautiful," he whispered, a moan drawing out his breath.

"How much of this goddess do you want to see tonight?" she teased.

He grabbed her hand, guiding her back to his front. His cock grazed her thighs, the thick head pressing against her belly as she centered herself in front of him.

"Turn around. Let me look at you, *all* of you," he said, dropping his hands to her hips as she spun. His palms worked over the stretch marks, his cock tracing against her skin as he kissed her neck and shoulders.

She backed into him, working her ass into his hard length.

His hands gripped her center, caressing her stomach.

She lowered her hands onto the mattress, bracing herself for his thick entry.

He teased her clit with each thrust as he circled himself around her opening.

"I want you to fuck me," Selia said.

"Not until I've tasted you," he said, lowering himself to his knees behind her.

She flipped around and slid onto the mattress as his tongue dove into her. He lapped and sucked on her until she was brimming for release.

Thunder rumbled overhead, the sound vibrating through her body as Damien brought her to the edge.

"Stop," she said, grabbing his hair. "Don't finish me yet. I want you to come with me."

Damien rose from between her legs. He clasped her hands, forcing her wrists over her head. His chest and arm muscles bunched as his hips rolled forward, and he finally plunged into her.

Selia reeled in the sensations of him claiming her again. How tight he felt with each thrust against her walls. Pleasure became pain as he thrust harder and faster.

He lowered himself onto the bed, dragging her on top of him. "Ride me."

She straddled his core, grabbing his hands as he supported her.

As he bucked his hips, she accepted ever pulsing inch of him. Damien was both her reality, and her escape. She could fall into his strong yet gentle soul and become completely lost in him.

"Selia, look at me," he said, his jaw clenching. "Look me in the eye when you come."

Damien's face blurred beneath her as she thought back to their first night together. How much had unraveled between them. Lovemaking was so much more than just sex with him.

With their sexual appetites finally appeased, Damien sat up in bed, tucking Selia beneath his arm. He held up the Italian takeout. "Bon Appetit!"

While Nyssa slept in her bassinet, they both dove in to their dinners of bread, pasta, and tomato sauce.

"Okay, this isn't the most romantic dinner in Paris, but it still works," Damien said as he slurped down his first bite.

Selia dove her fork into her heaping plate of pasta, then brought the first bite to her lips. The savory tang of tomatoes worked magic over her taste buds. "This brings back great memories. Remember the first night I visited your art studio, and you made Italian food?"

"You could say the Celtic Sea was the origin story of our relationship," Damien said, chuckling. "That must say something about my choice in first date food, because here we are almost a year later, eating the same thing with you." He ran his hand past her face, clearing a hair out of her eyes. "Have I told you how sexy you are when you eat?"

Selia's phone chimed.

Damien grabbed her phone and tossed it to the edge of the bed. "Deidra can wait. I want seconds, maybe even thirds tonight." He set his hand on her thigh, working his fingers up her leg as she swallowed another bite of pasta.

Selia grabbed his wandering hand.

"What's wrong?"

She glanced down at her food, suddenly overcome with confusion. "I met the new employee Dr. O'Connor hired."

"Oh?"

"Yeah. It was such a bizarre encounter. Never did I imagine that I would come back to the museum and find someone working where I did. He said that her position was only temporary due to her other research."

"What other research does she do?"

She shrugged. "I'm not sure. Something about her just seemed off. I can't put my finger on it."

"Are you jealous that someone took over your old job?"

"No. He was right. I needed to get out of there," she said, looking at crystal. It sat next to Nyssa in her bassinet, where she was sleeping soundly. "It's strange. I'm feeling oddly similar to this crystal. It's lost its origin, and I don't really know which way is home."

Damien wrapped his arm around her. "You know what? I was honestly feeling the same way. It's like we're stuck in some strange limbo."

Selia leaned into him, setting her head on his chest. "What do you want at this point?"

He kissed her forehead, then squeezed her. "I want to marry the woman who gave birth to my daughter."

Selia kissed him back, her breath hitching as she did.

His eyes dilated. "That's still what you want too, right?"

"Of course it is," Selia stammered. She gazed back at the crystal.

He grabbed her hand and threaded his fingers through hers. "But there's something else, isn't there? Something else that you need to feel whole?"

She stared up at the ceiling, where the crystal reflected its light. "I want to know why Naunet ran away and abandoned her duties as the midwife of the sea. The memories I have of her don't match what Zakai described. Abandoning her work with the Codex? Her people in Egypt?" She squeezed his hand. "Something doesn't seem right. Naunet was fiercely loyal to her work and her people. She served them with her whole heart."

"Do you feel like she abandoned her duties, and in turn, abandoned you?"

Selia's heart shuddered at the thought. "I never thought of that. Maybe in some strange way, I do." She gazed down at her food. "I guess that becoming a mom has made me realize that the timing is never perfect. It's something that changes your life forever. There is no going back."

His gaze leveled with her. "I hope you don't want to go back to the way things were before."

She squeezed his hand. "That has never crossed my mind. I just want to ensure that our salt auras develop together and that she's healthy. How did you convince Balfour to give me back the crystal, anyway?"

He shrugged. "He just needed some guy time is all. Apparently he had a falling out with his eldest brother, whose name is Mestor."

"Mestor, huh? How many other brothers does he have?"

"At least six other than himself. He was really upset with himself for trying to form this tidal bond with you, which apparently he did to save you from Masika?"

She shrugged. "I had no idea that he did so to save me. All I remember was the cavern filling with flame and smoke as the salt venom caught on fire."

"He must really care about you if he was willing to risk waking his brothers up."

"Do you know what it was that he became so upset about when he looked at that statue?"

"Oh boy. Where do I star? Long story short, Balfour has a memory of seeing Nephthys in his father's temple in Atlantis. She was the last individual he saw with his father, before he found him dead."

"What a horrible thing to walk into."

"I know. He was really spooked about it. But that's not the half of it. After he found is father dead, he and his eldest brother, Mestor, began to argue over his death."

"Did they suspect that Nephthys killed him?"

"That's the problem. They couldn't prove anything. They still don't know the truth about how Poseidon died. The only way they can answer what caused his death is to find this crown, which is apparently a bunch of ancient storm dragon territories out in the middle of the ocean. That's about all I could get out of him before the alcohol took over." He squeezed her hand. "Selia, I want to help him find the crown. He has done a lot for us."

"I'm glad to see that you're growing fond of him. I was worried after what he did to have you retrieve my inheritance that you two might never get along."

His cheeks dimpled. "After he opened up to me, I asked him to be Nyssa's godfather, or god dragon, whatever you want to call him."

Her heart leapt. "Really? How did he respond?"

"In normal Balfour fashion, he got really grumbly and started making thunderous sounds."

She laughed. "That sounds just like him."

"I told him that he needed to discuss it with you if he accepted the duty or not. He also mentioned there was a ritual of sorts involved."

"The more I get to know him, the less I feel I truly understand about storm dragons."

PART 3
WHEN DRAGONS AWAKEN

21

STEALING THE SEA DRAGON

Amy

Moonlight dappled across the damp pavement Amy padded upon late that evening. Setting out to track down Mestor wouldn't be easy, but her mother was counting on her. While Lachlan and his fishing buddies were deep in their drink, she jumped at her opportunity to hijack his boat.

Wind whipped through her clothing and hair as she descended the stairs to the marina. Fishermen had docked their fleets in preparation of the oncoming storm. Lachlan was sure to be deep in the drink and gambling well into the wee hours of the morning.

Boat hulls jostled against one another, creating an unsettling melody as waves swept into the harbor. Amy's nose burned with the electricity and cool moisture of an oncoming weather front. She was very familiar with the scent—the calm before a storm. It had been far too long since she'd been behind the helm of a sea vessel amidst the violent rain and winds associated with North Atlantic weather.

She walked from boat to boat, ducking under a few fishing nets until she spotted the barnacle-crusted hull of the *Sea Dragon*. Little Blue launched herself from Amy's robes onto the boat. She landed on the metal railing, scuttling back and forth as though encouraging Amy to jump aboard.

"Yes, I know you are ready for this adventure," Amy replied, half amused at the little crab's insistence. She hopped aboard and walked into the inner quarters, finding it eerily quiet. She reached into her bosom, tugging out the crystal fragment of the star of the sea. The light it put off, while dull, was enough to illuminate the inner quarters of Lachlan's boat.

She approached the controls, eyeing all of the knobs and levers that were too complicated to read. Nautical equipment had changed so much over the past few decades. A key stuck out next to the steering wheel, which she turned to the right. The engine puttered a few times, then quickly died.

Great. How was she supposed to get the sea dragon to set sail if it had no fuel to begin with? She needed something to power a boat that didn't have sails or a running engine.

Little Blue scurried along the boat's dashboard, dodging levers and fuel gages as she maneuvered to the crystal in Amy's hand. With a swift swipe of her claw, she snatched it up, scurried down to the floor, making quick work toward the boat deck.

"Hey!" Amy stammered as she left the inner quarters, following the crab is it darted to the port side of the boat.

The playful cries of a sea creature erupted from the water. A pod of dolphins began circling the *Sea Dragon*. Their lively chatter echoed off the boat, making Amy's heart sing.

She set her hands on the railing where Little Blue scuttled about, flailing the crystal in her little claw. Apparently the crystal attracted ocean life. She leaned over to watch a dozen rubbery grey dorsal fins slap the water as the curious dolphins flashed their toothy grins.

"Can you help me get this boat moving?" Amy pleaded with the playful porpoises.

Tail fins thrashed as another eruption of playful chatter sounded from below.

Amy snatched the star of the sea from little Blue and held it over the water. Something inside shifted, appearing as liquid light. While she didn't know how to speak to the dolphins, something inside of the crystal seemed to know how to communicate with some of the sea's most intelligent creatures.

Amy was thrown backward as the *Sea Dragon* jostled. A rope strung tight above her head. She'd forgotten to untie the boat...

Luckily, Little Blue seemed to sense her distress. She'd already scuttled over to where the rope was now taught. With a few swift pinches of her claw, the rope snapped.

The boat bobbed forward, now free to drift out into the sea.

"That's it! Keep going!" she cried as the dolphins worked to steer the boat out of the marina and into deeper waters. The dolphins kept thrashing their tails, generating enough momentum to force the *Sea Dragon* forward.

"Hey! What are you doing!"

Amy spun toward the disgruntled voice. White-eyed and furious, Lachlan was jogging next to the boat, his arms thrashing at his sides.

22

RETURNING TO THE CELTIC SEA

Damien

The next morning brought clear skies to Paris. Balfour must have gotten the sleep that he needed, because the stormy weather retreated. They packed their things in preparation for the train ride from the city to the Celtic Sea. The ride from Paris to Le Conquet, France, was roughly four hours—plenty of time for him to sketch what he'd been dreaming about over the past few nights.

The real weight of the day settled upon Damien's shoulders. What would happen when they arrived at his art studio? Would Maera be there? If so, what would she expect from his artwork?

Selia tucked the crystal into into her bag. "Should we track down Balfour and see if he wants to fly us?"

"*I wouldn't suggest that,*" Balfour rumbled into their minds. "*I'm nursing a hangover.*"

Selia's mouth flew open. "How much did you guys drink?"

Damien chuckled. "I might have bought him a second round, maybe even a third."

"*Make sure that Glitter Wing doesn't go flying up my nose again.*"

Selia's brows drew up. "What did he just say?"

Damien chuckled. "Balfour apparently has nicknames for other fae creatures, especially those who fly. That's his name for Zipper. You should hear what he calls Peppercorn."

At Damien's words, Peppercorn nudged her way out of Selia's hair, her tiny brown face swiveling with curious intelligence. She let out a furious *screeeeech*! then withdrew out of sight.

Damien grimaced. "To me, she's still a nose biter."

Zipper too, came flitting into the scene. A trail of golden light illuminated his shimmering wings. Instead of landing on Selia's other shoulder, he took to Damien.

"Great. I get the one with six legs and eyes that are terrifying," Damien stammered.

"Would you rather have a set of sharp teeth nuzzling your neck all afternoon?" Selia scolded.

"Nope. I'm good with the little golden guy."

Zipper tucked his wings down, repositioning himself so that he camouflaged next to Damien's shirt. "I thought dragonflies couldn't fold their wings," he said.

"He's not a normal dragonfly, he's *fae* dragonfly, remember?"

A gentle nudge became a tug on the tuft of his hair. "Right. Fae bugs and bats. You can't get any better than that."

Selia spun in front of him, making the aquamarine fabric clinging to her hips graze his leg.

"That dress looks good on you," he said, his words feeling out of place. Selia was beautiful in anything she wore.

"Thank you. Deidra gave it to me. I thought it would be more comfortable to wear after having you ravish me," she teased, brushing her leg against him.

Damien's chest swelled. He had a bruise on his arm from their evening having reunion sex. He would wear it like a trophy and hoped to earn more of them.

Selia strapped Nyssa to her front. "Okay. We have two fae creatures, and a baby. I think we are ready to go." She picked up her phone as another text came through. "Deidra has texted me a dozen times asking when we are going to arrive."

"I take it that dryads are not very patient?"

"Not her."

"Why don't you just call her?" Damien asked as he grabbed their bags and hoisted them onto his shoulders.

Selia grabbed the strap of his art satchel. "Or we could just call everything off, and I could take you back to bed with me."

Damien would have done anything to take Selia up on her proposal, but their quest to find the other two crystal fragments relied on their journey. Besides, as romantic as Paris was, he wanted to marry her where they first met—on the beach at the Celtic Sea.

Their group boarded the first train set to leave Paris. They nestled into one of the compartments and shut the door. Peppercorn disappeared into luggage rack, tucking herself between their bags for a mid-day nap. Zipper too, went missing as soon as they settled in. Damien suspected the dragonfly hid himself on the other side of the train car to prevent being preyed upon by the bat.

While Selia propped Nyssa onto her lap and tugged out a few toys, Damien pulled out his art journal and supplies.

Nyssa gripped one of the toys and tossed it onto the ground.

"I think she's bored," Selia said, grabbing it from the ground and giving it to her again.

Nyssa tossed it much harder, this time letting out a squeal.

His daughter's eyes kept darting over to him. He sketched what he could of her and Selia, trying to capture their energy as Selia struggled to keep her still. He drew her little round face, her pudgy arms and legs, then held up his drawing for them to see.

"See how your daddy can make art?" Selia said, bouncing her on her leg.

Nyssa's body wiggled upright.

Damien's mouth dropped open. "Wow, did she just sit up?"

"I think she did," Selia replied, catching her as she fell backward into her lap.

"That usually doesn't happen for a few months," Damien said.

"Well, she was born two months early," Selia protested. "I wouldn't be surprised if she develops much quicker than a normal baby."

"She's absolutely adorable. I love watching her play like this."

Selia set Nyssa with one of her toys into her carrier and fastened her in. She sat next to Damien locked the door to their compartment. Her hand grazed over his knee. She brushed her fingers over his jeans, tracing along his inner leg.

His cock twitched at the desire in her touch.

"Have you thought about making another one?" she asked as she continued to explore him.

"I thought we'd wait until—"

"—I'm not waiting," Selia said, her blue eyes meeting his. She kissed his cheek, tracing her lips to his, all while grabbing his belt and undoing it. "Since last night, I can't stop thinking about you that way."

"Here? On the *train*?" Damien ground out as he glanced at the door. The windows were fogged, giving them a somewhat decent sense of privacy.

"Why not?" she teased, kissing him again. "We need to make up for lost time."

Damien grabbed her around the waist. "A quickie does sound nice."

While Nyssa remained preoccupied with her toy, her mother got busy with the bulge in his pants. His fiancé wanted him, *now*.

He tugged down his jeans, and she lowered his boxers. Her fingers caressed all of the right places, working over his full throbbing length. How he'd missed the magic of her touch.

As the train jostled, so did the rhythm of her hand against his cock. He leaned his head back against the seat and closed his eyes. "That feels amazing," he ground out, moaning as she continued.

"I don't have to be quiet with you in here, do I?" Selia asked, her voice breathy.

His eyes broke open. "People might hear us. The train isn't very loud."

A smirk tugged at the corners of her flush lips. She stood up, bunching her dress as she stood in front of him. She slid down atop his hard length, and he plunged into her.

Damien's body shook as the movement of the train and his fiancé. How perfect she felt around him. With each roll of her hips, her pussy tightened around him more. He grabbed her hair, tugging it as she continued to rock him. He loved how she fed off his pleasure, moving her body like a wave atop his center.

"Goddess, Selia. You are so fucking beautiful," he growled as she ground her hips into him.

She bounced her ass—her sweet, beautiful ass—against him as the train jolted. Her hips rolled, and he tugged on her hair. Her soft whimpers tugged something ravenous and mad out of him.

"Damien, don't stop," she breathed, her fingers gripping his knees.

He bunched the fabric of her dress, lifting it to watch how perfectly fit they were together. Watching him slide in and out as she begged him for more only made him harder. "You are my only sea nymph," he breathed in to her ear. "Tell me how much you want this."

"I want *you*," she panted, slamming down and digging her nails into the denim of his jeans.

He bucked his hips, bouncing her until their bodies synced like butter on bread. Her back arched as her body thrashed in wildness, tossing her mane of untamed hair. The sight of her made him loose control, taking him to a swift climax.

Breathless and sweaty, he buried his face into her hair. Breathing in her scent, he closed his eyes. He didn't want to let her go, not after taking her in such a spontaneous way.

She fell to his side, still breathing quickly. Her face and chest were flush from their intimacy. "I needed that," she whispered, kissing him on the cheek.

"I didn't realize how much I did too," he whispered back to her.

She grabbed a few tissues for them to clean up and repositioned her dress.

He tugged up his pants and fastened is belt while still catching his breath.

"Both of your pulses are racing. Is everything all right? What were you doing?"

"Nothing that you need to know about," Selia interjected as she sat next to their daughter.

Damien ignored Balfour's intrusive thoughts as endorphins surged through him. His heart would need some time to settle after the passion-crazed sex they had just shared together.

After a couple of hours of sketching, and intermittent play with his daughter, Nyssa began to doze for her morning nap. Damien got up to stretch his legs. His stomach had also started to growl, so finding food for him and Selia was a necessity.

As he maneuvered through the train to seek out brunch, rain pelted the windows. He placed an order within the food car, where he was instructed to wait until their order was ready. He sat down, not wanting to pass up a sketching opportunity. As rain pelted the train car, he imagined streaks of water to be like little ocean waves. As he maneuvered his pencil over his sketchpad, a woman sat down across from him.

Damien's hair stood on end as he glanced up at her. She had warm brown eyes, and long brunet hair.

She crossed one leg over the other, folding her arms across her center in quiet observation like she'd been there watching him for quite some time. "What are you sketching?"

"The sea," Damien lied.

He blinked.

The woman vanished.

He stood up, completely haunted by the encounter. Had he seen a spirit?

After he retrieved their food items, he made his way back to their car. Selia was walking with Nyssa in her arms, waving at the cows as they whizzed by. He didn't stop to tell her about the bizarre woman. He found an empty compartment and sat down. "*Balfour, can you hear me?*"

"*I'm hovering outside the train, why?*"

"*Can you keep an eye out for anything strange?*"

"*Define strange.*"

"*I don't know, random people appearing and disappearing?*"

A thunderous growl followed. "*Tell me exactly what you are seeing.*"

"*A woman was just here, then she wasn't.*"

"Maybe you should eat something."

Damien found his way back to Selia and Nyssa. They tucked into their train compartments to share their brunch. Suddenly, he no longer had an appetite.

Arrival in town brought cool, muggy skies. Damien grabbed their bags, along with his art supplies. They loaded onto a bus that took them from the train station to his beach-side cottage. Coming back to his art studio after being away for nearly a year suddenly brought on all kinds of anxiety. What shape would it be in?

As the bus pulled to a stop, Selia swaddled Nyssa to her front. The three unloaded and headed in the direction of his home. As they walked, Damien caught a glimpse of a woman with brown walking in the crowd.

His heartbeat jumped.

Was it the same woman he'd seen on the train?

If so, was she following them?

"No sign of Deidra, or Zakai," Selia said as she tugged out her phone. "I've texted her, and no reply."

Damien glanced over his shoulder, then grabbed Selia's free hand. The woman had vanished.

They rounded the street, where his foot scuffed over beach debris. Driftwood and pieces of seaweed littered the sidewalk. Winter often brought violent storms to the part of France that faced the Celtic Sea. He hoped that being gone as long as he had hadn't turned his cottage into a nightmare.

They ascended the hill, and his cottage came into view. His shoulder's rose and fell in relief. The roof was still attached, and shutters still protected his windows.

Nyssa giggled the entire way up the walk.

"Yes, I know. You get to see where your daddy makes all kinds of art!" Selia said, bouncing her.

Damien grabbed his key and pressed it to the lock. He jingled it back and forth and shoved his shoulder against the door.

It didn't budge.

"Great. I think the hinges are rusted shut," he stammered.

Balfour manifested next to him, mist billowing out from his sides. "*Move aside.*" He set his hand on the door and pried it open.

Sand came pouring out.

"What in the world?" Selia said.

Nyssa flailed her little arms in delight.

"*How did my studio get full of sand?*" Damien shoved past Balfour, eager to find out what the inside looked like. Sand was piled along the walls surrounding his art studio.

Selia's pocket began to glow. She pulled out the crystal and held it out to light up the dim room.

"Um, Damien? I think I know where all the sand is coming from."

Damien walked with Balfour to the center of his studio. A giant hole sat in the middle of the floor. "What in the world?"

"Well, whatever it was, they were looking for something," Selia said.

Hoards of blue items were piled in the center of the room. Blue aluminum cans. Blue stones. Even a pair of blue sandals were piled in the corner.

"I guess that's what happens when you abandon your art studio for a year," Damien said as he approached his painting supplies. He stopped beside an easel and glanced over his shoulder. He could have sworn Maria had been there, standing like she did by the painting he started over a decade ago.

23
MINCA

Selia

Since arriving at Damien's art studio, Selia couldn't shake the feeling that someone else was watching her. The haunting sensation wasn't from the hermit crabs that had burrowed into his home. But the feeling became stronger the closer she was to Damien's artwork.

She stepped outside onto the porch that faced the beach. Zakai and Deidra had to be close by. The sun peeked through the clouds, warming her face. Nyssa flailed her little hands into the air as she faced the sea. "This is the first time you've seen an ocean up close, isn't it?"

Nyssa's squeals confirmed her unbridled excitement. One thing was for certain. They needed to take a field trip down to the water. She also had a hunch about who was responsible for ransacking Damien's art studio.

The infamous Henrietta must be nearby.

Her phone chimed. Deidra finally replied to her text.

> **Did you see what washed up on the beach?**

Selia made her way down to the waterline. Her feet scuffed along the sand and debris.

A figure stood on a dune not far from her, overlooking the Celtic Sea. Zakai's characteristic robes flapped in the breeze.

Selia approached her, stopping where the dune swept down toward the beach. Long blue strands of something covered the beach for as long as the eye could see.

She blinked a few times, trying to take in what she was seeing. "Wow, when did this happen?"

"Last night it stormed relentlessly. This morning, the beach was covered in blue minca," Zakai replied. "Deidra and I have been watching the sea. It's only a matter of time before they show up."

Selia knew what the *they* was Zakai was referring to. Only a few months ago, she'd discovered where minca originated from—the tails of storm dragons. By the amount of it, there had to be more than one storm dragon nearby.

Damien emerged from his cottage. His mouth dropped open.

"Minca isn't the only thing that's washed up," Zakai said, taking off in one of her intense strides down to the waterline.

Selia and Damien took after her, with Deidra trailing behind.

Nyssa squealed the entire way, rattling off fits of laughter that made Selia laugh too.

Damien grabbed her hand. "I've got to see her first reaction to the water."

They trudged down the sandy dune, slipping and sliding as they went. The minca became thicker the closer to the water they became. Waves crashed on the shore, filling the air full of salt-crusted sea spray.

Deidra's long blond braid whipped in the wind as they approached. She stood with a pair of binoculars to her face, gazing out at the sea.

"What are you looking at?" Damien asked as he stopped next to her.

"Here, see for yourself," Deidra replied a she handed him her binoculars.

Selia squinted at the horizon as Damien pressed the binoculars to his face.

"Wow..." they said in unison.

"Is that an iceberg?" Damien asked.

"How is there sea ice drifting this far south?" Selia added.

"Wow, it's really big, and really blue," Damien said, handing the binoculars to Selia, who swapped Nyssa with him.

Zakai smiled. "Sea ice floating this far away from the arctic is a sign that other storm dragons are nearby."

While Deidra and Zakai continued to survey the beach, Selia and Damien found a dry spot in the sand. She propped Nyssa in front of her, who hadn't stopped wriggling. Damien picked up a handful of minca, letting it dangle from his hand in front of his daughter.

Nyssa grabbed the minca and tugged it down on top of her head. She giggled with glee, spreading her toes into the sand. Minca had been a myth—something that had only existed in the past. But right here, squished in her daughter's fingers? It was as real as any other species of kelp on the planet.

Nyssa reached for the blade of minca Damien dangled above her.

"Wow, you *are* sitting up," Selia said, releasing her hands from her sides. Nyssa crinkled her little toes into the sand, then grabbed damp fistfuls and tossed it into the air.

"That's miiiinnnncaaaa..." Damien said.

Nyssa clapped her hands together. "Minca..."

Selia's breathing stopped.

Damien's mouth dropped open.

Both of them stared at each other. "Did she just *say* something?"

"She's only a couple months old, and she's *talking*?"

Selia grabbed another item and held it in front of her. "Seeeeasheeeeell, can you say that?"

"Miiinca," Nyssa gurgled back.

Something shifted in the sand by Damien's foot. A pair of ink-drop eyes emerged from the shell she'd set in front of her daughter's wriggling toes.

"That's a crab," Selia said as the sand beyond Damien began to shift. "Oh, that's a lot of crabs..."

Nyssa squealed with delight as dozens of little hermit crabs came swarming toward her.

Selia spun around, suddenly aware of what had attracted the sea life. The crystal had fallen out of her pocket, and was glowing a brilliant blue next to her leg.

Selia snatched up the crystal, squinting at the horizon. "Are those dolphins?"

The clouds misted, and in a fit of membranous fins and fog, a stocky figure manifested next to her. Balfour folded his arms across his chest, seemingly unimpressed with her.

"Have you gotten over your hangover yet?" Selia asked.

Balfour merely grumbled at her. "*I would suggest keeping the star of the sea away from the water if you don't want to attract any unwanted ocean life.*"

Selia lifted Nyssa into the air, plopping her into his arms. "She likes you. I take that back. She *loves* you," Selia said, patting Balfour's arm. "You remember him? He's a draaaaagon."

"*No, I'm not just any dragon*," Balfour grumbled, blowing out his cheeks. "*I'm a Stooooorrrrmmmmmm draaaaaaaggggoooonnn.*"

"Storm dragon baby sitter, you mean."

One of Balfour's giant bushy eyebrows lifted. "*You want me to sit on your baby?*"

"No, you are going to watch her while her father and I go clean up the house for the evening." She patted him on the arm. "Oh, and Damien told me that he asked you to be Nyssa's dragon guardian. I want you to tell me about this ritual that is involved."

Balfour's nostrils flared at her statement.

Selia grabbed Damien's arm and began walking back toward the cottage.

"*Hey, you can't just leave me here with a baby. What if she poops?*" Balfour protested.

"Yes I can. You are her guardian now!"

Balfour shifted his giant feet in the sand as a swarm of hermit crabs came darting over to him.

24

ESCAPING IRELAND

Amy

Lachlan sprinted in a mad fury alongside the *Sea Dragon*. He brandished one of his arms in the air, rattling off a sling of Scottish curse words Amy could barely make sense of. "Hey! You crazy sea witch! Get back here!"

Amy's salt nodes burned at his words. She could handle sea star. But *sea witch*?

She leaned over the railing and clapped her hands at the dolphins forcing the boat out to sea. "Let's pick this up!"

The dolphins thrashed their tails, steering the *Sea Dragon* into deeper waters. Lachlan fell behind, his flailing arms disappearing from sight.

Amy heaved a sigh of relief. "There. I think we are free of—"

A thud behind her jostled the boat.

She spun on her heel, spotting the enraged fisherman.

Lachlan staggered toward her, his shoulders rising as he centered himself. "What in name of Poseidon has possessed you to steal my boat?"

She braced herself, anger rising in her chest. "Nothing that a sea witch can't take care of on her own."

Lachlan lunged for her, grabbing her around the center. They tumbled, their bodies jostling against the boat deck.

He fell atop her, his hands pinning hers over her head. "Have you lost your mind?"

"Let me go!" Amy yelled.

His grip on her wrists intensified. "I don't think so. I never should have let you out of my sight."

She kicked her legs, desperate to free herself from him.

He hooked her beneath her knees with one arm. In one quick movement, he set her upright, tugging her back against his hard body. His lips rasped against the cusp of her ear as he spoke, "you are not in any position to barter with the captain of this boat."

He tugged her back against him. He wasn't gentle like he'd been with her in the pub. His callused hands worked over her wrists, quickly tying them behind her back. "Try escaping now, my redheaded selkie."

Amy fell back into the fishing net as the boat veered violently to the side.

The dolphins thrashed their tails, sending a fit of sea spray into the air.

Lachlan grabbed her before she tumbled overboard. Cold ocean water doused them both, jostling them from their argument. He scrambled to his feet. "What kind of spell did you put on these sea creatures?"

"Why don't you figure it out yourself?" she snapped. The ropes binding her wrists burned her skin as she tried to free herself.

The boat spun violently, pitching left, then right as the current threatened to rip the vessel apart.

A shiny silver blade appeared in Lachlan's hand. He grabbed the net, steadying himself. "Okay. If I cut you loose, you have to promise me that you will get those wretched things under control."

Amy fought with the net, forcing herself up into a seated position. "I don't think I can. Something else has caught the boat that isn't the dolphins."

The boat began to spiral uncontrollably, knocking Amy against the net.

Lachlan was thrown across the boat, his back slamming into wooden kegs and lobster traps. His knife went flying. Thankfully, Little Blue had gotten to Amy in time. With a furious snip of her claw, the ropes binding her wrists sprung open.

Once free, Amy gripped the railing, steadying herself as the waves rolled and pitched beneath her. She'd spent many a century sailing aboard pirate ships, successfully steering vessels away from triton currents. But this was the first time she had been *captured* by one. The current tugged them out as though the *Sea Dragon* was a minnow trapped in a violent riptide.

Amy ducked as a giant swell rolled over the bow, dipping the entire boat forward.

Crack!

She and Lachlan knocked into one another as something struck the side of the boat.

"What in the bloody hell was that?" Lachlan stammered as he regained his footing.

Another violent *crack* made Amy's feet shuddered.

A long, serpentine tail thrashed out of the water, followed by a set of membranous purple fins. Scales shimmered along the tail as it fell with a thunderous splash into the sea.

They had a storm dragon surrounding them...

"Stop attacking my boat, you bloody sea serpent!" Lachlan cried as he backed away from the railing.

Another tail ripped out of the water, slamming down inches away from the boat. It repeated the same movements, it's long, web-like dorsal fins snaking through the water as it generated the current.

"We don't only have one, there are multiples," Amy corrected Lachlan.

Little Blue scuttled in front of her, making off with the crystal fragment.

Amy swiped up the crab, taking the crystal back into her possession. The last thing she needed was for it to fall into the sea.

The boat gave another nasty shake as another tail swung against the hull. Salt water, sea horizon, and sky tumbled over one another as Amy fell into the ocean.

Her body seized the moment the cold water surged around her.

A hard, sturdy arm wrapped around her center, tugging her to the surface. She gasped for air as Lachlan floundered next to her.

"Hold on!" Lachlan cried as he positioned himself in front of her.

Amy braced herself as another tail rose out of the sea, then slammed down so violently, the undercurrent tugged them beneath the surface.

25

A CRABBY THIEF

Damien

As evening rolled around, Damien and Selia finally whipped his cottage back into a somewhat livable situation. It was a good thing, because another storm was quickly rolling in. As the sun dipped on the horizon, Balfour brought their worn out daughter, along with the crystal, in from the beach.

"*I'm not liking this,*" he grumbled as he walked into the cottage, while Nyssa was fast asleep. The crystal pulsed in Balfour's hand, the once brilliant blue light inside darkening.

Damien took his sleeping daughter from Balfour's arms, while Selia eyed the crystal.

"*It's reacting to something,*" Balfour grumbled.

"To what?" Selia asked.

Balfour's eyes narrowed onto the crystal. "*Something in the ocean.*"

Damien's stomach pitted. What could cause the crystal to react the way it did? He didn't want it by his daughter any longer, not with the long, black wisps filtering through it.

He grabbed the crystal from Balfour's hand.

Zap!

He dropped it onto the ground, and a bright blue light pulsed out of it. The light illuminated the far wall of his studio.

Balfour waved his hand over the crystal. "*Do not touch it.*"

Damien stood in front of Selia, preventing her from getting any closer to the darkening light flickering inside it.

Shutters rattled as the wind picked up.

Balfour folded his arms in front of his chest, gazing down at the crystal as electrical light pulsed out of it.

Damien and Selia settled with Nyssa into the middle of his studio. Peppercorn and Zipper had found a spot to perch on his easels, overlooking a stack of old artwork.

The front door burst open, sending a gust of frigid air into the cottage. "Br-rrrrr, it's *freezing* out there! It's almost like a winter front is coming in!" Deidra stammered as she bustled inside. She rubbed her hands down her arms. "Does this place not have central air?"

"It does, but we don't usually get cold snaps this far south like this," Damien replied as he grabbed a few spare blankets from one of his closets.

Selia took one of the blankets and bundled it around Nyssa. "What in the world? Is it *snowing* outside?"

"Storm boy, can't you just sneeze or something and make this all go away?" Deidra scolded Balfour.

His stoic expression became a frustrated one as he ignored Deidra's question.

A swift eye roll from Deidra followed. "Okay, well. Ignore me all you want. I don't know about you, but I didn't sign up to go to the beach to play freeze my butt off in the arctic," she complained as she rubbed her hands together. Green sparks burst from her fingertips, followed by a few golden wisps of smoke. "I'll get us a forest fire going."

"A forest fire?" Selia asked.

"Don't worry, it's not what you think it is," Deidra replied as she scanned the studio. "All I need is a piece of wood to get it started."

"Will driftwood do?" Damien asked as he held up a warped piece. "I've collected a lot over the years."

Deidra snatched it with trembling fingers. "This will be perfect!" She tossed the piece of driftwood onto the ground in front of them. "Get over here, Zipper. Let's show them how this gets started!"

Zipper flit off the easel, darting over to where Deidra stood. She held her hands over the single piece of driftwood before her boots. She wiggled her fingers, then began to chant. "From the heart of the old-growth forests, I summon you to my home. Of mushroom, fern, and pollen, I ask that you share your warmth so that we are not alone."

Zipper darted over the piece of driftwood, his wings putting off an ethereal glow. Peppercorn swiveled her head, baring her pointy teeth as she tracked the tasty bug back and forth.

The piece of driftwood sizzled, then cracked. Warm, golden light erupted out of the sides, burning bright.

"And there you have it, we have fire!" Deidra yelled.

"Fiiirreeeee!" Nyssa squealed from Selia's arms.

"Oh my word. She's *talking* already?" Deidra exclaimed.

"Yeah. She's already got a few words under her belt from our beach adventure earlier today," Selia replied. "Minca is her favorite word so far."

"You sure you aren't going to burn down my studio?" Damien asked as he gathered a few chairs and positioned them around the warm, golden light now filling his home.

Deidra plopped down into one of them. "Jeez, you really think I'd bring something flammable inside?"

"When you said forest fire, that's what I expected to happen," Damien concluded.

Deidra set her hands out, warming them over the golden flames. "It's smoke free, too. The flames are completely pollen generated. All we need now is a good batch of hot cocoa and marshmallows."

Damien took a seat next to Selia, amazed at how happy his little girl appeared. He couldn't wait to see her take her first steps and watch her grow over the next few years.

"Nyssa had her first campfire at her daddy's art studio! This is going to make for a great ghost story one day!" Deidra said as Zipper darted overhead. "Hey, what's got you so spooked?"

Shadows cast from his easels danced along the walls. Something lumpy and multi-legged began to scuttle across the floorboards.

"Um, I think whatever made the hole is back," Selia said, standing up as the creatures jostled across the floor.

"Crabs!" Deidra screamed.

She jumped so high, Balfour caught her in his arms.

"What are they bringing in?" Damien asked as the crabs swarmed in with their claws held over their heads.

Selia picked up one of the knobby items. "Is this coral?"

Balfour dropped Deidra, where she landed with a clatter into Damien's easels.

Selia scanned the floor where Balfour stood. "Oh no, one of them just snatched up the crystal!"

As quickly as the crab swarm came, it retreated back into the hole.

"Now what do we do?" Selia asked. "Go after them?"

"Are you kidding? They're probably half way to China by now," Deidra said as she straightened herself out of the pile of easels. "Something very strange is going on with the ocean life around here, and I'm wondering if it has to do with something other than the crystal."

Damien tore across the room after the infuriating little pest.

"Damien!" Selia cried.

But he was already out the door. Fire blazed through him at the thought of what not having the crystal might mean for his daughter. Whatever the strange fae behavior was about, he wasn't going to have any of it, not when his daughter's health was at stake.

The blue light of the crystal bounced in the sand as he tore after the little crab thief. He took off in a run, tripping in the icy sand as the crab scuttled toward a building he was familiar with. The Blue Mermaid Beach Bar & Grill loomed on the horizon.

He bustled up the boardwalk, following the light as it dipped into the building.

A giant hand grabbed his shoulder, tugging him back before he could enter the door.

Damien spun on his heel, facing Balfour. "Hey, what are you doing?"

"*Protecting you from the dragons I don't want to see right now,*" Balfour mumbled.

"What dragons?"

Balfour's dark eyes flickered with the orange lights of the bar. "Say hello to my brothers."

Damien squinted in the direction of the water. Whitecaps crested the waves, offset by the large bulky silhouettes of towering muscle.

A group of large, shirtless men stood on the boardwalk, facing the Celtic Sea. The group thumped their chests and rooted into the rain. Their thick, wild hair was tossed in the freezing wind. Icicles clung to their beards and hair as they raised their mugs, sending electrical sparks flying as they clashed them together.

A thunderous chant erupted from what appeared to be three of them. "To our father, Poseidon! May the storms of the sea reveal your crown!"

Damien ducked as another bolt of electricity jolted. "Those guys are your brothers?"

Balfour kept his back to the wall, hiding himself. "*Yes. I recognized their voices on the wind as soon as you stormed out of your studio. They can't find out I'm here.*"

"Why?"

"*Didn't you hear them just now? They want to find my father's crown. As soon as they know I'm here, they will demand that I go with them.*"

Damien ground his jaw, slamming his hand into the wall. "I'm not leaving without the crystal. You punched me in the head once when I was drunk off my arse. I'm not afraid of facing a bunch of drunk dragons."

Damien fell into a lobster crate as Balfour's mighty hand tugged him back.

He grabbed Damien's hand, helping him up. "*Do not approach them. The more they drink, the worse it will get. I've seen them summon hurricanes while intoxicated before.*"

Damien rubbed his head as he glanced over at the three giant men fist-pumping the air. Their drinks clashed once again, this time sending an ear-shattering crack of thunder into the atmosphere.

A bolt of electricity struck Damien in the chest. He staggered backward, falling onto the beach. Like magic, wind and rain spiraled around his body, encasing him in a solid enclosure of ice.

26

THAW THE ICE

Selia

Selia spent most of the night huddled around the flames Deidra had brought into the studio, with Nyssa fast asleep. Damien and Balfour did not return, nor did they give any indication of where they went. As the storm raged, Selia thought back to the night Damien had gone out looking for his brother-in-law when his boat went missing from the harbor.

Her mind traveled back to Scotland, which she'd envisioned as her long-term home. Thoughts of Auntie, and Gwen, and Pixie's cozy Bat Blitz Coffee Shop came to mind, as well as their lighthouse. What she wouldn't do to be back tending to Pixie's greenhouse, or drinking one of her amazing lattes.

"They've been gone a while, don't you think?" Deidra said as Zipper flit over the fire, adding what appeared to be golden pixie dust down from his wings. The flames crackled and popped as he hovered above them.

"Yeah, they have," Selia replied, "but oddly, I'm not too worried. Balfour has a way of dealing with the weather, even if it becomes dangerous." She thought of Balfour's loyalty to her, and now, her family. She wondered what kind of ritual might take place to make him the guard dragon for her daughter.

Deidra glanced up from the fire, her pupils dilating. "We haven't really talked about my relationship with Alex, have we? And why I stopped texting you?"

"I remember her stating that she stepped in because you hadn't fulfilled your mission, whatever that means."

Deidra slouched. "She was right. I feel super guilty about her death. Had I been able to prevent Masika from getting you to open the ocean vault, she wouldn't have had to step in and get herself killed."

Selia squinted at her. "You blame yourself for Alex's death?"

Deidra's shoulders rolled forward. "She never should have had to get involved As soon as I found out that Masika discovered your whereabouts, I panicked." She shook her head. "I never should have tried to become an Iridescent."

"Is there some test that you have to past to become an Iridescent?"

"Stopping Masika from finding you was my test, and as you know, I failed miserably."

"How long have you actually known me?"

Deidra stared into the flames, nostalgia warping her expression. "Project Abyss was the name of the mission. When Balfour brought you back from the Abyss, the Order needed someone to help you integrate into modern-day society. You had to learn a new language, and obtain a new identity, which dryads are very skilled at accomplishing. I remember coming across the opportunity like yesterday. Alex was my mentor. She stuck her neck out referring me for the job of making sure you recovered an identity."

Selia's insides churned, emotions burning through her. Alex had partnered with Balfour to ensure she was taken care of. "She must have seen something in you to trust you with me."

"Dryads are good with helping their kin and other daughters of Gaia with blending in with human society. Many of us live in urban areas, thriving in environmental and fields of sustainability. Preserving nature-based rituals is one of our specialties."

"Balfour mentioned to Damien about performing some ritual to become a guard dragon for Nyssa. Do you have any idea what this ritual might look like?"

Deidra shrugged. "I wish I did. But storm dragons are super mysterious."

"What do dryad families look like?"

"I have two sisters, and believe me. They keep me super busy with their own relationship drama."

"Are you the oldest?"

"I am. Sylvia is the middle sister. The youngest is named Rae."

"Do dryads also have some kind of female hierarchy like sea nymphs?"

"As far as I know, all of Gaia's nymph daughters are maternal in origin. There are no male nymphs, just female ones. No fathers, or uncles, or brothers. Just lots of aunts and female cousins. Dryads are kind of like the mycelium network beneath the forest floor."

"The what?"

"Sorry. I realize not everyone knows what fungi look like deep within the soil. Anyway, my mother said she became pregnant with all three of us just by touching the roots of the sacred mother three in the old growth forest of Northern California."

"She became pregnant from touching an ancient tree?"

"Yeah. I know. Salt is what makes sea nymphs have babies, roots and pollen hold all of the fertility powers for a dryad. All this talk about fertility reminds me of my first real assignment working for the Order, back when it wasn't so hard to become an Iridescent."

"When did you start working for the Order?"

"Oh, shoot. I enlisted the same year that the National Parks Service was founded in North America. I remember my first assignment. I was a rookie unit working on transplanting redwood saplings into patches of old-growth forest."

"That makes you, how old?"

"A few centuries at least. I guess I'm like an old tree at this point. You'll have to count my rings."

"You said you enlisted? Is the Order some kind of military?"

"Nobody enlists in the Order to go to war. While historically battles have been fought, the primary purpose of serving is for a nymph to preserve Gaia's natural resources and ritual artforms practiced by her daughters."

"So in our cases, salt trancing and root reading?"

"Exactly. If a nymph rises to the rank of an Iridescent, she gains special access to the records housed within Gaia's Codex."

"That answers my question about becoming an Iridescent. But how does a nymph become a goddess? Is she born as one, or does she earn it like you are trying to do with becoming an Iridescent?"

"A goddess is a nymph who forms a special, and in many cases magical, connection with nature. In Amphitrite's case, it's always been anything star related. Starfish. Starlit corals, you name it. Her freckles mirror that magical connection she has with the sea."

"Can human women become goddesses, or only nymphs like us?"

Deidra shrugged. "That's a great question. I'm sure it depends on what mythology you believe in the most." She rubbed her hands together. "It kind of makes you wonder about this origin stuff, doesn't it? Where we all came from as Gaia's daughters? Does mother earth have a mother, or is she the original one?"

Selia gazed into the fire, wishing she had the courage to ask the deep questions about her origin that Deidra did. "I don't think you should feel guilty about Alex," Selia said, setting her hand on Deidra's arm.

Deidra sighed. "I wish there was a way to turn back time. The forest doesn't only grow upward, it expands outward, and inward, in all directions at once." Emotion cracked in her voice. "That's what Alex used to tell me when I started practicing root reading for the Order." She waved her hand over the golden flames, drawing them upward. A yawn stretched her mouth. "I think that should do for tonight. I'm super tired. Why don't we get some sleep?"

Selia retired into her bed on the sofa, tucking Nyssa beside her. Zipper remained hovering overhead, Deidra's warmth was contagious, instantly reminding Selia of Pixie. As she closed her eyes, she tried to imagine what it must feel like to be surrounded by a glowing, golden forest.

Bright daylight jolted Selia awake as Deidra withdrew the curtains. Her expression twisted into a frown. "Look. I came to the beach for sunshine and sand. And what do I wake to?" She made gesture toward the window. "This white shit? Are you *kidding* me?"

Selia rose from the bed and walked to the window. "Oh my goodness..."

The entire beach was covered in snow.

Deidra lugged on her boots, and her jacket. "Screw this. We don't need a couple of dudes to tell us if we can go on an adventure of our own or not. I say we go and find them."

Selia waked Nyssa, who was ready to nurse again. Once fed and changed, she wrapped Nyssa in her swaddle and strapped her to her front. Down to the waterline they went, where the snow quickly transitioned into a thick sheet of ice.

"Is that what I think it is?" Selia asked.

"The icebergs have washed ashore!" Deidra exclaimed as she took off in a half-run for the icy waterline.

As Selia's boots squelched through the snow, the icy beach began to transform. The ice looked like beautiful glass sculptures, striking blue in color. Oddly-shaped chunks of sea ice were scattered everywhere along the water line. Some were as wide as a car, while others were cracked and disjointed.

Deidra disappeared behind one of the larger chunks of ice that must have broken off from one of the icebergs in the storm.

"This is incredible," Selia said as she caught her and Nyssa's reflections staring back at them.

"Um, Selia? You might want to take a look at this. I might have found Balfour," Deidra said.

Selia's stomach hollowed. As she rounded the iceberg, a darker shape morphed into view. A man was locked inside of the ice. If it was Balfour, where had Damien gone?

His bulky arms and legs were covered in black serpentine tattoos. The symbols appeared Celtic in origin, knotting their way up his muscular forearms and torso. A dark blue tunic clothed him, complete with what appeared to be silver gauntlets. Dark hair tapered behind him, suspended in the frozen state. A beard decorated with beads concealed the lower half of his face.

Selia let out a sigh. "This definitely isn't Balfour. He doesn't have tattoos like that, or beard beads."

"Then who the heck is he?" Deidra asked, squinting with scrutiny at the giant man locked in the ice.

"I don't know. He's pretty hefty though. Maybe a viking?" Selia suggested, thinking back to what Damien had said about Balfour's brothers the night before.

His eyelids shifted.

Blue sparks jolted through the ice.

"Holy mushrooms! He's awake!" Deidra stammered, falling back.

With a terrible shudder, the ice cracked.

The giant man came tumbling out of the iceberg, stumbling forward, then back. His feet shuffled in the snowy sand as he shook his head, sending ice flying in every direction.

He towered over them, his long hair coated in ice and snow. Looming and terrible, he could have passed as an abominable snowman.

"Stormy!" Nyssa squealed.

"Shhhhhhh!" Selia whispered, clasping her daughter's pudgy little hands as she flung them into the air.

A scar across his eye twitched as his ice-laden brow furrowed, sending flakes of ice into his piercing blue eyes. He muttered something that sounded like a different language, his voice groggy and low.

He staggered forward, nearly collapsing. "Stoooormy? Whooo's thaaaaat?" he slurred, his words awkward and lopsided.

With a giant step forward, he began walking. Slow, fluid movements contradicted his size. He took off up the beach, his dreadlocks swinging with each of his powerful strides.

Selia and Deidra peered around the ice, both terrified about what had just occurred.

"Did he not see us?" Deidra panted.

"I guess not," Selia huffed.

As he trudged up the beach, he swung his giant arms, sending the chunks of sea ice spinning. "Deidra, I think we just saw one of Poseidon's sons. That was one of Balfour's brothers."

27

SAILOR'S & STORM DRAGONS

Amy

Cold, damp sand squelched between Amy's fingers as she blinked into the sunlight. Waves lapped at her toes, threatening to drag her back out to sea. She scanned the horizon. The *Sea Dragon* was nowhere to be found. Only low-hanging clouds danced across the ocean.

A sharp pinch to her finger sent her bolting upright.

"Ouch!" Amy shook her hand out. A hermit crab had pinched her thumb, drawing blood. Little Blue jostled away from her, flailing her claws into the air. Seagulls cried overhead, circling as they dipped down to the water to scoop up an unsuspecting fish or to tease a curious crab.

She scanned the beach, finding that something else had washed ashore. A half-naked man lay not far from her. He lay on his side, his back facing her. His shirt was torn, the fabric lapping in and out with the waves.

Lachlan...

She crawled over to him, grabbing his shoulder and tugging him so that he lay on his back. She pressed her ear to his chest. He wasn't breathing.

Pressing her lips to his, she exhaled, and Lachlan's violent movement sent water pouring out of him.

He lay on his side, coughing. "Curse you, Poseidon," he stammered. His eyes swept to Amy, the blue so bright that she struggled to gaze into them. "Well, lookie here. My rebellious little Sea Star thought she had gotten away," he stammered, his sodden hair falling into his face. "What have you done with my boat?"

She scoffed. "What have *I* done? I did nothing. The sea took it."

His face burned red as he clenched his fists and sat up. "But *you* stole it. Then you bewitched it to have your crazy dolphins come in and make off with it."

Amy's salt nodes burned as she remembered what it was that Lachlan had called her—a *sea witch*.

She attempted to stand, only to have Lachlan's wide hand grab her wrist and prevent her from doing so.

The scent of pine and wood smoke filled Amy's nose. "Look, I don't know about you, but I'd rather not spend my day soaking wet on the beach. I'd like to warm up and find some dry clothing."

She patted her sides. Something was missing.

The dragon scale...

Had she really lost it?

A seashell darted across the beach. Blue light caught her eye as Little Blue took off in the direction of a building.

She staggered to her feet and took off after the crab.

"Hey, where are you going?" Lachlan called after her.

"To find my missing treasure!" She followed the little crab, who had scuttled far too quickly up the beach toward a building she recognized.

She blinked at the giant wooden sign. It *couldn't* be. The Blue Mermaid Beach Bar & Grill? Had the triton current ripped them south, dropping them in the Celtic Sea?

Amy jogged up the beach, reaching the bar in moments. She shoved past the doors and walked inside. The familiar sight of the Blue Mermaid Beach Bar broke over her. No mermaid portraits along the far wall. A different aura lingered in the room, one that made her salt nodes tremble with thunder.

A giant man sat hunched over at the bar. Serpentine dragon tattoos coiled up his bulging arms. Long dreadlocks of hair draped down his muscular back. Every time he shifted his wide hand out to grab his drink, electrical sparks shot out of his fingertips.

Light pulsed from his other hand, which he held up to inspect. "Lykos, get over here," he barked, his voice full of rumble.

Another large man with dark skin and dreadlocks approached him. "It's about time you thawed out. Mestor, you were the last of us to escape from the ice," Lykos said, clapping Mestor on the back as he squinted at the shiny item in his hand. "Are you shedding your scales again?"

Mestor grinned, twisting his wide mouth into an awkward smile. "Ever since we thawed out of the sea ice, I can't stop losing them."

Amy's heart jumped into her throat. She'd found her treasure all right—it was sitting next to the storm dragon it belonged to. Mestor didn't seem to know, however, that there was a crystal fragment embedded in it.

She dug her heels into the rickety floorboards. Should she ask him to give it back? Her mother told her to find him, but she didn't say what to do *when* she did.

She simply said that she would meet her when the tides came in.

Lachlan bustled through the door. He approached her, stopping at his side. "Why are you staring at that guy?"

"He has something of mine," Amy said as she took a step toward the giant storm dragon.

Lachlan grabbed her arm. "Whoa, easy there, lassie. Even I wouldn't mess with a guy that size, no matter what the treasure." He steered her away from Mestor.

"What do you suggest we do then?" Amy shot back.

"We do as you requested. Let's dry off and get something to eat." He glanced over his shoulder. "Then we watch him for a bit."

Amy chewed her cheek. As much as she didn't want to admit, Lachlan was right. While Mestor tipped his drink to his mouth, the other dragon he named Lykos retreated over to a table full of other just-as-beefy men she assumed were other storm dragons.

Amy turned her back to the table, fearful. She'd never been in the company of so many storm dragons before.

Lachlan headed straight to the bar, ignoring the giant man who took up nearly half of it. He reached into his pocket, tugging out his soggy wallet. "What have you got on the grill?"

"Fresh catch from the day—cod," replied the bartender.

Mestor swung his massive head in Lachlan's direction, sending his dreadlocks swinging. "The fish here is not good. Wouldn't recommend it."

Lachlan grinned, propping his elbows onto the bar. "What would you suggest?"

"Getting a shot of alcohol instead."

Lachlan scanned the bottles. "I'll have a shot of Macallan."

Amy marveled at the fisherman's easygoing interaction with the storm dragon. She highly doubted that he was even aware that Mestor was likely one of the storm dragons responsible for catching them in the triton current.

She found a table by the window and settled onto a stool. Once Lachlan retrieved his basket of greasy seafood and his shot whiskey, he sat opposite of her at the table.

He set the basket down, pushing it forward as though it was a peace offering. "Eat. You look like you just washed out of the sea."

"Well, we both sort of just did," she chided, folding her arms onto the table. "Do you remember what it was that tugged us overboard?"

"What, the sea serpents?" he asked. "This isn't my first rodeo with them. Why do you think I named my boat the Sea Dragon?" He grabbed one of the greasy chips and tossed it into his mouth. In one bite, he gobbled it down. "I think our big bad bloke over there is similar to you."

Amy's chest swelled. "What does that mean?"

Lachlan's blue eyes settled onto her. "Neither of you are human."

Amy's stomach churned. "What makes you think that?"

Lachlan's cheeks dimpled. "Look. I've met a lot of crazy redheads in my time, but *never* in my life have I seen one summon a pod of dolphins and rip my boat out of the harbor."

Amy's robes trembled as a tiny blue claw emerged out of her sleeve.

Lachlan squinted at her. "Oh, who do we have here? *Another* sea creature?"

Little Blue pinched her way out of Amy's robes, promptly perching herself atop her shoulder.

"Dolphins, *and* a crab?" Lachlan chuckled. "Don't try and fool me. Like I said on my boat, you must be selkie folk."

Amy sighed, wishing more than anything that her mother's crab hadn't made herself known. "I'm not a selkie, or a siren, or a mermaid."

Lachlan's dimples disappeared. "Then what are you?"

Amy squeezed her fingers together tight enough that her knuckles ached. "Have you heard of nereids, or sea nymphs?"

Lachlan folded his arms across his front. "I've met a lot of women in my time, but never a sea nymph."

Amy frowned. This fisherman was no fun at all. He was more concerned with teasing her about stealing his boat than knowing who she really was. "Look, what happened on the water was not planned."

"Oh, so you didn't *plan* to steal my boat? What had you intended?" he scolded.

Amy huffed. "It's complicated."

Lachlan's mouth twisted, either from the whiskey, or from his disdain of her statement. He shifted in his chair, leaning back and propping his legs up on the stool next to him. "I don't think it's complicated enough to know that you and I might be searching for the same treasure."

Amy folded her arms on the table. "Define this treasure."

He grinned, flashing his dimples in a cocky sort of way. "Whatever treasure that bloke has of yours, I'm going to win it back over for myself."

"You can't," Amy stammered.

Lachlan downed his shot then slammed the glass onto the table. "Watch me, sea nymph."

Amy bit her tongue. Now both she and Lachlan were *both* fighting for her treasure.

Little Blue perched atop her shoulder, just as eager as her to watch the testosterone between man and storm dragon unfolded. She hung back, waiting to see how Mestor would react to Lachlan's confident approach.

"Can I buy you a drink?" Lachlan suggested from Mestor's right.

Amy bustled up to his left. "No, I'm offering."

Mestor's giant, meaty fists clenched on the bar. He swung his giant head from side-to-side. "Who are you both? And why are you pestering me?"

Lachlan threw his arm out, slamming his elbow onto the bar. He presented his hand to Mestor. "The treasure you have, you're going to have to arm wrestle me for it."

Mestor heaved a hearty grumble of a laugh as he set the scale on the bar between them. "Try me, fisherman."

As Mestor turned his back to Amy, she inched closer to the beefy dragon. She was so close to the towering wall of muscles and tattoos, she could practically swipe the scale and run off with it.

"Count us in," Mestor grumbled as he gripped Lachlan's palm.

"Three, two, one!"

Biceps bulged as testosterone surged between fisherman and storm dragon. As one arm strained against the other, Little Blue scuttled about the bar. She maneuvered quickly, dodging the jostling movements of the two males as they attempted to assert their dominance.

Mestor's gaze followed the crab, who with one fell swoop of her claw, took off with the dragon scale.

"What is this?" Mestor bellowed, electrical sparks shooting out of his beard. He slammed Lachlan's arm onto the bar.

Lachlan's face twisted in pain as he released his hand.

The door flew open. Another large man with dreadlocks entered. "We've located Balfour. He's not far from us."

Lachlan's eyes watered as Mestor stood up. His dreadlocks swung as the giant tattooed dragon stormed out of the bar.

28

THE GODDESS OF THE SEA

Damien

Damien's body trembled so violently, he thought he might pass out. He was sure that any moment now, hypothermia would kick in, if it hadn't already. He'd spent what felt like the past hours trying to free himself from the icy enclosure. Every time he shifted to the side, another piece of his clothing got wet. Water dribbled down from the ceiling, forming icicles that dripped freezing droplets on top of his head.

"I'm g-g-g-oing to k-i-i-ill him..." Damien huffed, his breath puffing out in front of him in white clouds.

"*No, I'm going to kill you,*" Balfour thundered into his mind.

"W-w-w-what? Wh-h-h-h-hy?"

"*You should have left the bar when I asked you to.*"

"Damien? Is that you?" a muffled female voice called from behind the ice.

"Selia?" Damien huffed back.

"Deidra! I found him!" Selia said with a muffled voice again.

"Selia, I'm in he-e-ere!" Damien stammered, kicking against the giant wall of ice. His foot broke through the spot he'd been pounding upon.

Damien broke out of the ice, landing on his feet. Deidra stood before him, as well as Selia and their baby.

"Stormy?" Nyssa giggled, reaching for him.

"Why did she just call me that?" Damien asked, grabbing her and giving her a tight squeeze.

"Because we just met another storm dragon," Selia said. "We saw this giant man locked in the ice, then he just took off. The question is, why were *you* also locked inside the ice?"

"Drinking between my brothers often leads to spontaneous ice formations. Damien put himself in harm's way by eavesdropping on them. Did this man you saw in the ice have tattoos?"

"Yes," Deidra concluded. "They looked like Celtic knots that resembled sea serpents."

Balfour's shoulders slouched. *"Did he have a scar across his right eye too?"*

Selia nodded.

Balfour's shoulders rolled forward. *"It sounds like you saw my eldest brother, Mestor."*

"Stormy!" Nyssa squealed again.

"Ah, now I know where she got Stormy from. Must be a nickname for Me*stooooormy*," Damien said.

"Why was he frozen in a chunk of ice like that?" Deidra asked as she kicked one of the larger ice chunks aside.

"I am responsible for putting Poseidon's sons into an icy slumber," a female voice echoed off the ice.

Damien turned around, finding another woman standing by the chunk of ice he'd been locked inside. Her eyes were a startling emerald, and her hair was long and red. She wore long, seafoam green robes, with lace that kissed the hems. The delicate designs were intricate and oceanic.

Her nose and cheeks were dusted in freckles shaped like starfish.

Sand and ice shifted as Balfour dropped to the ground, bowing his head. *"The great Amphitrite,"* he stammered.

"Should we also be bowing?" Damien asked.

Amphitrite waved her hand. "That is not necessary. Only in Atlantis, maybe. But not here, with thousands of years between us and the great city."

Selia and Deidra continued to ogle the sea nymph who had been called a goddess in numerous tales of Greek mythology.

Balfour climbed to his feet. "*I was wondering when we should be expecting your arrival.*"

Amphitrite's emerald eyes found the storm dragon. "The bond you formed with the Blind Moon has helped the stars align for us. My daughter and I will be needing you and your brothers' assistance when the time comes for us to turn the tides in our favor."

"Is Amy nearby?" Selia asked.

"I sure hope so. I gave her a few items that should show up if she has arrived safely." She scanned the beach, her bare feet shifting through ice, sand, and snow. Damien wondered how she wasn't complaining about the cold. Her gaze shifted quickly back to Balfour. "Bellerophon, your brothers have washed ashore much sooner than I had planned. Then again, I should have accounted for the alarming rate in which sea ice is melting."

"*What assistance must you request of them?*"

"If I am to find what remains of my Ocean Apothecary and your father's crown, I will need you and your brothers' help," Amphitrite replied.

"*I don't know if that is such a great idea. You know how my eldest brother's temper can be.*" Balfour protested.

"I expect some retaliation from Mestor after what I did to him." Her foot shifted past a patch of ice. "Ah, here you are." Amphitrite bent down, grabbing one of the pieces of ice as it shifted away from her. As she straightened herself, a tiny blue crab perched atop her palm.

"That's the little thief!" Damien yelled.

Amphitrite covered the little crab with her other hand. "I gave her specific instructions one what to do. All right, Little Blue. If you also worked according to plan, you would have hidden the treasure somewhere right here under our noses."

The crab snapped its claw, then hopped out of her palm and landed on the beach. In one swift maneuver, it darted between her toes and took off up the beach.

Amphitrite glanced between them. "Zakai tells me you have an art studio nearby?"

"I do. It's right up that dune," Damien said.

"Let's go inside. It will make more sense after I've shared a nice hot batch of coral tea with you."

Amphitrite took off after the crab, her green robes and red hair swaying as she went.

Selia arched one of her eyebrows. "Did she just say coral tea?"

Damien grabbed her hand. "Somehow I feel like we're going to be hearing some strange things about your inheritance from Amy's sea goddess mother."

29

CRYSTALS & CORAL TEA

Selia

Selia walked with Damien up the dune, trailing behind Amphitrite as she ascended the beach after the little blue crab. Deidra and Balfour lingered behind, neither of whom were very excited about the turn of events.

"*I don't trust this,*" Balfour grumbled, his thunderous voice echoing into Selia's head.

"*What don't you trust about it?*" Selia asked him with her mind.

"*Zakai informed me that Amphitrite would give insight on your inheritance, but she didn't mention the needing our bond to find my father's crown part.*"

"I agree with storm boy," Deidra concluded. "What do you think, Zipper? Doesn't this all sound a bit convoluted?"

Zipper flit ahead of Selia, following Amphitrite. A golden trail of pollen floated behind him.

"Traitor!" Deidra called after her rebellious dragonfly.

Zakai stood outside the cottage, standing by the front door. Her arms were folded in front of her chest, the wind catching and twisting her robes. She gave a small bow as they approached. "Amphitrite. Your timing is always as impeccable as the tides."

The blue crab darted past the Iridescent and disappeared inside the cottage.

Amphitrite hesitated. She turned around to face the group, her emerald eyes dilating. "I have realized just how incredibly rude I have been to you. I've been so focused on timing and the tides, that I've not even properly introduced myself, have I?"

Selia stared at the red-headed sea nymph, completely lost in her appearance. Everything from her heart-shaped face, to her dazzling emerald eyes, to the locks of curly red hair screamed *Amy*. Amphitrite was taller than Amy, and her freckles were darker. Their star-shape was what made mother and daughter appear so similar. "You look *exactly* like your daughter."

The corners of Amphitrite's mouth curved up just as whimsically as Amy's, although her dimples were deeper, and the lines that creased behind her eyes were more prominent. "And your daughter will look almost identical to you one day."

"How can you tell?"

Amphitrite glanced above Selia's head, her green eyes trailing down the length of her body. "I can see the salt aura around you both beginning to develop—it's incredibly healthy."

Selia glared at Zakai. "Wait, Nyssa's salt aura is healthy?"

Nyssa let out a squeal of delight, grabbing a handful of Amphitrite's thick red hair.

"Very healthy," Amphitrite replied. She reached into her robe, tugging out a small blue item shaped like a star.

Nyssa grabbed it, immediately shoving it into her mouth.

"Her teeth will be coming in soon, and she's going to need lots of those to keep her occupied," Amphitrite said, her voice full of delight.

Selia laughed. Amy's mother was just like her daughter, pulling tricks out of her sleeves at a moment's notice.

"If her salt aura is healthy, then can you explain why she would fall asleep and not wake up?" Selia asked as Nyssa continued to mouth her new toy.

"Sea nymph infants can sleep for days at a time. It's quite normal for them to pass out whenever they are bathed, and in some cases, only sprinkled with water. Historically, sea nymph mothers called these sleeping episodes rain naps. Whenever the skies open up, they can fall asleep for hours, even days at a time."

Damien glanced at his daughter. "That would explain why she's been sleeping so much. It's been incredibly rainy, especially with Balfour around."

Selia locked eyes with Zakai. "Why lie and not just tell us the truth?" she asked, furious at the Iridescent who had apparently lied about Nyssa's salt aura.

"Timing is everything when it comes to the star of the sea," Amphitrite countered, defending Zakai. "Zakai was merely doing as I asked. I knew that two new parents would only do as I requested if the health of their daughter was involved."

Selia's stomach pitted at Amphitrite's words. One of them was new at this—herself. "Then I take it you have information on the purpose of my inheritance? I still have no idea why Isis intended me to inherit my crystal fragment."

Amphitrite's gaze settled onto her, a seriousness to her expression that didn't seem to fit her personality. "The star of the sea has many powers, some of which are lost to history. But like the art of salt trance, that power is not used for a singular purpose."

Damien opened the front door and held it wide. "I don't know about you, but I think warming up over some tea and a story sounds nice."

As their group moved inside his studio, Selia took Nyssa over to the sofa.

Balfour busied himself with the tea kettle, while Deidra tried to track down Damien's stash of teabags. Zakai stood in her usual stoic fashion, arms folded across her chest, observing the group in silence.

Selia's foot brushed across an item on the floor. A bunch of beach debris lay scattered before her. More seashells, pieces of smooth driftwood, and even some more of the starfish.

"Who did this?" Selia asked, amazed at the additional assortment of items. She sat down on the sofa, propping Nyssa onto her belly so she could crawl. She scooted her way toward one of the starfish and shoved it into her mouth.

Amphitrite watched her daughter with amusement. "My crabs knew that a baby was going to be here, so I ask them to prepare the proper beach toys for her. I remember when my own daughter was young, and how she took after the starfish."

Selia squinted at Amphitrite, making a double take. Her vibrant red hair cascading down her shoulders brought back a flurry of frozen memories of the last time she had seen Amy at the winter solstice gathering. "The last time I saw your daughter, she was preparing to go on a journey. The last thing she said to me was that her window to the past had opened. What did that mean?"

Amphitrite faced her. "Amy used the fae queen to do just as she described, but I am afraid that her quest did not result in the way she wanted it to."

"Did she really travel to the past?" Selia asked.

Amphitrite nodded. "The fae do not know the boundaries of time, and their powers can sometimes allow our hearts to bleed through those boundaries, even if it is only for a moment."

"Why did she go?"

Amphitrite's shoulders rose and fell. "Her quest was for love. But I believe Amy learned that only true love transcends the boundaries of time, as it follows us wherever we go."

Selia grabbed Nyssa, hoisting her and the crab that had crawled onto her arm into her lap.

"All right, you've played with the baby enough," Amphitrite said, reaching out and grabbing the crab before it crawled any further. She set it on the table, where it plopped down and faced her as though waiting for another order. "What did you do with the crystal fragments? Mine, as well as the one you stole from Selia?"

The crab pinched its claws as the tea kettle screamed from the kitchen. It darted away, scuttling into the room where Damien's art supplies were kept. Apparently, the crab had a mission of its own to contend with.

"Do you have any knowledge of what Nephthys did with the third fragment?" Selia asked.

Amphitrite's emerald gaze fell onto her. "Who told you that Nephthys had it?"

"I did," Deidra said, coming up behind Selia and stopping beside her. "The last record the Order has of the third fragment was that Nephthys hid it somewhere."

"What the goddess of death did with her fragment is still a mystery," Amphitrite replied. "But Selia will be the one to find it."

Selia jolted. "Me? How?"

Amphitrite smiled. "By trusting in the bond between you and Balfour."

Right on cue, Balfour brought the hot water over to the table where Amphitrite and Selia sat.

"How many of us are there?" Deidra asked.

"Seven, I do believe, which is the perfect number," Amphitrite said. "We will include the baby, although she will not need to drink anything. In fact, it's best if she is sleeping for the ritual."

At Amphitrite's words, Nyssa's eyes began to close. Selia bundled her in her blanket and rocked her while she dozed.

Deidra set seven tea cups onto the table. Balfour filled them with hot water, while Damien sat down next to Selia on the sofa. The dryad and the storm dragon sat across from them, while Zakai remained standing behind their chairs.

Peppercorn perched atop the teapot handle, keeping her attention on the vibrant blue crab that scuttled back and forth between Amphitrite and Selia.

"So, what is this hippie tea setup all about?" Deidra asked as Zipper dipped down, landing on her shoulder.

Amphitrite scanned the room. "I know that Deidra has shared the creation story behind the star of the sea with you. You are also aware that it was fragmented by me into three pieces." Her gaze found Selia. "I'm inviting everyone into an ocean trance. What you see will determine your role in how you will assist Selia in retrieving the third and last piece of her inheritance."

"Is an ocean trance the same as a salt trance?" Selia asked.

"Hardly," Amphitrite replied. "Salt trancing is used to help a sea nymph sync her salt aura with the ancestral mother of the sea, the Abyss. Ocean trancing allows one to share the past with others on a much larger scale. In some rare cases, individuals may *relive* memories. And in some instances, they have gotten lost in them the starlit shadows that house those memories. Ocean trancing also allows one to visit the temple where the star of the sea was created by Isis and Nephthys."

Selia's heart leapt. "The Temple of the Three Origins?"

Amphitrite nodded.

"But Deidra told us that only goddesses and prior midwives of the sea could access this temple," Selia argued.

Amphitrite's eyes shimmered whimsically. "You are in the presence of a sea goddess, are you not?" She retrieved a pouch from her robes and undid the twine. She tipped the pouch over everyone's tea cups, spilling small amounts of white powder inside.

Selia's cup frothed as the powder she assumed was ground up coral mixed with the water. The liquid turned brown, then green, until it finally settled on a deep shade of ultramarine.

Amphitrite grabbed her own cup, holding it beneath her nose. She closed her eyes, and inhaled. Her freckles turned the same deep blue color as the liquid in her cup. "Star of the sea, your heart is purely shown. From the darkest waters of the ocean, let your origin be known." She opened her eyes, gazing around the table. "Now everyone, drink your tea."

Everyone grabbed their cup, tipped it to their mouth and drank.

Selia tipped her cup to her mouth last. The moment the hot liquid hit her tongue, her mouth cooled, filling with the bitter taste of salt.

Damien, Deidra, Balfour and Zakai all became transparent. Amphitrite, however, remained solid, except for a brilliant blue glow that surrounded her.

Blue mist rose out of everyone's teacups, combining at the center of the table. An image of the ocean appeared. No landmasses were present. Only large white-capped waves that surged against each other. A large structure came rising out of the water. Giant marble pillars framed the entrance of a building that blended so well with the sea, it could have been mistaken for coral.

"What is that?" Selia asked.

"The Temple of the Three Origins," Amphitrite replied. "Historically, the temple was where the star of the sea was kept. One of the main temple structures was located in Atlantis. Did Deidra share with you why the crystal was created?"

"Yes, she said that Isis and Nephthys created the crystal to help your sister Pherusa with her duties during her reign as the midwife of the sea. She said that the bond between her and Erebéus was weak, making her responsibilities difficult to do."

"Did she not give any indication as to *why* their bond was weak?"

Selia shook her head, *no*.

Shadows drifted out of the temple, tendrils of black smoke coiling around its base. A woman appeared. Her long black robes clung to her thin body. Ebony hair framed her honey brown skin. Something cold lurked in her liquid gaze that reminded Selia of Masika.

Amphitrite pointed to the woman standing before them. "My sister, Pherusa, had long desired Nephthys's powers, more than she did her sister, Isis. Her infatuation with death contradicted what the midwife of the sea stood for, a bringer of life. Erebéus knew this when he approached her with his attempt to bond, stating that she should first consult with Isis."

"Did she?"

"No. Instead, Pherusa consulted with me. She knew that Erebéus's descendant, Poseidon, was becoming ill. She saw Poseidon's weakness as a sign that his ancestor, too, wasn't in the best of health."

Selia's stomach hollowed. "Balfour told Damien that he has a memory of seeing Nephthys in his temple before he found his father dead on the throne."

"Does Balfour believe that Nephthys killed his father?"

"He doesn't know what to believe. But he's tired of fighting with Mestor and the others over the territories in their father's crown. He's tired of them trying to find it to prove what happened to Poseidon."

Amphitrite's eyes shifted to her, their emerald color darkening. "You don't have to find the crown for me to admit that my Ocean Apothecary is responsible for Poseidon's death."

Selia jolted. "What? How?"

Amphitrite's emerald eyes locked with hers. "That answer can only be revealed with your inheritance. This is where you come in, Blind Moon. I need you to help me locate the third fragment. Mending the crystal back together can only be done in the Temple of the Three Origins."

Selia's salt nodes shook with a terrible force.

Like an icy growl, the word *Ammmmphiiitrittteeee* filled her ears, waking her from the ocean trance.

PART 4
STORMY SEAS

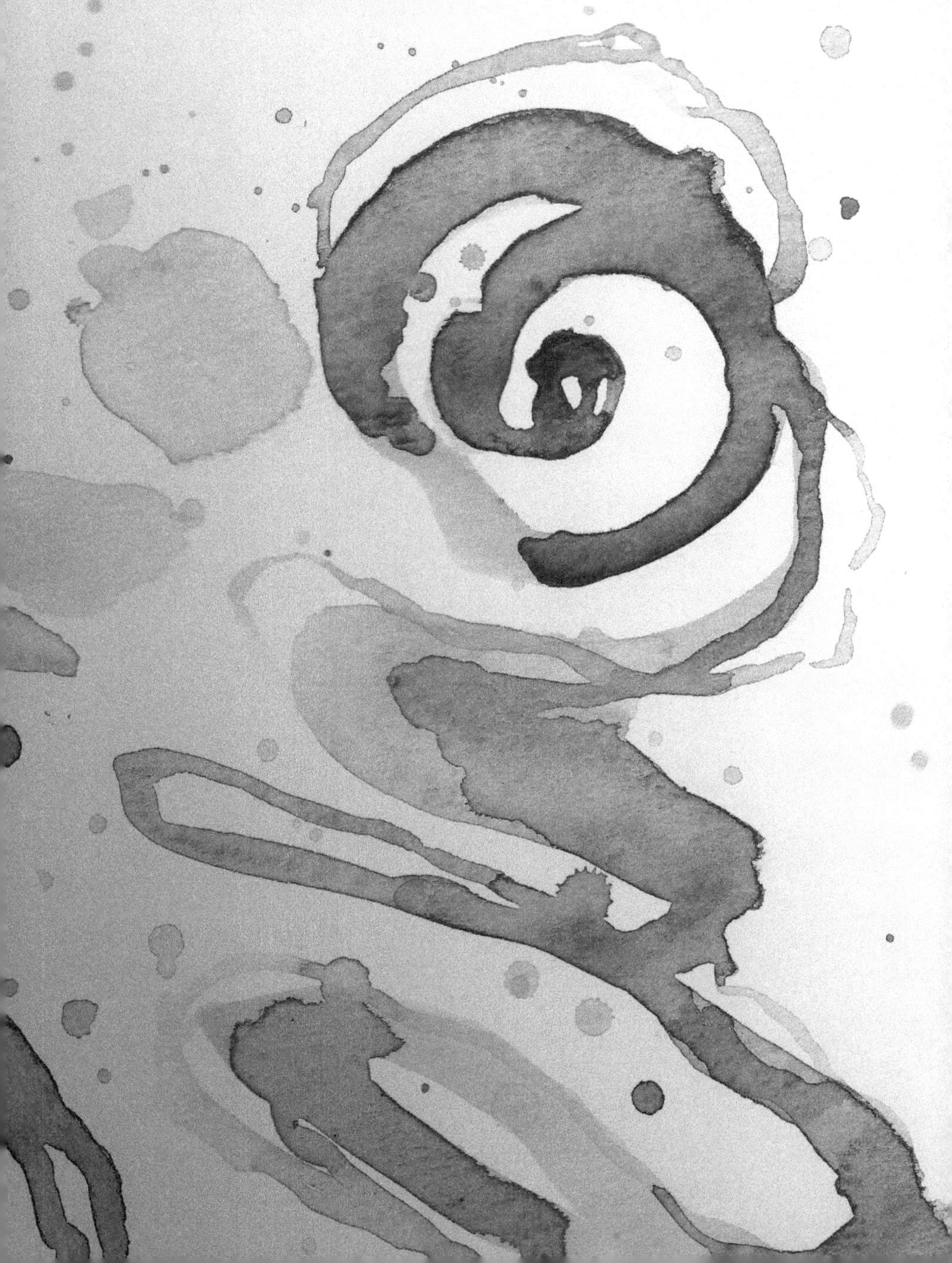

30
FORGETTING EWAN
Amy

After Mestor stormed out of the bar, Amy took it upon herself to gather her thoughts. She and Lachlan were both stranded, with no boat, and no treasure. Meanwhile, Lachlan tried to act like Mestor hadn't twisted his arm.

"I can't believe you challenged a guy three times your size to an arm wrestling match," Amy scolded him.

Lachlan sat on a stool at the bar, where he'd been for the past hour or so tending to a bruised ego, while flexing and bending his elbow. "He had nothing on me. He was all hot air and smelled like rotten fish. Had that other bloke not darted in and interrupted my focus, I would have won."

As he massaged his arm, his face twisted into a wince. "Who knows where that little crab darted off to with your treasure. Sounds like those big guys were looking for some bloke named Balfour," Lachlan stammered, flexing the arm Mestor could have easily broken if he wanted to.

Hopefully the crab's strange behavior meant that her mother was nearby.

Lachlan squinted toward the window. "Is that what I think it is?"

Before Amy could glance out the window, Lachlan took off in a mad run toward the door. "The Sea Dragon is back!"

Amy stood, but her leg didn't agree with her movement. A painful spasm shot up her calf as she put weight onto her foot. She hobbled after him, eager to see if his boat had returned to him.

She limped down the boardwalk, flexing her ankle as she tried to work through the shooting pains. His boat bobbed in the water just as it had in the Galway harbor. The currents, by however possible, returned the *Sea Dragon* to its owner.

Lachlan jumped from the boardwalk onto his boat, fisting his hand into the air. "I can't believe this! The sea gods are on my side today!"

As he clapped his hands and continued in his elated celebration, Amy folded her arms in front of her chest. "You have your boat. You don't need me any longer."

Lachlan hopped down onto the boardwalk, landing stiffly in front of her. "But you never finished telling me about the treasure you are after." He squared his hips, flashing his teeth in a curious smile. "Somehow, I think it's a bit different than what that little crab ran off with."

Amy spun on the wrong foot.

She buckled forward, nearly falling into the Celtic Sea.

Lachlan caught her around the center before she fell.

"Whoa, careful," he said, spinning her around to face him.

She settled into his strong arms. She breathed in his scent of wind and salt-crusted air, feeling his hard chest muscles beneath her palms.

"What's wrong? Are you hurt?" he asked, his voice tender.

"No, I'm just fine," she argued. She tried to step away from his embrace, but her ankle buckled.

"You can barely walk," he stammered, holding her up.

"That's not true," she whispered as the pain crippled her further. The hot, burning sensation was shooting up her leg now.

She didn't remember twisting her ankle. Where was the phantom pain coming from?

"I have medical supplies on my boat," he said.

Before she could protest, he grabbed her under her legs and hoisted her into his arms. He carried her onto the boat and into the inner quarters before lowering her beside him. "We'll sort this out. You must have injured yourself from our tumble in the surf."

With Lachlan's help, Amy limped inside of the cabin. Once again, she was overwhelmed with the presence of Ewan. How much she hated how Lachlan reminded her of the giant huntsman. His hospitality. His generosity. His genuine warmth.

She didn't deserve that kind of relationship with anyone, not after she'd left him to die atop that frozen mountain. His memory was trapped in the past, still burning like a hot ember in her heart. If only she could find a way to make the burning fire of Ewan's memory go out.

Lachlan steered her toward a bench in the corner. "Sit here. I'll grab some supplies."

Amy did so, thankful for not having to put weight on her bad leg.

He busied himself with a dresser not far from the bed, tugging open a drawer and pulling out various articles of clothing.

He tossed an item at her. "Here. You look cold."

She held up the item. "What is this?"

"A hide from a red deer. They have some of the warmest fur in Scotland. Just imagine what it was like to have the hide of an Irish elk. They went extinct long ago."

She tucked the fur around her legs, grateful for the added warmth.

Lachlan kept his back to her, tugging his shirt over his head.

Amy's body heated from the hide, and the sight of the shirtless Scotsman standing before her. Lachlan wasn't a huntsman, but a fisherman nonetheless. The peaks and valleys of his back muscles flexed wonderfully.

As he rummaged through the drawer, Amy's breath caught. The skin over his left shoulder blade was splotchy and discolored. "How did you get that scar?"

"Shark bite," he said, continuing to toss clothing aside.

"From what, a one-toothed shark?" Amy protested, noticing nothing else but a singular mark.

Lachlan shrugged. "I guess that joke only works on some. I like to think it's a scar, but it's not." He turned to face her, his bare chest catching the dim light. "It's a birthmark."

Amy stared at his well-developed chest, tracing the edges of his muscles that formed strong, hard lines along his neck. She blinked, not fully understanding what she was seeing.

"What," he said, cheeks dimpling. "Have you never seen a man without his shirt on before?"

"Can you turn around for me?"

Lachlan held his arms out as he spun in place. As he turned, the haunting mark appeared upon his back, and chest.

How could someone have a birthmark that mirrored itself?

Unless, a weapon had penetrated his body. Perhaps, an *arrow*?

Why did her nose suddenly sting with the cold of Winter Forest?

"Can I stop spinning?" Lachlan asked.

"Sorry, yes," Amy stammered, feeling slightly nauseous.

Lachlan faced her, propping his hands on his hips. "Are there other places of me that you would like to see as well?"

Amy held her gaze level with his. "The birthmark is also over your heart."

Lachlan's shoulders rose and fell. "Yes. It's odd. I don't think I've met anyone with a birthmark with two sides." He clapped his hands together. "All right. Let's get to your leg then," he said as he tugged his new shirt over his head, ruffling his hair. A satisfied half-smile, half-smirk tugged at the corners of his mouth. He grabbed a handful of bandages and a first aid kit, then sat down next to her on the bench.

Amy swung her leg onto his lap. She propped her back against the wall, wincing as he maneuvered a callused hand along her shin.

He traced his fingers down her calf, pressing gently as he explored her skin. "It's pretty swollen. I hope I can make it feel better."

Amy stifled a whimper before it became a sound of pleasure.

Lachlan pulled his hand away from her skin. "If I'm hurting you, tell me when to stop."

"Don't," she whispered.

Lachlan's hazel eyes flicked up to her as he further explored her leg. The mark he stated was a birthmark peeked out from his shirt.

Amy's fingers flexed, desperate to touch it. *No.* She had to be imagining things. There was no possible way. Even if Lachlan did remind her of Ewan, even if he had by some means of magic returned to her, she didn't deserve him.

Lachlan tugged up her legging, revealing a patch of red skin.

Amy's stomach hollowed. She'd seen that black, oily film before. Had she somehow gotten infected with salt venom?

"It's bruised is all. That's good," Lachlan said with confidence that didn't transfer to Amy.

Desperate to distract herself from the wound on her leg, and the idea that Lachlan was so similar to Ewan in too many ways, she forced her thoughts back to their encounter with Mestor. "You mentioned at the bar that you believed the man you arm wrestled and I weren't human. Now that you know I am a sea nymph, I must know. What did you assume Mestor was?"

"It doesn't matter who or what he was." He traced his lips along the back of her hand. "Right now, I want to focus on making you feel better."

Amy pulled her hand away. "Ewan, stop."

Lachlan glanced up at her. "What did you call me?"

She could have kicked herself for stating his name aloud. "It hurts."

His brow furrowed. "What hurts?"

She glanced at his birthmark again. "Sometimes there are things from the past that we can never heal from."

"Tell me what it is," Lachlan said, his voice desperate. He grabbed her hand, dwarfing her own in his big callused one. "I promise, I can and I *will* make it stop hurting."

Amy's body went numb. She didn't need to feel close to anyone right now. She didn't need to let anyone, not her mother, nor the memory of Ewan down.

"I can't do this," she stammered, tugging her leg away from him.

"Do what?"

She stood. As soon as she stepped down onto her leg, the pain burned up the back so fiercely it felt like she might pass out. But the physical pain was nothing compared to the hole the past had burned into her heart.

"Wait a minute, I haven't even dressed your leg yet," Lachlan stammered as she also stood.

Amy limped to the door.

Lachlan grabbed her arm. "You aren't going anywhere. You can barely walk."

"Watch me. It's not like I needed you to help me, anyway," she stammered and shoved past him.

Lachlan's brow furrowed. "Wait just a minute. I'm pretty sure I *did* help you, at least my boat did," he said, darting after her.

As she approached the doorway, Lachlan grabbed her shoulder and spun her to face him.

"Leave me alone!" Amy yelled, slamming her fist against his chest.

He didn't flinch as he propped his arm against the door frame, pinning her against the wall. "No. I'm not done with you yet."

"Oh, aren't you?" Amy said, fury rising in her voice. "I was done with you the moment you showed up in my life again."

A look of hurt reflected in Lachlan's blue eyes that reminded her too much of Ewan. "You don't mean that."

"Yes, I do. Now get out of my face."

Lachlan released her from the wall, stepping aside. "Amy, you're making a mistake," he whispered. "I...didn't mean to upset you."

Amy tore past him. She scrambled down from the boat onto the boardwalk, furious with the situation. She didn't need him, or his boat. What she needed was for her mother to show up.

Was she crazy for leaving the warm chambers of his boat? Probably. Had she made a fool of herself? Absolutely. There was no sense to be made of how she was feeling, or why she was acting this way. Maybe she wanted to feel the pain in her leg. The more she focused on the burning sensation building in her muscles, the less connected she felt with Ewan's memory.

She trudged down the boardwalk, making her way toward the water. Another figure made its way up the beach. Was it finally her mother?

31
MESTOR

Damien

Damien's feet were wet and cold. Stars—trillions of them—shimmered above. So *this* was an ocean trance? Why was there so much starlight? Amphitrite was preparing to share something about how they would assist Selia with retrieving the third crystal fragment of the star of the sea, right?

He squinted at the horizon. Neither Balfour, Deidra, nor Zakai were here. The last figures he'd seen had been Selia and Amphitrite, but they had also disappeared. He was completely alone, gazing out at the open water of the ocean.

"Damien," a woman whispered.

He turned, finding a figure standing by the water. Her long brown hair twisted in the wind as her equally brown eyes swam toward him. Maera had reappeared, more vibrant and starlit than ever.

"What do you want?" Damien asked, stepping backward into the water.

The waves crashed around his ankles as Maera walked toward him. "Zakai might not have needed your artwork, but I do."

"Ammmmphhiitrrritteeeeeee."

Damien jolted, blinking into the daylight of his art studio.

Maera was gone.

Where was all of the yelling coming from?

He squinted past his teacup, finding a large, burly figure emerging outside the window. He had to be hallucinating. Someone who looked like Balfour was making his way up the beach toward his studio.

"*Stay here*," Balfour ordered as he made his way to the front door and opened it.

Damien followed the storm dragon out to watch the confrontation unfold.

"*Mestor*," the real Balfour said as he descended the stairs and stopped on the beach front.

The storm dragon who stood outside his cottage was far larger than the ones he'd seen at the bar the night before. Sure, Balfour was big for a guy, but his older brother had him beat tenfold.

Mestor's hair was long and matted, some of it clumped into dark brown dreadlocks. He wore a blue tunic that bunched around his chest and arms. A thick, wiry beard framed his square jaw. His eyes were a piercing blue that made the sky look tame. A scar traveled from his thick brow, crossing over his eye and a good way down his cheek.

The beefy storm dragon wouldn't look Balfour in the eye. He remained focused on Damien, his nostrils flaring as veins bulged in his forearms. "Where is the sea goddess who is responsible for putting Poseidon's sons into a terrible, icy slumber?" he growled thunderously.

Damien shuddered. Mestor's voice was twice as deep and threatening as his younger brother's.

"Amphitrite!" Mestor bellowed. "Come out here, now! I know you are here!"

Both Zipper and Peppercorn disappeared at the terrible sound of Mestor's furious voice. One thing was different about this storm dragon. He spoke aloud, not telepathically. But his voice was not any less loud out in the open. Seashells bounced in the sand, vibrating as his explosive words tore through the air.

Selia emerged from the cottage, grabbing Damien's arm. "He sounds very upset."

"Upset? No. He's flipping pissed," Deidra chimed in as she emerged next to Selia.

"Stormy pissed!" Nyssa cried from Selia's arms.

"Did she just say what I thought she said?" Selia asked, laughing.

Despite the circumstances, Damien doubled over at his daughter's hilarious observation.

Balfour stood before them, taking a defensive stance in front of his much larger brother. Mestor's shadow nearly devoured Balfour. "*Stop yelling. You have no right to come barging up here like this.*"

An icy blast of air burst from Mestor's nostrils, forming icicles in his beard. He swung his arms at his sides, flexing and stomping his feet in the sand. "Amphitrite, I'm waiting. You know what happens if you ignore a storm dragon too long. He will blow your little shack to smithereens if you mock him."

Damien's stomach hollowed. He didn't like the idea of a storm dragon destroying his cottage, or the fact that Mestor wouldn't even acknowledge his little brother.

Mestor threw his head back, cracking his neck while laughing. "All right. Brace yourself for the consequences." He clapped his hands together, sending sparks out of his metal gauntlets.

Balfour took a step toward his older brother as electricity bolted through the air toward the studio.

A thunderous *crack* exploded in the air, grounding Mestor's electric attack. "*You will do no such thing, not while I am here,*" Balfour growled back.

"Leave him alone!" Selia cried as she handed Nyssa to Damien, then padded down the steps to Balfour's side.

Mestor cocked his head sideways, his heavy brows furrowing. "And who is this? A sea nymph who knows not how to bite her tongue?"

Selia recoiled as Mestor grabbed a strand of her hair and twirled it in his thick fingers.

Damien tried to hand Nyssa off to Deidra, but Balfour's voice thundered into his mind. "*Stay where you are. He needs to know who I am to the Blind Moon, and her family.*"

Balfour approached Mestor and shoved his hand against his beefy shoulder, forcing him to release Selia's hair. He grabbed Mestor's giant arm, which was nearly twice the size of his own. "*You can ignore me all you want, but I will rip your tail off if you touch her, or threaten her family in any way.*"

Mestor turned his thick neck, his dreadlocks falling into his face. "You will do no such thing to your eldest brother."

Balfour wretched his arm sideways, ripping one of Mestor's gauntlets off. He tossed it to the ground, where electricity sparked from it. "*I am bound to Celaeno's moon daughter,*" he growled, thunder rumbling out of him like an earthquake. "*Meaning I am also bound to her mate, and her offspring.*"

Mestor's giant hands flexed, balling into fists, then releasing. "Celaeno's moon daughter means nothing to me."

"She will when you witness the bond she and your brother have formed together," Amphitrite said as she emerged from the cottage. She descended the stairs, walking with grace toward Balfour and Selia. "I would suggest not threatening the storm dragon and the sea nymph who formed a bond that will help locate the crown of your father."

Mestor's eyes shifted to Amphitrite. "Oh? That's your plan now? Had my brothers and I not planned to do so before you put us all into an icy slumber?"

"You will show both your brother and Selia respect," Amphitrite corrected him.

"Or what? You'll freeze our tails off?" he chuckled, his voice low and hard.

"Oi, Mestor! We've got a catch!"

Two other giant men appeared behind Mestor, lugging a fishing net up the beach.

Mestor spun on his heel, swinging his massive arms as he faced them. "Can't you see I'm having a serious discussion with the sea goddess who locked us in the ice?"

With a last effort, the two slung the net to the side, which was full of shellfish.

One of them approached Mestor and clapped him on his beefy shoulder. "Don't care right now. You aren't setting us out to sea to find our father's crown without having a proper meal first."

As late afternoon rolled in, and tempers died down, Balfour's brothers got to work preparing a bonfire on the beach. While Mestor was all business, Balfour's other brothers seemed to have other festivities on their minds. Damien did his best to stay out of the way as they sorted out the roles each would perform.

The beach was soon crowded with the presence of seven large, muscular men, all of whom wore blue, brown, and green tunics. They sported long deadlocked hair and thick, unruly beards, and trudged through the sand barefooted. Mestor had nothing to do with the meal prep, keeping his back facing inland as he gazed out at the sea. Meanwhile, Balfour mingled with his other five brothers, each who seemed less distant that the eldest toward him.

Deidra and Selia took Nyssa out and about to play scavenger hunt with the little blue crab, who helped them track down driftwood for the fire. Zakai kept Amphitrite company as she kept her sights on Balfour's eldest brother.

While two of the dragons began shucking oysters, Damien grabbed Balfour's attention, waving him over to where he sat on a large chunk of driftwood. "What are their names?"

Balfour stopped next to Damien, folding himself so that he collapsed onto the ground. *"I'm sure they will all be introducing themselves before the night is over. My brothers never fail to put on a good show when they can. Their names are Hopleus, Idas, Pelias, Taras, and Lykos."* Balfour swung his head toward the stocky silhouette facing the sea. *"You already know Mestor."*

Bits of fragmented words were spoken between Balfour's brothers. Damien assumed it might be a residual language they spoke in Atlantis.

He propped his elbows onto his knees. "If these guys were all sleeping in a bunch of icebergs for a few thousand years, how are they all speaking English? Wouldn't there be some kind of language barrier between now and when they lived in Atlantis?"

"Storm dragons have never seen language as a barrier. Because our first means of communication was telepathy, speaking through the weather, we acclimate well to any language."

"Meaning, you basically adapt to the climate of any culture's language?"

"We can mimic the language spoken by any human, and many different oceanic creatures."

"I don't like how Mestor refuses to speak to you," Damien said.

"Well, I don't like how you keep looking over your shoulder," Balfour replied. *"You seem spooked."*

Damien shook his head, thinking back to his encounter with Maera. Did she really need his artwork for something? "Ever since that ocean trance, I've not been right."

"Me neither. Something was off about that tea," Balfour agreed with a growl.

"Amphitrite mentioned that we would all see something that would show us how we could help Selia find the third crystal fragment. I don't even know what Selia experienced yet."

"You should ask her. I have a feeling Amphitrite showed Selia something important about her inheritance. It was a good few thousand years not having to deal with Mestor's nasty temper."

Damien watched two of his brothers shuck clams off each other's heads. He glanced sideways at Balfour. "What did you see during the ocean trance?"

Balfour gazed up at the sky. *"Stars for as far as the eye could see. Before my brother awoke us all, I thought I might get lost in them."*

"I saw stars, too," Damien said, quickly thinking back to the haunting words Maera had said to him.

32
ORIGIN BONDS

Selia

As the evening rolled in, and Balfour's brothers continued to prepare the bonfire, Selia found herself wishing she had a reason to join in with their festivities. Amphitrite had shared something startling with her during the ocean trance.

She had admitted that her Ocean Apothecary had been responsible for Poseidon's death...

How, Selia still didn't know. Had Poseidon's death been an accident? Or had it been intentional?

Nyssa began to doze in her arms, her little nose and cheeks red from the cold.

Damien sat next to her, nudging her with his arm. "You look tired. Want me to take her for a bit?"

Selia handed him their drowsy daughter.

"Is everything okay? You seem a bit grim," he asked as he tucked her into her blanket and propped her against his chest.

"Everything is not okay," Selia replied, gazing across the firelight at Balfour's brothers. "What I saw during the ocean trance has been weighing on me."

"I figured. Can you tell me what you experienced?"

Selia's stomach hollowed as her gaze fell onto Amy's mother. Amphitrite appeared so beautiful, so innocent even, sitting where she was next to Hopleas as he passed her a skewer of cooked fish, which she politely refused.

How could Amy's beautiful sea goddess mother possibly be responsible for Poseidon's death?

"I think it's best if we wait a bit. I don't think what I saw will help the tension between Amphitrite and Balfour's brothers," Selia replied.

"Are we going to light up this fire, or shiver our butts off all evening?" one of the storm dragons grumbled as he slung another giant piece of driftwood into the fire.

"I'd like for Poseidon's sons to introduce themselves. The sooner we discuss the crown of your father, the sooner I can reunite with my daughter," Amphitrite said, her tone lively.

"Fine," Mestor grumbled. "Pelias, show this goddess of the sea what you can do. As soon as we've introduced ourselves, and have eaten, it's back to business."

Pelias approached the fire and held out his arm. He struck one of his wrists past the other, striking his metal gauntlets together. Electrical sparks jolted out of his hand, setting the driftwood ablaze.

Selia held her hands over the flames, thankful for the spontaneous heat.

"Pelias is our pyro. He can get a fire roaring from just about anything that washes up from the sea," Mestor stated, and Pelias flicked his thick fingers, sending more sparks into the inferno.

Two others tugged in a net full of fresh fish and mollusks and set them by the fire as Mestor continued in his introductions. "Hopleus and Idas have long been the ones who provide food. Your stomach might hate you after you are done with them."

Fweeeeeeet!

Selia jumped as a high-pitched sound trilled into the air. The last two dragons had created a whistle-like flute out of some of the driftwood. Both of the dragons hobbled about, trilling out a Celtic tune in a ruse of dueling flutes.

Mestor sighed. "Lykos and Taras are our musicians. They can turn anything they want into a musical instrument."

"What about Balfour?" Selia jumped in, eager to hear about her storm dragon's personality quirk.

Mestor propped his feet up onto one of the logs, his dreadlocks swinging across his beefy shoulders. "First of all, stop calling him by that atrocious name the

Order gave him. If you are to know about my youngest brother, you will call him Bellerophon."

"I don't care what you call me, as long as—"

"Silence," Mestor broke in. "Our father gave you a name, and you will honor it by having everyone around you address you as so."

Balfour sank down into his seat, shaking his head.

Mestor kicked one of his feet out, knocking a log into the flames. "Bellerophon is the quiet before the storm. He rarely speaks aloud. But when he does, he has been known to summon a stampede of waves unlike any other."

Selia thought back to her first memories of meeting Alex's henchman. Balfour was a giant, quiet man who wore a black leather jacket with a dragon that snaked up his massive shoulders.

He'd only started speaking to her a couple of months ago.

Nyssa began to stir in Damien's arms, letting out a cry.

Taras handed Selia a couple of seashells that he'd fastened together with some twine. "For the little one."

Selia handed Nyssa the seashell instrument, which she quickly snatched up. It rattled as she shook her little arm.

"Oh, she's a natural," Lykos said with a grin. "She's going to make us look like fools when we all play together."

"Stormy!" Nyssa cried as she shook her seashells. Soon, their bonfire turned into a festivity of music and food. While Idas and Pelias shucked oysters, and skewered fish, Balfour arranged them over the fire.

"You like sea urchin, right?" Idas asked, flashing his giant white teeth.

"Not a fan," Damien replied, his face turning white.

"How about shark?"

"Definitely not."

When Selia couldn't take the tension any longer, she grabbed Damien's arm and tugged him aside. "I need to tell you something about the ocean trance."

Damien tipped his head toward her as everyone began to feast on their dinner.

Selia whispered as quietly as she could into his ear. "While we were in an ocean trance, Amphitrite admitted to killing Poseidon."

Damien's eyes got huge. "What? She *murdered* him?"

"Shhhhh!" Selia stammered, sucking in a breath that would hopefully mask Damien's outlandish statement. "I don't know. All she told me was that her Ocean Apothecary was responsible for his death."

Damien's expression darkened. "Do Balfour and the others know?"

Selia shrugged. "Amphitrite expects that I move forward with retrieving the third fragment of the star of the sea and mending the crystal back together somehow. She said that only then will the truth behind Poseidon's death come to light."

As the group ate, Mestor folded his arms across his chest, his gaze once again leveling with Amphitrite. "I think it's time you explain to my brothers and I just why you've summoned us back from our icy slumber. I am not here to settle our differences over food and wine. I will scour the sea until I take back what is rightfully mine."

Everyone around the fire went quiet. Only the crackling *hiss* and *pop* of the flames sounded.

One of Amphitrite's red brows lifted. "You still believe that you will be the one to recover the crown of your father?"

Mestor glared at her. "I am Poseidon's eldest son from the West." His blue eyes scanned the others as he spoke. "None of my brothers dare compete with me for the ancient territories within our father's crown. When we find it, I will be the one to claim it as my own."

"You haven't asked Bellerophon about what he thinks," Amphitrite interjected. "All you've done since you've reunited is ignore and hush him."

Deidra let out a laugh, which she quickly quieted as Zakai shot her a glare.

"Fine then, "Mestor stated. "Bellerophon, what do you think? Will you be the one to recover our father's crown?"

Balfour merely dipped his chin and gazed into the fire.

Mestor chuckled darkly. "See? Silence, like always. Balfour has never been one to speak up."

"Maybe if you weren't so rude to him he would actually talk." Selia said before she could stop herself.

Mestor's bushy brows waggled as his blue eyes swept to her. "Oh, look. Celaeno's moon daughter will be the one to speak up for him now?"

"Mestor, I swear to the Great Storm, that you still haven't put our father to rest," Balfour grumbled aloud.

Selia shuddered at the sound of his voice out in the open. It was so different not being confined to the corners of her mind. The sound was smooth yet jarring, sending shivers of electricity up her spine.

Mestor swung his head toward Balfour. "How dare you swear upon our origin. Are you saying that the storms I created were a result of not properly processing our father's death?"

"You know why we fought, why we raged over the seas after the sinking of Atlantis. Those storms could have been much less violent had we only come to terms with our disagreement," Balfour grumbled in protest.

The fire cracked and popped as his voice filled the atmosphere.

"Maybe if you didn't have such a tsunami for a temper, Amphitrite wouldn't have had to put all of you to sleep," Balfour continued.

"And what, you think you are better than all of us for holding your tongue?" Mestor snarled back, his dreadlocks swinging. "A storm dragon should always speak his mind, no matter what."

"Even if the storms he creates harms others?" Balfour countered.

Mestor propped his elbows onto his knees as he leaned toward his youngest brother. "You do not honor our father with your silence. The reason his crown was so great, the very territories that made him the god of the sea, was due to the fact that no other storm dragon could replicate the weather patterns his bonds created. Don't you dare come to me after all this time and expect me to change my mind. I still stand by my belief. The only thing that will reveal who killed our father is to find what remains of his crown. When we find it, I will be able to reveal who murdered him, and finally bring him justice."

Selia glanced at Damien, then Amphitrite, who showed no sign of giving away her secret.

"Or, you could ask your ancestor, Erebéus. He has access to all death records of his descendants," Amphitrite said, not flinching as she spoke.

"Do not speak his name here," Mestor growled. "Storm dragons do not tread on or speak of the ground our ancestors have walked upon."

For the first time since Selia had observed Balfour's cocky older brother, she saw uncertainty in him. The mention of his ancestor's name sent a ripple of fear through his outward confidence.

Amphitrite folded her arms. "I must inform you that awakening you and your brothers from the ice was not my doing. Forces between the moon and Balfour are responsible for it."

Mestor spat out his drink. He wiped the back of his hand against his mouth, his eyes bulging. "A *tidal* bond?"

Amphitrite nodded, not taking her emerald eyes off Mestor.

"And the lies continue!" Mestor roared, his voice drunken with thunder. "Well, where is the great tsunami that sank Atlantis? Show it to me."

"You forget that the power of the tide originates from the moon," Amphitrite challenged him. "That power is not always something that we see."

Mestor's blue eyes watered with tears from his laughter. "The power of that bond might originate from the moon, but it is experienced through the storm dragon who channels it." His blue eyes narrowed onto Selia. "Tell me, Blind Moon. What do you know about the formation of storm bonds that originate from celestial objects?"

Selia thought back to what she'd learned from Masika. "I know there are seven storm bonds total. I know that the storm dragon chooses the bond, not the sea nymph."

"The tidal bond is an origin bond created by our ancestors, the great architects. The powers of these bonds originate from one of three celestial bodies. The moon is one of them. Can you guess the others?"

"Is the sun one?" Selia suggested.

Mestor nodded. "The third, is the stars. Origin bonds reach beyond the nymph a storm dragon bonds with." His eyes swept to Damien, and to their sleeping daughter. "As Balfour stated earlier, if he truly formed an origin bond with you, he is bound not only to you, but to your family. Origin bonds are not restricted to one place or time—they are enhanced by great distance."

"In other words, an origin bond extends through the boundaries of time?" Selia asked.

"As time goes on, the bond strengthens. Origin bonds never break, not even in death. The bond extends to a nymph's family, both to her ancestors, and her descendants."

"Then in theory, this bond could extend into the past, correct?" Selia asked.

Mestor's brow furrowed. "I am not understanding why you are concerned with the past."

"You said that origin bonds extend to the family. Does that not mean that it could also touch those who have touched me from another time?"

"Answer her," Amphitrite said.

Mestor leaned forward, his giant biceps glowing orange with firelight. "Who in your past could you possibly want to reach?"

Selia's stomach pitted as everyone's gaze landed on her. "I want to reach Naunet. I spent a good deal of my life blind to my own origin. Nobody deserves to live without knowing where they come from. They deserve to know what their family members sacrificed to keep them alive."

Mestor's brow furrowed. "You wish to know a mother who is not truly your own? Are you not a moon daughter of Celaeno?"

"Selia has the right to connect with whoever she chooses to as long as I am involved," Balfour said aloud.

Selia was grateful for her storm dragon's voice, because it broke the intense emotions reflecting in Mestor's eyes—a mixture of anger, sadness, and immense loneliness. All were the things she'd seen floating in Damien's gaze as he coped with his incredible loss.

Mestor folded his arms across his chest. "Tomorrow, at first light, Amphitrite and I will decide on how we will address the crown of our father. Balfour will need to speak up and put this bond of yours into play, and which route he will take if he is to help us."

Selia locked eyes with Mestor's blue ones, the color turning violently orange with the fire. Would the bond between her and Balfour help him in his quest to find his father's crown?

If so, would the quest also help her to learn what happened to her Egyptian mother?

182

33
THE QUEEN REBORN

Amy

The pain shooting through Amy's leg forced her to slow. She didn't know what hurt more. The pain itself, or the fact that Lachlan didn't come after her. She was alone, wandering the beach in an endless line that blended sand, and sea.

The figure she'd seen before disappeared, probably a hallucination from the pain. The fire in her leg became so fierce, her vision began to blur. Her leg buckled, and she collapsed onto the beach. The gritty texture of damp sand pressed through her fingers.

Her eyes closed, and the beach became no more.

Her body rocked from side to side, no longer stagnant. The pain in her leg was gone. A soft, warm mass shifted beneath her—the same warmth and texture of the deer hide Lachlan had given to her.

Giant red-barked trees lined the path. She lifted her head, finding the snow-capped trees were really the red giants. A massive burst of air erupted in front of her.

She sat up, fully aware of what she was riding on. A mighty crown of antlers rose and dipped with every step the giant fae king took. This had to be a dream.

She was sitting atop the mighty fae king, Errindoor.

"Where are you taking me?" she asked, knowing that he likely couldn't understand a word she said.

Errindoor let out a burst of air from his nostrils, letting a bugle erupt from his throat. The brush shifted ahead, sending snow cascading down from the boughs of the giant trees. A white doe pranced in front of him, flicking her ears forward as she shifted her long, elegant legs.

Amy dug her heels into the stag's sides, bracing herself for the chase to come. Errindoor bound after the doe. Unbridled wildness brimmed through him as he pursued her into the forest.

He leapt through the trees, his mighty hooves beating into the snow. As his muscles flexed beneath her, Amy sank into his powerful, graceful movements. How much she wanted to get lost in the frozen heartbeat of this enchanted forest.

He bound over a log, banking to the left as the doe took off up a snowy slope. No blood from the fighting, or Ewan's mangled body lay in the trees. She'd traveled back to the forest as she'd wanted to experience it—white, quiet, and full of pure, untouched wilderness.

As Errindoor chased after his doe, he ascended the mountain, leaving the trees below. His movements slowed as he reached the snowy peak. Wind whipped through the snow, but it was no problem for the mighty fae king. He trudged through the icy blast, forcing Amy to press herself firmly against his back to avoid the wind.

When she thought her fingers might freeze, Errindoor dipped down along a rocky slope. He bowed his mighty head and lowered himself to the ground. Amy slid off his back. She landed in the snow, finding her own footprints there, next to Ewan's massive ones.

Emotion stung her chest. She and Ewan had looked at these ruins together, ruins from the temple of Salt, Storms, and Starlight.

She ran her fingers along the stone wall where he'd stopped and given her history about the old and new kingdom of his people. This was where she'd learned from Ewan the meaning for the name of Errindoor—it meant fallen, or *crownless* king.

Errindoor lay next to her, sheltering himself in the ruins as another icy blast that ripped over the mountain.

Amy journeyed along the wall, finding the symbols Ewan had shown her. Yellow light pulsed out of them. She pressed her hand to the symbols, and her fingers warmed. The stone pulsed with bright yellow light that dulled as one of the stones at her feet crumbled away.

A serpent-like shadow reached for her ankle. Burning pain shot through her leg, crippling her. She fell to the ground, tumbling into an icy passage.

Her legs folded beneath her as she slid to a halt. She shifted, finding a pile of Errindoor's antlers stacked on top of each other. Brilliant golden light erupted from the center of the antlers, setting fire to what had been the fae stag's crown.

The silhouette of a giant man manifested in the flames. Locks of auburn hair framed his handsome face. His gaze dropped until his hazel eyes found her.

Amy sucked in a breath, exhaling. "Ewan..."

The huntsman's face blurred before her, becoming transparent. Ewan's features shifted behind the golden light.

The huntsman transformed into a fisherman.

"Lachlan?"

Smoke billowed out of the fire, catching in Amy's lungs. She coughed, throwing her arms up to shield herself.

"Amy, stay with me," a female voice said from behind her.

A tickling sensation on her wrist forced her eyes open. The smoke vanished, revealing a pair of gorgeous blue wings fluttering against her skin. No longer surrounded by the flames, Ewan, and Errindoor's antlers, Amy startled. She was encased in an icy structure, completely encased by blue and grey walls.

A minca moth fluttered away from Amy's wrist, drifting over to another figure. Light from its wings illuminated her features. A sea nymph stood before her, dressed in long blue robes. The design on the fabric reminded her of coral.

Amy gasped. "Maera?"

Maera approached her, crouching to where she sat on the ground.

Amy tried to move her leg, but the pain was so severe, she let out a cry.

"Don't move," Maera said.

"I don't know what I did to myself," Amy whimpered as the pain crept up her leg and into her torso.

Maera placed her hand onto the ground between her and Amy. The minca moth fluttered down, illuminating her fingers as shadows pulsed out of them. She closed her eyes and began to chant. "Star of the sea, let your power be known. I request that you return her body to its healthy origin."

Little shimmering lights pulsed from the ground and the walls. Amy focused on the illuminations that reminded her of starlight. As the lights faded, so did the pain in her chest and leg.

She flexed her ankle as the pain vanished.

"How did you do that?" she asked, gathering her breath.

Maera flexed her fingers, revealing a glowing item in her palm. A dark crystal fragment shone at the center, reminding Amy instantly of the black crystals of salt venom. "Take it. I've retrieved the third fragment of the star of the sea from Nephthys. It is yours."

Amy refused, backing away from the crystal that had shadows pouring out of it.

She wanted to keep that wound in the past and lock it away forever, but now she wasn't so sure that she could. What if the pain kept coming back? How could she control the symptoms?

"You want to keep your symptoms under control, don't you?" Maera replied, a glimmer of something that could be a threat shining in her eyes. "The only way to remedy a wound inflicted by salt venom is to connect with the star it originated from."

Amy squinted at her. "I don't understand, the star of the sea was created by Isis and Nephthys long before salt venom was ever born from the blood of Celaeno's fae queen."

Maera's eyes flickered with the shadow-filled light emanating from the crystal fragment in her palm. "It was created from the starlit corals, but it was forged in the light provided by the soul of a fae queen."

At her words, one of the lights descended upon them. It landed on Maera's wrist, its brilliant wings haloed by the shadows spilling out of Maera's palm. "When a fae queen dies, a new one is reborn. But the death of Celaeno's salt pod meant no other queens could emerge from her origin in the ocean."

"I don't understand, is this a *new* fae queen?"

Maera nodded. "Like your mother said, you going to the past has given us an opportunity we have long waited for. Your quest to the past has allowed Celaeno's fae queen to be reborn."

At Maera's words, the fae queen batted her wings, taking off in flight.

"You must take the crystal, while I will take her," Maera said, tipping her palm toward Amy. "As long as you do not tell your mother that you have the crystal in your possession, the pain will not return."

"Why must I keep the crystal a secret from her?" Amy asked.

Maera's eyes darkened. "Your mother has been keeping secrets from you about the power of the starlit corals." She took a step back, retreating into the shadows.

"Wait, where are you going?"

Maera faced Amy, her long brunet hair catching in the wind as her gaze lowered. "Like you, I was once in love with a son of Atlantean kings. It's time I finished what I started with him long ago."

She disappeared into the shadows flooding the cavern.

Amy's eyes began to close. As she clutched the crystal fragment between her fingers, the pain in her leg numbed. Her mind drifted, filling with the task ahead. Could she really keep the crystal a secret from her mother?

And what was the secret that her mother had been keeping from her about the starlit corals?

34
STORM RITUAL

Damien

"Wake up. I need to perform the ritual with you and Selia before I join my brothers."

Damien's head hadn't stopped throbbing since he'd dozed off sometime during the wee hours of the morning. Having Balfour jostle him out of his slumber with the few hours he'd slept was not ideal. The night at the bonfire left him restless.

The argument between Mestor and Balfour raged like a storm in his mind. The mystery behind Poseidon's death was somehow linked to Amphitrite's Ocean Apothecary. Why hadn't she admitted anything to Poseidon's sons the night before?

He sat up on the sofa, dazed by the amount of daylight flooding into his cottage. He caught the subtle movement of a small creature shuffling across the ground.

The crystal thief was back...

He launched himself up from the sofa, darting after the little crab. As he maneuvered into the kitchen, he slammed into a hard, muscular back.

One of the storm dragons turned to face him, a spatula and frying pan in his hand. "Breakfast?"

Damien winced, pressing his palm to the place on his face that had slammed into his solid body. "What?"

"Sit down at eat while Hopleus makes you a proper meal," Idas said as he tugged out a chair from the kitchen table.

Damien did so, grateful for a plate of sausage and eggs instead of the seafood from the bonfire. "Where are Selia and the baby?"

"They've already eaten, along with the others," Idas said as he pushed a cup of tea toward him. "We wanted to make sure you slept in before you joined them outside. I'm sure you slept horribly after last night. Mestor has a way of getting everyone rattled when he wants to."

Damien forked the sausage and eggs together, grateful for the brothers' hospitality in his own home. He ate quickly, downing his tea before he made his way outside to meet with the others.

A pile of blackened driftwood and ash remained not far from his cottage from the night before. Taras and Lykos stood next to Deidra and Zakai, while Selia faced Balfour. Nyssa's pudgy arms kept flailing for their storm dragon as he gazed out to sea.

Mestor was nowhere. Neither was Amphitrite.

Damien approached Selia, stopping at her side.

"There's your handsome daddy," Selia said as she rocked Nyssa in her arms toward him. "Did you eat breakfast, love?"

"Yes. Those two are better at cooking than I thought. Where are Mestor and Amphitrite?"

"Apparently they were the last to leave the fire, according to Pelias," Selia said as she eyed the dragon piling new driftwood into the fire pit.

"*They are deciding how to proceed with a storm calibration,*" Balfour answered into their minds.

"What in the world is a storm calibration?" Damien asked.

"*It's a formula used when generating a triton current. They plan to use a triton current to access my father's crown.*"

"I'm guessing that our tidal bond will impact this formula?" Selia asked.

Balfour nodded. "*Our bond will be the one to dictate how the current forms and behaves once unleashed into the ocean.*"

Selia sighed. "Well, I have no intention of going with them. I'm still trying to locate the third crystal fragment. It sounds to me like Amphitrite and Mestor both have plans of their own."

"We don't even know where the other two fragments went," Damien said, keeping an eye out for the little crab who'd likely buried them somewhere on the beach.

"I feel like we're at a dead end," Selia sighed.

"Pssssst, Selia, Damien," Deidra whispered, waving her hand over her head "I need to talk with you two."

Selia walked with Damien over to where the dryad stood, looking somewhat smitten.

Deidra shoved both of her hands into her pockets. "Look. I've been thinking. Amphitrite said the ocean trance would reveal something to all of us that would help us track down the last crystal fragment." She withdrew one of her hands from her pocket, tugging out a lumpy tan item. "This is what I found when I was walking along the beach in the trance."

"You found a rock?" Damien asked.

Deidra shot him a furious glance. "Um, excuse me? How can you *not* be excited? This isn't just any rock. Do you know what this is?"

"No idea," Damien grumbled, annoyed that they were admiring rocks instead of coming up with a serious plan.

Deidra held the rock up to the light. "This is an extinct marine invertebrate—it's a fossil of an ammonite!"

"How is a fossil going to help us figure out how to track down the third fragment of the crystal?" Selia asked as Nyssa flung her arms toward the ammonite. A spiraled seashell appeared at the center of the rock.

"This is a tool we need to explore," Deidra said, her cheeks dimpling as she beamed at the fossil. "There is only *one* archive I know of that houses other extinct fae specimens like it—Gaia's Archive."

"Gaia has an *archive*?" Selia and Damien said in unison.

"Oh yeah, and it's freaking spectacular. Gaia's archive was created by the Order long ago to help preserve and protect the knowledge, artforms, and artifacts that pertain to Gaia's nymph daughters." Her eyes dilated. "I think we could use this ammonite fossil to help us gain access to Gaia's Codex. The Codex should have answers not only on where to find the third crystal fragment, but how to access this Temple of the Three Origins.

"But neither you or I are goddesses," Selia protested. "Even if we do learn how to access the temple, I don't think we could enter it."

"Amphitrite *did* just put us all into an ocean trance, did she not?" Deidra countered. "I remember her stating that ocean trancing is one way to access the temple. Amphitrite seems like one to pull some strings, if you know what I mean. If our goal is to find the third crystal fragment and restore the star of the sea, we must gain access to the Temple of the Three Origins."

"Where is the archive?" Selia asked.

"Museums all throughout the world have special access points to the archive. While Mestor and his brothers pair up with Amphitrite and her daughter to set out to sea to find the crown, we will track down the third fragment. I suggest that we start at the British Museum in London."

"Why the British Museum?" Damien asked.

"The museum houses an Egyptian artifact that serves as an access point to records within the Codex that originated from Isis's temple."

"You mean, records that Naunet worked on?" Selia asked.

Deidra nodded. "Exactly. These are the records we need access to if we are to locate the remaining crystal fragment." She glanced between him and Selia. "But this does meant that we need to travel, possibly for days. Some of the locations are not, how should I say this, baby friendly?"

"She's right," Damien said. "If you are going with Deidra to the museum, you can't take Nyssa."

Balfour set his hand on Damien's shoulder. "*Before you decide on anything, I would suggest that we move forward with the ritual.*"

As Selia walked with Deidra down to the waterline, Damien slowed himself. This was the perfect opportunity to put his own plan for a ritual into action. "Balfour, hold up," he said as he trudged behind the group.

Balfour slowed his pace, falling back with him.

Damien reached into his pocket, tugged out a piece of paper, and handed it to him.

"*What is this?*" Balfour grumbled as he crumpled the paper in his massive hand.

"Something I want to include in your ritual."

Balfour squinted at the paper. "*You want me to have you kiss each other by the water? What kind of ritual is this?*"

"I wanted to surprise Selia with an elopement, remember?"

"*Oh, a marriage ritual?*"

"Yes, marriage."

"*You've already created offspring together. Doesn't that mean you are mated to one another?*"

"By modern day standards, no."

Balfour shrugged. "*Making babies with each other meant you were mated for life, at least it did in Atlantis. I'll blend the rituals together. Mine doesn't involve words, it involves rain and sunshine.*"

Damien's heart leapt. "That sounds perfect."

Selia slowed her pace, stopping once she reached the waterline. "Is this a good spot for your ritual, Balfour?"

Balfour and Damien stopped behind her.

"*Blind Moon and her mate, I need you both to position yourselves before me. Turn your backs toward the sea.*"

"What about the dryad?" Deidra chimed in.

"*You can stand aside. This ritual does not involve anyone but those participating.*"

A thunderhead brewed on the horizon, but it wasn't enough to distract Damien from this moment. Selia stood before him, her blue eyes catching the lightning in the distance. Balfour took his position between them, his back facing the sea. He clutched the paper Damien had given him to read from.

Damien's heart thundered in a way it hadn't in years. Even though he couldn't have his family here to witness their event, that was okay. Auntie was sure to give him an earful later, but it would be worth it. Their spontaneous beach elopement, in all of its spectacular awkwardness, couldn't be more perfect.

Drops of rain fell onto Selia's cheeks as she faced him.

Damien held his hand over his head. "We'd better get on with it. Balfour? Speak out loud. I want the ocean to be our witness."

"Witness to what?" Selia asked.

"Right," Balfour grumbled. "We are gathered here today to celebrate the joining of Damien Malloch, and Selia Fontaine. Together, they will form an everlasting bond that will rival the beauty of starlight."

Selia made a double take. "What is this ritual about?"

"Keep going," Damien said, encouraging Balfour.

"Is he *marrying* us?" Selia cut in.

"Holy mushrooms, you two are getting hitched right now? Why didn't you tell me to get the heck out of here?" Deidra stammered.

"Why don't you make yourself useful and take a few pictures?" Damien suggested.

While Deidra busied herself with her phone, Damien buried his hand into his pocket, tugging out the ring.

"I wasn't prepared for this. I don't have anything for you," Selia said, worrying ringing in her voice.

"You don't need to give me anything, love. You and Nyssa *are* everything." He slipped the ring onto her finger.

"By the origin of the seas, and the house of Poseidon, I Bellerophon, pronounce you husband and wife."

Damien jolted as Balfour cut to bottom of his vows before stating them.

Selia handed Nyssa to Balfour and grabbed his hands. "Damien Malloch, I can't tell you how much I love and adore you, from the moment I met you here at the Celtic Sea."

Damien's mind blanked. All he could see was her blue aura. Her light. The impossible beauty she'd brought back into his life.

She grabbed his face and pressed her lips to his before he could say anything.

His body filled with a rhythm of impossible force. The sound seemed to contradict itself as it rumbled against his chest. His heart thundered, the force of it threatening to rip out of him as Selia pressed her lips to his.

He closed his eyes, savoring the moment, never wanting it to end.

Whatever the force originated from, the sea, the moon, or the tide. Everything pulsed through him in some invisible way he didn't need to justify.

As their lips parted, and their foreheads rest against one another, Selia whispered, "I will love you to the moon and back until the end of time."

A brilliant display of rainbows bloomed over them.

"I will love you past the moon, and into the stars," Damien said, kissing her again.

35
CURRENT CALIBRATION

Selia

With the ritual complete, and the colorful rays of the rainbow fading overhead, Selia grabbed her new husband's hand. "Wow, it finally happened. We're married," she said, holding up her finger to marvel at her ring again. The gemstone sparkled, catching the brilliant colors of the rainbow misting over head.

"Took long enough," Damien concluded, kissing her again.

Selia glanced at her ring again, noting how the colors surged against one another. "It reminds me of the colors blending in one of your watercolor paintings. It's so beautiful!"

"*Baby, anyone*?" Balfour said as he thrust a giggling Nyssa forward.

Selia almost forgot that she'd handed him their daughter. She took Nyssa back into her arms, cradling her.

"How touchingly spectacular," a low, thunderous voice sounded behind them. Mestor approached, clapping his hands slowly as he sauntered over to them. "Housing your bond within a gemstone, now are we, brother?"

Balfour turned his head, revealing a vein pulsing in his thick neck. "I thought it was fitting, considering that her mate also had a ritual of his own to perform."

Mestor folded his arms across his chest as the rainbow above them evaporated. "Now we get to see if those colors fade or not."

"Stop being so conceded. I thought it was a beautiful ritual," Amphitrite said as she stopped next to the cocky storm dragon.

"Stormy!" Nyssa squealed as she spotted Balfour's brother.

Mestor arched one of his bushy black brows. "You haven't seen my stormy side yet, little one."

Balfour glared at his brother. "I take it that you and Amphitrite have calibrated for the triton current?"

"We are almost done," Mestor replied as the corners of his mouth curved into a smirk. "I don't think you're going to like how inconclusive the results are."

"Don't just talk about the results, show them," Amphitrite chimed, a slyness to her tone. She waved at Nyssa, who reached for one of her locks of curly red hair, then slipped one of her baby toy starfish into her pudgy little hand.

Mestor held out his palm, revealing a metal item made of multiple metal rings. They whirled around one another, sending out little sparks of electricity.

Selia recognized the device instantly. "A beaconing device?"

"Beaconing devices were used in Atlantis to calibrate storm bonds so they could be used to generate triton currents," Balfour said.

"Apparently they have uses other than teleportation?" Selia asked.

Damien's brows drew up. "Wait, you can *teleport* with that thing?"

"Alex and I did multiple times," Selia concluded. "While you were in a coma, she used the one in our lighthouse to bring me to a glacier, where I heard Balfour's voice for the first time."

As Mestor spun the outermost ring, five bulky outlines appeared behind him. Apparently, he could summon his brothers by manipulating the rings. Each ring had a different symbol on it, ones Selia remembered from the storm scrolls Gwen had shared with her along with a folktale about selkies.

"There are still a few variables that will impact our voyage," Mestor said as his blue eyes swept to Selia. "What does the Blind Moon plan to do? Are you coming with us?"

"No, I'm not," Selia concluded, glancing at Deidra. "We still haven't found the third crystal fragment, but we have a plan that could help us locate it while your party is searching for the crown."

"Well, then. That will change some things," Mestor stated as he gave the rings another whirl.

Amphitrite nudged Selia's arm. "You should have seen how these discussions went in Atlantis. They could last for weeks, even months at a time. In a few instances, years. The governing forces of storm dragons has always originated from weather."

"What determines how the current generates?" Selia asked.

"The storm bonds each dragon involved possesses. Ocean currents are one of the largest weather generators on the planet. Everything from temperature, to humidity, to geographic location is taken into consideration. Having Balfour added to the equation with your tidal bond has added some complexity. There is a high chance that someone will need to sit out this adventure."

"How is our tidal bond going to help with this process?"

"The moon is what will help us navigate the triton current once we are in the open ocean."

"Our bond is like a compass then?"

"Exactly. Like Mestor said last night, origin bonds are storm bonds married to celestial objects. In your case, the moon."

Selia grabbed Amphitrite's arm and tugged her away from the group. She glanced over her shoulder at Mestor's muscular build as he and his brothers observed the beaconing device. "Isn't it risky? I mean, what's going to happen when he gets to the crown and finds out the truth about your Ocean Apothecary and Poseidon's death?" She swallowed "I am assuming that his death was not intentional, but an accident?"

Electrical sparks erupted from behind them.

Amphitrite approached the storm dragons. Selia followed, her question still unanswered.

The rings whirling in Mestor's hand came to a stop. He squinted at their new orientation. He shook his head, sending his dreadlocks swaying. "Too much wind and rain. Not enough ice." His blue eyes swiveled between the other dragons. "Meaning that one of you must stay behind."

"Who stays behind?" Balfour grunted.

"It's between Lykos, Taras, and Pelias," Mestor concluded.

The three brothers faced one another, flexing their arm muscles.

"There's only one way to settle this," Lykos said, forming a fist and holding it in front of him. "We play sails, swordfish, and clams over it."

Taras and Pelias mimicked Lykos's fist.

"Ready?"

"Sails, swordfish, clams!" they rumbled in unison.

Each dragon threw out their hand, creating a different gesture.

"Pelias? You're out," Mestor ordered his pyro brother. "You stay with Damien while we set out with Amphitrite to find the crown."

A burst of blackened smoke erupted from Pelias's nostrils. "Fine. But that doesn't mean I'm not helping."

Mestor faced Amphitrite. "We leave at noon today. If you have any other members who will be joining our voyage out to sea, I suggest that you retrieve them shortly."

Amphitrite nodded.

Mestor turned on his heel, leading the others toward the sea. Pelias left too, but he took off in a run for the bonfire instead of joining his brothers.

Balfour didn't budge. He remained rooted in the sand next to Amphitrite.

Panic burst through Selia when she realized that she, Balfour, and Damien were going separate ways.

Not to mention little Nyssa...

Tears burned her eyes. Since she'd been born, this was the first time she'd separated from her daughter. "I don't think I can do this."

"From one mother to another, and for one who spent far too much time away from her own daughter, this will be a growing experience for you both. She will be much happier asleep while her mother is away. If you agree, I will put her to sleep, and she won't even remember that her mother was missing."

Selia nodded. "I would prefer that."

Amphitrite held out her hands. "May I hold her?"

Selia handed Amphitrite her daughter.

Amphitrite took Nyssa into her arms, who reached out and touched her cheeks and nose. "You have a heart for the stars little one, don't you?"

Nyssa squealed as Amphitrite's freckles darkened. Her eyes hooded and she dozed.

Amphitrite handed their sleeping daughter to Damien, then reached into her robes and pulled out another silk bag. "Use this to wake her when you arrive back at Damien's art studio."

Selia nodded, taking the pouch from the goddess of the sea.

"I'll be here when you get back, we both will," Damien said as he took Nyssa back into his arms.

"Zakai is already waiting for us," Deidra said.

"Right," Selia said, blinking the tears away.

She grabbed Damien's face, kissing him.

"We'll find out about Naunet, all right? You deserve to know what happened to her," he said.

Selia's chest burned.

Naunet.

She was doing this for her, right? Was she willing to leave her own family behind to reconnect with her Egyptian mother?

Naunet was living somewhere, her story untold. Her past was likely preserved in some dusty museum as an artifact that needed to be uncovered. Just like *she* had been, working at the Louvre, unseen and unknown, until she'd met Damien.

Why was Naunet hiding? What was keeping her from reconnecting with those who still loved her? Memories of the plague filled Selia's mind. If anything, she was doing this to uncover her story, like Alex and Balfour had done for her.

She wanted to see Naunet's story.

Deidra stopped a few paces away from the sea. A giant piece of driftwood sat on the beach. She picked it up.

"Is this another forest fire, or are we beaconing there?" Selia asked as she approached the dryad.

"Oh no. We're not using ancient Atlantean technology to transport to the museum. That's not my style." She clapped her hands together. "We're tap rooting our way there."

"There's not a single tree out here," Selia said, wondering how they could possibly accomplish anything with a root.

Deidra glanced at the sky. "That's where Zipper comes into play."

Golden light appeared overhead as the fae dragonfly zipped over them.

"Stand next to me and take my hand," Deidra said.

Selia did so, facing Amphitrite and Damien. They both watched as the light spiraled around them.

"Hold on, here we go!" Deidra yelled as she gripped Selia's hand tight.

Damien's face disappeared behind the brilliant golden light enveloped them both.

36

HIGH TIDE

Amy

A loud grinding sound grated against Amy's ears, jolting her out of her dream. She squinted at the horizon, hypnotized by what was floating in the sea. Her fingers grazed her palm, gripping a cold, sharp item. Maera had given her the third fragment of the star of the sea and told her not to tell her mother.

The crystal was so cold that it burned her skin. It's blackened sides shimmered darkly in the sunlight, making it appear deformed. Something about its imperfect shape and color made it beautiful.

The grinding sound grated against her ears again. Why was the sea ice breaking apart? And why was a giant man wearing a tunic with dreadlocks storming down the beach toward her?

Amy tucked the crystal back into her pocket, then ducked behind one of the chunks of ice as Mestor stormed past her. Four other men wearing tunics followed after him, one of which lagged behind the others.

Balfour?

Balfour slowed his pace, swerving toward her. He must have heard her thoughts as he quickly located where she was hiding.

"*Amy?*"

"Yes?"

"*Your mother is looking for you,*" he said, stopping not far from where she sat in the sand.

A sharp pinch to her skin sent her bolting upright. She scrambled to her feet, bracing herself for the burning pain to return to her leg.

Instead, she found a crab dangling off her behind.

"Really? Is this what you do? Pinch the heck out of folks when you find them?" she scolded Little Blue.

"There you are. I knew Little Blue would find you," her mother said as she stopped next to Balfour. "Are you hurt? Why are you out here on the beach all alone?"

Amy swallowed. She could have sworn she saw Maera standing behind her mother. She plucked the crab off her backside and tossed it aside. "Nothing. Well, something did come up."

"Amy!" a man yelled from further inland.

Amphitrite squinted toward him. "Is *he* the something?"

Amy glanced around the ice. Lachlan was scouring the beach, turning up tufts of sand as he tore across the waterline.

"Is that man looking for you?" her mother asked.

"Just ignore him," Amy said as she turned her back to him.

Her mother's emerald gaze found her. "Let me guess, you had that man drink what I gave you in the pouch?"

Amy stared at her mother. So much had happened since she'd left Ireland. She'd nearly forgotten about turning Lachlan's pint of Guinness green with the mystery ingredients in the pouch. "I did. And well, I *was* able to steal his boat to find my way here. Why?"

Thunder cracked in the distance. Drops of rain began to fall from the sky.

"If the seas are going to reveal Poseidon's crown to his sons, we need to go, now," Amphitrite grabbed Amy's hand. "Balfour, help us get this voyage under way."

Balfour nodded and walked toward the spot where his brothers gathered by the water. Their dreadlocks tossed in the gale force winds blowing in from the ocean.

Amy ducked her head toward the wind as they approached Balfour's brothers. "I'm confused!" she yelled as the violent crashing waves drowned out of her voice. "I thought you said we needed to bring all three fragments into Poseidon's crown to mend the star of the sea back together! I should tell you that I lost the fragment that you gave to me!"

Her mother held out her hand, stifling the wind with a wave of her fingers, allowing them to speak without yelling to one another. "Amy, you did your part in finding Mestor. As for the crystal fragments, they will find their purpose soon enough. Right now, we need to focus on this triton current if we are to have any hope of reuniting them."

Amy's stomach wallowed as the surf surged before them. Waves crested with white caps as they rolled and crashed upon the beach. "Just how big is this triton current?"

"It depends on the weather Poseidon's sons use to generate it," Amphitrite replied. "Remember, we are sea nymphs. They are storm dragons. They might create the weather patterns on the planet, but we are the ones who can manipulate them once they manifest."

Amy swallowed. She'd manipulated waves and wind and rain in small doses before, but never on the scale that her mother was eluding to.

Balfour took up his position next to his brothers, who were all slightly larger than him. They all stood in a circle, their backs facing them. Only when the two sea nymphs approached did they part for them.

Mestor glared at Amy's mother. "Ah, here she is. The goddess of the sea who has, how should I put this, so eloquently graced our presence with her rebellious spawn?"

Amphitrite dug her heels into the sand. Her red curls fanned, offsetting her like a painting against the sea. "Leave your comments about my daughter on the beach, or I promise to make your journey on the high seas a turbulent one."

Mestor chuckled darkly at her sea goddess mother. "Fair enough."

Amy's attention dropped to the device in Mestor's giant hands. Metal rings whirled around one another, sending off jolts of electricity.

Lightning bolted overhead as the rings whirled faster.

She jumped as electrical sparks jolted out of the item.

"It is time for our departure," Mestor growled just as thunderously as clouds above. "Follow us toward the surf."

Poseidon's sons took off toward the sea. Balfour didn't move, waiting for the two sea nymphs. He held out both of his hands, which Amphitrite graciously took. "You are far more of a gentleman than your eldest brother."

"*He has never been one for making impressions. When it comes to generating triton currents, he's all business.*" He held out his other hand for Amy.

She took it, feeling slightly jealous. Selia was so lucky to have such protective and gentle storm dragon to bond with. She felt oddly childlike next to him, forgetting how much taller than she and her mother he was. "How are we going to navigate our way to the crown?"

"*I'm hoping to put the tidal bond I formed with the Blind Moon into action,*" Balfour replied, an edge hardening his voice. "*I just hope that I don't let you and your mother down.*"

"Amy and I are here to help you," Amphitrite said from Balfour's other side. "We are going to make some waves your eldest brother will be envious of on this voyage."

As they approached the sea, the movement of the waves quieted, calming the water to the point it appeared still enough to walk upon. Each storm dragon took off in a run for the sea. The moment their bodies came into contact with the water, they evaporated into mist, disappearing.

Balfour stopped where the sand became wet and released their hands. He closed his eyes, sucked a deep breath through his nose, and exhaled.

The water surging between Amy's toes thinned. Waves receded, tugging out seashells and seaweed with them. The waves shifted and morphed, taking on the form of creatures as they churned and thrashed.

"I haven't seen the water horses since Atlantis!" Amphitrite exclaimed. "What a marvel to look at!"

The water horses pranced about, tossing their elegant heads. Manes of seafoam green cascaded along their bodies, breaking as waves.

"Careful with your approach. They've been known to accidentally trample those who become too infatuated with their beauty," her mother warned as she approached the water.

Balfour remained rooted on the beach, his eyes still closed as he chanted something about the moon and the tides.

Amy stepped toward the horses, terrified as the surf surged toward them. Their frantic movements frightened her. She kept close to her mother, who held out her hand, bending the horse's manes and tails as though they were pieces of fabric. The water cocooned around them as the sea floor emerged.

No longer men, Poseidon's sons had transformed into their dragon forms. Long coiling tails thrashed through the surf, each varying in color.

"*Lykos*, take her daughter," Mestor grumbled as his sharp, jagged fins sliced through the water. "*I'm taking the sea goddess for myself.*"

Amphitrite rolled her eyes. "If you must."

Lykos extended his tail down to Amy, scooping her up. "*Keep your knees bent,*" he spoke into her mind. "*My fins don't always cooperate when confronted with the tides.*"

Mestor's purple fins emerged from the waves, cascading toward Amy's mother. They were long and sharp with spines, much fiercer looking than the other dragons.

Amphitrite grabbed onto one of his fins, hoisting herself up behind the spine that sliced through the water.

The scent of diesel fuel stung Amy's nose as a puttering sound echoed over the water.

"*It's that fisherman again!*" Taras grumbled, thrashing his massive tail against the waves. The waves broke open, dousing Amy and her mother in a fit of sea spray.

"*We should have sunk his boat when we had the chance,*" Idas added, his voice just as grouchy as Taras.

A fin tore out of the sea, slamming down hard into the surf.

"*Time to have some fun and sink it for good,*" Mestor growled.

Amy bit her lip. What could she do to make sure Lachlan wasn't tugged out to sea? Mestor's long spines cut through the water, aiming for Lachlan's little boat.

How would the *Sea Dragon* fare against one of Poseidon's sons?

37
STORM SMOKE

Damien

Damien stood on the beach as a broken chain of emotions blew through him. Making sense of how he felt was well beyond his abilities, even with his background as a freelance illustrator and an art therapist. Here he was, alone with his sleeping daughter, and another storm dragon who only seemed to want to play with fire.

In the amount of time it took for Selia and Poseidon's sons to leave, Pelias had arranged three other piles of driftwood on the beach.

He approached Pelias, who was crouched over one of the driftwood piles. "What are you doing?"

"Mestor thinks that I can't help them recover our father's crown. Well, he can go shove a scale up his—" He stopped himself mid statement. "Never mind. I'll figure something else out without him." He grabbed another piece of driftwood and arranged it in a tepee arrangement.

Damien retreated into his art studio with Nyssa. He desperately wanted to be alone with her, even though she was sleeping.

Once inside, Peppercorn flit in front of him, seeming to sense his distress. She flew over to Nyssa's crib and perched herself atop it.

Anger flared in his gut. Even the *bat* had a purpose for something, to watch over their daughter. What was he supposed to do? Just sit here and wait out the storm while Selia worked with Deidra, and Amphitrite took to the seas with Balfour and his brothers?

He felt so helpless. So *useless*.

Amphitrite stated that what he saw during the ocean trance would dictate his role in how he would help. All he'd seen was his past, brutally reminding himself of how worthless he felt after Maria died.

He tucked Nyssa into her blanket, then kissed her on the forehead. "Sleep well, my little dolphin."

A ringtone chimed from the sofa. His heart stopped as his phone lit up. Gwen's number appeared on the screen. His sister was calling.

He grabbed the phone, holding his thumb over the answer button. What if Gwen reported his whereabouts to the authorities, and they came after him?

He jammed his thumb into the button and brought the speaker to his ear. "Yeah?"

"Damien, is it really you?" Gwen whispered. "Where are you?"

Damien went silent.

"Please don't hang up."

"It's me, Gwen," he admitted, his voice harder than normal.

Gwen's whimper became an elated laugh that danced with hysteria. "I'm so glad that I got a hold of you. There were rumors that you showed up at the mental hospital. Then when they called and told me that there was no record of Selia in their system? I nearly died. Where are you and Selia and the baby? Her due date was close to now."

Damien sucked in a breath and let out a long exhale. Sea nymphs were only pregnant for seven months, not nine. But he really didn't want to have that conversation with his overly dramatic sister.

"Gwen, we're all right."

"I couldn't forgive myself after I admitted her to the mental hospital, but you should have seen her. Frozen, bleeding, and insane, screaming at the ocean for you? I thought for a moment that I'd lost my mind."

Damien squinted out the window as Pelias caught his eye. He was crouching down, aiming his backside toward one of the bundles of driftwood. "Gwen, I love you. But right now isn't the best time."

"Damien, please don't go. Your family is worried sick about you. I love you so much. If anything ever happened to you. And Auntie, bless her heart. She has struggled more than I thought she would."

"Auntie?"

"She's not well. I think it's all of the stress associated with you missing."

Damien watched Pelias as he repeated the same posture again, bending over and wincing.

This time, however, a giant inferno erupted out of his behind, lighting the driftwood ablaze. "Gwen, I've got to go. I'm pretty sure the dragon on the beach is lighting his farts on fire."

"A dragon is doing *what*?"

Damien ended the call and left his cottage. He staggered onto the beach, waving his arms. The inferno sprouting from the bonfire was too close to his cottage for comfort. "Hey!"

Pelias ignored him.

Damien stopped before the flames billowing up out of one of three driftwood bonfires while Pelias crouched. "First of all, not cool. I've never seen anyone light a bonfire like that before. What are you trying to do? Send out smoke signals?"

Pelias stood, and a fiery belch erupted from his mouth. "Whatever Hopleus cooked for us last night, it's not sitting well with me at all."

Damien eyed the beginnings of a new structure at the center of the three piles of driftwood. "What's up with all of the blue smoke?"

Pelias squinted at him. "You can see it?"

"Of course I can. It's about as blue as blue can get."

Pelias's thick brows worked. "Only sea nymphs and storm dragons can see storm smoke. The last humans to see it lived in Atlantis."

Damien stared at the blue rising up into the sky. "Nope. I see it all right. What is storm smoke?"

"It is the sacred breath of the first storm dragons born into the sea. It is created by burning dried pieces of blue minca kelp. Storm smoke has many purposes. Human shamans have used it for many things, including vision quests, and to ward off unwanted spirits."

"What about communicating with spirits?"

Pelias's eyes dilated, flecks of red and orange glinting in them. "Is someone haunting you?"

"Possibly."

"If you can see the smoke, that must mean that your ancestors have a message to deliver to you. If want to see what the spirits have to say, then grab a piece of wood and start helping me."

38

HECATE

Selia

Selia's fingers became transparent as the golden light whirled around her and Deidra. Her ring began to slip, wiggling like it had when she'd been in the mental institution.

Panic ripped through her. What if she lost her ring while they tap rooted to London? According to Balfour, it was where he'd housed their tidal bond.

Deidra's hand slipped through her fingers as she was thrown backward into the golden light. The scent of damp earth filled her nose. She landed in a crunchy pile of leaves, their browns and reds and oranges washing over her.

"Deidra?" she called, crawling out of the leaves and combing them from her hair. A dark, damp tunnel encased her. "Where are we?"

Zipper flit overhead, creating a trail of golden dust as he hovered through the tunnel. The sound of bus and car horns blared overhead. The last thing she wanted was to be separated from a dryad in a rooty passage beneath London.

She followed Zipper through the tunnel, who seemed to know where to go. Deidra stood at the end of the tunnel, braiding her hair.

Deidra faced her as she let out a sigh. "There you are. Sorry. I think we both tapped into the roots of different trees. Good thing Zipper found you. It's been a while since I've tap rooted to a big city."

"Do you know where we are?" Selia asked as she approached Deidra, who started picking root threads out of her disheveled hair.

"I tried to get us as close as we could to the British Museum. But we'll know for sure once we leave the Tube."

The screeching sound of metal grated against Selia's ears. She suddenly realized that they were somewhere underground within London's metro system. The two nymphs set out down the tunnel, which was paved with ancient-looking cobblestones. They followed the sound of the train cars until they were stopped by a rusty metal grate.

"Don't just show off your sparkles, help us out little dude," Deidra instructed her dragonfly.

Zipper flit through the rusty grate, which glowed the same brilliant gold color as his wings as he drifted through it.

Deidra grabbed the metal bars and tugged on it, removing it with no problem at all. "There we are." She peeked her head out of the tunnel. "Come on, this is our window."

They both climbed out of the tunnel and into the Tube station, hurrying along until they found a staircase. Zipper tucked himself into Deidra's braid the moment they hit daylight. The air in the city wasn't fresh, but it was much better than it had been within the London Underground.

They passed through a small park. Selia wondered if one of the trees Deidra had tap rooted them to belonged to one of the giant oak trees that towered overhead.

Deidra's braid swung against her back as she propped her hands onto her hips and pointed down the street. "Well, would you look at that! I wasn't perfect, but I got us pretty darn close, what do you think?"

Selia spotted the British Museum through the trees. It's Greek architecture stood out amongst the other brick buildings. Giant white columns lined the front entrance, giving the building a majestic, ancient vibe.

Deidra set off down the sidewalk. Selia followed. They both ascended the staircase and entered the museum. Once inside, Selia's salt nodes thrummed with a sound other than visitor voices. She'd spent years working with the familiar background noise at the Louvre, but never had she heard a sound so haunting before.

Something in this museum that was calling out to her—an ancient song of some sort.

"Is everything okay?" Deidra asked as she flashed the admission desk a badge, allowing them entrance.

"This way." Selia led the way through the museum visitors, following the sound. It reminded her of ocean waves, but far less liquid. How that made sense was beyond her.

As she walked through the crowd, all she could think about was Damien and Nyssa. While she'd only just seen them, it felt like she'd been away from them both for eons.

The gemstone on her ring darkened as she rounded the corner. A female voice filled her ears, whispering words she couldn't make sense of. Her sound was cool and powerful, reminding her of Nephthys.

Was the Egyptian goddess of the dead trying to tell her something?

She stopped before a crowd of people who were all crowded around an artifact housed in a glass enclosure. A dark grey stone engraved with small, intricate writing sat before them. It's top was lopsided, appearing to be carved irregularly, erasing bits of the hieroglyphics that decorated the smooth surface.

A dark shadow drifted above the stone artifact.

Selia's pulse stopped as a low buzzing sound filled her salt nodes. She backed away, bumping into Deidra. "I should have brought Peppercorn with us, she eats these things."

"What does she eat?"

"You don't see the dark aura hovering over there?"

"No, I don't. What are you seeing?"

The bitter taste of salt welled up on the back of her tongue as memories of the salt flies and their horrible hallucinations came swarming back into her mind. A dark shadow silhouetted the stone, offsetting the people observing it through the glass. Shadows swept into Selia's periphery, erasing Deidra and the museum guests from sight. She was alone with the artifact everyone had been staring at.

She approached the glass enclosure, reading the display tag.

The Rosetta Stone

A tall, slender woman appeared behind the artifact. Her dress was as dark as the stone, with brilliant lunar symbols decorating the silky fabric. A triple moon emblem rested upon her chest. Her brilliant white skin accentuated her dark, full lips. Hair as dark as night cascaded down her shoulders, tapering above her breasts. "I recognize you as the Blind Moon. You are Celaeno's moon daughter."

"How do you know who I am?" Selia whispered, her voice echoing in the strange, shadow-filled chamber she'd found herself in.

"I recognize your salt aura from Isis's temple," the woman replied, her words silky and warm despite her cold appearance. "I remember your light when you were first learning to salt trance."

"Are you Nephthys, the goddess of death?"

Not two, but six eyes found her, blazing with green flames flickering in their irises. Her face was not one, but three separate faces. "No, but I am one of Nephthys's friends. I am Hecate, the goddess of crossroads and magic."

Selia took a step back as the giant three-faced goddess towered over her. "Hecate, where am I?"

"Those in ancient Egypt call this place the Duat, or Amenthes. It is the shadow realm one's soul journey's through to reach the afterlife. It is within these shadows that Gaia's Codex resides."

Selia touched the shadows tendrilling out of the Rosetta Stone. They were cool and soothing, nothing like they appeared. "I'm trying to locate Gaia's Codex. Is the Rosetta Stone part of it?"

The eyes from Hecate's central face met hers, dark fire flickering in them. "Yes, the Rosetta Stone is but a small piece of a much larger document. I have long watched over what remains of Naunet's work that was not erased by the salt venom."

Selia's heart leapt. "Can you tell me where Naunet is?"

"I can tell you that she no longer goes by the name from her life in ancient Egypt."

"But she's at least alive. And she's healthy?"

All six of Hecate's eyes found her. "The health of one's body and one's soul are two different things."

"Can you tell me where she is? Could I meet with her and discuss her unfinished work with the Codex?"

Hecate loomed over her, her ominous eyes darkening. "Naunet's whereabouts are not mine to give away, daughter of the moon. Although, I can say that she has missed you greatly." She held out her elegant hand, and the shadows spilling out of the Rosetta Stone turned from black, to blue. "What I can do is share what remains of her work."

The glass evaporated, leaving nothing to separate Selia from the Rosetta Stone. An energy pulsed out of its onyx surface.

The top part of the Rosetta Stone reformed, ancient writing manifesting in the shadows. A missing fragment of the stone appeared—symbols that included the celestial bodies of the sun, moon and the stars.

Hecate waved her hand through the symbols, making them shimmer. "The Codex documents the natural forces that shaped our planet. It houses the bonds between Gaia's daughters, and the great architects. Salt venom corroded Naunet's work documenting the cycling of the ancestral salt pods within the Abyss, and the formation of triton currents."

Shadows crept into the celestial symbols, separating them.

Hecate disappeared.

Selia fell backward, her back hitting a solid surface. She slammed into a piece of glass. Dozens of people were staring and pointing at her.

"Help me!" Selia yelled, slamming her hands against the glass enclosure she was trapped in.

39
TIDAL STAMPEDE
Amy

As Amy gripped onto Lykos's thrashing fins, her feet dragged along his serpentine body. She'd been in the sea with one storm dragon before, but never this many. Nor had she ever been on the back of one. The storm dragon's back was ridged in places and smooth in others. Everything she touched was slippery, except for a patch of scales that had a rough texture. Neither barnacles, nor algae grew on the keeled scales that offered her a foothold. She wedged her fingers into a ridge just above his muscular shoulders.

Waves cascaded around her, siphoning in great whirlpools that fed one another. The force Poseidon's sons generated with their tails was enough to send Lachlan's boat into spiral. If she didn't do something, Mestor and the others were going to capsize the *Sea Dragon*.

Lykos swam through the waves, taking Amy with him as his fins sliced through the water. Amphitrite surged ahead atop Mestor, her long red hair trailing behind her storm dragon's large shark-like fins as they came dangerously close to Lachlan's boat.

"Amy! I won't let the sea take you!" Lachlan yelled as he came running to the helm of the *Sea Dragon*.

"Damn it," Amy spat. The stupid fool had followed her. If only he hadn't done so, she wouldn't be in this situation.

"Who's ready for a game of sink the sailor?" Mestor growled, his thunderous voice echoing off the waves surging around them.

"You will do no such thing," Amphitrite said as she gripped Mestor's jagged dorsal fin. A massive scar was gouged into his scales that was nearly as long as Amy's mother was tall.

"Silence, sea nymph!" Mestor bellowed. "It would do you well not to come between a storm dragon and his prey."

With a gnash of his teeth from a mouth wider than it was long, Mestor banked into the waves, giving Amy a good look at his appearance as her mother held on for dear life. The upper half of his body was darker in coloration, contrasting with the light silver scales that lined his belly. His back and shoulders were a brilliant navy blue with hints of ultramarine. Vertical gill slits lined his neck, tapering behind a pair of dark blue fins that fanned out behind his jaw. His fins were heavily scaled, with the edges meant for slicing through the most violent waters of the ocean.

The scales varied in shape and size along his neck and torso, enlarging into triangular shapes as they swept to his tail. More scars appeared, massive gashes where large chunks of scales had been ripped away.

Amy wondered what other dragon would dare attack Mestor that way. Definitely not Balfour, or his other brothers. Did he possibly have an enemy at sea?

She counted five coiling storm dragon bodies that surged through the surf. They were missing one. Where was Balfour?

Lykos banked to the left, his massive green fins bursting out from his sides.

Amy ducked as one came dangerously close to her neck, its long spines nearly slicing her. A low strumming sound erupted from his fins as they caught the next wave crashing into his body.

"Sorry, I'm still not used to the waves. My fins have spent far too long frozen in the ice," Lykos apologized.

As the waves crashed over him, his fins trilled out another sound. Combining with the wind and the sea spray, Lykos's fins created an ominous tremor that made Amy's salt nodes ache.

He and Taras thrashed their fins, creating an aquatic melody.

"We're not making music right now," Mestor scolded the two musical dragons as their fins drooped back into the sea.

"We're calling for Bellerophon," Lykos barked back at his brother. "He's not answering."

Mestor chuckled as Lachlan's boat spiraled closer to him. "Too bad. He's going to miss out on the fun we're about to have with this fisherman."

Amy caught Lachlan's white-eyed gaze as he grabbed onto a fishing net before a wave knocked him overboard. Panic gripped her chest. Mestor thought that torturing him was a *game*?

Hopleus swam close, his indigo scales shimmering. "Mestor, you've always enjoyed playing with your prey. I say we put him out of his misery already."

"No, don't!" Amy cried, digging her heels hard into Lykos's sides.

Lykos tossed one of his fins up, spraying salt water in Amy's face. "Why, do you know this man?"

She looked at Mestor square in his massive blue eyes. "I think you are a giant jerk to even consider killing someone as entertainment."

Mestor's thick neck surged upward, nearly knocking her mother into the sea. He thrashed his fins, tossing his head from side to side. "That's it. It's time to reinforce who's in charge out here."

Amy gripped Lykos's scales as Mestor cut through the water, sending waves crashing into his brothers' faces.

Another wave surged in front of Mestor, knocking his giant body to the side before he could reach Lachlan's spiraling boat.

Amy's heart leapt as the *Sea Dragon* was spared once again. But it was only a matter of time before Mestor stopped playing with his fisherman prey and capsized him.

As the wave receded, the scaly head of another dragon emerged from the surf. Dark purplish-green fins branched out of his face, and long black and silver whiskers furled from his muzzle.

"Balfour?" Amy said, both relieved and blatantly in awe. She'd forgotten just how impressively terrifying Celaeno's ex guardian was in his dragon form.

While Bellerophon was nowhere near the size of Mestor, he made up for size what he possessed in beauty. Onyx scales lined his body, making him appear as a dark jewel against the swirling sea. Purple and viridian opalescence shimmered along the scales behind his eyes and on his nose, creating the illusion that he was wearing a mask, or war paint.

"*All of you must dive,*" Balfour rumbled, bubbles muddying his voice as he spoke into their minds.

"*Why?*"

"*Because I've summoned a tide that will force this current out into the open ocean. If you don't, it might rip your tail off.*"

"He's summoning a tidal stampede!" Lykos growled.

Amy dug her heels into Lykos's sides as his fins wrapped around her. She sucked in a breath, preparing for the descent. With a thrash of his body, he took her down into the sea.

Mestor gave the surface water one last thrash of his tail, which ended in tragedy. The sharp *plunk* of a body hitting the water confirmed that Lachlan had fallen into the sea.

Amy watched helplessly as he floundered above, his body being tugged down from the drag created by their descent.

Balfour was the last to dive, his dark body spiraling down like the powerful storm that he was. Blades of minca erupted out of each storm dragon's tail, shielding them from the darkening wave that was barreling across the surface.

Amy's mind blurred with panic. Lachlan didn't have salt nodes that could stabilize the tons of pressure the sea put upon an individual when diving to great depths. Even if the current did reach him and tug him down, he wouldn't be able to survive the pressure.

Amy's salt nodes burned. She kicked off Lykos's body and was instantly ripped away from him by the current.

"*What are you doing? Don't let go!*" Lykos growled.

Amy grabbed one of the blades of minca furling out of his tail as the current caught it and ripped it upward.

Lachlan's body came closer with each kick of her feet. He floated in the current, his body limp as the current tugged him down.

She grabbed his hand, wrenching him upward.

A dark shadow loomed near the surface as the entire sea bowed. A tidal wave crashed overhead, hooves from the water horses tearing into the water as the wave barreled above them.

40

PYROS

Damien

Damien observed Pelias's shamanic ritual, assisting him in any way he was instructed. In a matter of an hour, they'd finished creating a fourth structure that sat amidst the three other piles of driftwood. Together, they built what Pelias called a storm hut.

"There, it's almost perfect," Pelias said as he set another piece of wood onto the teepee shaped structure. He wiped his brow with the back of his hand. "We need something to trap the storm smoke."

Damien scanned the beach. There wasn't anything hardy nor flexible enough to cover the storm hut. "What about paper?"

Pelias arched a one of his bushy brows. "What kind of paper?"

"The kind I've painted on?"

Pelias grinned. "As long as it can withstand lots of moisture, we could make use of it."

Damien walked into his studio, eager to find the large sheets of watercolor paper he'd saved over the years. The only purpose it served now was to collect dust. Why not make use of it for the storm smoke ritual?

Nyssa was still sleeping soundly, undisturbed in her crib. His art supplies, however, didn't appear so similar to his daughter. Easels were shifted, and paintings he'd seen the day before were rearranged. Pieces he hadn't touched in years were stacked in the front on display.

"Must have been that bat," he stammered, finding her perched atop one of the easels with her wings outstretched. "Peppercorn, did you do this?"

She swiveled her fuzzy brown head, letting out a protesting *screech*.

"Right, I'm glad we had this conversation."

He glanced at his phone. Gwen had tried to call him back multiple times, which he'd ignored. He didn't want to tell her anything, although it pained him to think that Auntie might not be well. He grabbed one of the paintings that had been moved to the front of the others. He thumbed through the thick parchment, finding the concept paintings he did of a map he'd made for Maria long ago.

Emptiness filled him. Seeing his abandoned artwork made him feel even more useless. There was something to be said for the countless hours he'd spent listening to Maria's descriptions of her research at sea. He didn't need the original designs anymore, and had only kept them in case he needed reference material for when he did complete a larger work for her. The paintings were as good as trash at this point. There was no need to revisit what he'd created almost a decade ago.

He checked on Nyssa again, who was still sleeping soundly. He gathered the parchment and rolled it up, and walked back onto the beach.

Pelias glanced up from the rocks he'd piled together.

The moment Damien unraveled the parchment, Pelias's eyes went wide. "I recognize this artwork. I remember seeing it within the hall of our father in an ancient temple my father used to reside in when Atlantis was still around."

Damien squinted at the storm dragon. "I'm sorry, what did you say?"

Pelias bowed his head. "You have impossible talent, being able replicate something so beautiful."

"How could I have possibly painted something that existed in Atlantis?"

Pelias shrugged. "Beats me. First you tell me that you see the blue storm smoke, and now you show me these paintings?" He squinted into the sunlight. "You must be a Son of Atlantean Kings."

"Balfour called me that, too. I still don't know what that means."

"Poseidon's crown established the boundaries between territories created by Poseidon's sons. After Atlantis sank, the crown broke apart, destroying the boundaries." He glanced at Damien's artwork. "These boundaries were illustrated by the High Kings of Atlantis in an effort to understand the hierarchy of the seas and storm dragon kind."

"How were these territorial boundaries illustrated?"

"With the three celestial bodies that help form origin bonds—the sun, the moon, and the stars."

Damien's throat seemed to close. His moonlit paintings—did they depict something from a much larger piece of historical artwork? Zakai had mentioned that Maera had been studying the crown, which apparently had something to do with territorial boundaries of storm dragons. Then, he'd had the haunting interactions with her regarding his artwork. Was she trying to send him a message? If so, could revisiting the artwork he'd abandoned a decade ago possibly reveal that message to him about these territorial boundaries once owned by Poseidon's sons?

Blue smoke coiled up out of one of the fire pits, setting Damien's nerves on edge. After Maria's death, the only color he could see was blue. Not until he met Selia, and she had opened the vault, did his color vision return back to normal.

Damien set the paper aside. "I want to see what your plan is with this storm smoke, and to see if there is indeed a spirit who is trying to send me a message."

Pelias grabbed one of the stones he'd piled outside the shelter. "Then help me arrange the stones. Storm smoke won't reveal its secrets unless we honor our starlit ancestors—the great architects."

PART 5
SALT & STORM SMOKE

41

PHERUSA

Selia

S elia's wrists burned as the abrasive shadows constricted them. They coiled around her forearms, slithering like black serpents.

A hand wrapped around her arm, tugging her toward the Rosetta Stone. She braced herself, preparing for impact as she crashed into the solid stone. Instead of crashing into the artifact, she fell forward, her palms hitting the hard, cold surface of the museum floor.

A tall, looming figure stood before her. Porcelain hands mixed with the shadows as they curled around elegant poised fingers. The figure flexed their wrists, seeming to beckon the shadows back into their palms.

Selia was surrounded by sterile onyx walls with dark water dripping down them. "Who are you? And where have you taken me?"

The figure stepped forward, tendrilling shadows curling at her feet. Her face remained hidden, concealed by the darkness that seemed to fill the strange chamber.

A hiss escaped her lips as she threw out her hand.

A shadow serpent erupted from her fingertips.

Selia gasped. How much the shadows reminded her of Masika's vaporous salt venom serpents. Her hands were bound together and yanked behind her back. "Let me go!"

"Hecate isn't the only individual who has watched over Naunet's work, Blind Moon," the figure said in a cool, silky tone. A harshness in her voice made Selia's salt nodes burn.

The figure disappeared, leaving Selia to contend with the claustrophobic space. The water dripping down the walls came closer to her face. She closed her eyes, bracing herself. She didn't know what was worse—being encased in the Rosetta Stone exhibit, or this new shadow-filled chamber that wanted to suffocate her.

In a panic, she began to recite the salt trancing principles through her mind. *Breath. Memory. Salt.*

She opened her eyes to rain pouring atop her. If she didn't do something, she would drown...

She backed into the wall behind her, and her wrists broke free. She threw her hands out to her sides, which met the freezing water. Closing her eyes again, she imagined Damien, and Nyssa. Her pulse thundered in her chest as a vision appeared.

Balfour was swimming in the sea, his long onyx tail branching out behind him. A boat trailed in his wake, which Amy and another man she didn't recognize stood upon. A cloud of mist morphed the vision, redirecting Selia to land. Damien and Pelias were busy on the beach, brilliant blue smoke billowing out of one of the bonfires.

Golden sparks rained down on her.

The vision vanished as a dragonfly zipped in front of her face.

"Selia, can you hear me?" a muffled voice echoed behind the liquid wall.

"Deidra? Is that you?"

"We're going to get you out! Zipper, stop goofing off!"

Zipper flit through the water, his wings forming a golden halo above her.

Selia fell forward, her body breaking through the water.

Deidra caught her as she tumbled forward.

She staggered to her feet as Deidra helped her to regain her footing. "Where was I?"

"One of the barriers the Order uses to conceal the archives. Apparently you got sucked into one near the Rosetta Stone. Sorry about that. Museums are full of the entry points."

Selia grabbed her sodden hair and wrung it out. "Are the entry points always so wet?"

"Zipper, help her out, would you?"

Zipper hovered overhead, his wings whipping out a warm wind that worked over Selia's body. In a matter of moments, her hair and clothes were completely dry.

She glanced around at her new surroundings. The room was large, with tall, vaulted ceilings that branched overhead. The beams that supported the ceiling appeared more like giant roots than wood. Light fixtures hung from the beams, their varying shapes illuminating a group of tables below. Walls supported shelves with rolling ladders that individuals were busy maneuvering back and forth. They appeared to be sorting boxes and organizing the shelves. Other women were grouped around the tables, handling items and inspecting them.

Deidra propped her hands onto her hips. "Welcome to the inner quarters of Gaia's Archives—the Library of Gaia."

Selia's mouth dropped open. "Gaia has her own library?"

Deidra smiled. "She sure does—one the Order specifically works out of. You should see the Smithsonian. They have an entire research devision dedicated to Dryadology."

"What is that? The study of dryads?"

"Heck no! While I do wish woodland nymphs could take credit for the study, Dryadology is the study of fairies, or fae beings who disguise themselves in the form of common day flora and fauna species. The nymphs there even dabble in researching extinct fae species."

"What are they doing?" Selia asked, pointing to women busy handling what appeared to be a large bone.

"This is collections, where nymphs serving in the Order obtain and artifacts that have historical significance to Gaia. They inspect and sort newly acquired items according to their ecosystems, focusing on their natural environments." She waved her hand. "Come on. I'll give you a quick tour."

"Do the humans who work at the British Museum know about this hidden archive?" Selia asked.

"If they do, they have no way of accessing it. Only nymphs have the ability to pass through the access points and enter the archive."

The nymphs at work didn't look up as Selia and Deidra walked through the room. They kept their heads down, only addressing their peers when they had a question about the artifacts they handled. Selia caught the wording on a few of the paper labels stacked in a pile next to what appeared to be a massive fossil. She caught the word *biome*, followed by *woodland, oceanic, desert, river, mountain*. Next were two labels separated as *flora* and *fauna*. Beneath those labels were two an assortment of boxes labeled *fae species*, and *non-fae species*.

Oddly, the boxes reminded Selia of the cardboard box she'd first received her salt trancing talisman in. Had it somehow passed through this archive before she received it?

"If this is a library, does that mean that items can be borrowed?" Selia asked.

"Only by individuals who have the proper clearance."

Selia's salt nodes burned at the cool voice that slithered inside of her ears. A tall, slender woman approached them. She wore a form-fitting dress as black as her hair. Her skin was smooth and honey in color—her lips as red as a rich wine. Black hair clung to her scalp as it was tied up into a tight bun. A few strands curled out from her face, framing her high cheekbones.

As sinister as the nymph sounded, she was stunningly beautiful. Her dark eyes reflected a liquid fire that reminded her of Masika.

"Are you Hecate?" Selia asked.

The nymph laughed, tipping her head back as she did so. One of her elegant hands raised to her mouth, her knuckles grazing her lips as she chuckled. "Hecate only appeared to you because I sent her to inspect who had penetrated through the archive's access point. She isn't the only individual who watches over my daughter's work."

Selia's mind blanked. Earlier, she'd said something similar—Naunet's work. And here she was admitting that this work belonged to her *daughter*?

"That must mean, you are Amphitrite's sister, Pherusa?"

The nymph's eyes narrowed onto her, cat-like. "Yes, I am Pherusa, the last sea nymph to reign as midwife of the sea prior to the sinking of Atlantis."

"Don't tell her anything," Deidra cut in as Zipper flit between, his wings buzzing twice as fast as usual.

Pherusa's eyes darted to Deidra. "You must be the dryad who screwed her assignment up, resulting in Alexandra's tragic death."

"Deidra didn't screw anything up," Selia countered as Zipper flit between her and Pherusa. "Your daughter, Masika did, when she tried to kill me."

Pherusa's mouth made a wicked motion, contorting in a way that didn't seem natural. "Maybe if the Order actually did their job for once and protected what they said they would, sea nymphs like my sister wouldn't have to seek out the assistance of Poseidon's sons to remedy the mess with the plague victims." Her gaze fell onto Selia. "I overheard you telling Hecate that you have two fragments of the star of the sea, meaning one of two things. Either the Order is shoving its nose into business it shouldn't again, or my sister sent you to search of it."

"I am searching for the third crystal fragment so I can find your daughter."

Pherusa's face contorted, her expression something between rage and disbelief. "You believe you can find Naunet? Are you insane?"

Selia stood her ground. "The only insanity that I've encountered had to deal with Masika attempting to kill me."

"You might be a salt daughter of Celaeno, Blind Moon. However, you do not know the horrors that comes with mothering one of her children." Pherusa sneered, her lips curling as she spoke. Shadows tendrilled our of her hands, coiling like ebony serpents.

The nymphs behind them glanced up for the first time since Selia had entered the archive.

Pherusa took a step toward them, boldness blackening her aura. "No daughter of Gaia goes searching for the Book of the Dead without first sacrificing a piece of their own soul. That is the first rule of anyone who accesses the Codex."

"Which is exactly why I'm here," Selia countered. "I need access to the Codex so I can track down the third crystal fragment of the star of the sea."

Pherusa laughed, her voice both high and cold. "The Codex will not help you find the third crystal fragment. Neither of you have access to the artifacts that hold information about it."

"Zakai is an Iridescent, and I report to her," Deidra argued.

"Zakai isn't here, not is she?" Pherusa scolded. Her cold stare—how Selia wondered if this was what Naunet was forced to contend with in her mother, or if she had been kinder in her earlier years. "Only Iridescents have access to the shadow archives, not dryads who pretend to be them. Neither of you are able to step foot inside of the archives without the proper clearance."

Selia squinted at Deidra. "Shadow archives?"

"Get out, both of you. Or I'll see that Hecate's hell hounds escort you to Nephthys, and you will see just how unkind the book of the dead has been to the plague victims."

Selia checked her pockets. "You took them."

Pherusa smiled. "As far as I'm concerned, the fragments of the star of the sea became property of Gaia's archive the moment you stepped foot inside." She spun on her heel, her long, slender body breaking into shadows once again. She disappeared around the corner, smoldering like the liquid flame she embodied.

Deidra blew out her cheeks. "Wow, she's nasty. Everything I read up on about Pherusa is that she is nowhere near as pleasant as her sister." Deidra sighed.

As Selia took a step toward Pherusa, Deidra grabbed her arm. "Selia, wait."

Selia spun to face her. "We can't just let her take off with the crystals! That's my inheritance!"

Deidra tugged her aside. "Let her go. We still have this, remember?" She reached into her pocket and tugged out the ammonite fossil, and handed it to Selia. "You're going to use this to get into that shadow archive and find what Pherusa is trying to prevent us from discovering about her daughter."

42
LACHLAN'S APOLOGY
Amy

As hooves tore into the sea, the tidal stampede surged around Amy and Lachlan. The water horses crashed above, tearing downward into the ocean. Their power and elegance transferred to the water, mixing oxygen with sea foam in a magical way.

Amy held onto Lachlan for dear life as the wave barreled around them. The horses blended with the sea, breaking apart and shattering like beasts of liquid glass. Lachlan's body broke through the wave, taking Amy with him.

She sucked in a breath, gasping as she found the surface.

Lachlan, too, gasped and coughed as he floundered in the surf. He bobbed next to her, his hair a wild sopping mess across his forehead. Instead of panicking, he was all smiles, his mouth gaping open as he jumped between gasps and haughty laughter. "Did. You. See. That?"

"See what? The wave?" Amy asked, slightly perplexed at his question.

"Everything! The storm? The waves? The *dragons*?" Lachlan cried as he fisted the air. "That was fucking amazing!"

Amy jumped as something crashed into the sea, splashing her from behind.

She and Lachlan spun around, finding themselves gazing up at his boat. Sails were in tatters, and the mast was snapped in two. But the *Sea Dragon* was still afloat.

They bobbed in the surf as the ocean finally calmed. The coast was gone. The only thing that surrounded them was open ocean.

Lachlan grabbed one of the fishing nets that dangled over the side of his boat and climbed aboard. He helped Amy to do the same, tugging the net up and assisting her over the railing.

She staggered in front of him, her sodden clothes heavy with salt water. She grabbed a handful of her hair, ringing it out before him.

"And you…" he breathed, his sodden hair dripping in front of his eyes. Half naked and chest heaving, Lachlan looked stark raving mad.

He closed the space between them, lumbering forward and catching Amy around the waist. She nearly slipped, startled by his awkward embrace.

He grabbed her face with his damp hands, tilting her chin up so that she met his fierce blue gaze. He closed his eyes as his salty lips crashed against hers. It felt like she was being tumbled by a tidal wave all over again. This one, in some impossible way, however, had much more force behind it.

His kiss was sensual, and passionate, and he didn't dominate her.

She kissed him back, tugging at his bottom lip as they finished.

He pulled away, wresting his forehead on hers. "I told you I wouldn't let the sea take you, my Sea Star. I couldn't let you leave me, not after how I treated you."

Amy searched his cerulean eyes, which were now suddenly brimming with emotion. "How did you treat me?"

"Well, I tried to take care of your leg, which looks like now you're doing all right," he stammered. "Amy, please accept my apology."

She blinked at him, half forgetting where she was, and what he was apologizing for. All she could focus on was the thrumming of his heart against hers.

He pulled her into an embrace, grabbing her sodden hair and. "I didn't want that to be the last time I saw you."

Amy sank into his embrace just in time for a wave to crash into the side of the boat. A pair of scaly nostrils appeared, followed by a blast of hot air that sent Amy and Lachlan's wet hair.

"Well now, not just an any fisherman," Amphitrite said as she appeared on Mestor's shoulders. "A fisherman who kisses my daughter."

Amy burned hot at her mother's statement. Amphitrite emerged atop Mestor's back, her red hair and green eyes stunning against the sea and rippling storm dragon scales beneath her.

Lachlan jumped as Mestor let out a snort, sending his spiny whiskers furling toward him.

"That's the one who tried to kill me," Lachlan said, pointing at Mestor's giant dripping head.

"Who says I've given up on doing so?" Mestor grumbled back, his voice as thick as his shuddering neck scales that lined his gills.

Lachlan's eyes went wide. "They *talk?*"

"What did you think we did, communicate with a bunch of belches and farts?" Mestor grumbled, his neck bulging as he spoke.

Lachlan laughed. "Wow, and apparently this one is very grouchy?" He set both of his hands on the railing. "Hey, big guy. What's your name?"

Mestor's giant brow, if a dragon's brow could furrow, did so, making the silver ridge of scales between his eyes become much more prominent. As blue-eyed dragon stared into equally blue-eyed sailor, Amy wondered if the two recognized one another from the pub.

"Why do you look so familiar?" Lachlan asked, flexing his right arm.

"Amy, dear. While the males are sizing each other up, why don't you introduce us to this gallant man whom you seem to have a relationship with?" Amphitrite said as she grabbed one of Mestor's giant fins that frilled out next to his gills and gave it a tug.

Amy joined Lachlan at the railing as the sea bowed with the cresting fins and spines of Mestor's brothers as they swam toward the boat.

"Wow, how many are there?" Lachlan asked.

Each dragon appeared so different. Amy marveled at their colors as their heads rose up, dripping out of the sea. The most variation occurred with their fins and snouts. She recognized Lykos from his purple fins and viridian opalescence upon his scales. Hopleus was as a deep indigo color, contrasting Idas's creamy olive green. Taras was far darker in his green coloration, mossy with sharp hints of viridian.

Balfour, however, refused to surface. He snaked outside his brothers, keeping his beautiful onyx head below the water. His dark scales reflected a gorgeous iridescence that created dark swirling rainbows, reminding Amy of oil.

"Lachlan, this is my mother, Amphitrite," Amy said.

"I was wondering if the two of you were related, you look exactly alike." Lachlan reached out, grabbing her mother's hand, then kissed the top. "Hi, I'm Lachlan. Your daughter and I had a bit of a tumble back there in the surf."

"Tumbling, I'm sure," Amphitrite said with a twinkle in her eye.

Amy's cheeks burned again as Lachlan wrapped his arm around her and stared Mestor square in his giant blue eye. "And you are?"

"Skip the introductions, fish boy," Mestor grumbled, spines Amy hadn't seen before bulging beneath his jaw. "You've caused a problem with our expedition."

"Expedition? Where is everyone going?" Lachlan asked.

"Bellerophon tidal stampede has swept us far out into the sea," Mestor grumbled. "But we did not gain the momentum we needed to," he growled, swinging his giant head toward Amy. "All because *you* decided to spare a fisherman who smells like shallots?"

Lachlan raised his arm and took a whiff. "Hey, I don't smell bad. If anything, I think you're smelling your own breath."

Mestor's muzzle curled, revealing a set of sharp, greenish-yellow teeth. He frilled his neck fins toward Lachlan. "This voyage to the crown has not started with the force it needs. We might as well abandon it now."

"No, you will not," Amphitrite cut it. "I have waited too long to embark on this journey."

"So this is what it's like if you get lost in the Bermuda Triangle?" Lachlan said. "You get caught up in an argument between a sea dragon and a sea nymph?"

"*Storm* dragon," Mestor corrected. "Your stupid boat is the odd dragon out." With a thrash of his tail, he tore back into the water, taking Amy's mother with him.

The *Sea Dragon* began to trail behind the current generated by the dragon's tails as they ventured further into the sea.

"I still don't know what this expedition is about," Lachlan said as he popped the top of a wooden barrel off and reached inside.

"Did you not catch what Mestor mentioned about his father's crown?" Amy asked.

Lachlan's eyes went wide. "Mestor is his name, huh? And his father is Poseidon?"

Amy nodded.

He withdrew his hand from the barrel, clutching a shiny red apple. "You've got to be kidding me. Why didn't you say anything about this when we met? I told you that I was searching for his crown."

"I didn't think you would believe the myths."

He tossed her the apple while he fished another one out of the barrel. He crouched down, propping his back against the barrel.

Amy did the same.

"I told you that I wanted to find the crown. Trust me, sweetheart. You're safe as long as you stick with me. These chumps don't have anything on the *Sea Dragon*." He took a chunk out of his apple and began to chew.

Amy bit into her apple, the tart juices erupting into her mouth.

He grabbed one of Mestor's shiny silver scales that had shed onto his boat deck. "You've got to be kidding me. That bloke at the bar? Mestor was the big bad silver and blue one?"

Amy nodded. "All of the storm dragons swimming alongside the boat are searching for their father's crown.

His cheeks bulged as he chewed. "Why are they searching for it?"

"My mother put them into a sleep long ago because of an argument they were having over the death of their father. Finding the crown will answer how he died."

He swallowed. "Do you know what killed Poseidon?"

Amy bit her tongue. "I don't."

"Liar," Lachlan said, his tone full of amusement. "You don't lie well."

"What gives me away?"

"Your freckles look more like stars when you lie. As for anyone navigating the seas, the stars always tell the truth, no matter what."

Amy flushed. "Well, according to my mother, this voyage is going to be dictated not only by the stars, but the moon as well."

Lachlan's cheeks dimpled. "I'm all about a good time under the night sky. Darkness has never scared me off."

The taste of his lips brought her back to the warm nights she'd spent with Ewan in the frozen heart of Winter Forest.

43
STORM SMOKE RITUALS
Damien

By the time Damien finished laying the stones around the fire pit at the center of the driftwood hut, he'd broken a sweat. He and Pelias made multiple trips down to the sea and back up with pails of water he imagined would be used in case one of the bonfires got out of control. He still didn't know what the purpose of the central structure was, other than to trap the storm smoke. The more he watched this bizarre ritual unfold, the less he liked how things were starting to turn out.

Instead of using his artwork to trap the smoke, Pelias created an altar for the concepts Damien had abandoned years ago. He placed them around the hut, the illustrations of the moon and sea facing toward the center. Seeing his paintings—a wash of black, blue, and white images—made him feel oddly vulnerable.

His pulse hadn't beat this quickly since he learned his daughter was coming into the world early. Since Amphitrite put her to sleep, he wondered how long it would take for Selia to return to wake her. He hated not being able to hold Nyssa in his arms and play with her...

Pelias set one of the pails down next to the driftwood structure at the center of the other three piles of wood. "Last one," he huffed, sinking down to his knees. He motioned for Damien to do the same.

Damien knelt down across from the Pelias with the stone circle between them. It occurred to him that he had yet to see how he started the fire to begin with.

Pelias grabbed a seashell and dipped it into the pail, scooping the water, then poured it over the stones. "Now we begin our offerings."

Damien grabbed a seashell and dipped it into one of the pails, then mimicked Pelias's movements. "Are we trying to start a fire with water?"

Pelias dunked his seashell into the pail and repeated the same motion. "The sacred fire of our ancestors is only lit in one way—with salt, storms, and starlight."

"Right," Damien said, trying to comprehend the bizarre nature of this shamanic ritual.

After they emptied the first pail of water, Pelias set his seashell down. He rested his hands into his lap, folding them so that his palms faced up. He closed his eyes. His nostrils flared as he inhaled. The beads on his dreadlocks swung as a breeze swept into their makeshift dwelling. "You must meditate with me. Allow the sacred flames to build inside of you."

"I'm sorry, what?"

"Close your eyes, and observe," Pelias instructed as he opened his eyes. "If you can see the storm smoke, then you should be able to see the flame that forms it."

Damien wondered how meditating could possibly help him in any way connect with Balfour and the others at sea. Pelias's instructions were contradictory. How could he observe anything with his eyes closed?

He clenched his eyes shut, hoping that this ritual wouldn't somehow return him to the Temple of Isis. He'd learned from Balfour that storm dragons couldn't step foot inside of a temple their architect ancestor dwelt within. He resisted the urge to grab his throat, remembering what it felt like to have Erebéus's shadows constrict him. Instead, he focused on his breathing until splotchy blue spots appeared behind his eyelids.

"Do not open your eyes before I say so," Pelias said. "If you do, the storm smoke will not form properly."

The air became muggy as Damien focused on his rhythmic inhale and exhale. He tried to sync his own breathing with the melody found in the waves crashing in the distance.

To distract himself from the humid air, he focused his thoughts on the recent memories he had with Selia and Nyssa. He remembered their daughter sitting on the beach, her pudgy little hands flinging into the air as she experienced the sea for the first time. And Selia had admitted vulnerability about her body with him.

His cock twitched just thinking about the intimate adventure they shared on the train together. How broken of a man he would still be had he not met her.

With each breath he took, warm, humid air filled his lungs. Eventually, the air became so hot and muggy that it became difficult to breathe.

The horrible realization of what was happening dawned on him—this was a sweat lodge ritual.

The amount of sweat pouring down his face made him cough. He doubled over, tears squeezing out of his eyes as he opened them. "Pelias, I can't do this," he stammered. "I'm going to suffocate."

He fell forward, his wrists hitting the ground. No sand spread through his fingers. The stone circle vanished.

The rhythmic sound of the waves was replaced with the crackling sound of flames. Three separate fires burned in the giant room, each with the same orientation of the fire pits Pelias had created. But the heat filling the room originated from another flame—one that cast blue light into the room adorned with giant marble columns that looked like something from the Greek Parthenon.

Damien climbed to his feet, mesmerized by a piece of artwork hanging above the blazing blue flames—a tapestry. Two dragons coiled vertically up the wall, each facing one another. The dragon on the right was bulkier in shape and size, while the one on the left appeared more like a serpent. Both had vibrant blue and black scales with silver fins that framed their snarling mouths.

A central pillar separated the two dragons. With their claws reaching and muscular necks arched back, they framed a star perched atop the center of the tapestry.

He took a step back, overcome by the spectacular imagery.

"You found the Tapestry of Tridents," a female voice said from beside him.

A woman appeared beside the giant blue hearth. White linen robes adorned her body. Her long brown hair cascaded down her shoulders. She wore golden earrings and a necklace decorated with blue beads that shimmered in the light.

Damien took a step back, nearly stepping into one of the fire pits. "Maria?"

"Maera," she corrected, taking a step toward him. "I was hoping that Zakai would at least give you my true name."

"Maera, where are we?"

"The Temple of Salt, Storms, and Starlight."

44
FOSSILS
Selia

As Pherusa disappeared from sight, Selia gazed at the ammonite fossil Deidra had given her.

Deidra beckoned her over to one of the tables covered with various natural history artifacts. The nymphs working to sort through the materials didn't look up as Deidra grabbed one of the seashell fossils from the table and held it in front of her face.

As Selia approached the table, she glanced over her shoulder, half expecting Hecate's hell hounds to come darting down the hallway to as Pherusa so horribly put it, escort them to the goddess of death. "Where exactly are the shadow archives located? And how in the world am I supposed to use a fossil to access them?"

"I thought I told you two to leave," Pherusa snapped as she spotted them from across the room.

Deidra grabbed Selia's arm. "Quick, take the fossil and see if you can find any others similar to it. We've got to be getting close to where the other specimens are held. I'll hold her off. Just make sure that you follow the shadows."

Pherusa strode toward them, making quick work of the room as she approached.

Zipper flit between the dryad and Pherusa, forcing Deidra to dodge his rapid movements. Her arm knocked into one of the boxes full of artifacts, scattering rocks and animal bones all over the sorting table.

"Oh, clumsy me," Deidra stammered enthusiastically. "I'm so sorry, I never should have let my pesky dragonfly in here."

While Deidra kept Pherusa's attention, Selia pocketed her ammonite fossil and slipped around the corner, barely able to think. *Follow the shadows?* What did that mean? Since entering the archives, Pherusa was the only individual who possessed shadows. And they were super nasty.

She backtracked down the way they first entered the archive, noticing the hallway they'd ventured through had another route. She followed the route where the root-like wooden beams thickened into tree trunks. This archive, however bizarre it was, reminded her of a giant tree. If she needed to follow the shadows, then she likely needed to go deeper into its root system.

She ventured down a staircase, finding layer upon layer of dirt. A musty scent filled her nose as she continued. Another room appeared, one with far less nymphs sorting artifacts than in the room before. The workers wore white robes, making them stick out against the dark walls.

Her salt nodes burned as a melody rang through them. It was the same ominous sound she'd heard calling to her upon entering the museum.

Taking a turn down yet another flight of stairs, she found herself stumbling over uneven ground. The stairs were no longer stairs, but more of a layer of oddly-stacked stones.

No tables cluttered the space. No ceilings arched overhead. Selia found herself wandering through a tunnel of complete darkness. If there were shadows down here, she couldn't see them. Hopefully she wouldn't run into any of Pherusa's shadow serpents.

Her hands swung at her sides, both appearing brighter than before. She stopped, holding them in front of her face. Her fingers and wrists were completely transparent, putting off a dull, silver light.

Was her salt aura activating? If so, why?

The walls of the tunnel weren't solid—they were moving.

Silver lights flickered and danced, morphing alongside the surface. Something large and oblong shifted before her. She ducked as a large fin grazed over her head, seeming to expand out from the wall and into the tunnel.

Her breath caught as the creature revealed itself, branching like a silver ghost above her head.

A *whale?*

No, it couldn't be.

Another fin passed overhead as the creature dipped its face to see her. A giant blue eye glowing with intelligence shone back at her before it swam off into the inky walls.

The darkness was ocean full of starlit sea creatures...

As she walked, the tunnel illuminated as other marine life broke out of the darkness, fins and tails and eyes as bright as stars sparkled in the liquid cloak of night. Gaia's archive didn't only house artifacts of dead creatures fossilized in stone—it held a living essence within it of those lifeforms.

Some of the creatures were brilliant in their complex beauty, while others floated above, barely recognizable. Jellyfish, and ancient sea organisms drifted above that resembled brittle stars. Time, in essence, did not exist in this tunnel. She was witnessing a record of all ocean life, their spirits lingering, separating, then rejoining again.

How much she wished Damien was here to see this impossible display of the sea's beauty and imagination.

As she continued through the tunnel, guided by yet another massive whale that swam overhead, the ground began to level out. Her feet became damp. The further she walked, the deeper the water became.

Plop!

Deidra's ammonite fossil fell out of her pocket.

Frantic, Selia crouched to the puddle, feeling around for where it might have gone. Her fingers grazed across a smooth item. She grabbed it, bringing it out of the water. A seashell dripped between her fingers. She turned it over, searching for an opening. She became transfixed at the light glowing off the shell's surface. What appeared to be little stars decorated the exterior. She held the shell up to her ear. A soft melody crashed inside, sweeping in and out with the fluid rhythm of the tide.

Something grazed past her ear. She pulled away, glancing inside the opening. Had she seen a tentacle? Was a marine creature still alive inside of the shell?

"Can you hear me?" she asked.

"*Of course I can. And tell your dryad friend to stop calling me an ammonite. I am a rare blue ammonite—are you one of Naunet's scribes?*"

Selia jumped. Had the fossil that she dropped into the water somehow come alive? And did the creature, who apparently could speak to her thoughts, believe that she worked for Naunet? "I am. I need you to tell me what you know about the star of the sea."

The tentacle retreated back into the shell. "*I know that Pherusa's sister fragmented the star of the sea in Atlantis. Naunet told me this was because Erebéus did not trust her. I believe it was three fragments in which the crystal was separated.*"

"Do you have any idea where the fragments went?"

"*That would require me to share what Naunet told Maera about her bond with the god of shadows.*"

Selia's stomach hollowed.

Maera?

The woman she met at the Louvre—did she somehow know Naunet?

45
SECRETS

Amy

Amy's back and neck ached from the constant movement of the sea breaking against the hull. While Lachlan busied himself with tidying up his boat, she found a place behind a pile of wooden crates and dangling fishing nets to address something that had been bothering her since climbing aboard. As the *Sea Dragon* ventured further into the ocean after Poseidon's sons, her precious cargo made itself known.

The crystal Maera had given her felt like a stone in her pocket. She dug it out and held the fragment of the star of the sea in her palm. The surface had turned a murky blue color. She swore something was moving inside. Was it smoke?

A large onyx dragon head emerged next to the boat. Balfour's nostrils flared as he scented her. "*I smell something odd, and it's not seaweed,*" he grumbled quietly. "*It smells like smoke.*"

Amy clutched the crystal in her hand, regretting the moment she closed her fingers over the sharp edges. The prominent edge nearly pierced her flesh. "Maybe it's your breath," she said in a tone that was unusually high, even for herself.

Balfour's head shook, sending water and little bits of algae flying from his fins toward her. "*What are you hiding? It's not like you to make fun of me.*"

Amy glanced over her shoulder, noticing Lachlan was still busy shifting items around his boat. "Have you ever kept a secret from someone because you thought it was the right thing to do?"

He dipped his massive head, making his dark purple fins sway in the breeze. "*I wish my brothers hadn't woken up. Now I can't keep secrets from them at all.*"

Amy looked into Balfour's giant dark eye, completely lost in his calm. Even though Balfour was the youngest of the dragons, his eyes housed a truly ancient soul. "I kept secrets, and I ended up hurting those I loved." Her mind went to Ewan dying atop the sacred mountain.

"*What makes this secret you are keeping different from the last one you kept?*"

Amy's fingers relaxed over the crystal. "This time, I'm not the only one keeping a secret. I think someone I love is also keeping one from me."

"*Who?*"

"My mother."

"*What kind of secret could you mother be keeping?*"

"I don't know all the details, but I think it has to do with her Ocean Apothecary."

The whiskers jutting out of Balfour's muzzle thrashed, then relaxed behind his nostrils. "*Well, according to her, the remnants of her Ocean Apothecary are tied to my father's crown. How the two are connected is only known by her, and not us. It sounds like you and your mother need to have a heart-to-heart about this quest.*"

At Balfour's words, Amy caught sight of her mother sitting atop Mestor's ridged back. Her long red hair caught the wind, trailing out like the wild and free spirit that she was. A pod of dolphins swam in their wake, jumping and flirting with each other as they trailed behind her.

Amy's heart leapt at the sight. While her mother might take for granted, Amy would always see her as pure magic in her eyes. "You forget. I haven't seen her since Atlantis sank. Distance has grown between us that makes it hard for us to communicate."

Lachlan made his way over to where Amy was busy chatting with Balfour. Amy clutched the crystal in her hand as he approached.

Balfour dipped back down beneath the waves, resuming his place behind the boat.

Lachlan propped his elbows onto the railing and eyed the water. "Darn it. He must have seen me coming. Maybe he's shy? I barely got a good look at him."

Amy turned her back to Lachlan, wishing he hadn't interrupted their discussion.

"Oi, what are you up to back there?" Lachlan asked as he propped his back against the crate and leaned over the top.

"Nothing."

He swung his head over her, craning his neck. "Can't be nothing if you are back here hiding." He maneuvered around the crate, facing her. "I wanted to see if you could help me with something at the front of the boat that could use two people."

Amy followed him to the stern, finding a new item she'd not seen before. Sitting on a metal post was an item that reminded her of the beaconing device Mestor used to calibrate the triton current.

A flat brass sphere sat atop the post. Little gears squeaked as Lachlan set his hand on the device, which flipped back and forth. "All right. Hold onto this little lever. I'm going to adjust the pole."

Amy did so, pinching the small metal lever between her finger and thumb.

Lachlan crouched down next to her, squinting up at the device. He lined it up with the sun, tweaking the pole until it became level with Amy's chest. "There we are," he said, brushing up alongside her as he stood. "Definitely looks pretty up here, but not as pretty as the redhead accompanying me on this voyage."

Amy blinked, looking away from his vibrant blue eyes. "What is this nautical device?"

"It's an astrolabe. I figured that if we are going on a quest to find Poseidon's crown, it might be fun to actually chart where we are in the process, old school style."

"Do you plan to use the stars to chart where we are?" Amy asked, the idea suddenly sounding far more romantic than it should.

"You bet I am. If the grouchy big mouth your mother is riding thinks I'm just going to sit back for the ride, he's got something coming for him. It's not every day that a sailor gets to sail the high seas with a bunch of dragons and a hot redheaded lass." His cheeks dimpled. "For reference, that hot redhead is you, not your mother. Although both of you are impeccably gorgeous."

Amy's cheeks burned at his second attempt to flirt with her. "Have you ever used an astrolabe before?"

Lachlan shrugged. "Not really. But it can't be any different than a compass, right?"

"I guess that depends on if you trust in magic of the stars or not."

His shirt still hadn't dried all the way, making the fabric cling to his chest. She caught sight of the birthmark over his heart, a place an arrow had been.

No. She was imagining the impossible again.

Lachlan set his hand onto her waist as he leaned toward her. "I think there is more than one force of magic on this boat."

Amy remembered the salty taste of his lips on hers, combined with the graze of his stubble across her cheek. For a split moment, she was transported back to Winter Forest, sitting with Ewan as the first stars appeared in the inky sky.

Somehow, the journey atop a sacred mountain in the past wasn't that different from this voyage into the sea. Not even the boundaries of time seemed to separate the moments her heart recognized as the same. They were both rediscovering something vastly beautiful and deep—something only starlight could allow her to see.

The boat shuddered, and Amy was knocked sideways as Balfour's tail swept into the hull. The crystal fell out of her pocket, landing with a glassy *thunk* onto the deck.

"Balfour, stop that!" she scolded the storm dragon who was obviously listening to their discussion.

Lachlan had already dipped to the ground and retrieved the crystal fragment. "Well, now. What is this beautiful piece of treasure?"

Amy reached for the crystal, which he quickly held over his head. "Give it back!"

"Not until we discuss more about the stars and their magic."

Maera said she couldn't tell her mother about the crystal, but she never said anything about keeping it a secret from others.

"Give what back?" Balfour rumbled as he slid his massive onyx head up beside Lachlan.

"There you are," Lachlan said as Balfour's purple neck fins thrashed toward him. "What's your name?"

"I'd like you to meet Mestor's youngest brother, Bellerophon," Amy said, fear gripping her stomach. "He goes by Balfour for short."

Lachlan craned his neck backward as Balfour towered over them. "Wow, Balfour. You're the youngest?" He leaned forward, squinting at Balfour's onyx scales. "Between you and I, you look way more intimidating. I think your big brother looks like an over-sized puffer fish."

"What is this treasure the two of you are keeping?" Balfour grumbled aloud.

Lachlan tucked the crystal into his pocket as he looped his arm around Amy's waist again. "Amy is the treasure, haven't you seen her?"

Balfour's giant eye rolled. "Your flirting makes my gills tremble with sea sickness." He dipped his head down into the water again, resuming his place alongside the boat.

Amy let out a massive sigh. Lachlan had kept the crystal a secret from Balfour.

He released her. "If anyone is going to keep secrets on this voyage, it should be between us, you hear?" He handed the crystal back to her. "I'd recommend keeping it closer to you if you don't want to lose it again."

Amy nodded, appreciating the fact that he hadn't given away her secret. Their voyage might be doomed before they'd even started if he had. She squinted at the horizon, where blue smoke billowed up into the sky.

46

THE TAPESTRY OF TRIDENTS

Damien

Blue smoke filled the room where Damien stood before the hearth. The flames illuminating the tapestry flickered, catching the silvery threads, which quickly burned out. As the smoke rose up into the air, it coiled into a circle, creating a symbol Damien had seen many times before.

The smoke created the moonlit symbol he signed his artwork with.

"Did the Sgàthan clan make this tapestry?" he asked, mystified at the imagery.

Maera continued to wave her hand, dispersing the smoke. "Your ancestors from Atlantis did. They passed the smoke symbols the Tapestry of Tridents creates down to their Sgàthan clan descendants, who after Atlantis sank, inhabited Scotland." She faced him, her golden earrings shimmering. "I remember the day you found the folktales that depicted the moonlit symbol in your Auntie's closet. I had been pregnant with Sophie at the time."

Damien shivered as damp coldness rippled up his spine. "I started signing my artwork with this moonlit symbol after you died." His voice shuddered. "It was my way of reflecting on our life together."

Maera's gaze met his, the blue flames from the hearth flickering in her eyes. "I remember you reading the folktales to Sophie, the tales about the fae, dragons, and selkies."

Damien blinked, suddenly unable to look Maera in the eye. Something about her didn't seem right. Maybe it was all of the smoke in the room that was making his vision blurry. "You wanted me to create a children's book out of those folktales for her."

Maera's expression softened. "Damien, when I left you, my work with the tapestry was not yet complete. And I currently do not have an afterlife to return to. Do you remember what I said to you about the last piece you worked on? The map you had worked on for years in an attempt to illustrate my marine studies?"

"Yes. You said that even the brightest stars find their origin in the darkest waters of the origin."

Maera gazed at the wall again. "This tapestry is what I was referring to."

Blue mist filled the room, clouding Damien's vision. When the mist parted, two men stood beside one another, each facing a pillar with a crystal atop.

"Mestor, come forward," a low, powerful male voice echoed into the room. The man on the right approached the pillar on which the crystal was displayed. A brilliant rainbow of colors shone out of the crystal, which looked more like a star. Just as it had been depicted in the tapestry, it had seven total points, each sourcing a different color.

Another giant man sat atop a coral-crusted throne beneath the crystal. His deep blue eyes followed Mestor as he approached. Long ultramarine and red robes cascaded down his front. His muscular arms were bare. Gauntlets—one silver, the other gold—covered his forearms. Sandals dressed his feet, with leather bands that wrapped up his calves, stopping at his knees. Facial hair concealed the man's mouth and chin. Dark brown hair framed a regal face fit for a king.

A discolored patch of skin on his arm caught Damien's attention. The kingly man shifted his silver gauntlet down to cover the mark.

Mestor knelt before the man sitting on the throne. He propped one of his arms atop his knee, bowing his head as he spoke. "Father, you wish to speak with me about your crown?" he asked, his voice far less wholesome than what Damien remembered of him.

Poseidon's giant hands gripped the armrests of his throne as he answered. "Yes. I need to discuss the territories within the Abyss that make up my crown."

Mestor looked up, meeting his father's intense blue gaze. "Your sons from the Orient do not respect your crown."

Poseidon dipped his chin. "Kai tells me that you have taken it upon yourself to claim not one, but multiple territories within the Abyss. He claims that you are attempting to guard all seven on your own."

Mestor dipped his head. "I thought you would be proud of me, father, taking on more than one. Is it not still expected that we serve the Abyss by forming a territory around the ancestral salts before we establish territories in the deeper waters of the ocean?"

Poseidon shifted on his throne. "This effort is overzealous, even for my strongest son in the West."

"Why are you worried? Do you not believe I can accomplish my goal? None of my brothers have communicated any interest in the Abyss's seven territories other than I."

Poseidon propped his elbows onto his knees and leaned toward his son. "I believe that I should disperse the responsibility between my sons from separate trident. Besides, Bellerophon has expressed his interest in one of the salt pods—Celaeno."

Mestor scoffed. "You would give your youngest son in the West the territory of the Abyss's darkest star?"

"Bellerophon tames my storm horses," Poseidon argued. "He possesses the strengths found in quiet, and patience. He will be a great guardian of Celaeno one day."

Poseidon grabbed his gauntlet, repositioning it over the blemish on his arm.

"Father, I request permission to speak," another voice rumbled, his voice much lower than Mestor's.

Damien jumped. He'd forgotten about the other man standing in the room.

Poseidon raised his other arm, his golden gauntlet reflecting the light as the newcomer stopped beside Mestor. "Kai, walk forward."

Long, sleek black hair tapered down Kai's back. He was tall and slender, yet his build was not any less powerful than Mestor's bulk. What he lacked in size he made up for in grace as he approached Poseidon. His gauntlets were not silver like Mestor's, but gold. Red robes fell at his sides as he stopped next to his brother.

Damien didn't remember Kai. Who was this other mystery brother of Mestor? Was he witnessing some kind of sibling rivalry? And why was Balfour in the middle of it?

"For the Abyss to remain healthy, you cannot treat the territories of our father's crown as though they are separate from one another," Kai sneered, orange flames licking up his forearms.

"Kai is right. The Abyss has long required the unified protection of storm dragon territories," Poseidon cut in as he shifted his silver gauntlet down his arm.

Mestor's gaze fell toward his father's gauntlet. "She's made you ill, hasn't she? Do her ancestral salts not originate from the Dark One?" He took a step toward Poseidon. "Did the midwife of the sea spread this illness to you?"

"There is no proof that Pherusa has made me ill," Poseidon protested, not glancing up from his arm.

"I see how you avoid her advances," Mestor growled. "I've seen how she insists that you bond with her." He threw out his hands, sending electrical sparks flying out of his fingertips. "You want to know what I think? I think she's somehow poisoned you because she's jealous of your feelings for her sister."

"Silence!" Poseidon roared, his voice making the room tremble. The windows above him shook, fracturing the daylight into a brilliant display of color that streamed through them.

Damien's breath caught. How magnificent the stained glass windows were. Seven in total formed a circle above Poseidon, each one a different color. Seven different sea nymphs were depicted in each, all of who illustrated the Abyss together. One of the windows was darker than the others. The sea nymph at its center held her hands at her sides as she focused the colors of all the other windows down toward Poseidon.

Mestor dropped his gaze to the ground. "Forgive me, father. I cannot look past what I see. If Amphitrite refuses to bond with you, then she should at least find a remedy for your illness with her Ocean Apothecary."

Poseidon's blue eyes shifted between his sons from the East and the West, great worry reflecting in them. "Amphitrite has no cure for my illness. In an effort to preserve my tridents, I have resorted to speaking with my ancestor, Erebéus."

Both Mestor and Kai jolted.

"You speak his name?" Mestor asked, his voice breaking.

"My lineages in the East and in the West will crumble if you two do not work together."

Kai lowered himself before Poseidon in a bow. "Father, know this. When the day comes that you are no longer with us, the seas will become ill. But unlike Mestor, I will not flee from this illness, I will fight it." He glanced up, red embers flickering in his liquid eyes. "I will not rest until I burn all of it."

Damien's eyes hooded as the scent of smoke filled his nose. Blue mist filled the room as the vision of Poseidon and his two sons evaporated.

47
OPAL

Selia

The seashell Selia had heard a voice echoing from illuminated in her palm. The names *Naunet* and *Maera* filled her salt nodes, unsettling her. Who was this god of shadows the ammonite had mentioned?

The shell wriggled in her hand. "*Let me free. I can tell you more about Naunet's work with the Codex, and her history with Erebéus.*"

"Selia!"

Selia jumped as Deidra's voice echoed into the tunnel.

"*Selia is your name?*"

"Yes."

The stars on the shell glowed brighter. "*Naunet spoke so much about you to me when she was documenting the storm bonds. She even spoke of you after she fled Egypt and found refuge in the Orient.*"

Selia's heart leapt. "I want to know what happened to Naunet after she left Egypt."

"*I can do more than tell you. I have the power to show you, but only if you are who you say you are.*"

"How do I prove who I am?" Selia asked.

"Selia, are you in here?" Deidra called again.

"*Take me with you, but don't let anybody know you have me. Dryads in particular tend to be very nosy when it comes to ammonite records. Our memories are extraordinary.*"

Selia tucked the ammonite into her pocket. "Deidra, I'm over here!"

"Wow, this is incredible," Deidra said as flit between them. His wings created an everlasting glow that illuminated her face. "This must be one of the oceanic tunnels. They house records of life that first originated from the sea."

Shadows filled the tunnel. Hecate appeared, her faces manifesting as three separate masks. "Knowing Naunet's past comes with consequences, I must warn you."

"There will be no such thing occurring in the archives, not while I am in charge here," Pherusa's voice cut through the tunnel. She stormed past Hecate, grabbing Selia's wrist. Black shadow serpents tendrilled out of her hand, constricting Selia's arm. "I said get out, now."

"We aren't leaving until you give us back the crystal fragments," Selia snapped, wrenching her arm way.

"Or what, you'll find your way into the shadow archives yourself?" she laughed, high and cold, releasing Selia's arm.

The goddess of crossroads stood between Selia and Naunet's furious mother.

Pherusa threw her hands out, sending her shadow serpents coiling along the walls. The oceanic scenery disappeared from the tunnel. "They are not to pass through any of the origin tunnels without the proper clearance." She shot Deidra a nasty look. "Especially those who are non-Iridescents."

Deidra's braid frizzed as Pherusa spewed another nasty statement about her ranking.

Hecate held out her hand, sending Pherusa's shadow serpents retreating. "These nymphs can gain access to the origin tunnels if the god of shadows grants it to them."

"Impossible," Pherusa spat. "The only individual Erebéus has ever given access to has been the midwife of the sea."

Hecate's three faces separated again—each porcelain white, displaying on their forehead one of three phases of the moon. "Pherusa, let them through. The Blind Moon and her friend are allowed to explore this realm of the archive without you."

Pherusa faced Selia, liquid fire burning in her dark eyes. "I hope you embrace the darkness, salt daughter of Celaeno."

Selia felt her hair stick on end as Pherusa watched them walk past. When they were almost out of earshot, Deidra turned and cupped her hands around her mouth. "Nice knowing you!"

Selia's pocket squirmed.

A liquid *thunk* told her that the ammonite had fallen from her pocket into the water.

"*Follow me. I'll guide you through, all right?*"

"*I don't even know your name yet,*" Selia replied with her mind.

"*Naunet used to call me Opal. She believed I shimmered like one of the gemstones that resembles starlight.*"

"I've never been this far back in the archives before," Deidra said as she followed Zipper through the tunnel. The water they walked through began to empty, draining alongside the pathway.

How was Opal going to help her if she had nothing to swim in?

Another room emerged, this one much different than the collections from before. Instead of shelves with boxes, giant brass contraptions surrounded them that reminded Selia of the beaconing device Mestor had used for his storm calibration.

Giant armillary spheres surrounded them, their massive golden rings swirling around each other. Some moved fast, while others were slow. Each made a different pitched sound as they synced with one another.

"Selia, look at this!" Deidra said as she pointed up. Zipper had already flit up toward the ceiling, which didn't appear as a ceiling at all. His golden body disappeared into a blanket of hundreds of shimmering stars.

Her breath caught as she stopped next to one of the spheres that made a low *whooshing* sound as the rings slowed.

"*Opal, where are you?*" Selia asked with her thoughts.

"*I'm up here.*"

An outline of her shell drifted across the ceiling, blending with other starlit sea creatures. The stars created dozens of constellations.

"I'm digging the astronomy vibes in here. I have a feeling that records are stored differently in this room than they were back in collections." Deidra said as she approached one of the giant telescopes. "This is amazing, let's take a look at what's up in that sky!"

"Do you recognize any of them?" Selia asked as she stopped beside Deidra. A table sat next to the telescope, where some hand-written notes had been taken. She recognized the names of the ancestral salt mothers.

A circle had been drawn around Celaeno, with a note beneath it that read: **Darkest when paired with his starlit origin.**

"Look, the Pleiades!" Deidra said as she removed her face from the eyepiece. "You need to have a look!"

Selia glanced through the telescope. "Was someone studying the Abyss?"

"I'd say so," Deidra replied as Zipper flit down to the armillary sphere.

Selia noticed how one of the spheres slowed, while the other twelve or so continued to spin at full speed. She repositioned the telescope, aligning it with what she observed from the notes about Celaeno.

The giant armillary sphere stopped.

She grabbed a knob sticking out of the ring. A star with seven points decorated the surface. When she tugged on the knob, the ring opened, revealing a stack of papers inside. She grabbed the papers and withdrew them.

As she flipped through the notes, another label appeared.

Star of the Sea
Poseidon's Crown
Origin study artist: Damien Malloch

Selia's stomach hollowed. Why would Damien's artwork be here in Gaia's archives?

The armillary sphere began to smoke, ebony mist spewing out of its rings as all twelve of them began to spin out of control. She was thrown back into the mist as the sphere swallowed her whole.

48

SIRENS

Amy

The crystal in Amy's hand had changed form. No longer oblong in shape, it had seven points, one of which was more prominent than the others. The edges became smoky with a bluish-black color.

What was causing it to darken so quickly?

Lykos's head rose out of the water next to the *Sea Dragon*. His viridian fins flared as his nostrils let out a burst of hot air. "Something smells like burned fish."

Taras's mossy head bobbed in the surf next to his brother, his nostrils flaring more aggressively.

As the dragons scented the wind, Lachlan covered his face with his handkerchief. "Wow, that's rank. One of you must have let one rip."

Amy lifted her hand to shield her nose from the putrid smell. Where was it coming from?

Lachlan grabbed Amy's arm and spun her. "Look."

She squinted toward the stern. A plume of bluish-black smoke billowed up into the sky. "Is it coming from land, or sea?"

"No idea," Lachlan replied. "But that smoke doesn't look normal."

Amy's stomach churned with anxiety.

As Mestor's lumpy back maneuvered toward the boat, Amy's mother jumped from his shoulders and landed next to her. "It looks like Pelias is trying to send us a message."

"With what? I've never seen smoke like that," Amy said.

Water churned against the boat as the dragons' heads rose out of the water, including Balfour.

"I agree with Amphitrite. Pelias has sent us a signal," Mestor chuffed, his spiny whiskers frilling.

"What for?" Amphitrite asked. "He's not trying to summon us back to shore, is he?"

"It's not like him to summon black storm smoke," Lykos said, his grumbly tone uneasy.

Something dark shimmered in the water not far from the boat.

Mestor swung his giant head in observation of the murky water. "Everyone stick close. Oil ahead."

Amy stood between Lachlan and her mother as the storm dragons maneuvered the boat away from the blackness floating in the sea. As they shifted their tails, they generated a current powerful enough to keep the boat drifting.

A dark fleck appeared before her. At first, Amy thought it to be a piece of debris floating on the water. It hovered in the air, its wings buzzing fast and low, filling her salt nodes with a horrible whine.

An entire cloud of salt flies hovered over the oil. They were surrounded by fae parasites. The brackish water churned as the stench intensified to the point that Amy wanted to retreat into the boat.

Her mother set her hand on her shoulder. "This isn't oil."

"What the heck is that?" Lachlan asked as he squinted at the glistening black mass.

Something shifted in inky blackness.

A grey hand reached into the air before disappearing back into the oil.

Amphitrite grabbed Amy's shoulders and tugged her back. "This isn't oil—it's salt venom."

"Sirens!" Lykos roared.

Water crashed into the boat as the dragons panicked, sending their fins and tails into a coiling fit.

Amy grabbed the railing as she was nearly thrown overboard.

"Counter current, now!" Mestor ordered.

At his command, Idas thrashed his tail. He and Hopleus continued the thrashing movements, siphoning tons of ocean water with their long keeled scales.

A whirlpool formed, sucking the boat away from the oily water that seemed to have a mind of its own.

One of the sirens latched onto the railing, its clammy, grey hand gripping for Amy.

"Oh, hell no," Lachlan stammered as he flicked open his knife. With one swing of his arm, he sliced through the net the siren had grabbed onto.

With an angry *hiss*, the siren fell back into the water. As quickly as it surfaced, it disappeared, leaving nothing but an oil-slick coating where it tumbled back into the ocean.

"Dragons, and now siren-infested waters?" Lachlan said as he closed his blade. "Wait until I share this story with my buddies at the pub."

The patch of oily salt venom they'd encountered disappeared behind them.

"Why were they out here?" Amy asked.

"That was too close," Mestor grumbled as he swung his head up from the water. "Something attracted the sirens. They don't just attack a group of storm dragons like that."

"What are you saying?" Amphitrite asked.

The scales on Mestor's brow crowded together. "Somebody in our party is keeping secrets from the rest of us. Hopleus? Taras? Search the boat."

Amy's gut hollowed. What if Mestor was right? Was the crystal fragment Maera gave her responsible for attracting them?

Hopleus and Taras thrashed their tails in the water until a cloud of mist formed. They manifested as men on the boat deck.

Lachlan held up his arms. "I swear I'm not hiding anything," he said sending Amy a sideways glance.

Her mother joined in with the dragons, turning over barrels and crates.

Amy panicked. How long would it take them to figure out what she'd taken with them to sea? How long would it be before the sirens attacked them again?

As Amy ventured to the stern, a hand gripped her wrist and spun her around, facing the sea.

A low, threatening voice rasped against her ear, "Don't move, or I'll make sure the sirens find you and your secret treasure."

49
DRAGON LINEAGES

Damien

Cold water splashed into Damien's mouth, sending him upright. He coughed as smoke and ash burned his nose and eyes.

"Damien? Are you awake?" Pelias asked.

Damien coughed, wincing into the daylight. "Where am I?"

Pelias leaned over him, his dreadlocks grazing his arms. "You passed out. The storm smoke turned black, so I had to pull you back." He straightened himself, worry clouding his eyes. "Black smoke is a bad omen."

Damien stared at the dark smoke rising up into the air. The stones they had poured water over were steaming with. All he could remember was the tapestry with two coiling dragons reaching for the star of the sea. He remembered the discussion about Pherusa passing on an illness to Poseidon, possibly out of jealousy of her sister, Amphitrite. He remembered the brilliant stained glass windows shimmering above Poseidon, specifically the star Poseidon and his sons called the Dark One—Celaeno. Her light had been the darkest.

"Well? Did you see something?" Pelias asked as he set the pail aside.

Damien climbed to his feet, trying to remember the events the Tapestry of Tridents revealed to him. Poseidon knew he was dying. So did two of his sons—one from the East, and one from the West.

He stood up, shaking the sand from his pants and arms.

"Where are you going?" Pelias asked as he doused the still-smoking stones with water.

"I need to call my sister," Damien replied as he took off in a run for his cottage. He went inside retrieving his phone. It took two and a half rings before Gwen picked up.

"Oh, Damien. Thank goodness, I—"

"—Gwen, I need to ask you something about dragons."

"What? Are you kidding me? Why?"

"What do you know about Eastern and Western dragons? Specifically, what separates them?

"Eastern and Western dragons are entirely different in origin."

"What if Poseidon was a dragon?"

"I've never heard of that myth before, but I'd be open to discussing it."

"I don't have time to discuss it. I need to dissect it."

"I know that Poseidon possessed a trident, which symbolized his power over the sea."

The Tapestry of Tridents flashed before Damien again.

The tridents—they were Poseidon's *lineages*.

Mestor was Poseidon's son form the West, and Kai, from the East.

"I gotta go," Damien said as he hung up his phone. He went back out to the fire pits, which Pelias had put out with the last pail of water.

"Poseidon's sons have not only one, but *two* lineages. You have brothers from the Orient."

Pelias squinted at him as though this was not new knowledge. "Yes. Mestor and the rest of us all originate from the wester trident. We were born from the sea ice and glaciers that reside in the Atlantic Ocean."

"I thought sea ice formed in the north and southern seas near the poles."

"Form, yes. But when the ice breaks off, it combines with the currents that take it into the Atlantic and Pacific oceans."

Damien stared at the smoke that still issued out of the stones. Watching it burn reminded him of the last words Kai said as he addressed his dying father. "*Unlike Mestor, I will not flee from this illness, I will fight it.*" He glanced up, red embers flickering in his liquid eyes. "*I will not rest until I burn it all.*"

"I saw an event unfold between your father, Mestor, and another storm dragon named Kai," Damien said.

Pelias's eyes locked with his, worry flickering in them. "Ryu Ren Kai is a pyro like me. He and Mestor have long argued over who is to blame for our father's death."

"Meaning the two are still at odds?"

"Absolutely. I'd hate to think what might happen if they crossed one another again."

"Was Kai locked in the sea ice like you and your brothers by Amphitrite?"

"No. Not even the coldest sea ice could conceal his fiery soul."

Both Pelias and Damien gazed at the blackened smoke, realizing the sign of the bad omen.

"We need to reach Mestor and the others, now. Kai is out there. If they cross him, they could be in danger," Damien said.

He darted back into his cottage. What should he do with Nyssa? He couldn't just leave here here, but taking her skyward with a pyro didn't sound safe, either.

He walked to the crib, finding the blankets disturbed.

His stomach caved in. "No..."

He reached into the crib, searching for his daughter. "Nyssa is gone..."

50
THE GOD OF SHADOWS

Selia

Golden light branched out of Selia's fingertips, but not quickly enough to stop the ebony mist billowing out of the armillary sphere. Deidra and Zipper disappeared, leaving her to face the presence lurking in the darkness.

She fell into the black hole the shadows created. The whirling *whoosh* of the armillary spheres filled her ears as she was thrust into the black mist. Her body became weightless. Disembodied voices whispered, filling her mind with flashes of light.

As she fell, memories flashed before her eyes. Starlight illuminated the most powerful recent memories of her life.

Meeting Damien.

Opening the vault.

Releasing the fae queen.

Masika's vaporous threats entering her mind.

Hearing Balfour's thunderous voice for the first time.

The birth of their daughter.

Then, Damien disappearing into the night…

Her throat constricted. The last memory wasn't a memory at all. Why had she seen Damien walking away, consumed by the starlit shadows?

Her legs compressed as the gravitational force released her. She stood, her knees buckling as she tried to grasp where she was. She stood in the sky, the universe spilling around her like a starlit sea.

"Where am I?" she said, taking a step into the darkness.

A shelled creature swam up to her, encased in the liquid starlight.

"Architect, this isn't funny!" Opal said, her voice echoing out into the void of the new cosmic surroundings. *"Show yourself!"*

The universe around Selia trembled as a low voice broke. "Daughter of the moon, you witness me as I am. You are the one who has ventured into my soul."

"I'm *where?*"

"As above, so below. So I hear the riddle goes," the architect said, his voice echoing like thunder. "The great architects were created by Gaia, but our souls originate from the cosmos."

Blackness clouded out the constellations, settling around Selia as the ebony mist formed again. A giant sphinx manifested. He stood before her on four legs, a tail swishing in his wake. Shoulders scissored, and a muscular spine flexed. Every time it moved, the stars blurred, blending as though a paintbrush would mix pigments in a painting. His mane poured over his massive shoulders, offsetting him from the universe behind him. His eyes possessed the same expansive space she'd seen while gazing into the telescope—a sea of starlight.

"Who are you?" Selia asked, her voice sounding muffled in the sphinx's presence.

"I am the last architect who remains on the planet," he shifted his massive paws, each almost as big as Selia. He lowered himself, crossing one of his feet atop the other in an almost nonchalant way. "I am the god of shadows, Erebéus."

Selia held her hand over her head, shielding herself from the golden beams that poured out of his mane. For a god of shadows, he sure put off a lot of light. Damien made it sound like you were a monster."

A low, thunderous chuckle followed. "I do not appear as soft and warm to most humans. To Gaia's nymph daughters, however, I present myself much more pleasantly." His massive face came inches away from her, the strong bridge of his nose crinkling.

Selia took a step back as his whiskers grazed her.

Two giant golden eyes narrowed onto her, nearly crossing as he took her in. "You are the Blind Moon. I recognized your scent on the man who came to retrieve your inheritance from Isis's temple."

"You tried to harm this man who is my husband."

Another low chuckle erupted from everywhere this time. "Your mate is not like most men. He didn't back down when I threatened to suffocate him. Maybe I should try decapitation next time."

"You will do no such thing," Selia snapped at the cocky sphinx.

He lulled his massive head from side to side, his whiskers frilling in what could have been amusement. "How you have not made use of your inheritance by now is beyond me. I am to believe that your mate confronted me for no reason at all."

"I brought the two crystal fragments with me, but Naunet's mother confiscated them as soon as I entered the archive."

A low rumble escalated, quickly becoming a roar. His muzzle quivered in an unmistakable fit of laughter. "How is it that you let the witch of the Nile take it?"

Selia didn't know if she should laugh, or be angry with him. "If you are going to mock me, then let me go."

He shifted his massive paw forward, the pad of his foot expanding around her. "You cannot leave the stars until the other secret your heart desires is known."

Selia's mind drifted to Damien's artwork, and the notes about Celaeno. "Who took those notes about the Abyss? Was it you?"

Erebéus lowered his gaze, his giant eyelids drooping. "No. Naunet's loyal scribe still visits the cosmic center of Gaia's archive from time to time. You have no right reading them. Only I do."

"Why not?"

"I guard what remains of Naunet's work. I am highly protective of any and all of her observations of my historical greatness." He shifted his massive paws, crossing one over the other. "Why do you come to Gaia's archives, Celaeno's moon daughter?"

"I am trying to locate the third fragment of the star of the sea. I want to know what happened to Naunet after she left Egypt. Do you know where she is?"

His tail thrashed, painting the sky behind him in starlight. "I do. But even I am not able to connect with her the way I used to. My desire has long been to resurrect the bond we once had, but my descendants are making my reacquaintance with her difficult."

The way his voice drooped like his eyes made Selia wonder—what kind of relationship did Naunet have with this moody sphinx?

"Selia hasn't come all this way to listen to you complain about your bond with Naunet." Opal interjected as she swam between them, her little shell bobbing between shadows and stars. *"She needs to find the Temple of the Three Origins so she can access Gaia's Codex."*

Erebéus batted his giant golden eyes, and a great wind swept around her. "For what purpose do you need to access the Codex?"

Selia swallowed. "I am trying to find the third and last crystal fragment of my inheritance."

Erebéus blinked his giant golden eyes three times, seeming to withdraw into his own thoughts. "An inheritance that I requested Amphitrite to fragment, a choice I regret to this day." He crossed one paw over the other. "The Codex resides in the Temple of the Three Origins. Entering the temple will require you to answer a riddle. I am the one who decides who enters, and who leaves the temple."

"Why do you regret having Amphitrite fragment the star of the sea?"

Erebéus lowered his head. "One does not question the great sphinx before he presents his riddle."

Well then, present it to me."

"A riddle presented by an architect can be dangerous. One must be willing to give a piece of themselves in exchange for entrance."

Selia studied his regal face, searching for any sign that he might be lying to her. His ears flicked back and forth as he awaited her answer. "I'm guessing this temple is named after three separate origins, correct? That means I would need to give you not one, but *three* answers to your riddle?"

"Yes. The temple houses three chambers, each granting passage to souls as they depart the world of the living and move on to the next. Record of these souls are all documented within Gaia's Codex."

Selia thought back to what Mestor had said about what made origin bonds so special. "Origin bonds do not break, not even in death."

"You know more than what I had assumed of you, daughter of the moon. Do you even know what the three origins are? Rather, do you know the true name of the temple?"

Selia shook her head. "No, I do not."

"Then the riddle is settled. If you can guess the name of all three origins, then I will grant you access not only to Gaia's Codex, but to the temple."

Selia straightened herself. Guessing three different names shouldn't be that difficult, right? "What happens if I get your riddle wrong?"

A low rumble echoed around her as Erebéus's laughter filled the universe. "Your soul will remain with me in the temple. You have one opportunity to get it right."

"Selia deserves to see some clues, which I will provide her. She's smart. She will figure your riddle out." Opal chimed into her head, her voice an octave higher than it had been.

Selia swallowed. Opal sure seemed to have faith in her ability to outwit the god of shadows.

PART 6
ORIGIN RIDDLE

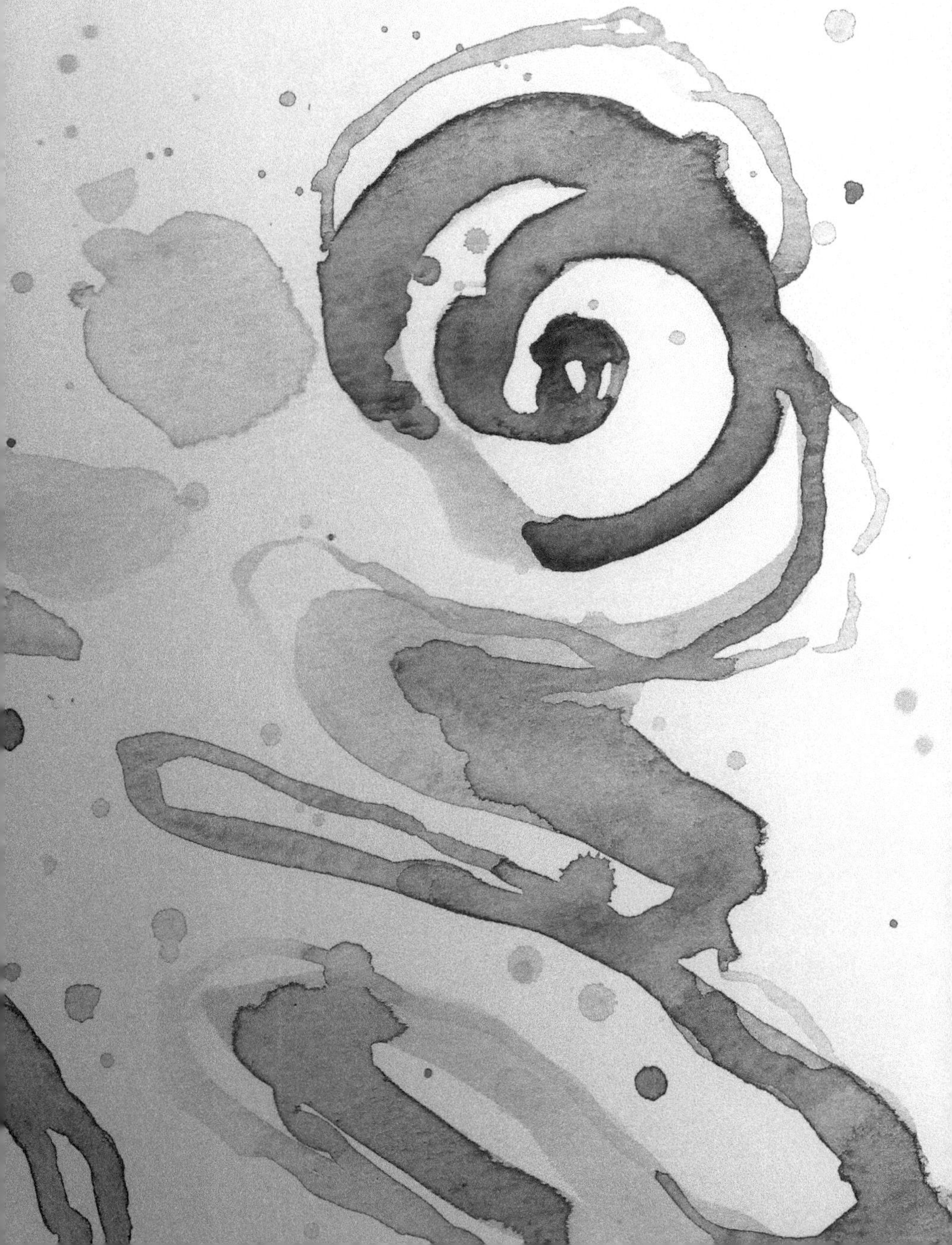

51
RYU REN KAI

Amy

Amy's wrists were tied behind her back. She was tugged into the hard body of whoever had taken her hostage. A firm, callused hand gripped her arms, restraining her.

"Amy!" her mother cried.

Lachlan grabbed Amphitrite's arm, pulling her back. Both had fear and anger glinted in their eyes. The blurry image of Amy's captor reflected in them.

"Back off now, or she's dead," the man breathed across the cusp of Amy's ear as his long black nails grazed her neck.

"What do you want?" Amphitrite asked, her voice breaking. "Please don't hurt my daughter."

Amy's body shook as her captor strung her closer to his body. "I want Mestor to show his ugly face and stop cowering away like he always did when it came to the wishes of our father."

Amy's body seized as adrenaline coursed through her. He mentioned *our* father. Did that mean he was also one of Poseidon's sons?

Hopleas and Taras appeared behind Lachlan and her mother. "Ryu Ren Kai, the lotus dragon from the Orient," they both said in unison.

Amy's mind blanked. Since when were there oriental storm dragons? The only sons of Poseidon she knew of were the ones who lived in the Atlantic sea.

A plume of mist blew onto the boat. Mestor manifested between the others. His dreadlocks swung into his face as his chest and arm muscles flexed. "Go back to the orient, Kai," Mestor growled back at him. "Or have you forgotten what my tail feels like against your ribs?"

Kai snarled, his hard body forcing Amy forward. "Who is navigating in your party? You're in my territory, Mestor. Go back to the Western sea ice, or I'll send you there myself." He swung her around. Tossing his arm out, he threw Amy toward her mother.

Lachlan grabbed her, slinging her back behind Mestor.

Amy got a glimpse of the oriental storm dragon. A long red robe dressed his body. He wore black pants and no shoes. His arms were gauntlet free. Tattoos that resembled smoke coiled up his arms, branching out into black flames that licked up his taught neck muscles. His build was nowhere near as bulky as Mestor. But what he lacked in size, he made up for in elegance. His body was long and lean, his face narrow, with high cheek bones and eyes that flickered more than they swam.

Kai's dark eyes flickered red as he stared down his brother. "The moment I smelled your scales, I thought I was dreaming. But no. You and your brothers are back in the sea, making waves over something that should have died long ago."

Mestor's back muscles clenched so tightly, his shoulder blades cracked. A ridge of sharp scales rippled along his spine, slicing through his tunic. "You have no right to interfere with my mission to find our father's crown."

"I question your loyalty to our father." Kai shot back, his eyes burning like red embers. "Our father became ill with the salt venom because you abandoned Celaeno's territory."

Mestor tossed his hands into the air, making his silver gauntlets quake. Electrical sparks flew, raining down on Kai.

The oriental dragon didn't flinch. The sparks ignited his robes, burning out as quickly as they formed. He took a step toward Mestor, making the entire boat shift. "Your abandonment meant one thing—the death of our father, you murderer."

Amy glanced at her mother. "Is Kai blaming Mestor for Poseidon's death?"

Amphitrite sighed. "Yes. The Fighting between these two was what caused me to put Mestor into an icy slumber. They nearly ripped each other apart."

"Why did you put Mestor and his brothers into a sleep, and not Kai?"

"Kai's temper is flammable. Not even I was able to keep him locked within the ice."

Kai shook his hands, which both began to glow orange. "You are no longer in the Atlantic, but the Pacific Ocean, meaning one thing." Flames sparked out of his fingers. "You've come into the Eastern territory."

Mestor threw his head back, sending his dreadlocks swinging as he laughed. "Impossible. We departed land well within the range of Western Seas."

Kai's eyes darkened. "Have you lost your ability to navigate?"

"There's only one way to find out what sea we are really in," Mestor concluded as he squared his hips, dipping his shoulders forward.

He lunged for Kai.

In a fit of muscle and mist, Mestor grabbed Kai around the center and took him overboard.

Amy ran to the side of the boat as both dragons plummeted into the sea. A cloud sea spray erupted, sending icy sparks showing over the boat.

"Great. We're going to want to move, now," Taras said.

"What are they doing?" Amy stammered as the clouds above the *Sea Dragon* darkened.

Hopleus grabbed her and Amphitrite's hands, steering them away from the railing. "Rivals from the East and the West are doing what all storm dragons do to settle an argument—they're building a cyclone."

The sea and sky came alive in a matter of moments. Lightning bolted between clouds, sending violent rumbles of thunder overhead.

Lachlan remained at the edge of the boat, craning his neck as the storm manifested. "Are you kidding? A dragon fight?"

Amy wrenched away from Hopleus, grabbing Lachlan's shoulder and tugging him back. "What are you doing? We need to get your boat away from them!"

Lachlan disappeared into the inner quarters of his boat. Amy followed.

The motor revved to life, jolting the boat forward.

As soon as the scent of exhaust filled the cab, sparks jolted out of the dash.

"Shit," he stammered, backing away from the smoke. "They've short-circuited my engine."

"What do we do?" Amy asked.

"I'm not going to hide in here and wait out this storm," he said, grabbing Amy's hand. "I'm going to watch."

A thrill of panic and excitement danced in Amy's stomach as she dashed with Lachlan out onto the boat deck. They climbed onto the upper level, taking the ladder up above the cab.

Mestor and Kai swam alongside each other, sizing each other up. Scars lined their bodies, likely from territorial disputes with one another. Kai's body was long and angular, but not any less intimidating than Mestor's shark-like dragon form. His head was slender, with a dark red snout that tapered into brighter yellow, white, and orange scales that formed a strong ridge above his orange eyes. He resembled a manta ray with his long, sleek fins, paired black and white coloring. Kai was quick and agile, slicing through the waves with little to no effort.

What agility Mestor lacked, he made up for with brute force. He slammed into Kai's side, ripping a chunk of scales from his dorsal fin as he ran one of his jagged spines past his dragon rival from the orient.

Kai's tail thrashed as a shower of red and orange scales spilled into the sea. "You were always quick to turn your fins into daggers when threatened."

"Strike first, ask for forgiveness later," Mestor growled. He swung his tail this time, which Kai quickly ducked beneath.

Membranous fins sprang from Kai's spine, transforming his back into a brilliant display of red, orange, and yellow. Black spikes layered each fin, attaching them together. The oriental dragon thrashed his body, waving his fins in a way that created an illusion that the sea had caught fire.

"Who rules the seas now, Mestor, son of the Western ice," Kai hissed, his fins stretching and retracting. As he arched his head back, and opened his long, lean mouth, a horrible sound churned from deep within his throat. Flames poured into the sea, igniting the salt venom.

Amy jumped away from the railing as the flames tore up into the air. The heat was warm enough to singe the tips of her hair.

While Mestor thrashed his tail, the water near him froze, forming into a glistening sheet of sea ice.

Lachlan grabbed Amy around the center. "Okay, I think it's time we shelter ourselves."

Lachlan descended the ladder first. Amy followed.

Mestor swung his massive tail, slamming it down not far from the boat. The ice shattered, sending shards flying into the air.

As Mestor's tail rose from the sea in another attempt to shatter his icy creation, a fiery blast of air burst up from the sea, forcing Amy to release her grip on the ladder.

She hit the water, spiraling down into the current. Surprisingly, the water was much calmer beneath the terrible tempers flaring on the surface. Tails coiled, and fins thrashed as the battle ensued. She kicked her legs and dove, hoping to distance herself from the cyclone as ice and flames danced with one another.

She blinked a few times, blinded by a bright silver light. Something large and luminous pulsed beneath her. A massive silver orb glowed beneath the two dragons, its warm yet cool light beckoning her.

Balfour's onyx tail coiled around the silver sphere. His fins sprang out, framing his large glowing head as he coiled upward. Brilliant silver light poured out of his eyes as he swam through the orb.

"*Ceeeeleeeeaaanooooooo*," he bellowed, his voice filling the ocean.

The light blew up into the current, ripping apart the cyclone.

Amy gasped as she surfaced. Seafoam coated the waves as ice melted and flames were extinguished.

Mestor bobbed in the water in his human form, mangled and defeated.

Kai was nowhere.

Amy swam for Mestor, grabbing his arm and tugging him onto Balfour's scaly side. A chunk of his hair was missing, and a giant blue gash spread across his arm.

52
MAERA'S MESSAGE
Damien

Damien had turned over his studio three times before he collapsed to the ground. Nyssa had been sleeping in her crib, and now she was gone.

Pelias crouched next to him, his features blurring from all of the adrenaline. "Don't panic yet. Could she have crawled out of her crib?"

Damien shook his head. "I don't know, I..." His voice trembled so violently, he thought he would be sick. "How am I going to tell Selia?"

Pelias's brow furrowed. "We will find her."

Peppercorn flit between Damien and the storm dragon like she had for the twentieth time. Damien had lost count of how many times the bat almost clipped him with her wing. She landed onto one of his easels, making one of his paintings bow.

A piece of paper fell out from the concept he'd painted for Maera over a decade ago.

He grabbed the parchment and unfolded it. His moonlit signature had been drawn in blue ink at the top.

Damien,

Your daughter is with me. I have taken her to the place where I know Selia will find use for her inheritance. In order to find me, you must bring me the two crystal fragments of the star of the sea. To

**find your daughter, you must seek out the darkest
star in the ocean.**
   Only the ancestor of Poseidon knows my origin.

Maera

Damien dropped the note, shaking.

Peppercorn landed on his shoulder. She immediately began to make soft chirping sounds. While the noises might have been her attempt to comfort, all it did was annoy him. "Why would she take her?"

Pelias's gaze hardened. "She? Who else did you encounter from the storm smoke?"

"It's complicated."

"Complicated enough not to discuss who took your daughter?"

Damien's fists clenched. "All right. My deceased wife has been haunting me over the past few days. I only learned recently that she was a sea nymph."

Pelias's grabbed the note from the ground and began to read it. "*Maera* has been haunting you?" He glanced up from the letter. "Why didn't you tell me sooner?"

"Do you know about her?"

"*Know* about her? All of Poseidon's sons were required to report their storm bonds to her, both in Egypt, and Atlantis. As Naunet's scribe, we were responsible for reporting any and all bonds we could form with sea nymphs as they were a vital component for keeping the Abyss healthy." He handed the letter back to Damien. "During Atlantis, the record of these bonds were woven into a giant tapestry."

"The Tapestry of Tridents?" Damien asked.

Pelias nodded. "Yes. This tapestry illustrated the two storm dragon lineages. It was housed in the temple of Salt, Storms, and Starlight."

Damien's mind returned to the interaction he'd seen inside the temple. Above the argument between Poseidon and his two sons from the East and the West, artwork of sea nymphs had been depicted in a brilliant display of stained glass.

Celaeno's window, despite her darkness, had stood out the most against the six others.

"The darkest star, that must mean Celaeno," Damien said, eyeing the letter. "According to Selia, this is where her salt ancestry originates from."

"But Celaeno's territory no longer exists within our father's crown," Pelias argued.

Damien eyed the note. "This part about only Poseidon's ancestor knowing her origin? She's saying that I need to speak with Erebéus." He grabbed his hair, spiking it out from his head. "We can't do anything until we've met with Selia first. She has the other two fragments of the crystal. Maera stated in her letter that she needed them."

He left the cottage, followed by Pelias. "We need to find Selia now. Spread your fins and take me to her!"

Pelias shook his head. "We cannot leave. If we do, we could miss a message from our ancestors."

"What are you talking about? Are you crazy? I need to find Selia, now!"

Pelias ignored him, grabbing another piece of driftwood and piled it on top of the others. "Before we do anything, we must ask our ancestors for guidance by turning to the storm smoke."

53

THE THIRD ORIGIN

Selia

As Erebéus retreatedinto his shadows, Selia weighed her options. Either she could try and solve his riddle to gain access to both the Codex and the Temple of the Three Origins, or she could pick up where she and Deidra left off trying to explore their way through the archive.

Either way, she wasn't leaving the museum until she took back the crystals Pherusa had stolen. After mocking her, the god of shadows admitted to having the same goal—to find the last midwife of the sea.

What had prevented him from finding Naunet if they had bonded with one another? Could origin bonds die? If so, what would it take to resurrect one?

The universe surrounding Selia changed, morphing into a landscape. Her heels sank into warm sand. The scent of spice drifted on the air as a temple came into view.

Her breath caught. The Temple of Isis manifested before her.

"*Let's go inside*!" Opal said as she swam alongside Selia in the Nile.

As Selia ascended the stone steps to enter the temple, Erebéus manifested before her again. He resumed the form of a sphinx, folding himself at the top of the stairs as he guarded the entrance.

His giant golden eyes settled onto her. "I will give you but one clue. The Temple of the Three Origins pertains to the origins of sea nymphs, storm dragons, and the great architects."

"I know the name of the origin of sea nymphs, the Abyss," Selia replied.

Erebéus thrashed his tail. "The Abyss is not the correct answer."

Selia's stomach hollowed. Had she already failed?

Erebéus lowered his head, propping his muzzle onto his massive paws. A look of amusement took over his expression. "What constellation is the Abyss composed of?"

"The Pleiades, or the seven ancestral salt mothers."

Erebéus blinked once.

Selia's heart leapt. *"Salt* is the first origin?"

Erebéus blinked a second time, his eyelids lulling over his giant golden eyes. "You are correct. Salt is the first chamber within the temple, which symbolizes the origin for sea nymphs. But you have two other origins to guess before I can grant you access."

"Meaning storm dragons are next," Selia said as a giant crack of thunder rumbled overhead. Raindrops dolloped onto her head and shoulders as lightning riped through the clouds. "Balfour called it the Great Storm."

Erebéus blinked once. "The Great Storm is not the correct term. There is another name you must give to me, one that is equivalent to the Abyss."

"*I know,*" Opal bubbled. "*Think about what a storm out at sea is called, the one that creates big, powerful waves.*"

"A hurricane?" Selia suggested.

"Silence!" Erebéus bellowed as he shook his head, sending raindrops into Selia's face. His mane stood on end, making him appear as a giant sun.

Selia remembered what Balfour had compared Mestor's temper to during the bonfire. "How about a *tsunami*?"

Erebéus blinked twice. "You are correct. Storms is the name of the second chamber, which is also called the Great Tsunami. This is the origin of storm dragons."

"Two down, one to go," Selia said, hope brimming in her voice.

Erebéus stood, his giant form evaporating as his voice echoed around her. "To know my origin, you must know the sea nymph to which I was last bonded with."

Selia squinted toward the temple's entrance. Two figures were fast approaching her. She ducked down the stairs and tucked behind the papyrus as two sea nymphs strode down the bank of the Nile. The second sea nymph had dark hair, honey brown skin, and dark liquid eyes.

Selia's stomach hollowed. Naunet was walking next to another sea nymph. She followed them, keeping a safe distance as to not be seen. The two sea nymphs weren't children, but they weren't quite adults, either. They both appeared to be somewhere in their teen years.

Naunet stopped along the trail, and Selia dipped back into the reeds as the other sea nymph grabbed her hand. "Your mother requested that I work as your scribe in the temple as you and I share the same salt ancestry. Is there anything you need of me?"

Naunet's shoulders rolled forward. "Maera, I wish you could help me convince my mother not to pass along her responsibilities to me before I'm ready."

Maera nodded, releasing Naunet's hand. "That's why she requested that I help you. I'll see you at the temple later. I can't wait to hear about how your initiation goes with Erebéus."

Naunet glanced away from her. "If it's anything like my mother said hers went in Atlantis, I'm not going to be excited for it."

As Maera headed back to the temple, Naunet kept walking toward the river.

It took all of Selia's strength to not reach out and touch her.

Naunet walked past her crouched in the reeds, heading for where Opal's blue tiger striped shell bobbed in the water. She bent down, scooping the ammonite into her hands. "Wait until I tell you what I learned about being the midwife of the sea today," she said, her voice younger than Selia remembered. "Mother wants me to bond with Erebéus before I'm ready."

"You will be a great midwife of the sea. Take it from me. I remember some issues your mother had in Atlantis with him, but that doesn't mean you too, will experience them. Why does she want you to bond with him early?"

"She wants to pass along her responsibilities to me. As you know, she and Erebéus have never gotten along with each other."

"I can't wait for you to take over. You care about extinct fae like me."

"But you're *not* extinct."

"Not everyone believes that," Opal said back. *"Unlike your mother, you are one of the few sea nymphs who finds a useful purpose for me."*

Naunet's shoulders rose and fell. "What if Erebéus doesn't like me?"

"Don't be afraid. Architects aren't as scary as they seem. They're all riddles and shadows, but Gaia created them that way for a purpose."

"Mother makes it sound as though he's a monster at times."

Opal thrashed one of her tentacles out of her shell. *"Sometimes monsters make things interesting."*

The sound of crying filled her ears, followed by a horrible stench. Her feet burned hot in the sand as a red horizon burned in the distance. She couldn't differentiate what was water, and what was the night sky. A dark, oil-slick film coated the entire surface of the Nile.

Selia took off in a run. The mangled remains of sea nymphs were scattered along the riverbank. A mother's hand outstretched to grab her infant.

This wasn't a memory—this was *hell*.

She dug her heels into the sand as another figure appeared.

Pherusa crouched over one of the mangled bodies. Her face was tilted down, disheveled strands of her sleek dark hair tumbling across her face as she tended to one of the victims. A sob escaped her. "Maera is dead. You will no longer have the assistance of your faithful scribe. She's been claimed by the salt venom, just like your sister."

Tears streamed down Naunet's face, streaking through the dirt and blood caked on her skin. Her hands were coated in the black oil-slick substance. "Mother, please. I can't do this, I—"

Slap!

Pherusa straightened herself after she struck her daughter. "This is *your* fault," she scolded. "You *never* should have formed that bond with Erebéus without first consulting with me."

Naunet held her hand to her cheek, her blood mixing with the black substance on her fingers as she wiped both her blood and tears away. "I didn't know this would happen. I didn't know so many would die."

"They are not dead," Pherusa corrected. "Celaeno is. The victims of the plague have no origin to return to, no afterlife."

The hum of salt fly wings buzzed in the air as the fae parasites swarmed around them. "You are the sea's midwife. It is your responsibility to tend to the souls of sea nymphs—both who enter this world, and those who leave it. As the new midwife of the sea, you must come up with a solution on how to fix this."

Naunet's eyes swept over the carnage, white with fear, and black with the mangled bodies the salt venom had claimed.

Selia's throat closed.

She couldn't breathe.

"Please, Opal," she wheezed. "I can't see anymore of this. It's too much."

"*Hold on*," Opal said.

The gentle sound of water trickling through stone filled Selia's ears as a new memory manifested. Deciduous trees crowed the landscape. A red temple with strong curved beams framing the roof loomed in the distance. The air was full of moisture, and the landscape supported a river that was clean.

A brilliant wooden red bridge arched over the river, on which a tall, lean man stood. He wore long red robes. A black and white mask concealed the upper half of his face.

A woman wearing a red kimono approached him, stopping at his side.

He pulled her into an embrace. He held out his other hand and unfolded his fingers, revealing a beautiful blue bloom. He tucked the flower into her hair. "You are safe from your mother and my ancestor while you are with me, my Dark One."

The scene changed, thrusting Selia toward the temple behind the river. Large white doors framed the building.

A platter of tea cups sat atop a table surrounded with cushions. The same woman who the man with the dragon mask had embraced knelt at the table, and began pouring the tea.

"Naunet," A woman said from the far corner of the room.

Naunet glanced up from her teacup. Her face was so different from before. New lines creased behind her eyes, and her mouth appeared sour. "Maera? Is that really you?"

"Yes, Naunet. It's me."

Naunet nearly dropped the tea kettle as she stood. "How are you here? How did you *find* me?"

"The salt venom tells me things that I know you too have begun to hear," Maera said, her eyes dipping to the tea Naunet had prepared.

"You died. I saw what the salt venom did to—" Naunet's gaze as she reached out and touched her face. "How is this possible? My mother and I disposed of your body."

Maera grabbed Naunet's hand and lowered it to her side. "I exist in a place between life and death. But I can only visit you temporarily."

"Why? What prevented you from becoming a siren like the other plague victims?" Naunet asked. "Why have you come to the Orient?"

"I did something in Atlantis that I never shared with you. Something to Poseidon." She glanced up at a man wearing a mask lingering in the doorway. "I cannot share what I did to him here. You must return to Egypt."

"I refuse. I do not trust the architect, nor do I wish to see him ever again."

Maera's gaze returned to the tea. "Erebéus allowed me to live on. You should not dismiss him so easily. His shadows have given me a new body. I am tethered to his origin."

Naunet's eyes widened. "This is Erebéus's doing?"

Maera nodded. You cannot hide in the East forever. Come back to Egypt. The Order needs you to pick up where you left off with the Codex. Your mother has been searching for you."

Naunet glanced down at the tea she was busy preparing. "The salt venom has changed who I am." She glanced up at Maera. "I doubt that my mother will even recognize me."

"It has changed me, too," Maera said, taking up Naunet's hand. She set a crystal into her palm.

"Why have you brought a piece of the star of the sea here?" Naunet asked.

"As your scribe, I need to know what you intend for it. Isis is no longer present within her temple. I need to know if should you disappear, who you wish to inherit it."

"Nobody would find use for a broken star. Erebéus had the crystal fragmented because he did not trust my mother. But I do not trust him. I've considered severing my bond with him."

Maera's brow furrowed. "By what means? I cannot imagine how an origin bond could ever be severed."

Naunet grabbed a small vase, tipping its contents into her tea. A single drop landed in her cup, changing the water from green, to ebony. "By using the substance that destroyed my people. Why can't I use the salt venom to destroy the bond I have with him?"

As Naunet and Maera faded, the starlit universe returned to Selia's surroundings. A silhouette appeared before her. No longer a sphinx, Erebéus took the form of a human man. His upper torso was bare. A kilt dressed his lower half. He stood barefooted before her. The headdress of a pharaoh adorned his head and neck, draping over his shoulders where there had previously been a golden mane of fur.

He towered over her, darkness spilling out of his sides. "You have seen pieces of Naunet's past as fragmented as the crystal you desire to possess. Now you must answer the final piece of my riddle—what is the name of my origin?"

"I have some questions I need you to answer first. Maera died, but stated that you helped her. She said she is tethered to your origin within the temple. She's trapped, isn't she?"

"One could say so."

"What did she do to Poseidon that resulted in her becoming trapped in the temple?"

"I cannot say."

"You are lying. You are a god of shadows. Even Amphitrite said you have a record of all of your descendants. You cared about Naunet. You should know who cared about her after she left you."

Erebéus shifted his feet, not taking his eyes off her. "I will give you but one final clue. Darkness held in the deepest places of one's soul is what separates the Great Storm from my origin. Tell me the name of my origin, Blind Moon. Answer correctly, and I will grant you access to the temple."

Selia shivered. Something wasn't right. "I don't feel comfortable guessing the name of your origin yet. You haven't show me what you're hiding in your shadows about Maera."

His eyes shifted, great pools of starlight shining from their ebony depths. Had she outwitted the riddling sphinx?

"You risk losing your inheritance if you neglect my riddle," Erebéus said. "What is borrowed from the Codex must return to the shadows, eventually."

"Then I'll wait."

Erebéus's body withdrew into the universe he embodied. "As you wish, Blind Moon. Naunet would be proud of you."

54
BONFIRE AT SEA
Amy

Mestor's body floated in the ocean, blue pouring out of him. Amy hadn't seen a storm dragon bleed before, but she assumed the blue liquid spilling out of the gash on his shoulder was blood. It pooled around Mestor's arm, coating his silver gauntlets as it trickled down his thick forearms.

She bobbed in the current, quickly finding refuge in Balfour's mass as he coiled around her and his eldest brother's mangled body. Mestor floated face up, his mouth blue with his own blood.

"Amy! Are you all right?" Lachlan yelled from the boat.

"I'm fine," Amy replied, glancing down at Mestor.

Lachlan tossed a net into the water. "I'll pull you up!"

Amy didn't grab the net. She clutched a handful of Mestor's thick soggy dreads, refusing to let him go.

"Let me tend to him," Amphitrite said as she approached the gruesome aftermath of the fight between the two dragons. She grabbed one of Balfour's membranous fins drifting in the water and hoisted herself onto his back. Hair dripping, and eyes bright with concern, she inspected the victim of the fight.

"Is he going to be okay?" Amy asked, scared beyond reason. What would they do if the storm dragon leading their expedition couldn't lead any longer?

Her mother leaned down, grazing her lips past his forehead.

Amy blinked a few times, trying to register what she witnessed. Did she just *kiss* him?

Mestor's nose bunched, and his lips quivered. His eyes remained closed.

"I think he's going to be fine," Amphitrite said as she straightened herself.

"What about Kai?" Amy asked.

Lykos's viridian fins sliced through the water as he rose his head out of the sea. "Hopleus and I have checked, he's long gone. He either blew into the next sea, or dove so deeply that we've lost his scent."

All five dragons lifted their heads out of the sea to inspect their eldest brother.

Balfour's onyx head, however, remained beneath the water.

Amy heard him mumbling something under his breath about how *stupidly cocky* his brother was. Another grouchy fragment of his voice drifted into her head, "*all because he had to prove his tail was bigger.*"

"He's still unconscious," Amy said, gripping onto Balfour's fins.

Amphitrite said as she set her wet hand on his forehead. She closed her eyes, and chanted. "Salt from the sea, I ask that you send. A remedy for this dragon's body, so he may quickly mend."

The wound sealed, new silvery blue scales forming along his shoulder as they quickly formed a scab. She glanced around the group. "I think there has been enough adventure for the day. We need to rest and prepare for the last stretch of our journey." She glanced up at the sky. "Besides, tonight the moon will give us clarity on when we need to dive."

Amy worked with Lachlan and the other dragons on the boat to prepare for their evening at sea, while Mestor remained unconscious. They'd hoisted him on the boat deck, and wrapped him in a few blankets, and propped against a stack of crates. Her mother checked on him ever once in a while, touching the scales where his wound had been, or simply to brush his lumpy dreadlocks out of his eyes.

In the passing moments, it occurred to Amy that she had never seen her mother love another in a romantic way. Sure, they had been apart for centuries. She could have had multiple lovers during that time. But her mother's love for the sea and her creatures always took priority over forming a relationship of her own.

"Oi, that's the last of it," Lachlan said as he pried open another crate with food rations.

"Idas, help me out!" Hopleus yelled as he tugged a net full of fish up from the water. The two storm dragons began sorting through their catch.

"Had it not been for Balfour, Kai and Mestor might have ripped each other to pieces," Taras said as he released an octopus back into the sea.

"At least we got rid of him," Lykos said.

While Lachlan worked with the others, Balfour approached Amy. He reached out his hand. A blackened crystal sat in his palm. "*This is what Kai was searching for.*"

Amy's stomach pitted. "Give it back."

Balfour's nostrils flared. "*You've had this on you the entire time,*" he said, anger trembling in his voice. "*This crystal fragment once belonged to the goddess of death. How did you come into possession of it?*"

"I don't need to tell you that," Amy replied.

Balfour withdrew his hand. "*Someone must have given it to you and told you to keep it secret.*"

Amy jolted. Did Balfour now about Maera?

"Balfour, stop slacking and help us! We don't know how to get a fire going without Pelias!"

Before Amy could harass Balfour to give back the crystal fragment, he spun on his heal and headed for his brothers.

"Kai!" Mestor yelled as he sat up. His eyes bulged as his arms swung forward.

"Kai isn't here," Lykos said, abandoning the net and grabbing his brother's swinging arm.

"What happened? I had his neck in my teeth," Mestor spat, reaching his finger into his mouth and tugging out an orange scale. "That bastard got away, didn't he?"

"Your brother from the Orient is no longer a threat, for now," Amphitrite said as she approached Mestor and dropped to his side. "But I suggest we use the moon tonight to plan on when we dive to find the crown. The sooner, the better."

Mestor's blue eyes swept to Amy's mother, dilating as he found her. "What's preventing me from going after him again?"

"He took a chunk out of your arm," she scolded.

"Kai's teeth are no match for mine," Mestor growled up at her.

Amy didn't dare make eye contact with the blue eyed dragon. But blue eyed sailor would do. Lachlan kept gazing at her, a smirk on his lips.

He knew what her secret was. Would he continue to help her keep it?

Mestor grabbed her mother's hand, bringing her fingers to his lips, which he kissed. "I would go to the end of the sea to ensure you are safe from Kai's flames."

Amphitrite flushed as she stood, pulling her hand away from him. "You will do no such thing."

Mestor gazed down at his shoulder. "You did this to me, didn't you? I recognize the mending techniques of a sea goddess. Your touch makes my scales shimmer like the moon."

Orange daylight painted Amphitrite's face as the sun kissed the horizon. Her freckles turned bright red as Mestor's gaze returned to her. The sea nymph and the storm dragon gazed upon one another, timeless forces making Amy wonder if either knew what to do with their quest forward.

Once a few metal barrels were rolled together, the evening festivities could finally ignite. Lykos threw his arm out, clashing his gauntlet past Hopleus's. Sparks erupted into the barrels, igniting the driftwood inside.

Amy's stomach hadn't stopped doing somersaults ever since Balfour walked off with her crystal fragment. What was he planning to do with it? She had to steal it back from him.

"Let's get this fire started. I'm hungry," Hopleus stammered as he layered fresh fish skewers across the top of a barrel.

"You're always hungry," Idas scolded, layering more food across the flames licking up toward the night sky.

"Didn't you just eat fifty clams before we swam our asses out here?" Lykos asked as he carved a long pinky finger claw across a piece of driftwood, hollowing its center.

"Bottom dwellers aren't what they used to be," Hopleus grunted. "A storm dragon with my appetite needs to act like he's eating for at least twenty."

Amy couldn't help but laugh. Somehow, this journey to sea reminded her very much of Winter Forest. While she wasn't landlocked and surrounded by thousands of snowy trees, she was still surrounded by far too much testosterone. And unlike Ewan's men, each one of Balfour's brothers had a very prominent personality. They didn't do blindly as they were told, but argued while still enjoying each other's company.

As her mother sat by the fire, the flames turning her already flaming hair aglow, memories of Amy's own childhood in Atlantis began to play before her with the help of Poseidon's sons. The music. The festivals. The gatherings, all long gone. Events her ancestors used to spend weeks celebrating had been buried in her past for so long.

"Amphitrite, I thought you said the moon was going to help guide our voyage," Mestor grumbled, glancing up at the sky. "There is no moon. Look how dark she is tonight!"

"It's a new moon. Sometimes darkness is what we must cross in order for us to see the light in our journey," Amphitrite replied.

Amy caught her mother's gaze from across the fire. She knew what darkness she was referring to. Losing two people she had loved was not something she ever wanted to experience again.

Balfour stood across the fire from Amy, folding his arms across his chest. He kept his dark eyes settled upon her, a glare unlike any she'd seen in the usually calm and collected storm dragon.

Lykos trilled out a Celtic tune on his flute. Taras joined him, their dueling jig reeling until the flames in the barrels burned up into the air.

Idas and Hopleus rotated the skewers over the flames. As they prepared the food, they began to sing in an Atlantean language.

"What are they saying?" Amy asked.

"*A song of the old storms, the ones that originally shaped the skis and seas. How the moon cried her tears, marrying them together,*" Balfour replied to her mind.

Amy glanced over at her mother with Mestor. "What does it translate to?" she asked, knowing the language of Atlantis was long gone.

"Only when the stars meet the sea, will my truth be known," Balfour replied, his voice ringing out into the open. "Even the brightest stars in the sky find their origin in the darkest waters of the ocean."

Amy's heart trembled at the sound of his voice out in the open. Maybe it was the words, or his sound. But the magic it brought to the atmosphere made the music die.

Lykos and Taras quieted their driftwood whistles.

"Your voice is beautiful," Amphitrite said. "I wish you would speak aloud more often."

At her words, Mestor shot a jealous glance toward his youngest brother.

With one swift movement, Balfour tilted his head up and leaned back. A giant *splash* confirmed he'd fallen into the sea.

"Balfour, wait!" Amy stammered as she jumped to her feet.

"Oi, he's gone for a night's swim is all," Lykos said, waving his hand. "After the stress of today, I might consider joining him."

Panic erupted in Amy's chest. What did he plan to do with her crystal fragment?

As the music continued and the festivities heated up, Amy left the fire, too emotional with the turn of events. She found herself standing at the edge of the boat, trying to come up with a plan.

"Amy, come look at this," Lachlan's voice rang from the dark.

She followed his voice, trailing away from the chanting around the fire. As soon as the firelight faded, the cloak of night embraced her. The cold. The dark. The salt. How long had it been since she'd gazed up into the inky blackness so full of the light of her ancestors?

"Where are you?" she said, searching for the fisherman.

Lachlan climbed the metal ladder, hoisting himself up onto the boat. He stood there, panting and dripping.

Her heart stopped. A glowing Celtic knot tattoo of a stag branched across his chest.

She looked away as he jumped onto the boat deck and shook out his wet hair like a dog. The last thing she needed was for him to think that she was checking him out.

He tugged his sodden shirt over his head and let it fall on the boat deck. Those well-defined muscles came out in the open, veins snaking up his forearms to his biceps.

"You are going to freeze out here," Amy scolded him.

Lachlan's damp stubble caught the light of the sea. His chest flexed as he reached over his head to stretch, further exposing his muscular physique. "Nah, I run pretty warm." He lowered his arms as he approached her. He came up behind her, setting his arms on the railing. His lips grazed the cusp of her ear. "It's not every day you get to see the heart of the sea light up with a sea nymph."

His heart crashed against Amy's back. His scent of fresh wind and salt washed over her. She found herself leaning back into his body, loving his solidness. Even if his pants were still dripping wet, his body put of an incredible amount of warmth.

His foot slipped out to her side.

She grabbed his arm as he tumbled forward.

In one swift motion, both of them fell overboard.

Cold water flooded Amy's senses as she surfaced. "You pulled me in!" she scolded.

"I did not!" He yelled back at her as he bobbed in the current.

They splashed each other. Their combined laughter erupted over the water.

Lachlan thrashed in the surf, his head dipping under. Soon, Amy was left bobbing in the ocean, great waves and pulsing light surging around her.

"Lachlan, this isn't funny!" she cried.

Bubbles erupted out of the water where he had been moments before.

Drat.

The current had caught him. She sucked in a deep breath and dove after him.

55

TWO FLAMES

Damien

Hours passed. Damien couldn't think. All he could do was watch Pelias prepare another one of his stupid bonfires as the sun set on the horizon. Anger branched through him, splitting up his spine.

He kicked one of the piles of driftwood, sending splinters and ash flying. "That's it. I'm done with this sitting around and watching this storm smoke shit."

"Hey, quit it," Pelias said, shielding his face from the ash.

"There's only so much you can count on your ancestors for," Damien spat at him. He took off in a mad run for the sea. "Maera! I won't let you do this to me!"

When he reached the waves, his heels tore into sodden sand, forcing him to slow. He fell to his knees, unable to see straight from the adrenaline blurring his vision.

Slamming his fists into the sand, a sob escaped him. His body had gone numb. Even the urge to breathe seemed pointless. He'd allowed his daughter to be taken away from him.

Vision swaying, he blinked. It had to be a mirage. A man walked toward him, long black hair draping over his shoulders. His black pants and red robe were ripped in places.

"What are you looking at?" he growled as he stopped before Damien, picking what appeared to be a sharp tooth out of his forearm.

"Who the heck are you?" Damien asked the newcomer.

"I followed the storm smoke, thinking that more storm dragons might be nearby. I didn't expect to find a man crying by the sea."

Damien blinked. Was he really that pitiful looking?

He staggered to his feet, quickly regaining his wobbly footing. "I'm sick of you storm dragons. Get the hell away from me."

"How did you know that I was a dragon?"

"You're cocky like all of them. And you smell like fish."

"Wow, your temper is pretty flammable," the newcomer patronized him. He tossed his hand out, and a flame burst from his fingertips.

"Oh, let me guess. You're a pyro too?"

His eyes shifted, half-amused, half dangerous. Something about this storm dragon was different than the others. He was difficult to read. While he wasn't dressed in a tunic, something about him looked familiar.

Damien made a double-take as the black bands coiling up his arms brought him back to the Tapestry of Tridents. "You're Mestor's brother from the East, Ryu Ren Kai?"

He is gaze leveled with him. "Yes, how do you know my cocky brother?"

Damien's memory blanked as he tried to remember the argument between Mestor and Kai before their father. How much should he let this rival of Mestor know?

Kai picked another sharp tooth out of his arm. Instead of his skin bleeding, it sealed over, instantly healing.

"How did you do that?" Damien asked.

"Minca is strong within the dragons of the East. Wounds mean very little to our bodies. Regeneration is something our brothers from the West have lost the ability to do," his eyes. "Unless, of course, you are in the presence of a sea goddess like Amphitrite."

Damien locked his gaze with the Oriental dragon. Something about him was off.

Kai didn't blink as his gaze rose skyward. "Well, if you have no business with my kin from the West, then I should—"

"—she's taken our daughter."

Kai's gaze returned to him. "Who has taken your daughter?"

"Maera took her. I don't know why. I need to find my wife, Selia. She's currently at the British Museum trying to find the remaining piece of her inheritance."

Kai's eyes did something strange. "Your wife is the *Blind Moon*?"

Damien nodded.

"I was wondering where that tidal wave in the middle of the sea came from." Kai squared his hips, crossing his black-banded arms across his chest. "That must mean that she is the sea nymph bonded with Bellerophon?"

"Damien, stay away from him. He's dangerous," Pelias growled from behind.

"Hello, little ember," Kai taunted. "Did big bad brother leave you behind in one of his quest to find our father's crown again?"

"You've come into contact with them, haven't you?" Pelias shot back.

Kai dipped his chin, making his long face appear sunken. "Mestor won't have any luck finding our father's crown—not when I know for a fact that they are walking into a trap."

"Traitor!" Pelias roared, throwing his arm and releasing a burst of flame from his fingers.

Damien ducked as the flame blew over him. The last thing he wanted was to get trapped between two pyros wielding their flames on the beach.

Kai tilted his head sideways, his ebony hair catching fire as the fireball blew past him. "I don't unleash my flames over petty matters, Pelias. My infernos are reserved for the shadows."

Pelias's nostrils flared. He took off in a mad run and lunged for Kai.

Kai shifted with fluid grace to his side.

A mess of dreadlocks and gauntlets tumbled in the sand as Pelias missed his target.

Kai spun on his heel, a snarl turning his profile into the danger Pelias warned about. His face changed into half man, half mask. White and black markings decorated the nose and cheeks, with bright red framing the eye holes. Wide nostrils flared beneath the eyes. Horns jutted from the mask's forehead.

Kai's red eyes flashed through the mask as he found Damien. "Go with me to find your wife, or stick with the chubby one who can barely keep a handle on his flames. It's your call."

Pelias snarled. "Go back to the Orient!"

As Pelias lunged again, Damien maneuvered to Kai's side. "Take me to find her."

Kai withdrew as graceful as he did before, dodging the burning sand as it kicked up into Damien's face.

He threw out his arms, and the black bands coiling up his lean muscles flew toward him. In a fiery wind of flame and burning embers, Damien was thrown skyward.

56

PHERUSA'S WARNING

Selia

"Naunet would be proud of you..."

Selia's heart swelled with an emotion that didn't seem to know how to fit inside her body. Her wrists and fingers felt swollen. Her mouth was completely dry.

As the universe faded, and the giant astrolabes surrounded her, the feeling ached worse than any bone or muscle could. The idea that Naunet could be proud of her after all this time of being apart? Something didn't feel right. She needed to leave Gaia's archives and get back to her daughter.

"Selia!" Deidra yelled as she darted over to her. Zipper flit overhead, a brilliant trail of his golden light illuminating above her. "What happened? One second you were looking through the telescope, and the next, you were gone! I almost had a panic attack!"

Selia found a place to sit next to the telescope. She glanced past Deidra, gazing up at the stars. "I met the architect."

Deidra's eyes went wide, darting up toward the ceiling. "Erebéus is up there?"

Selia nodded. "He appeared as a sphinx to me."

"What did he say to you?"

"When I told him that I was trying to gain access to Gaia's Codex, he informed me that he was the guardian of the Temple of the Three Origins. He presented me with a riddle to solve, stating that if I could guess the names of the three origins for sea nymphs, storm dragons, and the great architects, that he would grant me access not only to Gaia's Codex, but also to the Temple of the Three Origins."

Deidra's eyes went wide. "Well? Did you answer it?"

"I guessed *two* of the origins, which are Salt, and Storms. But I didn't feel comfortable with naming *his* origin."

"Why not?"

Selia shivered as an ache crept up her spine. "Erebéus shared a series of memories with me, stating that if I was to know his origin, that I would need to know the nymph he was last bound to. Each memory involved Naunet, along with her scribe, Maera. Maera died from the plague. But instead of becoming a siren, she became trapped in the Temple of the Three Origins."

"How?"

"After the plague, Maera found Naunet in the Orient after she fled Egypt. She wanted to tell Naunet something about Poseidon, but she wouldn't tell her unless she went back to Egypt. Maera did something to Poseidon that resulted in her becoming trapped in that temple. Erebéus wouldn't tell me what she did."

Zipper flit over to the astrolabe with water pouring down its giant spheres. Deidra shifted the sphere aside, inspecting the pool her dragonfly hovered over. "Oh, wow. Are you what I think you are?"

"*Don't let the dryad find me!*" Opal's voice echoed into Selia's head.

"Did you just *talk*?" Deidra asked.

"Opal, it's all right. Deidra is harmless," Selia said.

"Zipper, quit that," Deidra scolded her dragonfly, who promptly perched atop her head as she fished Opal out of the pool.

"*Gentle, my shell is quite delicate,*" Opal said as Deidra scooped her into her palm.

Deidra cupped both of her hands together. "I've only held one of you as a fossil. Are you really an ammonite?"

"*I am the fossil you retrieved during the ocean trance. Gaia's archive brought me to life.*"

Deidra nearly dropped her as she fumbled her shell.

"*Careful!*" Opal scolded her. "*And don't you dare think I'm a normal ammonite. I'm a rare blue ammonite, the only ammonite fae incarnate as,*" Opal corrected her, pride ringing in her bubbly tone. "*I admit, I was the one who helped Selia try and solve Erebéus's riddle by sharing memories I have of Naunet's past.*"

Deidra beamed. "So it's true about your telepathic abilities? Fae ammonites can share memories they remember with Gaia's daughters?"

"It's definitely true. I was inherited by Naunet after I served Pherusa in Atlantis. But between you and me, I much preferred Naunet over her mother."

Zipper buzzed his wings forcefully atop Deidra's head.

"Stop being so jealous," Deidra called up to him. "Just because I can admire more than one fae species doesn't mean that you are any less perfect."

Selia sighed. "After seeing the fragmented memories, I didn't feel like I could make that judgment, so I refused to answer."

"Uh oh...you turned down an architect's riddle?" Opal said. *"I was wondering why we left the stars so abruptly."*

"What would have happened if I guessed incorrectly?" Selia asked.

Deidra squinted at her. "Selia, something *is* happening to you."

Selia held her hands in front of her face. "I'm turning see-through."

"Do you think not answering Erebéus's riddle has impacted your salt aura?" Deidra asked.

"Not only impacted, but enhanced," a familiar female voice said.

Zakai emerged from behind one of the astrolabes. She closed the space between them, stopping next to the telescope and squinted through the eyepiece. "As the creator and guardian of Gaia's Codex, the architect's power is not limited to one location alone. Nymphs have been known to disappear entirely when turning down a riddle presented by him."

Selia waved her transparent hand in front of her face. "Is that what's going to happen to me?"

Zakai glanced between them. "How in the world did the two of you make it back here without my presence? This space is strictly reserved for research conducted by Iridescents."

"Hecate allowed me to," Selia replied.

Zakai dipped her chin. "And I assume Amphitrite's sister attempted to stop you?"

"Yes. I'm surprised that witch isn't here screaming at us for leaving fingerprints on these artifacts right now," Deidra said.

"She's defiantly a wicked witch of the Nile, that's for sure," Opal added.

Zakai's eyes shot toward Deidra as she tucked the ammonite into her pocket. "Who is this witch you speak of?"

Selia's hair stood on end as Pherusa's harsh tone filled the room. She sauntered over to them, her dark eyes full of smugness.

She stopped beside the astrolabe and grabbed one of its spinning spheres. The metal creaked as she stopped it from spinning. "Zakai, I was wondering if you were ever going to show up. I was convinced this dryad was lying about who she reported to."

Deidra glared at Pherusa. "At least I don't steal other people's possessions."

Pherusa's lips twisted as her cold stare swept to Zakai "What kept you? Let me guess, matters only the Order is allowed to know about Selia's inheritance?"

Zakai stood her ground, squaring her hips to face her. "Why would you steal the crystal fragments from Selia? You know they are of no use to the archives if not all three fragments are present."

Pherusa held out her hand, displaying the crystals. "You're right. There's no point in trying to preserve an artifact that will never served a purpose to begin with."

Selia grabbed the crystals, which were both frozen to the touch. She didn't expect anything different after they had been in the presence of such a cold individual.

Pherusa folded her thin arms across her chest. "I'm eager to know how Erebéus presented himself to you."

Selia rounded on Pherusa, a fire burning in her core. Erebéus's golden eyes flashed before her. Naunet's reflection burned like dark flames in their abyssal depths. "I don't need to tell you anything. But I will tell you this. I know that he's protecting Naunet's story to the point that he's not willing to show me the details. He's protecting her."

Pherusa smirked. "What an architect protects and what he wants are two separate things. You do not know what the god of shadows is capable of manipulating."

"As someone who has been blind to their past, I feel it is important to make decisions after you've seen the full story."

Pherusa's lips pursed before she spoke. "I will make myself very clear. What he shared with you via that stupid ammonite is *not* the full story, nor will you ever get it from him."

Selia's body stiffened as the memory of Naunet crying next to the carnage along the Nile flooded her. The bodies. The death. The sight of Naunet's mother striking her...

"Why did you blame Naunet for the plague?" Selia yelled.

"Origin bonds have been known to change the life cycles of fae species," Pherusa replied through bared teeth. "The toxic minca moth queen was no exception. I *never* should have forced her role as the midwife of the sea before she was ready. Erebéus's bonds have become manipulative attempts to overpower the earth mother goddess."

"You believe Erebéus is trying to overthrow Gaia?" Deidra asked. "*How?* Wasn't she the goddess who created him?"

Pherusa rolled her eyes. "Use your imagination. Erebéus has long rebelled against natural order. He has his own plans on how sculpt the planet, including the fae species who inhabit it. The plague that swept Egypt was likely *his* doing. He keeps his motives in the shadows like rest of the promises he fails to keep to the nymphs he bonds with."

Zakai spun on her heel and walked toward the exit.

"Where are you going? Don't leave us with this witch," Deidra called after her.

"I smell smoke," Zakai replied as she disappeared into the tunnel.

57

STARS BENEATH THE SEA

Amy

Amy kicked her feet as she swam deeper into the sea. The water was surprisingly warm, possibly from the flames Kai had created earlier with his blazing inferno. A band of silver light beamed through the water. The light pulsed and dimmed, seeming to come from multiple places at the same time. There was no once source of the light, only blinding silver rays that drifted endlessly through the ocean.

Was it some kind of electricity generated by the storm dragons when they generated the cyclone? Or was it light from the crystal fragment Balfour had stolen from her?

She grabbed the band of liquid light, threading it through her fingers. It pulsed through her, grabbing her like a rope, tugging her deeper.

Lachlan's limp body floated in the water below her. His skin was pale. His mouth gaped open.

Her heart stopped. She had to get to him.

The deeper she went, the cooler the water became. She grabbed his face and pressed her lips to his.

His eyes opened the moment she forced her tongue into his mouth and blew what breath she had into him. The liquid light pulsed around them, softening his expression. Life returned to his eyes as the current tugged them deeper.

The water shifted, thrusting them upward as the current released them.

She gasped, fresh oxygen flooding her lungs.

Lachlan climbed out of the water, elbowing his way onto the rocky ledge outside of the pool. He staggered to his hands and knees, coughing. His sodden hair whipped across his forehead as he glanced up. "Where are we?"

Amy climbed out of the water, resting on her side next to him. Judging by the damp stone walls and the sound of dripping water, they were in a cavern. A dull blue glow illuminated the ground and the walls. "I'm fairly certain we are in a section of Poseidon's crown," she said, running her hand over the rough, knobby structures on the wall.

"Why do you think that?" Lachlan said as he scrambled to his feet.

Amy did the same, further exploring the wall with her fingers. At her touch, the coral wall lit up. "The coral that grows in the crown doesn't grow anywhere else in the ocean."

He mimicked her, touching the wall. Light burst across the knobby structures, spreading and flaying like little rushing rivers, before fading down a tunnel. "I know that coral lives in shallow seas. Why is it here, growing in the deeper ocean? This isn't far from the surface. Is it floating?"

"From what my mother has told me, Poseidon's crown is unlike anything else in the ocean."

His face glowed blue as his cheeks dimpled. "What do you say we follow the starlight?"

She took the first step. Lachlan followed, soon falling into stride next to her. The two walked barefooted into the passage, which was oddly warm. No chill swept over Amy's body, even though her clothing was soaked through.

The air shifted through the passage, catching Amy's sodden hair as it changed direction. The further they walked, the warmer the air became.

The pathway seemed familiar, with its dripping walls and cavernous surroundings. Had she found the entry point to the Temple of the Three Origins? Was this the Chamber of Salt?

"Why do I get the feeling that this passage is breathing?" Lachlan asked.

Amy's own breath caught at the thought as memories from the chamber flooded her. "I really hope the sirens aren't down here."

She stopped, suddenly captivated with how different the passage had become. A rocky ledge stuck out of the wall, which tapered out into the widening passage. "Wow...look at all of them."

Lachlan's hard body bumped into her. He pressed his belly to her back, wrapping his arms around her front.

The room filled with the pulsing lights, each shimmering like little stars.

"This is incredibly beautiful," she said, hoping that her voice didn't make the pulsing lights disappear.

"I think we found where the strange lights have been coming from," Lachlan whispered, his lips grazing the cusp of her ear.

Amy closed her eyes, focusing on the soothing sensation of his voice as it mixed with the glowing light illuminating her eyelids.

"*Come watch the stars arrive with me,*" Ewan said, his words blowing cold air out into the night.

A memory flashed before her. She sat next to the giant huntsman, gazing up into the canopy of the giant trees—their blackened silhouettes completely framed by a blanket of stars.

She opened her eyes, finding the entire cavern was aglow. She turned herself toward Lachlan, facing him. "Ewan, I."

His brows worked. "Who is Ewan? This is the second time you've called me by that name."

Amy flustered at her slip-up. "I'm sorry, I—" She glanced away from his incredible blue eyes. "It's a name I'm quite fond of, actually."

He squeezed her. "Well, Ewan is my middle name."

She stared at him, lost for word. "Really?"

His cheeks dimpled. "My mother said it's Scottish Gaelic, but in some languages, it translates to *born of the mountain.*" He gazed up at the wall of stars, his neck and jaw ridged in the afterglow and chuckled. "And here I am, working my life away fishing."

"Lachlan Ewan Malloch," she said. "There is a nice ring to that name."

"*A king is nothing without his queen,*" Ewan's words rang from another time, filling the cavern and bringing the stars alive.

Lachlan set his hand on the wall behind Amy, leaning against her.

"What are you doing?"

"Returning the favor," he said, his lips dangerously close to her. Water dripped from his torso onto her chest. "I'm pretty sure I would have died had you not kissed me back earlier."

His lips worked over hers. Even with the roughness of his stubble, Lachlan's kiss was sensual, flooding her with incredible tenderness.

She kissed him back, taking his lower lip into her mouth. His tongue pulsed against hers, expertly maneuvering as he explored.

When he withdrew, they both stood panting, their breathing syncing with each other.

A creaking sound echoed up the pathway.

"Something else is in this passage," she whispered.

"I really don't care what's in here with us," he growled, his voice lowering. He buried his face into her neck, his lips tracing a scorching line down her jaw.

"Ewan..." she breathed, overcome by the force of his body.

He nipped at her earlobe. "You can call me that if you'd like." He hooked her under her knees and lifted her onto the rocky ledge.

Amy's body tensed. She knew where this hot, damp moment was quickly going.

Lachlan pulled away from her, his blue eyes catching the tiny lights shimmering around them. "You should see yourself right now," he stammered, raking his hand through her hair. "Your freckles are glowing."

She traced her finger along his jaw, wiping the beads of moisture away from his stubble. His face, while wholesome, lacked the hard lines she remembered from the ancient huntsman.

"What are you thinking right now?" he asked, gathering her hands into his callused ones. "About this place? About *us?*"

She glanced up at the ceiling and walls, unable to explain the feelings that surged through her like a storm. Regret and anger had forced her to withdraw from letting go and moving forward. "I've been so focused on trying to forget the past, to forget someone special, I was never able to love them in the same way they cared for me."

"Amy, what ever your past holds, *you* are something very special." He kissed the tops of her fingers, working his thumbs over her damp knuckles. "You are someone I can't ever let go."

Amy's gaze dropped to the birthmark on his chest. Silver light reflected off the splotchy skin, making it glow. She pulled her hands away from his and cupped his face. She forced her lips to his, kissing him until her cheeks burned. The salt tingled against skin as his stubble rubbed her raw.

He pulled away, grabbing the hem of her sodden dress that bunched between them. "Can I please relieve you of this?"

"Please do," she whispered, desperate to undress herself. Her clothing stuck to her body as the saltwater made it difficult to peel away.

He bunched the damp fabric and tugged it down while she lowered the straps from her shoulders. She kicked her legs, slinging her dress to the side. Suddenly naked, she sat before him, her breasts and skin and knees glistening in the warm humid glow of the cavern.

"Lift your hips. I'll do the rest, my Sea Star," Lachlan said as he cupped her ass in his hands and dove between her legs.

Her back arched as his tongue worked in circles. She grabbed his hair, guiding him to where she wanted his tongue to go. Heat rolled in her belly as he brought her to the edge, releasing her into a trembling fit of ecstasy.

He grabbed her arm as she lowered herself. His movements were all too familiar from what she remembered of the generous huntsman. Ewan was always the one to give her the first orgasm.

Once on her feet, she steadied herself by grabbing his arms.

Lachlan's face blurred before her as the rush of her pleasure settled. "Amy, I want you. I want to make love to you."

She grabbed his belt and ripped it away from his crotch. His pants fell in a damp heap onto the ground, releasing his cock.

He wasn't massive like Ewan. Thank goodness, because learning to walk after making love to a man nearly twice her size was not a pleasant thing.

His eyes went wide, his mouth quirking. "What, am I too—"

"—you're perfect!" she stammered, jumping into his arms and wrapping her legs around him. He gathered her hips, pinning her against the wall as he slid into her.

Amy's body embraced his entry. She didn't recoil like she'd done in the past due to their size difference. His movements were fluid and powerful. Shallow thrusts deepened as he surged against her. She rocked her hips, relishing in the sensation. It didn't feel like one of her ovaries would burst when he plunged into her.

"Tell me what you want," he ground out next to her ear. "Slower? Faster?"

She released her legs from around his waist and stood. The mating ritual from behind had never been her favorite position. Now she wanted to see how well they fit together.

She faced the wall and backed her body into him. His hard chest and core formed around her as he understood where she wanted him to go.

He set his hand atop hers. "I need to look at you," he said, grabbing her waist with both of his hands. "You even have stars back here."

Amy tried to spin toward him, but he kept a firm grip on her hips.

"I've got you right where I need you," he grunted, his body blending with hers.

She threw her hands out, gripping the wall as he bucked his hips.

A moan escaped her as his thrusting deepened. Longer, faster movements created a friction no man had ever given her before.

"Don't stop," she breathed as he quickened his pace.

He slapped her ass, his palm burning against her skin as she forced herself against him.

The pressure built, burning and surging as their bodies synced.

"Lachlan!" she cried out.

"Amy, my sea goddess, you are mine," he growled.

His body shuddered against her as the lights around them burst, shimmering and splaying as Amy's vision went dark. Her heart thundered as she tried to catch her breath.

Lachlan's hand remained atop hers on the wall, their fingers damp and intertwined with one another.

He lowered himself to the ground, propping his back against the wall.

Amy folded next to him and tucked herself beneath his arm. She closed her eyes, but the starlit corals remained glowing behind her eyelids. Maybe it wasn't such an outlandish idea that somehow, with thousands of years between them, Ewan's spirit had returned to her.

PART 7
POSEIDON'S CROWN

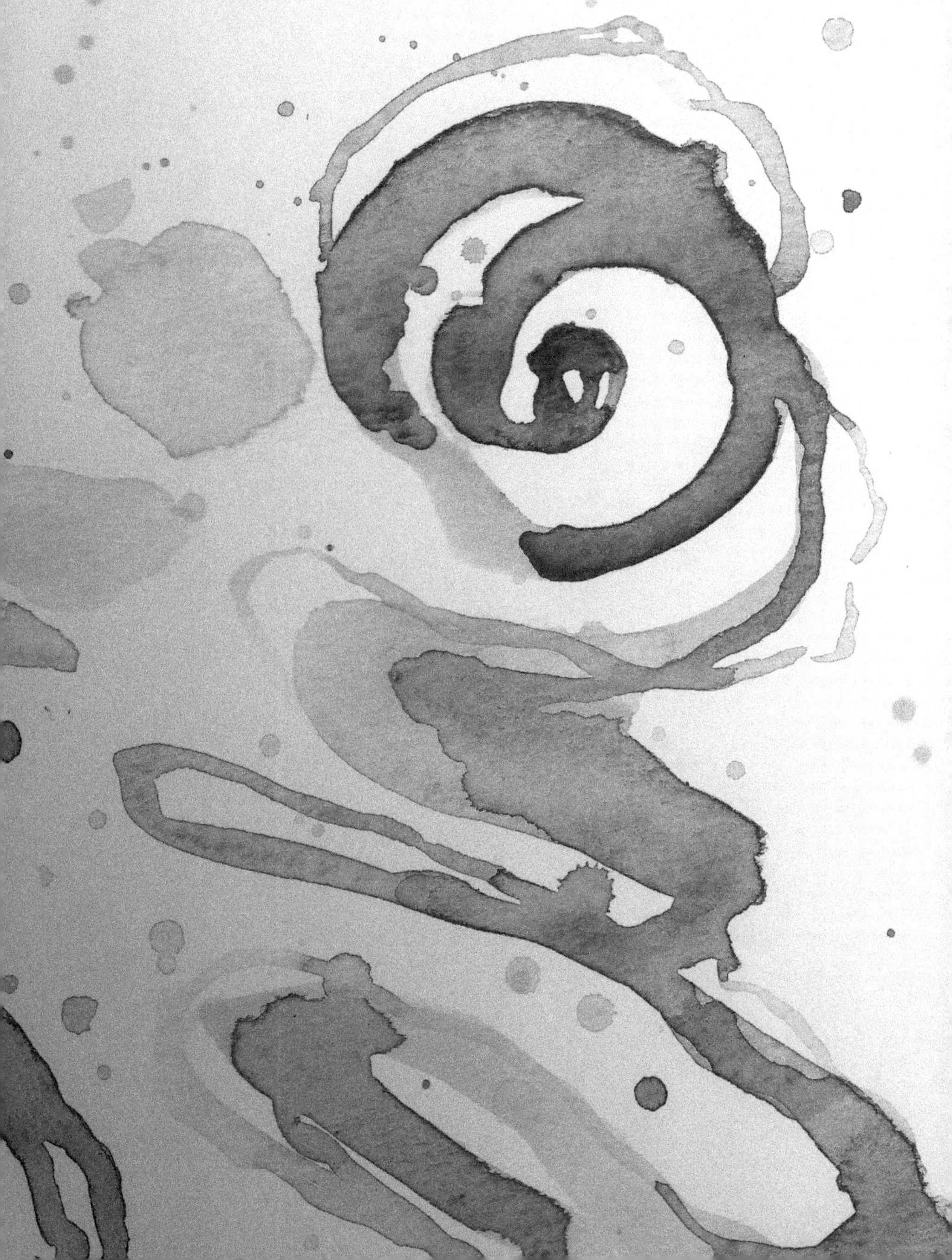

58

TO LONDON

Damien

As soon as the flame and ash swept Damien off his feet, Pelias's bonfires fell away. Being thrust into a smoky void wasn't the most desirable experience, but he had to get to Selia. Grit ground between his teeth, and a burning smell permeated his nose. As the smoke tunneled around him, he thought he might be sick. He closed his eyes just as the violent tunneling motion stopped.

His back hit a solid surface. Brick buildings and cobblestone streets surrounded him. He stood in a grimy alleyway crowded with dumpsters. He wiped the back of his hand across his face, smearing something dark. He was covered in soot from the flammable journey with a dragon pyro.

Kai, however, appeared much neater in appearance than he had been before. He resumed his human form across from Damien. His clothing was no longer torn. His dark hair was tied back into a ponytail that slung down his back. He wore a red sleeveless shirt, black pants and boots. Black tattoos wound up his forearms, appearing as flames.

His nostrils flared. "Something doesn't smell right." He grabbed Damien by the shirt and shoved him against the building. "You didn't tell me that Pherusa was here."

"I can't remember who Pherusa is," Damien spat, grabbing his forearm to prevent the storm dragon from moving his hand any closer to his neck.

"You should know the family names of the nymphs who your wife has history with." Kai released Damien's shirt and took a few steps back. "I've taken you to London. I'm sure you can figure out how to get to the British Museum."

"Wait. At least help me track her down? Can't you smell like every other dragon I've met has done?"

"I can try, but no promises. The moment I smell Pherusa's stench again, I'm gone." He leveled his gaze with him." Do you have something of hers that I can pick up her scent from?"

Damien patted his sides, then reached into his pocket. He tugged out one of Nyssa's tiny socks. His heart sank. How was he going to tell Selia that their daughter had been taken? "Will this work?"

Kai scented the sock, wincing as he did. "This way."

They left the alleyway and rounded the corner of the street, following the crowd of people moving about the city. He knew that Selia and Deidra both went to this museum, but Deidra made it sound as though they were going to access some records that only nymphs were aware of.

A woman with short blond hair stood on the sidewalk outside of a green area full of trees. The park sat across massive Greek-style building he guessed was the museum.

Damien instantly recognized the Iridescent as her gaze locked with him. He and Kai approached her. Zakai's gaze swept Damien from head to toe. "Let me guess. You found yourself here with the help of a pryo?"

Kai glared at the Iridescent, his dark eyes igniting. "If you want to discuss pyrotechnics, I suggest you do so in a space that is not so crowded with trees. They have a habit of going up in flames without warning."

Zakai took a step toward him. "I know who you are. I know how much Pherusa's daughter means to you. I will have you know that Naunet's moon daughter is on her way to discovering where she is located."

Damien stared at Kai. "Wait, you know where Naunet is?"

Kai's eye's focused across the park. Selia was making her way toward them. "It is her. Naunet's moon daughter is alive." He took a step back, flame and embers encasing him.

Damien grabbed his arm. One of Kai's tattoos ignited, sending a plume of smoke and ash into his face. In a fiery burst, the storm dragon vanished.

Zakai waved her hand, dispersing what flames were left over before they gripped the low hanging tree branches.

Selia came darting for Damien. "What are you doing here? And why are you all covered in soot?"

Damien swept her into his arms, breathing in her scent. "You have no idea how glad I am to see you."

Selia pulled away from him. "The man who was just here, I recognized him. Where did he go?"

"I don't know. He hated that he smelled someone named Pherusa. Then Zakai here got him to admit that he knew where Naunet was located."

Selia's eyes went wide. "That's two individuals who know where she is! Deidra and I uncovered some amazing information. Where is Nyssa? I can't wait to squeeze her!"

Damien's vision went blurry. "Selia, there is something I need to tell you." He took her hand and walked her over to a bench beneath one of the giant oaks. "I need you to sit with me."

She lowered herself onto the bench.

Damien sat next to her. He gazed down at his trembling soot-covered hands. How much of a failure he was. He glanced up at her, forcing himself to look into her blue eyes. "Selia, Nyssa has been taken."

Time stopped as Selia's face broke. Her eyes dilated, and her mouth dropped. "What do you mean, taken? By who?"

He grabbed her hand. "By another sea nymph I've been hiding from you."

She blinked, her expression hardening. "A sea nymph took our daughter? Why? Who are you hiding from me?"

He glanced up at Zakai, whose expression didn't waver. He'd asked her and Balfour to both keep Maera a secret from Selia.

"What did I miss?" Deidra asked as she approached them.

"Damien and Selia's daughter has been taken by Maera," Zakai said, removing the burden from Damien of having to repeat those horrible words a second time.

Deidra shot Zakai a glance. "Maera? Isn't that the name of Naunet's scribe? Why in the world would she want to steal Selia's daughter?"

Damien's heart broke as he watched Selia fall to the ground. She threw her face into her hands and cried.

59
DAMIEN'S SECRET
Selia

Selia's pulse thrashed so violently, she thought her heart might erupt from her chest. As her palms smeared against her face, she forced herself to breathe. Slow and steady. In and out. That's what she needed, just to breathe—not to believe what Damien had said.

Deidra grabbed her arm, helping her to stand. Her pupils were dilated, making the dryad's yellow-green eyes appear darker than they were.

Damien stood next to Deidra, with Zakai behind him. He reached out to touch Selia on the arm.

She pulled away from him, locking her gaze with his unfocused eyes. "I trusted you with Nyssa. How could you possibly let someone steal her?"

Damien's face paled. Soot smudged across his forehead and cheeks. His hair was windblown, sticking out at awkward angles. "I know, and I betrayed that trust in not telling you about her. I had no idea that she would steal Nyssa, and I have no idea why she took her."

The sound of his voice grated against her ears. What was usually smooth and sweet felt like sandpaper.

Selia spun on her heel and tore down the path.

"Selia, where are you going?" Zakai asked.

Anger burned through Selia, dulling Zakai's voice. She tore through the park, heading straight for the museum.

"Wait, I know what you're thinking," Deidra said as she caught up with her and began to jog alongside her. "You can't go back in there. Pherusa will be sure to steal those crystals away from you for real if you go in a second time."

Selia stopped and rounded on Deidra. "Didn't you hear him? My daughter is missing. She was taken by some sea nymph named Maera. The only way I'm going to track down this sea nymph who took her is by getting back into the archives and confront Erebéus. He's keeping secrets about her, too. I won't be lied to any longer."

"Selia, your hand," Deidra said, as her own hand slid through her arm. "Your salt aura is behaving strangely again."

Selia waved her hand in front of her, watching as the trees in the park appeared through her skin. The last time this happened, her emotions had been in turmoil, specifically about her daughter.

She gazed up at the trees, lost in their green canopy, and became suddenly transfixed by the golden sunlight shining through the leaves. A dark figure blurred in her periphery, pulling her attention down from the trees.

"If Maera took your daughter, then you should know who you are going up against if you choose to go after her," Pherusa said as she stopped a few paces away from the group. She folded her slender arms across her chest. "She is one of many individuals who stands between Naunet and I. The others are Hecate, Erebéus, and a storm dragon named Kai."

Selia faced her. "How was Maera able to take our daughter if she's bound to the Temple of the Three Origins?"

Pherusa's eyes narrowed. "While her soul is bound to the temple, she is able to leave temporarily for months, even years, at a time. As a victim of the plague, her soul had no origin to return to. Erebéus guards the temple, allowing her to come and go. Her body is a temporary one, provided to her by the god of shadows. She has long sought a way to escape her punishment."

Selia jolted. "*Punishment?*"

"Being trapped between two of the three origins only occurs when an individual acts against one of the primal threads written in Gaia's Codex—that all life is sacred. Even I do not know the truth behind that story. The only way to reveal what it was that she did would be to experience the memory as recorded in the Codex."

Pherusa spun on her heel, motioning to leave.

Selia grabbed her arm arm. "I witnessed memories of you and Naunet. I saw the horrible aftermath that you and Naunet had to dealt with after the plague killed so many of Celaeno's salt daughters."

Pherusa sneered at her as she pulled her arm away. "How dare you speak of that time as though you know it."

"You were *cruel* to Naunet. I watched you strike her."

A shadow drifted across Pherusa's thin face, coiling like a serpent along her neck. It's tail thrashed, slithering to where it disappeared into her dress. "Go on. Strike me. Strike me like I did her."

Selia's fingers darkened on Pherusa's wrist as her shadow serpents overpowered her. She wanted to hit her—to do what the voice had said so many times as Masika said it would.

"Taste it. Savor it. All salt daughters of Celaeno will surrender to it."

A horrible thought crossed her mind. Naunet had admitted to using the salt venom to sever her bond with Erebéus. What if she was slowly becoming addicted to it?

Selia threw Pherusa's arm away from her. "No. I won't hit you. I pity the mother who was never able to see what her daughter truly wanted."

Pherusa's upper lip curled. "That currently makes two of us." She spun on her heel and left for the museum.

"Good riddance," Deidra said as Zipper flit above, sending golden sparks into the air in what could have been a celebration.

The group checked into a nearby Inn to gather themselves and sort out a plan. Selia was exhausted, and Damien looked like a firework exploded all over him.

As soon as they booked a room, he grabbed her hand and steered her into the hallway in an another attempt to consult with her. "Look, I know we aren't okay right now. I can't blame you for being angry with me. But I promise you that we will find Nyssa."

Selia looked into his eyes for the first time since they'd reunited. Shadows lived there, blackened forms drifting behind his irises. "You must have been so scared when you saw she was gone."

He pulled her into an embrace, and Selia fell into him. His chest shuddered. "I can't tell you how scared I have been. This is a nightmare that I never thought I would have to relive again."

Selia embraced him back. "This isn't your fault. I shouldn't have been so angry with you."

He released her, wiping a strand of hair away from her eyes. "I need you to know that I am going to do everything in my power to find her, no matter what it takes."

Selia blinked away the tears forming in her eyes and pulled away from him. "Get cleaned up. When you get out, I expect you to tell me how you know Maera. No more secrets."

Damien nodded, kissing her cheek. "I promise."

While Damien retreated into the restroom, Selia sat next to Deidra, who had taken Opal out of her pocket. She removed flower clippings from a vase sitting on an entry table and set the ammonite into the water.

Opal's tentacles flared out of her shell as Deidra carried the vase into the sitting area. Zakai already stood by the window, her arms folded across her chest in her usual stoic fashion.

As soon as Deidra set the vase on the table before them, Opal's voice bubbled into their minds. "*We can find your daughter. Maera is smart, so we have to be smarter than her.*"

Selia sat down next to Deidra on the sofa. "When I found you in the archive, you asked if I was one of Naunet's scribes. *When* did Maera become her scribe?"

"*In the Temple of Isis.*"

"Did she become Naunet's scribe before or after Erebéus forced Isis out of her temple?" Selia asked.

One of Opal's tentacles thrashed, sending water into the air. "*I believe after, but I can't say for sure. All I know is that Naunet inherited me from her mother*" *as soon as they found refuge in Egypt after Atlantis sank. Maera used me to record Naunet's research and documentation within the Codex.*"

Selia glanced up at Deidra. "Something is very strange about this Maera individual. I saw her at the Louvre, and then she abducts our daughter?"

"That's not the strangest of it, either," Zakai said from the window.

Selia swung her head around. "What do you mean?"

Damien emerged, cleaner than he had been before.

"I think it's time you tell Selia about your relationship with Maera," Zakai said.

What color had returned to Damien's face drained. He blew out his cheeks as he sat down next to Selia. He grabbed her hand, squeezing it. "Right. There's no other way to say this." He locked eyes with her. "Maera is my deceased wife."

The words *deceased* and *wife* stuck to Selia's ears like spiderwebs funneling around a hole. "You're joking..."

Damien shook his head. "No, I'm not."

She glanced up at Zakai, then Deidra. "Did you both know this?"

"Holy mushrooms, no!" Deidra cried. "You're pulling our legs, right? How can a dead sea nymph steal a child?"

"Balfour and I both knew," Zakai admitted. "Deidra was not aware of this knowledge."

Selia rounded on Damien. "How is that possible? Did you know that Maera was a sea nymph when you two were a couple?"

"No," Damien answered. "I only learned of Maria's true identity recently." Damien reached into his pocket, tugging out a wrinkly piece of paper. "Selia, this is what I found in Nyssa's crib after I discovered that she was missing."

Selia grabbed the paper and read.

Damien,

Your daughter is with me. I have taken her to the place where I know Selia will find use for her inheritance. In order to find me, you must bring me the two crystal fragments of the star of the sea. To

find your daughter, you must seek out the darkest
star in the ocean.
Only the ancestor of Poseidon knows my origin.

Maera

Selia glanced up from the paper. "The name Maera means *shining one*. I remember finding the name in a magazine when I was researching baby names." She glanced down at her message again. "Why does she say here, *knows my origin*? I think Maera's letter might actually be part of the riddle that could answer what his origin is."

"What riddle?" Damien asked.

Everyone stared at Selia.

She took Damien's hand. "I encountered Erebéus in Gaia's Archives. He appeared to me, stating that if I could name the three origins, he would grant me access not only to Gaia's Codex, but also to the Temple of the Three Origins."

Damien's eyes widened. "That's easy. It's called the Temple of Salt, Storms, and Starlight."

"Starlight!" Selia yelled. "That's part of Erebéus's origin! How did you figure that out?"

Damien squeezed her hand. "After you and Deidra left for the museum, Pelias performed a storm smoke ritual on the beach. During the ritual, I saw Maera at this temple. She gave the full name of it to me. I also saw Poseidon. He was arguing with Mestor and another storm dragon named Kai about his crown in what appeared to be a memory. Poseidon also didn't appear to be in the best of health."

Selia shivered. "I also experienced a series of memories that all involved Maera. She died from the plague. But instead of becoming a siren, she became trapped in the Temple of the Three Origins."

"How did she become trapped?" Damien asked.

"Maera did something to Poseidon that resulted in her becoming trapped in that temple. Erebéus's wouldn't tell me what she did."

"Do you think Maera and Erebéus are working together?" Damien asked.

"Or *against* one another. Maera obviously wants to escape the temple. I think stealing our daughter might somehow help her to escape." Selia glanced at the letter again. "Damien, remember what you taught me about selkies? A selkie's identity *is* the sea. What if Maera wants us to discover her identity?"

Damien squinted at her. "What does revealing her identity have to do with recovering your inheritance? Or stealing Nyssa?"

Selia jumped up. "Why didn't I see this sooner? At the Louvre, Maera said something strange to me. She said that some of the greatest truths about marine discovery exist just beneath the surface of the water. These truths are like stars, only becoming visible in complete darkness." She turned to Deidra. "We know that she's spent a long time researching Poseidon's crown. What if this darkness she's referring to is really concealing what she did to Poseidon?"

"Do you think she could be linked to Poseidon's death?" Deidra asked.

Selia nodded. "I do. Erebéus became very suspicious when I questioned him. We almost have all three names for the three origins. Salt represents the Abyss for sea nymphs. Storms represents the Great Storm, or Tsunami for storm dragons." She picked up the painting of Damien's she'd discovered in the Celestial archives. "The only way we are going to figure out what Starlight represents for the great architects is by getting into the temple."

"But how?" Deidra argued. "Pherusa won't let us go anywhere near those archives again."

Selia traced her finger over Damien's artwork, finding a lone star shimmering above the sea. "I think I know how we can get inside the temple."

60

CORAL & DRAGON BLOOD

Amy

An eerie sound echoed through the cavern, stirring Amy from her slumber. Lachlan was still out cold next to her. She slid out from beneath his arm and crawled to her feet. Had she heard crying?

Gaia forbid, was it the cry of a siren?

The starlit coral had dimmed, making the cavern more ominous. She glanced down at Lachlan, who was still sound asleep. There was no point in waking him when he was still so satiated from their lovemaking.

Her clothing had dried in the time they had dozed. She tugged on her dress, grateful that the fabric no longer felt restrictive against her skin. Blinding silver light filled the tunnel, dimming as quickly as it illuminated the walls. As the light faded, the corals became brighter. Were the two sources of light communicating with each other?

Amy followed the brighter silver beam as it pulsed once again through the tunnel. With each step she took, the light pulsed brighter. As she entered another chamber, the sound of water trickling over stone echoed off the walls.

A figure appeared, offset by the light that seemed to originate from their body. Long elegant arms swept up into the air, bringing the silver light above their head, where it fell, showering over them.

The figure turned to face her. "Hello, Amy."

"Maera? What are you doing here?"

"Preparing for our visitors, should they find their way here," Maera replied. "Your mother has long known the secrets hidden within these starlit corals. They were some of her most powerful ingredients in her Ocean Apothecary."

Amy glanced down at the pool glowing at Maera's bare feet. Brilliant colors shimmered in the water.

Maera crouched to the ground, trailing her fingers over the pool. When she withdrew her hand, a brilliant silver moth climbed out of the water and perched atop her wrist. "The fae queen returned to me from this very pool, reborn anew. Had you not ventured to the past, none of them would have been able to locate the crown's location. Only when the moon is darkest does their light shine brightest."

Amy shook her head. Was *this* the secret her mother had been keeping from her? Starlit corals that emerged beneath the *new moon*? The way she had made the remainder of their journey sound make her think that they would need to dive deep beneath the sea. What if the crown was hidden just beneath the water's surface?

"Like blue minca, the starlit corals use moonlight to grow. The Abyss originated from these corals." Maera said, her thoughts entering Amy's mind.

"In other words, this coral is the mother of the Abyss?"

Maera's eyes found her, light from the pool reflecting in them. "Even the ancestral mother of the sea has an origin story of her own." The fae queen spun on her wrist and took off into the air. "I'm sure your mother has also told you that the star of the sea was also formed from this starlit coral."

Amy's began to tremble. How was she going to tell Maera that she lost her crystal fragment? And where had Balfour run off with it?

Light from the coral illuminated Maera's face, turning strands of her dark hair silver. "Speaking of your mother, where is she? The plague victims have long awaited her return. Not only those within this chamber, but also your friend, Masika."

"Is Masika here?"

"All of the plague victims are," Maera said. "Here, the lost souls of Celaeno's salt daughters exist with the starlit corals, unable to return to their ancestral mother."

Amy glanced at the coral. "The lights are their souls? I don't understand. I saw the sirens earlier."

"The salt in the sea returns them to their original state of being before salt venom took their lives. It's only above the surface that they appear as sirens."

Amy's heart thundered in her chest. She had wondered why the sirens disappeared so quickly when they fell into the sea. They had vanished as quickly as they came, leaving a dark oil-slick salt venom floating on the water's surface.

Maera lowered her gaze back to the pool. "The crown has been a refuge for the plague victims, along with Isis after she fled her temple."

"Isis is here? *Where?*"

Maera smiled, her hair turning from silver back to dark brown. "I'm sure she will reveal her self soon enough with the visitors we have arriving."

Amy spun around. Voices she recognized echoed in the passage.

"Amphitrite must be nearby. Keep searching for her and her daughter," Mestor grumbled.

Maera had disappeared from the pool, including the fae queen.

Amy ducked behind one of the rocky shelves as Mestor emerged in the room. His broad face illuminated just as Maera's had by the pool. Worry wrecked his expression. His dreadlocks fell into his face as he glanced down into the pool. He became half man, half dragon.

"You saw the magic she worked on the wound I gave you," Kai said as he stopped at Mestor's side. "The remains of her Ocean Apothecary reside here. I say we destroy it before she does the same thing she did to our father to us."

"No," Mestor argued. "We destroy nothing until we reach the Chamber of Storms. Only there will we discover the remains of his crown and reveal the truth behind his death."

A hand came to Amy's mouth. "*Don't scream. I have the crystal fragment.*"

She spun around, finding Balfour behind her. "What are you doing?" she whispered.

"*Come with me. We can't let my brothers find the crystal fragment. As you heard, they want to destroy it.*"

She took off after him into the tunnel, her heart thundering. Orange light erupted out of the passage, spilling with liquid flames.

"Kai," Balfour growled, his voice no longer concealed to Amy's mind. "How did you find us?"

"Kai? Are you kidding?" the storm dragon replied from the dark. Pelias emerged, his face blackened with soot. "You really mistook me for that nasty Oriental pyro?"

"Pelias, how did you find us?" Selia asked.

"The storm smoke brought me to you," Pelias replied. "If only Damien had been patient with me, it would have brought him to you too."

Balfour fell to his knees, a groan escaping him.

Another flame erupted in the passage, this one much more violent.

"Get behind me," Pelias barked at Amy, flames burning bright from his gauntlets.

Amy ducked behind him as the pyros faced one another. Their flames spit and crackled, illuminating the passage with brilliant yellow light.

Kai's eyes danced with the orange embers as they died. His face—a mask of white and black—illuminated in the dying flames. His gaze dropped to Balfour as he fell to the ground, blue blood spilling out of him.

"Balfour!" Amy cried, lunging for him.

Pelias threw out his arms, shielding Amy from another bout of flames as Kai sent them toward her.

She fell back behind him before the fire caught her hair.

"Pelias, stand down," Mestor growled from behind.

Amy spun, finding Mestor approaching.

Kai stood his ground, holding his hands out at his sides, flames spewing out of his outward-facing palms.

Mestor stopped next to where Balfour lay. His wide face caught the orange light of Kai's flames. "Amphitrite has betrayed us."

Amy swallowed. How had her mother betrayed Poseidon's sons?

Kai's gaze landed on Amy. "Take her with us."

Mestor grabbed Amy around the center and hoisted her over his shoulder.

"Wait!" Amy cried. "We can't just leave him!"

Balfour's body disappeared as Mestor carried her away. The starlit souls of the plague victims reflected in his blood as he took her deeper into the cavern.

61

MIRRORS & WINDOWS

Damien

Damien had only started to drift off when a golden beam of sunlight burst through the door. Surely the light was not the early signs of the wee hours of the morning.

Deidra poked her head inside the bedroom where he and Selia were cuddled in bed. "Rise and shine! It's time for a break in."

Zipper flit through the room, illuminating the walls with his golden light.

Damien withdrew the curtains. The streets of London were thick with fog. It was still night.

Something dark blurred outside the window.

"Looks like we have a nightly visitor," Selia said as she sat up from bed. She opened the window, letting Peppercorn flit inside.

Seven other smaller bats followed her.

"She brought her pups?" Damien stammered, ducking as he dodged one of the enthusiastic creatures.

"They know something is up," Selia said as one of the pups landed in her hair. It thumbed its way down to her sweater, swiveling its tiny head as it let out an excited *squeak*.

Zipper panicked, flitting toward Deidra's braid, where he tucked his wings and disappeared from sight.

Damien got dressed, mumbling as one of the pups dove through the air and disturbed his pile of clothing. He wished he could grumble to Balfour right now. Speaking of Balfour. He'd dreamed of something horrible before Zipper lit the room up with his golden light. He'd dreamed that Balfour had been in a horrible fight.

"Why do we have to break into Gaia's Archives in the middle of the night?" Selia asked as she tugged on her sweater.

"It's the time when Hecate allows visitors. And Pherusa is not there, according to a log Zakai was able to get access to," Deidra said as she poured out copious amounts of frothy brown liquid and handed out the mugs. "I already brewed everyone my special mushroom coffee!"

Damien took one whiff of the steaming mushroom concoction in the mug and set it back on the table. Apparently, dryads were early risers and didn't require the appropriate amount of caffeine before functioning.

Peppercorn landed on Damien's shoulder, nudging his ear with her wing.

Selia tucked the two crystal fragments and Opal into her pockets. "Let's go."

The group took off into the foggy London streets. Peppercorn and her pups flit silently through the mist that blanketed the gloomy city. Opal kept silent, a quite bubbling sound echoing in Damien's head that suggested she was still sleeping. Something about the quirky creature told him that she was constantly thinking.

"How did you and Deidra get into this archive, anyway?" Damien asked as they passed another lamp post.

"Deidra and I entered the museum first. Then I had an encounter with Hecate near the Rosetta Stone. I'm sure we will be meeting her," Selia replied.

"There are other ways to enter Gaia's archives," Zakai said as she approached one of the giant columns outside the museum's darkened entrance. She held her hand out, illuminating the surface.

A symbol appeared—one that resembled a tiny earth.

Zakai glanced over her shoulder before she chanted a few hushed words. "With the light of Gaia, I illuminate your knowledge."

The column began to glow a brilliant yellow.

Zakai waved her other hand, encouraging them to enter the illuminated tunnel.

One by one, they passed through the light barrier. As soon as Damien stepped foot past the threshold, he was surrounded by tendrilling darkness.

A woman with three faces appeared. She towered over them, her presence much more dominating than what he remembered of Isis.

"What brings you to Gaia's archives at this hour of the night?" she asked, her voice echoing out into the strange shadow-filled space.

"We've come to research the star of the sea," Selia said, presenting the two crystal fragments to her. "I need to access the shadow archives so I can locate the third fragment."

Hecate's eyes worked over the crystals as all six of them surveyed the group. "Before you may enter, you must present any and all fae you have accompanying you."

Selia turned out her pocket, exposing Opal. Peppercorn and her seven pups all darted out in the open. Zipper was the last to show, his golden wings trembling beneath Deidra's braid as the bats swarmed above.

"Three nymphs, ten fauna fae, and," her eyes hooded as her gaze lowered to Damien, "and a human."

"What's wrong with him?" Selia asked.

"Humans are not allowed to visit Gaia's archives without an architect escorting them," Hecate said, the two hounds sitting at her feet snarling. Their multiple eyes fixated on Damien as he felt oddly like he was being watched by something more than one goddess. Hecate wasn't like Isis—she exuded coldness, not warmth.

Selia didn't bat an eye as she approached the eerie goddess. "Erebéus can come find me when he wants me to try answering his riddle again. I expect that he's likely sleeping?"

"Sleep is not required by the god of shadows," Hecate replied, her pale face lacking expression. "He prefers to call his resting time contemplation."

Selia clapped her hands together. "Well, tell him that the only thing he should be contemplating is how we are going to get our daughter back from the nymph who took her."

Hecate's six eyes fell onto her. "Who has stolen your daughter?"

"Maera has. We are using her research in Gaia's archives to find her."

Hecate's three faces merged, her six eyes becoming two fierce ones. "Be advised. I am not responsible for holding back his shadows should they decide to imprison you."

"We are willing to take that chance," Selia said to the goddess.

Hecate stepped aside, both of her hounds dipping their heads as they walked by. Damien gripped Selia's hand as they passed through the barrier. A room appeared that was crowded with shelves. To think that Maera was coming here all these years, taking his artwork and using it for something?

How had his paintings helped her with her research?

"I will stand watch in case any unwelcome visitors decide to show up," Zakai said as she stood by the edge of the room. She folded her arms across her chest as Deidra took charge.

"All right, everyone, let's split up," Deidra said as she grabbed a stack of paper. "We're looking for anything that has to deal with what Maera mentioned in her note."

Damien's attention went straight to the magnificent ceiling. "Is this where you met Erebéus?"

Selia glanced up. "I sure did. He's up there all right. When he sucked me into his shadows, I went up there with the stars."

Damien scanned the stars, wondering if someone had painted it to make it sparkle. No pigments he'd ever worked with had that kind of powerful impact. It had to be magic.

His attention moved through the room, which looked more like an observatory than an archive. Giant astrolabes crowded the space, their cylindrical rings swirling around one another. Some moved fast, while others gave off an ominous *whooshing* sound as the rings juxtaposed.

One of the astrolabes caught his eye. Symbols decorated the rings—symbols he recognized from the Temple of Salt, Storms, and Starlight.

Selia stopped at his side. "This is where I found a note about your artwork." She flipped the metal ring on the armillary sphere sideways. "Someone has taken it."

"Let me guess, Pherusa removed something?" Deidra scolded as she rolled her eyes.

"What did the note say?" Damien asked.

Selia pressed her fingers to the bridge of her nose. "Something about the star of the sea, Poseidon's crown, and an origin study completed by you."

Damien grabbed a stack of old paintings he recognized from over a decade ago. He flipped through the old concepts, drafts of seascapes and Maria's detailed descriptions of the coral he assumed she'd been studying. Running his fingers over the old warped parchment felt oddly like coming home.

"Why take these concepts and file them away here?" Selia asked. "I still don't know what she was using them for."

"Maybe she was using them to study something else other than the crown," Damien said, glancing up at the brilliant starlit ceiling. It reminded him of the temple where he'd seen Poseidon sitting atop his thrown. "You said the Abyss is named after the constellation Pleiades, correct?"

"Yes," Selia replied. "That's what Amphitrite told me."

Damien glanced through the eyepiece of the telescope. "Selia, come here and look at this. I think there is something hidden up there that could be a clue on what Maera has been using my artwork for."

Selia looked through the eyepiece. "I just see a bunch of stars."

Damien held up one of his paintings. "Look closer. You see this here? What do you see when you look at it?"

Selia pulled her eye away from the telescope and gazed at his painting, comparing the two. "Is it a window?"

"That's what I thought. In the Temple of Salt, Storms, and Starlight, there were these massive, brilliantly colored stained glass windows above the Tapestry of Tridents. Each one depicted an image of a different nymph. I think the nymphs represented different stars within the Pleiades constellation, or the Abyss."

"What do you think the tapestry represented?" Selia asked.

Damien closed his eyes, trying to envision what he remembered. "There were two dragons depicted facing the star of the sea. Together, with the crystal at the center, they created a trident."

"What did the dragons represent?"

"Kai was the dragon from the East, and Mestor represented the West. They both represented Poseidon's two lineages." Damien watched the telescope shift in Selia's hand. "A star of the sea. Two dragons on either side." He grabbed the telescope, stopping it. "In order to find her, you must seek out the darkest star in the sea. Only Poseidon's ancestor knows my origin." He snapped his fingers. "That's it. Poseidon's sons don't have one, but *two* lineages. I think there are two names that will answer Erebéus's origin of Starlight."

Selia squinted at him. "How can there be two?"

"Think about the moon. It can be full, or new. Light, or dark. One is a mirror, the other is a window. One reflects, the other refracts." He pressed his eye back onto the eyepiece. "One is life, and one is death."

Selia grabbed his arm. "Could the answer involve Isis, and Nephthys?"

"It has to be. Isis and Nephthys were the original creators of the star of the sea." Damien said, pulling back from the eyepiece. "When Erebéus forced Isis out of her temple, her light left with her, casting her temple into darkness. *She* is the darkest star. Maera was using my artwork to reveal *Isis's* true identity after she fled her temple."

Selia squinted at her. "Why would Maera need to reveal Isis's identity? We know that she was an Egyptian goddess of life and fertility."

"But we don't know what happened to her after she was forced out of her temple by Erebéus."

Selia's brow furrowed. "Are you saying that Isis took on a different identity after she left her temple?"

"I think that Pherusa was right about one thing—Erebéus is manipulating something. I think he was the one to not only force Isis out of her temple, but in doing so, she lost her identity." He glanced up at the ceiling. "Only *one* of these stars are going to lead us to crack Maera's message and solve Erebéus's riddle. I think we need to match up the stars with the right colors."

"Hey, guys, look at this," Deidra said as she spun one of the rings on an astrolabe. It warbled back and forth, sending a beam of light out of its center.

The light landed on the base of the telescope.

"Why don't you put the crystal fragments in that spot, and we can see what happens?" Damien suggested.

Selia did so, and Deidra spun the astrolabe again. When the beam of light hit the crystals, it fragmented into colors, before quickly fading again.

"We need to find a way to filter the light so the colors match up with the corresponding stars," Damien said. He eyed the way the astrolabes were spaced. "We need something that's in the shape of a spiral."

"How about a spiral from a rare blue ammonite?" Deidra suggested.

Selia reached into her pocket and withdrew the creature. "Opal, we need your help."

"Set the shell right there," Damien instructed as he pointed to the base of the telescope where he set one of his paintings. "All colors in the presence of light are white. In the absence of light, they turn black. We need to figure out which of those stars up there is the darkest out of all of them."

"I'm glad you studied this, because I never would have thought about matching up colors with the stars," Selia said as she set Opals shell on the table beneath the giant lens.

Damien shrugged. "You do a lot of thinking when mixing pigments."

Deidra rearranged the crystals around Opal's shell, aligning them with the stars on Damien's painting.

"What do you see now?" Selia asked.

"I see the darkest star in the ocean," Damien said as he peered through the telescope. "Celaeno just lit up the night sky."

"What are you doing?" a voice shrieked from across the room as a woman appeared in Damien's periphery. "Get away from there!"

Pherusa tripped as Zakai waved her hand, sending a burst of light into her face.

Zakai's illuminations, however, did nothing to stop Pherusa's shadow serpents from reaching for them.

"Peppercorn, stop her!" Deidra demanded.

The mother bat dove, her pups swarming after Naunet's enraged mother.

The crystal fragments lit up as Deidra spun the astrolabe once again, showering the room in a brilliant burst of color.

Selia's arms became transparent as the colorful light erupting out of the crystals exploded into the air. "To the darkest star in the ocean," she said as she grabbed Damien's hand.

As her fingers gripped his, Damien's body too, became transparent. "Let's go find Little Origin."

62

TEARS OF STARLIGHT

Selia

Coldness embraced Selia as Damien's fingers slipped through her hand. In a blur of night sky and sea, he disappeared. A hard, damp surface slammed against her she fell onto the ground. The scent of salt water filled her nose.

She staggered to her feet, trying to make sense of her new surroundings. She stood in a cavern-like structure, with water dripping down the walls. The bitter taste of salt filled her mouth. Everything glowed with a strange disembodied light that had no source. The ceiling, if there was a ceiling, was completely concealed in vaporous mist. Her lungs became tighter with every breath. The atmosphere reminded her of the place she'd first encountered Hecate—a void space full of liquid echoes where time didn't seem to exist.

Had they entered the Temple of the Three Origins? If so, what chamber was she in?

"Damien?" she whispered, putting her hands out to feel for anything that might tell her where she'd gone. Tiny lights glistened around her, reminding her of stars.

Liquid covered the ground, reflecting the lights as it trickled down the path. She scrambled to her feet, following the blue liquid as it filled the chamber.

A low grunting sound echoed from ahead. A large figure lay on the ground. Selia slowed her pace, fearing that it might be Erebéus. What if the sphinx was lurking in the dark, ready to pounce?

She took another step, her foot splashing into the blue liquid that pooled around the figure. A man lay on his side, his arms and legs sprawled out. His face was covered in dark scales, membranous fins branching out behind his ears and jaw.

"Balfour? What happened to you?" Selia cried.

Balfour groaned again, his eyes flicking up to find her. What had once been deep pools of ebony had become dangerously shallow.

She dropped to his side. Something was happening to his body. He morphed between man and dragon, flickering like a dying flame. His tail shifted through the puddle, shedding scales as it it quivered to a stop.

The blue liquid was his blood...

"Who did this to you?" she asked, shivering.

"One of my brothers," Balfour replied, his voice thick with broken thunder. His eyes began to roll into the back of his head.

Selia's breathing stopped. Her storm dragon was leaving her. She set her hand onto his side, feeling for his pulse. Scales were splayed open on his ribs, revealing the throbbing mass of his heart.

Balfour wasn't just any storm dragon, he was *her* storm dragon. His heart trembled, beating like a wave that had no place to crash upon a shore. A horrible thought crossed her mind.

Was he passing into the Great Storm?

Her hand became transparent as her ring began to glow. "Balfour, don't leave me."

She fell into the mist blooming out of her ring. It swirled around them like silver ribbons. Balfour's body dissolved like she'd seen many times before. But this time, she knew his mist wouldn't reform.

"No, you *can't* leave," she begged, reaching out and trying to collect the ribbons of his soul. Tears ran past her cheeks as she was thrust once again into the empty void.

"*You have not answered my riddle, Blind Moon. My descendant will return to the storm from which his soul originates from,*" Erebéus said, his giant voice booming into her head.

"*I refuse to answer your riddle until I have my daughter.*"

"*Then Balfour's soul will return to his origin.*"

Selia glanced down at her legs and body, all of which were now aglow. She closed her eyes, focusing on the rhythmic sound echoing in her ears. Her pulse was sinking with something out of her reach.

Lightning flashed behind her eyelids, breaking her eyes wide open.

Balfour floated before her, half man, half dragon. He shifted between the two, storms of mist and lightning coiling around him.

Selia threw out her hands as she tried to reach him. "Bellerophon, I am bound to you. I won't let you go. I ask the tides to return your soul to me."

Ribbons of mist gathered around her hand, tethering between her fingers as they coiled up her wrists and arms. The stars fell away, and Balfour's body appeared on the ground.

Selia pulled her hand away from his side. The wound had been had sealed over, scales now lining his skin.

His eyes found hers, deeper than they had been before. The shallowness there before was gone. "Blind Moon?" he asked, his cold hand coming to hers.

"It's been quite a journey finding you again," she said, grabbing his large hand and bringing it to her face. "I'm so glad I found you when I did."

"Your tears, they look like stars," he said, sitting up and wiping one of the salty drops away from her eye. As it fell to the ground, light burst out of the liquid, shattering like a crystal.

"What's happened to you?" he asked as Selia's hands lit up. "You're glowing."

Selia wiped the remaining tears away from her cheek. They glowed silvery white, illuminating Balfour's worried face. "Balfour...she took Nyssa..." tears formed again, light pouring onto the ground as she sobbed.

Balfour straightened himself. "Calm down. I'm all right," he said, shifting closer to her. He tucked his hand beneath her chin, tilting her face up to look into his eyes. "Who took your daughter?"

"Maera did."

"*Maera?*" Balfour questioned, his voice lowering as well as his hand. "Why would she take Little Origin?"

Another sob escaped her. "Damien and I don't know. That's why we're here. Maera left a message stating that the only way we could find her was to find the darkest star in the ocean, and that only your ancestor knows her origin."

"Where is Damien?"

"I was hoping you could answer that. He must be here somewhere. Are we in the Temple of the Three Origins?"

"We are in the Chamber of Salt," Balfour replied. "My brothers are trying to find their way into the Chamber of Storms."

She caught a glimpse of the scales shimmering on his ribs where the wound had been. "Which of your brothers did this to you?"

"I don't know. Before you showed up, I heard Mestor say something about Amphitrite betraying them. Then Mestor grabbed Amy before they both left me here to die."

Selia's hands burned with silver light. Something shimmered in the puddle of Balfour's blue blood. She grabbed the item, bringing it to her face. A crystal fragment glistened in her fingers that made her salt aura pulse.

She stood up and grabbed Balfour's arm, tugging him up to his feet. "Nobody treats my storm dragon like this and expects to get away with it."

63

CHAMBER OF SALT

Amy

As Amy pounded her fist into Mestor's beefy arm, visions of Balfour's bloody body flashed before her. How could Mestor side with Kai and abandon his brother? "Turn around! My mother can heal him!"

"Your mother abandoned the boat shortly after you and the fisherman did," Mestor growled as he carried her further into the cavern. "None of us have seen her."

Amy's stomach pitted. Why would her mother just abandon their quest?

Maera had mentioned that Isis was nearby before the two storm dragons injured Balfour. Did her mother know that Isis was here somewhere in the strange cavern full of starlit corals?

Kai stormed ahead, illuminating the coral with the flames spewing out of a set of fins that flared out of his black spines.

"Hold it, Kai," Mestor barked as he repositioned Amy so that she couldn't grab a fistful of his hair. "You haven't kept your part of the bargain."

Kai rounded on his brother, flames licking up his mask as his dark hair fell over his shoulders. "There is no bargain when it comes to Celaeno's remains. All we have is what the goddesses of life and death have promised us."

Amy's breathing stopped. Did the Chamber of Salt contain *Celaeno's remains*?

"There is no goddess of life here," Mestor argued, his voice shaking. "Only death lingers in this place. I wouldn't be surprised if we ran into our ancestor lurking in the dark."

"Then we use her as bait," Kai said, his voice thickening like the smoke billowing out of his sides. "We will see how long it takes for mother and daughter to reunite."

Amy jolted. *Bait?*

Mestor lowered her to the ground.

She slammed her hand into his chest. "You are horrible, you know that? Leaving your brother to die back there? How could you!"

Mestor didn't flinch as she scolded him. He grabbed one of his dreadlocks and ripped it from his head. He tugged Amy's hands behind her back and bound her wrists with it.

Amy kicked her legs out, trying to free herself. But she was no match for Mestor's powerful grip. "I thought you and Kai were enemies. Now you're working together?"

Kai leered over her, his mask spitting flames out of the holes made for the nostrils. His brooding silence made Amy feel even more infuriated with him. She sank down into a crouched position, propping her back against the wall. How did the two dragons plan to use her to reveal her mother's whereabouts?

Guilt wrecked her gut. *Lachlan.* Since she'd been kidnapped, she'd not even thought about her gallant fisherman.

Mestor straightened himself, slinging his dreadlocks over his shoulder. He spun on his heel, following Kai into the center of the strange, dimly-lit room.

Amy couldn't tell where the walls, ceiling, and floor separated. Everything was damp, echoing with the trickling sound of water. Dark silhouettes moved about the space as Balfour's other brothers emerged in the cavern. Lykos and Taras entered, followed by Idas and Hopleus. Pelias, however, was still missing.

"Still no sign of Amphitrite?" Lykos asked as he approached Mestor.

Mestor shook his head. "No. Until she shows herself, none of us are returning to the surface. We cannot enter the Chamber of Storms without her."

As Mestor surveyed the group, Kai walked around them, his movements swift and predator-like.

Amy still didn't understand why the dynamic between the dragons from the East and the West had changed. They were obviously rivals, seeing one another as competition over oceanic territory. Why had Mestor and his brothers sided with the dragon from the Orient who attacked them on the surface?

"She's sure to come for her daughter when they enter the cavern," Kai said, backing away from the pool.

A hiss sounded from the mist separating over the water.

Amy shivered as the familiar sound the sirens slithered toward her.

Arms and wrists emerged out of the pool as they clambered over one another.

The pain she'd felt—searing hot pain—broke through her body as they clawed their way closer.

She no longer had the crystal fragment. What would the sirens do to her? She closed her eyes, trying not to think about what might happen next. She knew what they were searching for. They wanted the crystal she no longer had.

Would they rip her limb-from-limb as they searched for it?

"Try to imagine what it's like when the venom seduces you," a voice hissed, forcing Amy to open her eyes.

Masika's face blurred in the mass if horribleness crawling out of the pool. In the sea of deformed arms and grey skin, her friend emerged as a vaporous mist.

"I tried to save you. Stay away from me," Amy ground out.

Masika's face came inches away from her. "You have nothing to save. The salt venom and I are one in the same." She pressed her lips to Amy, kissing her.

Amy recoiled, choking as the bitter taste of the salt venom filled her mouth.

Masika bit down onto her lower lip, sending white-hot pain jolting through her.

Amy's eyes closed as pain seared through her, striking every nerve in her body. A terrible storm of regret, loneliness, and grief blew through her.

This was it. She was dying...

"Hey!"

Amy fell backward as someone grabbed her around the waist. She tumbled through the sirens, falling with her captor as they forced through the mass of mangled arms and hissing faces.

Down they went, sliding into a crevasse hidden beneath the mist. They spun and spiraled until the passage opened into another layer of the cavern.

She landed in a soft heap of something much less menacing than the mangled swarm of sirens. Minca kelp bloomed around them, great plumes of the blue fronds unraveling like ferns in the night. The minca's texture was soft and feathery, not slimy like most seaweeds and kelps.

"That was too close," Lachlan said, falling to the ground beside her. One of the blue fronds unraveled, arching over them both.

Amy threw out her arms, her wrists now free. She touched her bottom lip, which was bleeding. The searing pain, however, was gone. She swallowed the iron-rich taste of her own blood.

"Do you see them? The stars, how bright they are?" Lachlan said, a smile curling upon his lips as more fronds of minca arched over them "Why do they make me think of snow and the mountains?"

Amy crawled to where he lay, blue minca sheltering them both. The fronds were glowing, each with tiny silver lights. The flickering lights reflected in liquid pooling on Lachlan's chest.

Amy's breath stopped.

He'd been wounded by the sirens...

Lachlan didn't seem to notice. He gazed up at the minca, his blue eyes reflecting the thousands of tiny silver lights. "I'd love to take you there one day. Just you and me, and a cabin in the woods. How does that sound?"

"I would go with you in a heartbeat," Amy replied, her voice breathless and weak.

"I'm a hopeless romantic, what can I say?" he said, his words slurring as his eyes rolled back. "I know you are much too bright of a star to fall for a fisherman like me."

Amy took his hand into hers, his calluses working over her palm. How perfect he felt. How little reasoning there was for this reckless, pointless adventure into the heart of the sea. "I can't loose you again," she whispered, taking Lachlan's body into her arms. His blood felt cold. This couldn't be happening.

She had lost him then, and now, *again.*

What cruel fate had made her endure history repeating itself?

"Lachlan Ewan, I never told you then, so I'll tell you now. I love you from the bottom of the sea, to the top of your sacred mountain."

She bent down, pressing her lips to his. Time melted away as the taste of iron from her blood, and the winter-rich memory of Ewan dying atop the sacred mountain flooded her again. Her memories of the past blended with the present, mending like a stitch over a wound not even time could heal.

Salt crystals jutted out of the blue minca as the giant fronds coiled over them.

64

CHAMBER OF STORMS

Damien

Damien's sense of direction dispersed as quickly as Selia's hand left his. A vortex of wind and darkness funneled around him. Thunder rumbled in the distance as lightning tore overhead. The scent of smoke burned his nose as a room manifested.

His legs buckled as gravity grounded him into his new surroundings. Blue flames rose out of a crackling hearth. A giant tapestry hung above the flames, with blue smoke rising up toward the ceiling. His breath caught.

Had he returned to the Temple of Salt, Storms, and Starlight?

"Selia?" he said. The echoing sound of his voice unsettled him. He approached the flames. Something about this place wasn't like he remembered.

He glanced up at the ceiling, searching for the magnificent stained glass windows depicting the seven stars of the Pleiades. The room was so blue with the smoke. A thick haze clouded Celaeno's dark window.

A figure appeared to his left, a woman he recognized meeting him here before. She wore white linens, a golden necklace, and earrings decorated with blue beads. "Welcome back, Damien."

Damien gripped his hands together, his fingernails digging into his palms. He had to keep himself calm. The last thing he wanted to do was for her to harm his daughter. "Why have I returned to this temple?"

Maera stopped a few paces away from him, her long brown hair swaying. "The Temple of Salt, Storms, and Starlight has three separate entry chambers. You have entered the Chamber of Storms, where the Tapestry of Tridents resides."

"Where is Selia?"

"She is in the Chamber of Starlight. Amy and Poseidon's sons are currently within the Chamber of Salts."

"I'm not understanding. I thought Amphitrite and Poseidon's sons set out to find Poseidon's crown. How did we all end up at this temple at the same time from separate locations?"

Maera approached the hearth, standing next to Damien. She waved her hand, sending the blue smoke away. More of the tapestry emerged, above the two dragons and the star of the sea. A snow capped mountain, framed by a blanket of stars. "There are three ways to visit the temple. Through the ocean, through smoke, or with the help of an architect. All three of you have seen these places. All three chambers house memories that Isis and Nephthys used when they created the star of the sea. It is a timeless temple, full of ancestral spirits, and memories."

Damien tried to wrap his mind around the concept of a temple existing outside of time, let alone being part of a crystal.

Maera folded her hands in front of her. "All three of you are required to be present for Amphitrite's Ocean Apothecary experiment."

Damien glanced around the space, searching for any sign of an experiment taking place. "What experiment?"

"You have long been familiar with the Sgàthan clan belief? That memory and spirits reflect one another—that they are one in the same. Have you ever wondered where that belief originated from?"

"Let me guess, this temple?"

Maera nodded. "The Chamber of Storms, specifically. This chamber houses a memory pertaining to the creation of the star of the sea."

Damien blinked, trying to take in the details of the artwork before him. When he'd seen the tapestry before, he'd been fare away. But from this perspective, it didn't look like fabric. There were thousands of smaller images—all paintings he'd completed long ago.

The tapestry was a mural of his watercolor paintings of the ocean.

"It is a mural of memories. Not only from you, but originating from your ancestors as well." Maera gazed up at the mural before them. "I find that like the stars, the images appear so different from when far away. But if you gaze at them more closely? You can see how every image, every memory, has a purpose in a much larger piece."

Damien lowered his gaze. "Maera, you must give our daughter back. Selia and I have been worried sick about her."

"Your daughter is not in danger," another voice sounded from behind.

Damien spun, finding another sea nymph entering the chamber. Long red hair folded over her shoulders. Amphitrite's star-shaped freckles darkened as her emerald eyes drifted up from the infant bundled in her arms and locked with him. "I asked Maera to bring Nyssa here."

Damien's heart stopped. His body stiffened, adrenaline surging through him. It took all of his strength not to lunge toward the sea goddess and take back his daughter. "You asked her to steal her without telling us?" he bit out, his voice hard. "You put her to sleep so you could *experiment* with her?"

"All I needed from you, Damien Malloch, was but a simple memory your artwork has helped to preserve," Amphitrite said as she took a step back, retreating into the smoke.

Maera's eyes flickered from brown to a startling blue. She also disappeared, her body evaporating.

"Stop!" Damien cried, lunging for the blue smoke that swallowed them both.

65
CHAMBER OF STARLIGHT
Selia

Selia and Balfour followed the lights shimmering along the path. They synced with her heart, quickening with the rhythm of her pulse. She held the crystal fragment in front of her, using it to guide their way through the dark.

"*Stop,*" Balfour said from behind. "*Something is not right.*"

Selia glanced down the tunnel where she'd heard a high-pitched *hiss*.

Were the sirens here?

Balfour grabbed her hand, tugging her away from the wall as blackened crystals jutted from the surface. The crystals jostled against one another, shattering as a red-haired sea nymph came tumbling out into the open.

She landed on the ground, brushing her hair out of her eyes.

Selia fell to her side. "Amy?"

Amy's gaze leveled with her. "Selia? How did you get here?"

"Damien and I went to Gaia's archives, but we got separated in the process. Where are we, exactly?"

"I was in the Chamber of Salt, until Balfour's brothers found me," Amy replied as she sat up. "The storm dragons have gone mad. They turned on Balfour and attacked him."

Balfour emerged from the shadows, stopping next to Selia. "I appreciate you trying to stop them," he said aloud, his voice more hushed than normal.

"Thank goodness!" Amy cried. "I was so worried about you. What happened to the wound on your side?"

"The Blind Moon healed me," Balfour replied. "Her salt aura has come alive with a brand new ability."

"Or, it was this crystal fragment that helped me to heal you," Selia said as she held the crystal in front of Amy's face. Balfour's blue blood still coated the surface. "Is this what they were fighting over?"

"I thought so, but then they took off and didn't seem to notice that Balfour had it." Amy said as she climbed to her feet. Her hand grazed the wall as she steadied herself.

"Don't touch the crystals. You are going to hurt yourself," Selia said. When she tried to grab Amy's arm, her hand passed through her.

Amy's mouth dropped open. "What's happening to you?"

Selia withdrew her hand. "I don't know, but it looks like it's happening to you, too."

Amy held up her arm, which had also become transparent. "Our salt auras are reacting to something."

"Celaeno's coral remains have long housed the salt crystals that hold the power to blend the past with the present," a voice said.

Selia and Amy both spun, finding a figure emerging from within the crystals.

Balfour stepped between them, guarding them as a vaporous mist filled the room.

Masika manifested. Her appearance was just as menacing as Selia remembered of her. Long, matted hair draped over her shoulders. Her pale skin glimmered in the dim light. Her fingernails matched her dark, liquid eyes.

Selia's stomach hollowed as the nightmare from her past resurrected itself.

"Stay back, you witch," Balfour growled, his thunderous voice shaking the cavern.

Masika didn't hiss, nor did she make any attempt to assault them. "You currently reside inside the Chamber of Starlight within the Temple of the Three Origins. You are surrounded by what remains of your ancestral salts—the darkest star."

"Celaeno's coral remains are the darkest star?" Selia asked.

"They were, until your daughter was born," another voice said.

Maera emerged from the wall, stepping out into the open. She waved her hand, and Masika's vaporous form evaporated.

Selia's body went cold. "Maera, give Nyssa back to me."

Maera folded her hands in front of her as an icy coldness crept into the room. "Even if I did give her back to you, you wouldn't be able to fully revive her."

"What does that mean? Why do you want her?" Selia spat, her salt aura flaring out in sharp bursts.

Maera's eyes swept between the three of them as she spoke. "All salt daughters of Celaeno must be accounted for if the Abyss is to be remedied. The ancestral mother of the sea cannot be whole without them. All souls must be gathered in one place to restore the darkest star of the ocean."

Selia glared at her. "But Naunet isn't here, neither is her mother. I know their salt ancestry originates from Celaeno."

"Both Pherusa and her daughter served as midwives of the sea. They are not required to be present as they have both bonded with Erebéus," Maera replied as her eyes dropped to the crystal glowing in Selia's hand. "It appears the Blind Moon has recovered another piece of her inheritance. But where are the other two fragments?"

"I don't have them. And even if I did, I'm not going to give anything to you to mend until I have my daughter."

Maera's mouth curled. "There is no need for the crystal fragments to make the Abyss whole again. They were only needed to unite all of you here, so that I could continue on with Amphitrite's Ocean Apothecary experiment."

"I don't understand," Selia stammered. How can you possibly restore the star of the sea if you don't have the fragments? And why do you need my daughter?"

Maera's blue eyes met hers. "Selia, look at yourself. You *are* the crystal. The darkest star lives inside of your heart, your blood, beating with your pulse this entire time. You only needed visit the Chamber of Starlight to see it."

Selia lowered herself to the ground, focusing on her pulse. As she breathed in, and out, the dark crystals lining the cavern lit up. The crystal fragment in her hand transformed. Coated in the blood of her storm dragon, the crystal grew three times its original size.

"Blind Moon, be careful," Balfour warned as the crystals began to jut out of the ground.

Selia blocked out his voice. She didn't care. This sea nymph had stolen her daughter, and she was going to get even with her.

"The only thing I've realized is just how toxic you are!" Selia cried as she raised her hand with her crystal dagger and lunged for Maera.

PART 8
THE THREE ORIGINS

66

STARLIT CORALS

Amy

As Selia lunged for Maera with the crystal dagger in her hand, a cold vapor gripped Amy around her center. The chamber went dark as she struggled with the new sensation. Pain struck her chest as though Selia had plunged the crystal into her own heart.

Yet somehow, the pain she felt went far deeper.

By the time the vapor settled, Selia and Maera disappeared, along with Balfour.

A woman with long red hair came into view. Amphitrite was crouched by the water, trailing her fingers over the surface.

"Mother, what are you doing?" Amy said as she approached her.

Amphitrite was not well. Her skin was pale. Her freckles were dark and splotchy, no longer star-shaped.

She doubled over, coughing. Black, oily liquid spilled from her mouth into the pool.

"No!" Amy screamed, darting for her mother. She fell to her side, unable to think. Like herself, her mother's arms had become transparent. Amphitrite's once beautiful fire red hair became silver. "Mother, what is happening to you?"

Amphitrite propped herself onto her hands, digging her fingers into the salt crystals forming around the pool, "Isis," she whispered as she gazed into the water. "I finally see her."

Amy gazed into the pool, searching for the goddess of life. A fae creature she recognized swam between the coral branching just beneath the surface. Her silver wings pulsed as she maneuvered between the brilliant white structures.

The fae queen...

The coral appeared bleached. In any other shallow sea, it would be a sure sign of death. But here, the water was swimming with life. Fish swam between blades of blue minca that framed the coral. Did these corals really possess some kind of starlight? If so, what could it show her?

As the fae queen swam between the corals, the water began to churn.

The faces of her friends were there, mixing with one another. Selia and Damien stood on a beach together, with Balfour standing between them. A giant moon rose in the distance, sending silver beams of light across the ocean.

The light broke over the water, branching like lightning as it mimicked the shape of the jagged white corals. A vision appeared within the pool.

Her mother appeared, standing before Poseidon in his temple. She turned away from him, her face stricken with tears as he held his hand toward her.

As Amphitrite left the temple, a shadow followed her. She stopped on the marble steps as a figure manifested before her. "Why have you refused him again?"

Amphitrite gazed up at Nephthys as she waited for an answer. "Please, I cannot continue to break his heart like this," Amphitrite said to the goddess of death. "He cannot know what I am suffering from. Nobody can, not even my daughter."

Amy shuddered at the fear in her mother's voice. What was she suffering from that she felt she needed to hide it?

"If you stay in Atlantis, your salt aura will continue to suffer," Nephthys replied. "Your only choice is to take what remains of the star of the sea and to leave at once."

"I know," Amphitrite replied, her voice shaking as she winced again. Her hands and arms became transparent. "How do I make sure that my daughter doesn't come searching for me?"

"She will search for you, but Isis and I will make sure that she never finds you. We will ensure that what survives from your Ocean Apothecary after the great city falls is sent to your daughter." She set her hand on Amphitrite's shoulder. "Never forget the truth about the starlit corals, no matter how dark and lonely the seas become toward you, Amphitrite, goddess of the sea."

Amphitrite nodded. "I wish from the depths of my soul that I can one day find a way to have my daughter forgive me."

The vision vanished from the pool. The water settled, leaving Amy feeling helpless. She glanced up at her mother, whose eyes were glassy with emotion. "I know why you refused Poseidon's attempts to bond with you. Mother, you were the one who was ill, weren't you?"

Amphitrite's emerald eyes met hers, truth glinting in them. "Yes. As a result of fragmenting the star of the sea, I in turn, damaged my own salt aura. I became very ill. No matter what I tried, I could not find a remedy for the illness I had brought upon myself."

"But you did as Erebéus requested! Could he not find a way to help you?"

"Erebéus withdrew into the Temple of Isis shortly after I fragmented the crystal. Eventually, he forced her to abandon her crystal fragment and fleet her temple."

"What about Pherusa? Could your own sister not help you recover?"

"No. As I told you before, I chose not to follow her and her daughters to Egypt. I did not want to risk contaminating the new life they began after the great city sank."

"Where did you go? For all of that time, where did you hide from me?"

"This temple, and the Chamber of Salt, became my refuge as I tried to find a remedy for my symptoms. Not long after Naunet became the next midwife of the sea, the plague of salt venom broke out, and Maera became a victim."

"That's when she became trapped within the temple?"

Amphitrite nodded. "With Celaeno's ancestral salts contaminated by the salt venom, I knew that not only was I ill, but so was the sea. That's when she and I pondered the idea of restoring the crystal. Erebéus would allow her to leave the temple temporarily. I had one crystal fragment, and she had the one that Nephthys gave to her. But we could not accomplish our goal without the fragment that Isis had left in Erebéus's possession. And only Isis knew who should be the one to inherit it."

Amy's fists clenched as anger coursed through her. "You told me that you and Maera were working together to remedy the Abyss."

Amphitrite's gaze intensified. "I don't understand your concern."

"My concern? How about blatant fury?" Amy clenched her fists. "Did you ever think that maybe I would want to help my own mother?"

Silence filled the chamber. Amy's heart thundered so loudly, her blood pounded in her ears.

"You were dying. You *are* dying," Amy continued, her words sounding harsh and forbidden. "All you have done is try and protect your sister. You want to know what I think? I think Pherusa is selfish. All she could focus on was her jealousy. She never put you or me above herself or her own daughters."

"Amy, Please. I never wanted you to think that I abandoned you."

Amy's vision blurred as her mother's words gouged into her. "But you *did* abandon me. All because of what? You and Maera wanted to experiment with these crystal fragments?"

"There were other lives to consider other than myself. Think of the plague victims. Think of what what they have endured after Naunet abandoned her role as the midwife of the sea. The day she left, the only hope for remedying the situation with the Abyss passed on to me."

Anger rippled through Amy's body. "As long as I've known you, you have done everything to protect the ocean—to make visible a world that not everyone sees." Tears burned in her eyes as her words mumbled together. "But I can't continue to be alone like this. I can't, and I *won't*."

Amphitrite's voice cracked as she spoke, "I know how alone you have been. That's why I brought his spirit back to you."

Amy squinted at her mother. "What do you mean?"

"Have you not noticed the way Lachlan looks at you? Even after eons of time pass, two souls will recognize one another."

Amy blinked, thinking of Lachlan's face as he blended with the huntsman. "Why would you do that for me? And how is that even possible?"

"The fae queen's magic originates from the starlit corals she emerged from. She is the source of both death, and life. I wanted to give my daughter a second chance at loving one of the souls who cared for her. You are right. You deserve to be happy with someone who can be there for you, always."

Amy stared at the pool, unable to look at her mother any longer. The fae queen swam beneath the water. Her brilliant silver wings drifted behind her, pulsing with the light put off by the starlit corals.

"Come watch the stars arrive with me."

Amy's throat closed as Ewan's words echoed through her.

She reached into the water, grabbing one of the starlit corals. With a swift tug, she snapped off a sharp fragment.

"Amy, what are you doing?"

Amy glanced down at the water, the light of the fae queen spiraling below. There was only one way to free her mother and herself from the spell this temple and the starlit corals had put on them both.

Her mother reached for her. "If you do anything to harm the queen, Ewan's soul will vanish. Her timeless magic is the only reason that you can still be with him. You will lose everything you fought for—both in the past, and in the present."

Amy clutched the coral in her hand. She sucked in a breath and dove into the water.

67

STARS

Damien

The mist billowing into the room thinned as Damien regained his composure. Maera, Amphitrite, and Selia had disappeared into the blue storm smoke.

"Damn it," he stammered, coughing.

The Tapestry of Tridents appeared. A large, smoky figure silhouetted the work of art.

The ground shook as a low, thunderous voice echoed around him. "Who enters my chamber of storms?"

Damien staggered to his feet as the mist parted, revealing a figure where there used to be a throne. A giant man wearing blue robes emerged from the storm smoke. Metal gauntlets decorated his wrists—one silver, the other gold.

Poseidon manifested before him, looming like a giant through the storm smoke. He dipped his chin, his regal face illuminating in the dim light. "You are not one of my sons. What business do you have within my temple, human?"

Damien's gaze dropped to Poseidon's gauntlet as he repositioned it over his forearm. Blue liquid dripped from his skin onto the ground. "Are you hurt?"

Poseidon's eyes drifted up toward the stained glass windows towering above them. Tears streaked down his cheeks as he spoke. "As I gaze into your crown of starlit shadows, the Great Storm finds the light of my ancestors. My heart is broken. I seek out your help from the Oblivion."

Damien staggered backward as Poseidon fell to his knees.

The god of the sea hit the ground with such force that the flames shook in the hearth behind him. His massive hand landed up, his thick fingers flexing over a sharp item.

Before Damien could attempt to help Poseidon, both the tapestry and the great god of the sea vanished into the blue storm smoke.

"Damien?"

Damien spun on his heel, finding Selia running toward him. He grabbed her as she launched herself into his arms. "Thank goodness. I thought I lost you."

Selia's feet hit the ground and she pulled away from him. "Where are we?"

"We're in the temple of Salt, Storms, and Starlight."

"I know that. I was just in the Chamber of Starlight. Which chamber are we in now?"

"The Chamber of Storms," Damien answered as he wiped a strand of hair away from her eyes. He caught sigh of a shiny object clutched in her hand. "What is that?"

"A fragment of the star of the sea," she stammered, holding it out for him to see. "I found it along with Balfour earlier. Maybe we can use it to find Nyssa. Which chamber do you think she is in?"

"I'd say salt."

"Then we need to figure out how to get there," Selia said as she took off.

"Selia, wait," Damien said as he bent down and grabbed the sharp item Poseidon had left on the ground.

"What is it? A crystal? Or a dragon scale?"

"I don't know." his breath caught. "I think I witnessed Poseidon's last moments before he died."

Selia's mouth dropped open. "You saw Poseidon?"

Damien nodded. "Right before you appeared, he was standing right in front of me. He fell to the ground. He was bleeding."

Selia glanced up. "Oh, wow. Look at those windows!"

"Those are the stained glass windows I told you about, remember? The ones I thought represented the seven stars found in the constellation Pleiades?"

Selia squinted. "Look how they are shaped. Does their formation resemble a crown to you?"

Damien gazed up at the windows, repeating Poseidon's words from moments before. "As I gaze into your crown of starlit shadows, the Great Storm finds the light of my ancestors. My heart is broken. I seek out your help from the Oblivion."

His chest burned as something struck him.

He staggered backward.

"Damien!" Selia screamed as sharp crystal daggers rained down around them.

Damien fell, his body weightless. Lights flashed before him as the crystals ripped the tapestry to shreds. Stars—that's what they were. They were nothing to be afraid of.

He felt winded, out of breath. Still, his heart pulsed quicker as more of the crystals shimmered around him like a rainbow of liquid glass.

Electrical outbursts broke through the atmosphere as he sank deeper into the starlit sea. Brilliant lightning flashed overhead, striking through him as the coiling tails of the dragons spiraled.

A great storm—the one he'd seen every time he painted—it was right here in this temple. The energy it created pulsed through him. He glanced up, finding the stained glass windows of all seven stars of the Abyss raining down on him.

With a rippling *crack*, a bolt of lightning zapped through the shadows clutching Damien's throat.

"*Damien, hold on,*" Balfour said, his voice tumbling like a wave after him.

In a flash of onyx scales and fins, Balfour tore up toward the window where Celaeno's image used to be.

68
DEATH OF A KING

Selia

In a fury of blue smoke, Selia fell to the ground. Her crystal fragment was knocked from her hand. Her palms scraped against the jagged surface of the glass that had rained down atop Damien. She closed her eyes, trying to forget what she'd just witnessed.

Damien falling as a thousand shards of glass came raining down on him.

"You..." Selia breathed, her voice unrecognizable. She turned to face the spirit standing at the edge of the pool where Damien had fallen.

Maera's composure did not change. She remained standing, her hands clasped together at her front.

Selia blinked, tears and smoke burning her eyes. "First, you take my daughter. And now you take him? Why are you doing this?"

Maera's gaze leveled with her. "Damien solved the riddle you refused to answer. You should be grateful for his actions. Doing so means that neither you, nor your daughter, will have to face the same fate I have endured since I killed the great god of the sea."

Selia clenched her hands. "*You* killed Poseidon? Why?"

Maera took a step toward her. "Amphitrite and I might have agreed on one thing regarding the bonds between sea nymphs and storm dragons. They should only be formed when love is not woven within them."

"This is about love? Between who?"

"Unrequited love between Amphitrite and Poseidon," Maera replied, her voice hard. "Amphitrite refused to bond with Poseidon, a right she was free to choose. But her choice endangered the very symbol of Poseidon's power—his trident."

"I don't understand. How could refusing to bond with Poseidon endanger his trident?"

Maera dipped her chin, making the light dapple across her high cheeks bones. "It all goes back to when Erebéus requested Amphitrite to fragment the crystal."

Maera waved her hand, scattering the blue smoke that filled the room. A giant tapestry clung to the wall before her. Two dragons coiled up the tapestry, one red, and the other blue. A giant star shone above them, seven beams of light trailing down into the sea below.

She settled herself in front of the tapestry, gazing upward. "This tapestry illustrates Poseidon's two tridents, or lineages from the East and the West. It was created long ago by Damien's ancestors in Atlantis. During Poseidon's reign, Amphitrite's sister, Pherusa, served as the midwife of the sea. She attempted multiple times to bond with Poseidon, but he refused. He had his sights set on only one goddess of the sea."

Selia took a step back as the tapestry changed. The threads morphed around one another, illustrating two sea nymphs. One had dark hair, the other red. Poseidon stood between them, his regal face focused on the sea nymph with brilliant red hair.

Maera folded her hands in front of herself once again. "I watched in silence as time and time again, Amphitrite rejected the great god of the sea. With each rejection, jealousy from her sister, Pherusa, grew stronger. Until one day, Erebéus approached Amphitrite, requesting that she fragment the very crystal that her starlit corals drew their power from."

Selia held her breath as the tapestry changed. Shadows billowed down above Poseidon's throne, cloaking him in darkness.

Maera's face dipped into the shadows. "Despite my attempts to warn her, Amphitrite used the starlit corals to fragment the crystal. Soon after she did, Poseidon became very ill."

"People began to suspect that Amphitrite made him sick, didn't they?" Selia asked.

"Some say he became ill from her fragmenting the crystal. Some say his illness was a result of her rejecting his love," Maera's eyes leveled with her. "I knew I could use the dying sea god as a means to protect what I had devoted my life in preserving—the Temple of the Three Origins."

Maera waved her hand, making the tapestry change once again. Amphitrite strode away from Poseidon, who with his outstretched hand, had fallen to the ground. Long strands of what Selia assumed was blue minca surrounded him.

"All Amphitrite had to do was choose him. But her first love had always been the sea. She could never put a dragon and the storms he created before her true love of the ocean. Poseidon even offered to let her choose which bond to create. And still, she said no. Instead, she buried herself in her Ocean Apothecary, obsessing with her starlit corals. With the star of the sea fragmented, and Poseidon's death on the horizon, the great kingdom of Atlantis would fall. His death, when it did happen, quickly became something that I could control."

"How could you control when Poseidon died?"

Maera's eyes drifted up toward the wall. "By having Damien's ancestors create this tapestry." She crouched to the pool and dipped her hand into the water, withdrawing a strand of something blue. "Every time Amphitrite rejected his attempt to bond, one of his scales created a bloom of blue minca. But the minca was as ill as his heart had become, and withered into a strand like this. Amphitrite gave the strands to me, which I became inspired to create a work of artwork with. But even in death, minca can still bloom. It seeks after light from the moon."

"Strands of moonlight," Selia said, remembering back to the folktale that Damien had shared with her when they first met.

"That story dates back to the very strands woven together by Damien's ancestors. Combined with the salt of his tears, it continued to grow out of the tapestry it was woven into. Until one day, it reached the windows of his crown above Poseidon's throne." Maera waved her hands, changing the tapestry again. Poseidon stood with his hands at his sides, gazing up at seven colorful windows above him. "One day, Poseidon became so frustrated with Amphitrite's rejections, he returned to his temple and gazed up into the heavens as he said, 'As I gaze into your crown of starlit shadows, the Great Storm finds the light of my ancestors. My heart is broken. I seek out your help from the Oblivion.'"

Crack!

Selia stepped back as the tapestry morphed again.

Poseidon lay on the ground, his body mangled with blue pooling all around him.

Maera lowered her gaze. "Poseidon's prayers brought upon his death. Naming the origin of an architect caused the minca to bloom. Once it bloomed, the darkest star of Celaeno's window to shattered, killing him instantly."

"The darkest star from his crown," Selia said. "Celaeno's window killed the god of the sea?"

Maera's eyes darkened. "A king never suspects his own crown as his downfall. This temple became both my prison, and my sanctuary. Killing Poseidon meant that not only would I have access the records of the Codex located within the Chamber of Salt, but the Chamber of Storms as well. To access the Chamber of Starlight, I had to face the darkness of Erebéus's shadows after what I had done to his descendant."

"What was this darkness you had to face?"

"Erebéus would have given you but one clue about this darkness when he asked you to state his origin."

Selia remembered how empty his eyes appeared when she refused to answer him. "He said that darkness held in the deepest places of one's soul is what separates the Great Storm from his origin."

Maera smiled. "Darkness is all that separates me from what Erebéus guards of the Codex in the Chamber of Starlight. These records were the last records Naunet touched before she fled Egypt. The knowledge is sacred and powerful. It dates back to when Gaia first gave birth to her daughters, as well as when she created the first architects to serve them."

Blue smoke filled the room, crowding the place where Maera had been.

Selia backed away from the tapestry as the smoke settled. A giant man cradled a woman with silver hair in his arms.

"Mestor?" Selia said as she approached Balfour's eldest brother.

"She's gone," he whispered, his voice trembling with emotion. "Amphitrite, the great goddess of the sea, is no more..."

69

ISIS

Amy

As soon as Amy hit the pool, the coral in her hand lit up. The starlit corals came to life, blooming like brilliant displays of silver moonlight. The walls surrounding her fell away, deepening to the point Amy could no longer see the bottom.

The fae queen swam before her, wings of silver drifting ghost-like through the sea. How brilliant she was, dancing like a moon amongst the starlit corals. That peace, no matter how tranquil, wouldn't last for long.

Amy clutched the coral in her hand, ready to drive it where it needed to go. She kicked her feet, focusing on the trail of silver light the queen left in her wake. Her wings were no longer soft, but jagged like Celaeno's coral remains. Amy floated behind her, transfixed with how bright the darkest star in the sea truly was.

The fae queen turned, floating toward her. Her giant eyes reflected Amy's coral dagger as she approach. Intelligence lived inside of her eyes that housed an ancient soul.

Amy kicked in the opposite direction, slowing her approach. The corals faded around her, illuminating a memory of her own. She stood in the snow, facing Errindoor, his mighty starlit antlers framing the sacred mountain.

She knew the origins of sea nymphs, and storm dragons, and even the great architects. But when a fae died, where did its spirit go? Would killing the fae queen end her forever? Maera said she reincarnated herself atop that mountain in the past, but who knew what would happen if she took the queen's life before it was her time to go.

She remembered feeling so helpless when she'd been too afraid to slay the mighty fae king. Her hesitation had cost Ewan his life.

"Salt, storms, and starlight, of which we sing. Your light we find in the crown of a king."

Amy braced herself, her coral dagger trembling in her fingers. This small creature had given her a light of hope. Now, that light would go out.

"I'm sorry. Please forgive me," Amy thought. She drew her arm back, then dove the coral down into the queen's body.

The movement stopped Amy's pulse as the entire sea became silent.

The queen folded around the coral as the jagged edge plunged through her delicate form.

Amy's fingers warmed as silver blood poured out of her.

The coral remains of Celaeno flashed, pulsing brilliant white light into the sea. Faces and arms and legs emerged as sea nymphs swam out into the open.

Panicked, Amy kicked for the surface. Had she made the right choice, killing the fae queen? Where were all of these sea nymphs coming from? Were they the plague victims?

How beautiful the souls of Celaeno's salt daughters really were. Down here, they weren't mangled sirens.

One of the sea nymphs approached Amy. Her dark eyes lit up as she swam close.

"Masika?" Amy thought.

Masika reached out her hand, grazing her cheek. *"Thank you for being there for me."*

Amy's friend drifted before her, her face healthy and alive.

She choked.

Masika grabbed her hand, tugging her toward the surface. Amy closed her eyes as bubbles exploded from her mouth.

Amy crawled out of the water, gasping for air. "Masika," she breathed. Where did she go? Was her spirit free, no longer cursed by the salt venom?

"Masika will be all right, along with the souls of the plague victims, thanks to you," a voice sounded from the cavern.

Amy squinted toward the silhouette framed in silver light approaching her. A white dress draped over her bare feet. Long brown hair tumbled over her shoulders. Her eyes were dark brown, matching the color of her hair. "Naunet, is that you?"

The woman tossed a piece of jagged coral onto the ground.

Amy's mind blanked. "I'm sorry, who are you?"

The woman bowed slightly, revealing an aura that branched over her like wings. "Does my lunar light not give me away?"

Amy's eyes dropped the piece of coral she'd tossed to the ground, then back to the woman before her. "Are you the fae queen?"

"Isis," she corrected, the light in her eyes impossible to ignore. "Thank you for releasing me."

70

EREBÉUS'S ORIGIN

Damien

Balfour's onyx fins surged around Damien, carrying him upward, then down. They plunged into a different kind of storm—one made of pure shadow.

He clutched what scales he could, bracing himself as Balfour's body swayed back and forth. The movements felt different. Were they flying, or swimming? He couldn't tell. He had to get back to Selia, but every time he thought about her, all he could see was the window shattering above him.

"Human, you were not meant to guess my origin, only the Blind Moon was," Erebéus's thick voice ground out. *"How dare you take Poseidon's dying words and use them against me."*

Damien jolted. "The *Oblivion*? That's the name of your origin?"

Balfour banked to the left as shadow coiled around his leg.

"You will not escape death so easily," Erebéus threatened. A low chuckle echoed around him. "Too bad Maera killed you shortly after you gave your answer. Now you will have to contend with my origin."

Damien jolted. Did Maera kill really *kill* him? He didn't *feel* dead. In fact, he didn't feel any pain at all.

The entire event happened so fast, he didn't have time to react.

Wind tunneled around him, ripping through his hair. The gusts were so forceful, they threatened to rip him from Balfour's back.

"You've seen this place before, haven't you?" Erebéus taunted. *"You plunged into it when you lost Maera and your daughter. You have visited the shadows of death before, Damien Malloch. That's how you knew how to answer my riddle..."*

Damien whipped his head around, trying to find out where Erebéus's voice was coming from. He sounded annoyed, angry even.

The shadows surged around him. His spine buckled. The gravity they created was sure to crush him if he didn't do something.

"*Do not listen to him,*" Balfour thundered. "*Only if you believe you are dead, will the Oblivion claim you. I have the power to bring you back into the Great Storm.*"

Despite Balfour's attempt to comfort him, Damien began to feel ill. What if he became trapped between the two origins of the storm dragon and his ancestor?

Erebéus's shadows gained on them, drifting and billowing like smoke rising out of a fire.

Speaking of fire...

An orange burst caught Damien's attention from below. He gripped Balfour's scales, wedging his feet into the shallow hollows. "*Balfour, listen to me. You need to dive.*"

"*What?*"

"*Just do it. I think I know how we can get him off your tail.*"

Balfour dove, falling head-first into the smoke.

"*You won't rid yourselves of me that easily,*" Erebéus growled as he retreated back into the shadows.

With a heavy *thud*, Balfour's body slammed into the ground. Soot and ash blew into Damien's face as he dismounted. One of Balfour's brothers was hunched over a fire.

"Pelias?" Damien asked.

"Yeah?"

"What are you doing?"

"Lighting a fire to ward off the evil spirits in this place," he answered, shivering.

"Well, whatever you are doing, it's keeping us safe from the god of shadows," Damien said. Gazing up into the blue storm smoke rising upward, forcing Erebéus's darker shadows away. He faced Pelias. "Where are Amy and her mother, as well as your brothers?"

Pelias's eyes glinted up to him, fear flickering in them. "They're up there. Judging by the way it's all quiet, something horrible has happened."

Balfour manifested between them in his human form, a scowl upon his face. "What are we waiting for? Let's fly up there."

Damien grabbed Balfour's shoulder before he could resume his dragon form. "No. Don't fly. Erebéus's will find us." He glanced down at Balfour's foot, where shards of glass covered the ground. One of the shards, however, had Balfour's blue blood on it.

He bent down, retrieving the fragment Selia had in her hand before the windows shattered above him.

Balfour grabbed one of the stones on the wall next to Pelias's flames. A staircase emerged, shiny with firelight.

"*Selia, I'm coming for you,*" Damien thought as he pocketed the crystal, grabbed the stone ledge, and began to climb.

71

TIDAL STORM

Selia

Mestor's body shook as deep, heaving sobs rippled out of him. His torso trembled, sending his matted dreadlocks falling over his shoulders.

The other storm dragons, including Kai, stood behind him, watching their grieving brother.

"Mestor," Lykos said as he approached.

"Leave me," Mestor growled at his brother.

Lykos dipped his head along with the other dragons as Selia watched the pitiful event unfold. Maybe now wasn't the best time to tell the grieving storm dragon who had killed his father.

Mestor held Amphitrite, rocking her body as great tears streamed down his face. As they dolloped onto her cheeks, her freckles darkened into splotchy stars. "Our father wouldn't have wanted this. If we cannot protect what the Great Storm intended for us to, then what purpose does our origin have at all?"

Selia's salt nodes burned at his words. *Purpose.*

Damien's artwork had always given her a purpose for exploring the *past*. But what purpose did it have, if they weren't going to have a *future* together?

Mestor's blue eyes swept up to her, their vibrant color lost to grief-filled shadow. "I should have listened. I should have known. And I was too focused on finding our father's crown to care."

Selia's body had gone numb. She'd never seen a sea nymph *die* before. What would happen to the Abyss if Amphitrite wasn't there to mend it?

Mestor's body shifted as Amphitrite became transparent. Her silver hair, dress, and body evaporated, filling the room in a salty mist.

Selia blinked away her tears as the salt crystals spiraled around her face.

"Tell my daughter that I will always be with her," Amphitrite's voice echoed, then faded, her face and words blending with the mist.

Kai bent down, removing his mask. He set it the ground, waving his hand over the top. Blue flames burst from the eyepieces, to which he bowed.

Selia's breath caught. She had seen the beautiful blue bloom before. A blue lotus grew out of the ashes, blooming like a flame. It wasn't a flower—it was minca.

"Kai," she said, stepping toward him. "You were the dragon on the bridge with Naunet. You were the storm dragon from the Orient."

He glanced at Selia, blue flame licking in his dark eyes. "I don't know what you are talking about."

Mestor slouched, his body folding in a pitiful way. His shoulders rose and fell quietly, his breath quickening as he turned his head, glaring up at Kai. "You made her worse. You hurt her," he spat, rising up from the ground. A vein bulged dangerously in his neck as sparks jolted out of his silver gauntlets. "Kai!" he bellowed, clashing his gauntlets together. A giant wall of ice came bursting up out of the ground.

Taras grabbed Selia, tugging her away before one of the icicles crashed into her. "Stay back!"

"Mestor, not here!" Lykos said, lunging for his brother. "The coral, it's not stable! You will cause what remains of Celaeno to collapse!"

Mestor's arms swung forward, sending electricity into the air. In a grief-stricken rage, he threw out his hands, sending sparks into the air. "Amphitrite didn't deserve to die!"

Selia ducked as the electrical sparks bolted into the wall, tearing off a chunk of stone.

"He's always been a fool," Kai spat, dodging another icicle that jolted up out of the ground. "I just hope I can hold off his anger before he destroys our escape."

"Blind Moon, behind you," Balfour grumbled.

A thick arm flung over the ledge, followed by a man. Pelias climbed onto the ledge, hoisting Balfour up behind him.

Damien staggered over the ledge, huffing as he landed on all fours.

Selia lunged for him, dropping to his side. "All I remember was you falling," she stammered, grabbing him and tugging him close.

Damien squeezed her back. "I'm all right, but I still haven't found Nyssa."

Selia helped him to stand.

"Why is Mestor flinging icicles into the air?" Damien asked as he steadied himself.

"Amphitrite is dead," Selia replied. "And Mestor is not at all happy about it."

Damien's mouth dropped open. "What? How did she die?"

"I don't know," Selia replied. "One moment, she was was in his arms, and she just evaporated into a salty mist."

Damien withdrew the crystal from his pocket. "Is this the crystal fragment?"

Selia's eyes went wide. "Yes, where did you find it?"

"Get down!" Pelias shouted as he dove for them both.

Selia and Damien fell to the ground as an explosive flame surged over their heads. Her hand crumpled the blue lotus flower. She gazed at the bloom Kai created, transfixed with how simple it was to overlook and crush something so small and beautiful.

The memories Erebéus shared with her began to bloom in her mind, illustrating another side to his riddle. His deep voice echoed from a deep, unseen place within her, *"Darkness held in the deepest places of one's soul is what separates the Great Storm from my origin."*

"Nyssa isn't here, she never *has* been here," Selia said.

Damien's brow furrowed. "What are you saying?"

"This temple, all of its chambers and layers, is some kind of illusion that Maera is somehow manipulating. It must have something to do with the trance Amphitrite put us into."

"Wait, you think we're still in the ocean trance?" Damien asked.

Selia climbed to her feet, taking the crumpled flower with her. "Remember what Amphitrite said about ocean trancing before she served us all that tea? She said that in some rare cases, individuals can *relive* memories. And in some instances, they have gotten lost in them the starlit shadows that house those memories."

"In other words, we could all become lost in the Oblivion," Damien added.

"The *what*?" Selia stammered.

"I guessed the name of the third origin, and Erebéus isn't happy. He said I never should have been the one to answer it." He took Selia's hand. "But this still doesn't answer what happened to Nyssa."

Selia squeezed his hand. "Damien, you had your daughter taken from you before, didn't you? She died in the car accident when Maera returned to the temple. What if that memory is somehow blending with the ocean trance? What if in some sick way, Maera is making you relive it?"

"How could Maera use the ocean trance to manipulate us that way?" Balfour growled.

Selia faced her storm dragon. "Balfour, Maera admitted to me that she killed your father. She used his own grief and pain from Amphitrite rejecting his attempts to bond with her to kill him."

Balfour's face contorted between disbelieve and anger. "How?"

"Maera used a work of art Damien's ancestors created to weaken him—a tapestry that illustrated his *trident*. This tapestry was created out of strands of blue minca he offered her. Over time, your father became so weak and confused, that he eventually looked to guidance from his ancestors in the crown above his throne."

"The starlit window," Balfour admitted. "I remember seeing it above him in his temple. Father always said it was dangerous to gaze into the window that led to his ancestors. He never spoke of the name of its origin for that reason."

Selia nodded. "When he spoke to the Oblivion, his crown shattered, instantly killing him."

Balfour looked away from Selia, pain etched into his expression. His face and jaw tightened. "I always assumed his death had been from illness. But a sea nymph who took advantage of his unrequited love?"

Selia grabbed his arm. "Take a breath. This is what Maera *wants*. She wants us to relive memories that fill us with grief, so she can manipulate us."

"Why would she do something like that?" Damien asked.

"Maera told me that she currently has access to the records of Gaia's Codex held within both the Chambers of Salt and Storms. But she doesn't yet have access to records in the Chamber of Starlight."

"How does she plan to access the Chamber of Starlight if she's trapped?" Damien asked.

Selia sucked in a breath, exhaling slowly. "When Erebéus asked me to name his origin, he said that darkness held in the deepest places of one's soul is what separates the Great Storm from his origin. Now I know what that darkness is—it's grief."

"Maera manipulated us so she can gain access to the Codex in the Chamber of Starlight?" Balfour asked.

Selia nodded. "The Chamber of Starlight is where Erebéus keeps Naunet's last records within the Codex. She killed Poseidon so she could gain access to it. But instead of gaining access to the chamber, she became trapped between them. Now she's using us to try and bypass Erebéus."

"If Nyssa isn't here, then where is she?" Damien argued as he removed the crystal fragment from his pocket.

"I don't know," Selia said as she glanced at the crystal. "But I can feel her pulse. I know that she's safe, somewhere." She took the crystal from him. "I just need to have faith that somehow, we are all going to wake up from this nightmare."

Balfour leveled his gaze with her. "How do you suggest that we break ourselves out of the ocean trance?"

Selia grabbed Balfour's arm. "Balfour, you've always been the calm before the storm. This is your chance to *be* the storm. We need to destroy the tapestry. It's the only thing tethering Maera's spirit and us to this temple."

"What kind of storm are you suggesting that I create?"

"A *tidal* storm," Selia replied, glancing at the flames licking up Kai's arms as he seized up Mestor. The crystal lit up in her hand, turning Balfour's blood from blue, to silver. "And your brothers are going to help us build it."

"Stand with me, or stand down," Mestor ordered the others as he stood with his arms trembling at his sides. "It's time I put this dragon from the Orient in his place for good."

While Mestor and Kai faced one another, Selia focused on silver light pulsing out of the crystal. Her hands became transparent again. The light thrashed, clinging to her salt aura.

She closed her eyes. The light became an extension of herself. With it, she could feel the slightest fluctuation of the temperature and humidity in the air.

"Damien, move!" Balfour roared as Kai sent an inferno toward them. Red flames tore overhead, licking the walls and ceiling.

Damien tumbled to the ground. His arms and legs had become transparent.

Selia locked eyes with her storm dragon. Their bond had a new meaning here beneath the sea. The look in his eyes told her that the quiet she'd known of him would be no more.

"*Find the tapestry,*" Balfour said. "*I'll join you after I've taken your mate else-where.*"

"*Why are you removing him?*" Selia asked.

"*If Damien becomes harmed again, he won't leave this place alive.*"

As Balfour and Damien withdrew into his onyx mist, Selia focused on the energy unfolding into the room. A wave crashed into the chamber, shattering one of the walls. One by one, Balfour's brothers other than Mestor and Kai resumed their dragon forms.

Selia backtracked her way to the spot she remembered seeing the tapestry before Maera made it vanish. There had been a pool of water where she tugged the strands of shriveled minca from.

Her foot scraped against something jagged.

The sharp item grazed her ankle, slicing through her skin.

She spun, finding the wall behind her was covered in sharp white coral. Celaeno's bleached coral remains were closing in on them.

The room began to vibrate. Mestor drove his fist into the ground, forcing up jagged crystals of ice.

"You are no brother of mine, Ryu Ren Kai!" he roared, tearing yet another chunk of razor sharp ice out of the ground.

Watching the ice dominate the room gave Selia an idea. What if she could use it to break through the coral?

"Balfour, I need your help," she said. *"I need you to use our bond to create a wave."*

"Creating a tidal wave in here could kill all of us," he countered.

"Not if it's one made of ice," Selia argued.

As Kai dodged Mestor's ice with his swift movements, the dragon from the orient threw one arm into the air. The other he lowered to the ground as he crouched, where he began to chant. "May the fires of my soul bloom into a sea of inferno."

Selia's body heated as a Kai resumed his stance, twisting his arms as he summoned a coiling blue flaming serpent.

Mestor dodged the serpent's tail as it coiled and danced. With a thrash of its flaming body, the serpent devoured the ice, melting it in an instant.

Selia's plan for the ice wasn't going to work—not if Kai was going to melt it first. As the two dragons continued to hurl ice and flames at one another, Selia remembered who had fought for her. She remembered how Alex gave her life to save her from the venomous inferno in Masika's tidal cavern.

Anger and despair coursed through her. The anger these two dragons felt for one another was part of her. She couldn't escape it. She had to embrace *both* of them if she was going to find and destroy the tapestry that had ultimately killed their father.

She walked toward them, ducking as another chunk of ice flew over her. She held the crystal in front of her face. Energy pulsed out of it, deflecting another burst of flames.

"Selia, what are you doing?" Balfour grumbled.

"Trust me."

"It's my brothers that I have trust issues with, not you."

Selia walked into the surging cyclone of fire and ice. The crystal burned her hand, forcing her to drop it. It hovered in the air, absorbing the flame and ice that surged around her. In a brilliant display of red and blue, her salt aura ignited.

The explosive energy coursed around her—*through* her. Balfour's pulse flooded her chest as their bond activated. Weightless, she hovered in the air, her aura blending with the elements that bound to the storm she and her storm dragon created. His thunder was no longer distant, but erupted from her own heart. The sound made her bones tremble as the storm of his soul surged through her aura.

She was knocked back by another figure that entered the cyclone. "It looks like the darkest star in the sea is going to sacrifice herself to Poseidon's trident."

Selia clenched her fists, steadying herself as another wave of Balfour's pulse flooded through her. "I'm going to undo everything you've done not only to my family, but to Poseidon's sons."

Ice and flame spiraled up Maera's body as she manifested before her. "You will never find the tapestry, not with Celaeno's remains protecting it."

Selia glanced down at her legs. The cyclone had eroded away the ground, revealing a blanket of sharp, dead coral. She locked eyes with Maera. "Damien loved you and your daughter. How dare you make him relive the memory that almost killed him."

Maera's face twisted into a smirk. "Men who have soft hearts are the easiest to manipulate. But don't worry, all of you will soon be put out of your misery."

Jagged and pronged, a shimmering coral structure rose upward. It's shape and size resembled the one thing the tapestry had illustrated—Poseidon's trident.

Selia was swept up by Balfour's onyx tail as the coral trident ripped apart the cyclone.

She dove for Damien as another jagged piece of coral broke up from the ground. She caught Damien's arm as the room began to crumble. "I'm not letting you or our daughter go. Not now, not *ever*."

Damien grabbed her, pulling her away from the cyclone.

"Balfour, look out!" Selia cried.

They tumbled as Balfour's tail took the blow.

"Blind Moon, destroy the crystal, now!" Balfour bellowed as a tsunami of his voice surged through her.

Selia reached for the crystal that hovered above. Her fingers couldn't reach. Focused on the surging energy of her storm dragon's pulse, she forced her aura toward it.

With a burst of blue and orange light, the crystal exploded.

Ribbons of light tore around them as Maera's spirit evaporated.

The tidal storm surged around them, waves of ice and flame ripping what remained of the coral trident.

PART 9
STAR OF THE SEA

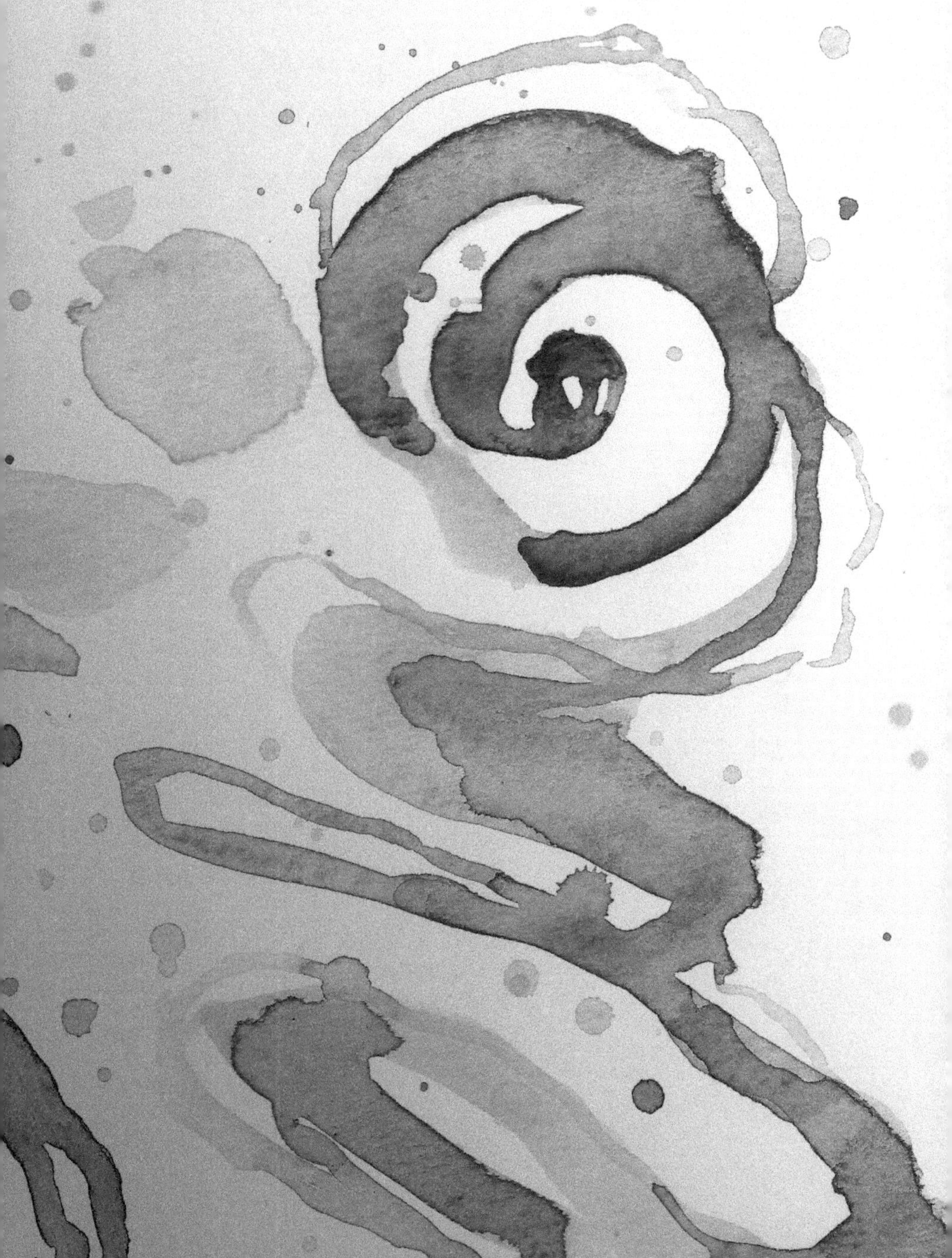

72

THE DARKEST STAR

Amy

Isis stood before Amy, her white dress furling out from her bare feet. Fragments of white coral clung to her long brown hair, creating the illusion that stars shimmered in the dark strands. Her shoulders rose and fell as she studied Amy. "I'm sure you have many questions about my true identity."

"I don't understand," Amy stammered. "All this time? The goddess of life was trapped in the body of a minca moth *queen*?"

Isis smiled, the corners of her eyes creasing elegantly. "Erebéus never forced me out of my temple. I left willingly when I learned from Naunet's scribe that your mother had harmed herself in fragmenting what Nephthys and I had created together." She took a step toward Amy, bathing her in an aura of warm silver light.

Amy held her breath as the goddess walked gracefully around the pool. "I need to know why you would ever incarnate as a fae being, a toxic one, of all things."

Isis crossed her hands in front of herself, gazing down into the water as she continued to walk. "After Erebéus convinced your mother to fragment the star of the sea in Atlantis, the Abyss's seven ancestral salts separated. This was never our intention for them. Nephthys and I discussed how we could remedy the Abyss. We agreed that making the Abyss ill was the only way to make her better, so I incarnated as Celaeno's fae queen and introduced salt venom into the sea."

"How could making the Abyss ill possibly make her better?"

Isis walked the remaining length around the pool, then stopped before Amy. "The Abyss is a maternal structure. Each of the seven salt mothers are sisters with one another. When one of the sisters becomes ill, the others tend to her, restoring her back to her original health. Nephthys and I believed that making the Dark

One ill would mend the Abyss back to her original identity as one unified salt mother."

"But that *didn't* happen," Amy argued. "A plague broke out in Egypt, killing off an entire salt ancestry."

Isis's face dipped into the shadows, her high cheek bones cutting against the light reflecting off the water. "Even a goddess of life cannot foresee the destructive power of fae beings. I was wrong to do what I did, attempting to mend something far more complex than I understood. My intentions to restore life to the Abyss resulted in a plague that killed many. Selia, the Blind Moon, as the midwife of the sea named her, had long been my intended cure for the illness I would send into the heart of Celaeno's ancestral salts."

"Wait until I tell my mother this," Amy said, her thoughts running amok.

A cool, dark mist filled the room. Nephthys manifested before her, wearing a long black dress. Like her sister, her blackened wings arched upward, framing her. Amy was bathed in both of the goddesses light and shadows as they embraced one another.

Nephthys pulled away from Isis. "My sister, I was wondering how long it would be until I saw you again."

Isis's gaze dropped to Amy. "I've incarnated, and reincarnated myself more than once, thanks to Amphitrite's daughter."

"Where is my mother?" Amy asked as she glanced up at the sister goddesses. Nephthys, however, had tears streaking down her cheeks.

The goddess of death lowered herself and knelt on one knee in front of Amy. "Your mother knew how strong you would be for her. She knew that in the end, you would want to stop her suffering. She had one last request, that her daughter would be the one to inherit what remains in the Chamber of Salt."

"The rest of what?" Amy asked.

"What remains of her Ocean Apothecary—the starlit corals."

Isis lowered herself as well and set her hand on Amy's shoulder. Her dark eyes became blue, luminous with tears. "Had it not been for your mother, the toxin I created would have done far more harm to the Abyss than it had. When she learned what I had incarnated myself as, she knew there was only one sea nymph alive who could set me free."

Amy's stomach hollowed. "What are you saying?"

"By bringing you to the Chamber of Salt, she gave of herself what Pherusa and her daughter Naunet could not. Your mother trusted that her crystal child would one day kill the queen and free me." Her grip on Amy's shoulder tightened. "But doing so has cost your mother her life."

Amy's breathing stopped. Isis, along with the light she created, blurred violently. "You are lying," she whispered. "My mother, she's not…"

"Amphitrite, goddess of the sea, has returned to her origin."

Amy's body trembled so violently, that she fell to the ground. "No, this can't be happening." She pressed her hands onto the ground as tears fell into the pool.

"You were always my crystal child," her mother said as her face appeared in the water. Her freckles shimmered like vibrant silver stars. "You were always meant to see the stars in the sea in ways that I couldn't."

"Please. I can't bare to say goodbye to you again," Amy whispered, reaching into the pool to touch her mother's beautiful reflection.

Amphitrite's hand came to her face as Amy's tears dolloped into the corals blooming out of her fingers. "I'm here with you, forever, and always. Amy, I am giving you what remains of my Ocean Apothecary."

Amy gazed into her mother's emerald eyes one last time before they closed. She withdrew into the pool.

"She knew she would return to the Abyss when I was set free," Isis said. "She knew that trusting her daughter to do the right thing was the only true remedy."

Amy's wiped the tears away from her face. "I failed her. I failed my mother."

"No, dear daughter of Amphitrite. You did what your mother could not. Mending a crystal as broken as the sea was not something her Ocean Apothecary could ever do alone."

"Then what's next? How am I supposed to move on without her?" Amy sobbed.

"The secrets held in the temple of Salt, Storms, and Starlight are far from being fully explored. Naunet will soon discover what remains of the starlit corals." Isis held out her hand, touching Amy's forehead. "Step into your name, the new Amphitrite. Take up what your mother has left you to inherit, goddess of the sea."

Amy closed her eyes as Isis's blinding lunar light filled her periphery.

73

STORMS & SHADOWS

Damien

Damien gripped so tightly onto Selia's hand that his fingers passed through her. He was swallowed by the mist that tunneled into the room. Mestor and Kai disappeared, along with the cyclone made of ice and fire.

A window appeared before him. Selia stood in the nursery at the lighthouse, rocking Nyssa in her arms.

"Selia!" he yelled, slamming his hands onto the glass.

She didn't turn to look at him.

A bold, bright light encompassed him as a white figure appeared to his side and said, "Time is such a simple, yet malleable thing. Sometimes I wonder if you think of it that way when you create one of your beautiful paintings."

Damien glanced sideways. "Isis?"

"If there was anything that my sister and I intended when we created the star of the sea together, it was to ensure that the cycle of life and death for sea nymphs remained healthy." Her long silver hair draped over her shoulders. "By taking your life, Maera has disrupted that balance."

Damien glanced back at the liquid wall, wishing with every ounce of his being that he could be with them. "But I'm not a sea nymph. I'm a human."

Isis dipped her chin. "While this temple might not house your origin, you made it here, didn't you?"

Damien swallowed. "Sure, but that doesn't mean I'm going to leave it." He glanced up at the lunar goddess. "Where do I go next?"

"That is up for you and Balfour to decide."

As quickly as Isis appeared, she was gone.

Damien blinked as her blinding light vanished.

"Great," Balfour grumbled as he resumed his human form. "That didn't go as planned, at least not on our part."

"What do you mean, *didn't go as planned*?" Damien asked, noticing how his hands had become transparent.

"The cyclone must have ripped open the Chamber of Storms," Balfour grumbled as he slammed his fist into the inky ground that consumed them almost instantly.

Damien glanced at Balfour, who was just as transparent as himself. "Where are we?"

"You've entered the Chamber of Starlight. Welcome to the Oblivion," a voice echoed through the onyx mist surrounding them.

Damien braced himself as the god of shadows manifested. There were no stars in this chamber, just an endless void. His pulse sounded muffled against the space that made gravity do horrible, painful things to his body.

That was if he was still *in* his body. With each passing moment, he became more transparent.

Erebéus crouched, lowering himself to his haunches as the great starlit sphinx resumed a less threatening pose. His great brows drew up, his muzzle crinkling in disgust, warping the strong bridge of his nose. "As much as I would adore flinging both of your souls into the Oblivion, I cannot lie over my oath to Gaia. The three origins have long been one of my responsibilities to guard."

Damien and Balfour glanced at one another.

"Are you saying—"

"Silence!" Erebéus bellowed, his whiskers furling as he spoke. "There are rules my kind must follow that no rock, river, tree, creature, or fae, can know. Unless, of course, an origin bond is involved."

Damien took a step back from the sphinx, who began to mumble under his breath. He seemed to have these contradictory conversations with himself frequently. "I need to get back to Selia and my daughter."

Erebéus's mumbling stopped, and his quivering muzzle became still. His giant golden eyes swept between Damien and Balfour. "Maera made a mistake. Killing you within the temple violated her agreement with me, leaving you two in quite the predicament."

"What happened to Maera's spirit?" Damien asked.

"She, along with the plague victims, have been released back to the Abyss. It is only a matter of time before the ancestral salts accept their spirits," he huffed, rolling his giant golden eyes. "Alas, I am presented with a problem. I am looking at *two* souls, one of which this temple does not house an origin for."

Damien frowned. "*Me?*"

"Yes, you, *human*," Erebéus huffed, his nose crinkling. "You should know that while you are currently the dominant species on the planet, Gaia did not intend for it. Had the other architects not resumed their molten slumber beneath the earth's crust, we would have gladly caused your extinction in an effort to cleanse the soil the great architects used to walk upon."

"Damien's soul isn't going anywhere," Balfour growled. "Not while I am here."

"Where human souls go when they die is not my concern," Erebéus huffed. "The only passage of souls I am concerned with are my descendants, as well as Gaia's sea nymph daughters."

"Well, he's your concern now," Balfour argued. "It's not his fault that Maera decided to kill him the same way she killed my father."

Erebéus flicked his tail, blending the stars behind him like pigment on paper. "What are you suggesting?"

Balfour locked his eyes with his brooding ancestor. "Damien died in the chamber of Storms, the house of my late father. He is bound to me, a son of Poseidon."

Erebéus's outline trembled. "State your request, son of the late Poseidon."

"First, I must know. Is it true? My father died, because he sought after your help? When he couldn't turn to his sons? When he was alone and helpless?"

"Stating the name of my origin has been known to draw storm dragons into the vast emptiness of the Oblivion. The Great Storm was born of my cosmic origin." His head dipped, great voids filling his eyes. "Loneliness is something the great architects know far more intimately than our descendants."

"Then I know what I must say to you if I am to ensure the Son of Atlantean kings is to return to his origin. His family—the sea nymph I am bound to, and his daughter."

"Balfour, wait," Damien argued.

But Balfour had already made up his mind. "From the depths of my origin, the Great Storm. I honor the crown of my father, in exchange for returning the mate of Celaeno's moon daughter to his family."

"As you wish, son of the god of the sea. But you are not allowed to visit the Blind Moon. Only your bond will live on." Erebéus's golden eyes swiveled between them as his tail stopped thrashing. "In exchange for Damien to return to his family, *both* of you must serve my shadows."

"But I thought architects were cosmic beings of starlight," Damien countered.

Erebéus's gaze leveled with him. "My origin encompasses both light, and darkness. You cannot experience the light of the stars without the great distance between them. As an artist, I can only imagine this contrast could entice your creativity."

Damien took a step toward the architect. "What do you ask of me?"

"You must create me a work of artwork. Only this time, you will not use the symbol Isis created." His muzzle rippled, revealing a set of sharp teeth. "You will use one created by me."

Balfour shot him a nervous glance. "I stand by your decision, whatever it is you make."

"Deal," Damien said without hesitation.

A roll of parchment manifested next to the sphinx's head, along with a stylus. "Sign, rather, paint, along the dotted line."

Damien grabbed the stylus, flicking the bristles across the blue pigment. Something about the color didn't seem normal as it was absorbed by the parchment. Then again, he was making a deal with a god of shadows. Who knew what kind of ancient magic he was dealing with.

74

A SEA OF STARLIGHT

Selia

Blue and red flames licked along an inky horizon dotted with a few sprinkled stars that offset the sky from the sea. It took Selia a length of time to realize that she wasn't falling headfirst into the tidal storm. Instead, she had been staring at a painting.

She stood before multiple images that spanned the length of not one, but five easels, each supporting a large piece of watercolor paper. Judging by how damp the parchment was, Damien must have just stepped away, or he'd been working on the pieces out in the elements.

Her heart jumped. The wall of windows behind the painting overlooked a familiar body of water—the North Sea.

Was she really back in the lighthouse?

Damien appeared, a cloth in one hand, which he wiped a paintbrush through. Blue paint smudged his cheeks, which both dimpled as he spotted her. "Do you like it?"

Selia ran to him, flinging herself into his arms. She breathed in his fresh scent of wind and salt. "What in the world happened? How did we end up back home?"

He squeezed her. "I don't know," he spun her so that she faced his artwork. "All I know is that during the ocean trance Amphitrite put us in, this is what I saw."

Selia blinked, blurring Damien's beautiful painting. "Stars for as far as the eye could see?"

He kissed her forehead. "There were so many, that I thought I'd lost myself in them."

Selia sank into his arms, disbelief washing over her. The Oblivion of those endless stars had brought them home.

A high-pitched cry pierced Selia's heart before it met her ears. She ran down the hall and dipped into the nursery at the beautiful cry of her baby.

Peppercorn was perched atop the crib, her fuzzy brown faze twisting back and forth as she peered down at the child flailing her arms into the air.

Selia reached into the crib and pulled Nyssa out, bundling her into her arms. Her tears returned, streaking down her cheeks as she rocked her. How incredible it felt to have her close to her again.

Damien stopped behind her, pulling them both into his arms.

She turned to face him. "Amphitrite knew she was dying. I think the ocean trance was all part of her death. But Maera, what happened to her?"

"After you and Balfour released that tidal storm, he and I were swept into the Chamber of Starlight."

"Let me guess, Erebéus was waiting for you there?"

He nodded. "Erebéus made it sound like Maera's soul would return to the Abyss along with the souls of the plague victims. Balfour was also there with us." His eyes drifted away from her. "Selia, I don't know if he is coming back to us."

Selia's stomach hollowed. "What do you mean, not coming back?"

Knock, knock, knock.

Peppercorn took off from her perch on the crib, heading straight toward the door.

Selia and Damien followed her.

Damien opened the door, revealing three women. The two who stood at the back were much taller than the shorter, elderly woman who gazed up at him. "Auntie? What are you doing here?"

Auntie's face scrunched as she scrutinized him. "I didn't travel half way across Scotland to have my nephew turn me away, now did I?"

"Oh, what a cute little baby!" Gwen cried as she waved at Nyssa.

Peppercorn let out a loud *screech* as she flit through the other woman's hair.

"Peppercorn, where are your manners?" Pixie huffed, her mossy bangs bobbing as she scolded her bat.

"Gwen? Pixie? What are you both doing here?" Damien asked.

"Gwen, the last time I saw you was at the mental institution," Selia said, her words slipping out of her mouth before she could catch them.

Pixie shot Gwen a look as the pastries in her arms shook to her nervous laugh. "Right, well. I'm glad that we're all on the same page about how this special day is going to turn out. Selia, maybe you should stop drinking my triple shot lattes."

"What mental institution? Are you saying I've lost my mind?" Gwen cried, hiking her head back and laughing. "I hope that's just a bad joke, because that will be a real banger to chat about come the next Winter Solstice gathering."

"Then why are you all here?" Damien asked as he squinted past the three women crowding their front door.

Selia noticed there were others behind them. Loud, boisterous laughter erupted from a few men chatting with each other.

"I came to babysit so you two could get prepped. It's your wedding week!" Gwen stammered as she shot her brother a dangerous look. "Don't tell me your forgot the date you're tying the knot. This wouldn't be the first time that we had to change plans at the last minute."

Selia glanced at Damien, who looked just as perplexed as her.

Gwen's auburn hair practically frizzed at her next statement. "I swear on our parents' graves, brother. If you've been wasting your time painting the day away again, we're going to have a very serious discussion."

"Right! Well then. Everyone inside!" Damien said as he wrapped his arm around his aunt and steered her toward the kitchen. Pixie followed them, her arms bulging with her famous pumpkin muffins.

Selia stepped sideways as a familiar golden dragonfly came zipping in after her.

"Selia, finally!" Deidra said as she walked inside. "I feel like it's been ages since I've given you a hug! Zakai is on her way. But she wanted me to tell you not to panic when you saw how everything unfolded after you escaped the temple."

"But, *how*? Did we go back in time?" Selia asked.

"I don't think so. I think time caught up with us the way Amphitrite wanted it to." Zipper flit overhead, sending golden light streaming down from his wings. "Remember the ritual Balfour performed with you three at the Celtic Sea?" She dug her hand into her pocket, tugging out a photo. "I took this of all of you during that moment."

Selia took the photo, a perfect memory captured between all of them.

"The ocean trance Amphitrite put us in must have brought you back to what you and Damien asked for when your tidal bond formed."

"Are you going to let us inside, or are we going to freeze our asses off out here in the cold?"

Selia jumped, realizing who the six giant men standing outside were. Instead of wearing tunics, Poseidon's sons were all wearing the proper Scottish garment—kilts. Hopleus and Taras walked in, followed by Pelias, Idas, and Lykos.

"I hope they aren't serving fish," Taras grumbled.

"Stormy!" Nyssa squealed as the last of the giant men walked inside.

Balfour's eldest brother stopped, dipping his head toward her daughter. "My youngest brother told me about you, Little Origin."

"Where is Balfour?" Selia asked, but Mestor was already across the room joining in with the others. A dull ache crept into her chest. She needed to find her storm dragon. She couldn't look at his brothers and not think of him.

75
STARLIT SECRETS

Amy

One Month Later
Galway, Ireland

Amy's focus had been confined to the same pile of salt crystals ever since she arrived back in Galway. She'd spent many a day and night, (beneath the full and new moons) attempting to bring to life the constellations she'd seen inside of Celaeno's coral remains. Isis had eluded to their origin, stating that even the fae had forgotten how they formed long ago. Their starlit secrets could reveal truths that not even her mother knew about the deepest, darkest places in the ocean.

She sat at the small wooden table upstairs above her mother's Ocean Apothecary shop, gazing into the crystals like a sea sorceress might do. Nothing appeared yet. Ripples of frustration traveled up her spine every time Little Blue decided to dart across the table and topple the crystals over.

The shop door opened. A man walked inside, his hands both at his sides and his vibrant blue eyes wide. "Amy, something just washed up in the harbor. You need to see this."

She blinked a few times, her brain not making sense of who she was seeing. A blue-eyed sailor squinted back at her. "*Lachlan*?"

He propped his hands onto his hips, studying her. "Yeah, what's up?"

She flung herself toward him.

Lachlan caught her around the middle as she pinned him against the wall. "Easy, lassie. What's gotten into you?"

She pressed her face to his neck, breathing in his windswept scent. "It *is* you…"

"Of course it's me," he stammered, taking her face into his hands. "I didn't think you'd miss me this badly over a few weeks at sea."

Amy grabbed his hands from her face, bringing them down to her front. "What do you remember last? Please tell me that you at least remember swimming with the starlit corals."

Lachlan's cheeks dimpled. "The starlit corals? That sounds amazing. Is this a fantasy of yours?"

Amy's breathing finally settled. This must have been Isis's doing. Lachlan returned to her unscathed, as though their time away from one another never occurred.

She pressed her ear to his chest. "I just need to listen to your heart for a moment if that's okay with you."

He squeezed her, resting his chin on her head as she listened to the quickening rhythm.

She pressed her fingers into his cotton shirt, unbuttoning the top. Something wasn't right. She ripped the fabric open, revealing his chest. "What happened to your birthmark?"

"First it's starlit corals, and now it's birthmarks?" He cupped her face with one hand, his blue eyes settling onto her. "Maybe I should go away more often, if this is the kind of affection you are going to greet me with."

She searched his eyes, the crown of Errindoor reflecting inside of them. The memory disappeared as soon as it came. Isis had mended the boundaries of time between them—both in the past, and in the present. "Lachlan Ewan, I've missed you so much."

He bucked his hips, rocking her up onto the table. "How much did you miss me, my Sea Star?"

Amy reeled. Here in her Apothecary shop, she must might need to recreate what she remembered of their lovemaking in the midst of the ocean.

Lachlan kissed her forehead and took her hands into his callused ones and helped her back down. "Let's go out to the marina, all right? Then we can pick up where you and I left off discussing this idea about swimming in starlight."

The two left for the harbor, their hands swinging together as they walked. Amy's thoughts traveled to her mother's last words she remembered inside the temple before she'd vanished.

"I'm here with you, forever, and always."

Amy shook her head, tears stinging the corners of her eyes. A splashing sound caught her attention from beach.

Two redheads, a mother and her daughter, were skipping sea shells into the bay. The little girl bent down and picked up an item, holding it high over her head. "Mom, look at this! It's a star!"

Amy's breath caught. Starfish covered the beach. They had washed all the way up to the dune grasses that swayed in the breeze as she and Lachlan walked onto the dock and approached the boats. Maybe seeing so many was a sign from her mother.

Speaking of sea creatures. A seashell that didn't belong to Little Blue scurried across the deck of Lachlan's boat.

Lachlan stopped beside the *Sea Dragon* as she bobbed in the surf. "Careful where you step. That crazy little thing has a mind of its own."

Amy climbed up first, Lachlan following. She was met by a pair of ink drop eyes that had too much intelligence swimming inside for them to belong to a normal hermit crab.

Henrietta had returned. The question remained—was it for some kind of vengeance as she had in the past? For one reason or another, this quirky fae creature always had a way of sabotaging her plans.

"What are you guarding this time?" Amy asked, noticing a soggy roll of parchment sat on the deck before her.

Another crab entered the scene, scuttling over to where Henrietta held her claws up in a fierce stance. Little Blue scuttled over to her, raising her blue claws in what could be an attempt to woo the infamous fae hermit crab who had led Amy down so many crab holes over the past few months, she could barely keep count.

"Well then, this is new," Lachlan started, eyeing the little crabs as they began to shift back and forth around the scroll. They joined their claws, scuttling between lobster crates and fish nets.

Amy swooped in, scooping up the scroll as the dynamic crab duo continued to dance. She skipped back to Lachlan, excited to have for once been the one to make off with stolen treasure.

Lachlan propped his elbow onto one of the crates, his dimples reappearing. "Nice work."

"Who is it from?" Amy asked, trying not to rip the sodden paper.

"No idea. I found it soon after I docked. I dare not touch it, because that little crab wanted to snip my thumb off."

Amy unraveled what she could of the scroll, finding another bound tightly inside with a red ribbon. A blue wax seal prevented it from opening. She scanned the writing on the first paper that bound the other one inside.

To Amphitrite's Daughter,

Give this scroll to the Blind Moon. Isis requested me to ask this of you.

Amy flipped the paper over. There was no signature.

"Who sent this? There's not even a signature. Just a flower that sort of looks like a star."

"Speaking of stars, Amy, my sea goddess," Lachlan said, his voice shaking.

Amy glanced up from the scroll, finding him lowering himself to the ground as he folded onto one knee.

The color in his face drained, making his blue eyes contrast against the grey ocean water behind him. "I need to ask something of you."

Amy folded the scroll and tucked it into her pocket. "What do you need to ask me? And why are you trembling?"

Lachlan locked his eyes with her. "While I was out there sailing on the water, alone at night, searching for Poseidon's crown, I realized something. I found a very special and rare star that I want to keep. I'm not whole without you." His voice shook as he spoke. "Amy, my Sea Star, will you have me as your fisherman, and maybe one day a huntsman, *forever*?"

Amy's heart leapt. She bound toward him, grabbing his arms and tugged him up to stand before her. She didn't even look at the box with the ring shaking in his hands as she cupped his face. "Of course I will!"

76
RAINBOWS

Damien

Montrose, Scotland

It didn't take long for Damien and his family to settle back into their home. Gwen had threatened him multiple times, stating that if they ever decided to try and forget about their big day again, she was going to unleash a dragon of her own wrath toward them both.

Over the last three months, Balfour, however, still hadn't shown himself, which had Damien very worried. He'd last seen the storm dragon in the temple.

Selia walked into the living room, where Damien was busy organizing yet another stack of letters from Amy. Peppercorn had been swooping down the chimney with her claws full of emerald green envelopes, all of which were addressed to Selia.

She stopped at his side. "You got another one?"

"This is the seventh one today," Damien replied, folding the corner over. He swore there was a pinch mark there, one that reminded him of a certain fae hermit crab.

Peppercorn swooped overhead and perched atop Selia's shoulder. "Why is it so quiet?"

"It's almost summer, and we've barely had any storms," Damien replied.

Selia sighed. "I've missed his voice rumbling in the distance. It feels so silent, so empty with him gone."

Damien grabbed Selia around the waist, tugging her down into his lap. "I never thought I would say this, but I miss him too."

Selia tucked herself into his arm. "I feel so horrible. I never got to say goodbye to him. He did so much for us, for Nyssa. He named her." She glanced at him, sadness dancing in her eyes. "Do you think he will ever show up again?"

"I wish I could say I knew," Damien said, knowing the only reason the three of them were still together was because of Balfour. "Selia, I love you and our daughter to the moon and back."

Thunder rumbled in the distance.

"Just in time! Nyssa will be out for a few hours with the sound of that," Selia said.

Through the thunder, Damien could have sworn he heard a mumbled, "*Come outside.*"

"I'm going to take the trash out," he said as Selia left for the nursery. He exited the back door, following the thunderous rumble as it echoed over the sea.

A shadow drifted by the trees, catching Damien's attention. Fog drifted before him, quickly manifesting as the storm dragon he and Selia had just discussed.

"Did you actually admit that you were starting to miss me?" Balfour asked, his voice echoing.

Damien chuckled. "I did. Selia misses you tremendously, we both do."

Balfour's dark eyes leveled with him. "You remember what Erebéus said. Me not speaking to the Blind Moon was part of his agreement," he growled. "But that doesn't mean that I can't pass along one last gift before I go."

Damien squinted at Balfour's body. He didn't appear much different, other than having the flog cling to his body like an aura. "Are you really, *dead*?"

"I guess if this is what you call death, then yes. My father still lives on in the weather patterns that all of his sons create. I assume I will as well." His eyes swam like Erebéus's did, filling with starlight. "I told you that I would die for all of you."

Damien's body went numb.

His throat closed.

This was it? Was Balfour *leaving* them?

Balfour clasped his hands at his front. "Make sure the storms keep raging on in your artwork. I expect you to complete the painting you abandoned one day for

Little Origin so she can grow up to chase after the images created by her father." He turned on his heel and began to walk toward the sea.

"Wait, where are you going?" Damien asked, taking a step toward him.

Balfour stopped, facing him. "To join my father in the Great Storm." He spun again, mist and fog billowing around his dark outline.

"Balfour, wait," Damien called, this time choking.

Balfour faced him a second time, the dark storms in his eyes lighting up. "Don't make this more difficult for me than it needs to be."

Damien sucked in a breath, exhaling as he spoke. "Thank you for being there for all of us. I know we couldn't have escaped that temple without you."

Balfour's eyes creased into a smile.

With a clap of thunder, and a brilliant display mist, he evaporated.

Selia came out with Nyssa, pointing at the sky. "Look at that! It's just like one of your daddy's paintings! It's a rainbow!"

Damien's heart might as well have evaporated too at the sight of the colors branching over them. He could have sworn that he saw two figures in the clouds, both standing with their hands clasped together. One was a red-headed sea nymph with freckles that looked like little stars. The other was a giant man with both gold and silver gauntlets shimmering upon his muscular forearms.

Both the god and goddess of the sea gazed down upon them. Maybe Amphitrite and Poseidon had somehow reunited at the Temple of the Three Origins.

77

KAI'S MESSAGE

Selia

The piles of mail tripled by the end of the month, so much, that Selia had resorted to shoving it into every nook and cranny she could find in the lighthouse. Envelopes spilled out of her kitchen cupboard and from a stack on the fireplace mantle, both of which Damien had threatened to toss into the flame. Amy had been sending her snail mail almost three times a day. Today was no different from the day before. The letters were all the same, with a single message scribbled across a rolled up piece of parchment.

```
I'm going to deliver a message to you personally,
once I get this stubborn fae creature to cooperate.
Amy
```

Peppercorn came swooping into the room right at her usual morning time. A stack of green envelopes dangled from her feet. She landed clumsily onto the sofa. One by one, her seven pups came fluttering in, each carrying their own little stack of envelopes. Thankfully, Selia had just put Nyssa down for a nap. She rarely awoke, even when stirred by the frantic wing beats of a fae bat.

Knock, knock, knock.

Selia stood up, walking to the front door. "I swear, if I have one more interruption," she stammered.

Damien walked to the door and opened it.

Two individuals stood outside. One had long, curly red hair, complete with a dark green dress and a purple shawl. The man standing next to her had auburn locks of hair, bright blue eyes, and wore jeans with a plaid shirt.

"Amy, you've finally arrived!" Selia said, rushing to Damien's side.

"I would have been here sooner, but, ouch!" Amy flung her hand out of her shawl, taking a small creature with it. "Henrietta wanted to be the one to deliver this message to you."

Selia eyed the little hermit crab dangling from the end of a scroll. "That sounds like her all right."

"Can we come in?" Amy pressed as she re-pocketed both Henrietta and the scroll. "I don't think she's going to stop pinching me until we do."

"Of course, we'll put on some tea," Damien said, opening the door wide.

"Just make sure there isn't any coral in it, okay?" Amy said as she bustled through the door in her flamboyant, Amy way.

"Hey, cousin. It's so good to see you!" the man who followed her said.

"Lachlan?" Damien stammered, taken aback.

The two men embraced in the foyer, clapping each other on the back.

Lachlan pulled away first. "I wanted to apologize. Turns out I missed your wedding *twice* now. I missed the one at the winter solstice gathering, and then the one a month ago at your old art studio."

Damien shrugged. "No hard feelings."

Lachlan turned to Selia. "My cousin is lucky to have you as his wife."

"Do you like to hunt by chance?" Selia asked, suddenly thinking about Ewan, even though Lachlan's eyes were much too blue to resemble anything she remembered of the son of Atlantean kings.

Lachlan shrugged. "One day. But for now, I've convinced Amy here to move into my boat with me."

Amy was already across the room, setting up a space on the coffee table. She set a blue silk bag atop the table and lowered herself onto the sofa. Her movements and mannerisms reminded Selia of her mother.

While Damien and Lachlan disappeared into the kitchen, Selia sat next to Amy on the sofa. A dull ache settled into her stomach. "I'm so sorry about what happened to your mother."

Amy didn't smile, nor did she frown. She gazed at Henrietta as the crab climbed onto the table and scurried about. She gripped the hems of her blouse, crimping the fabric. "Her death was a peaceful one that I have come to accept."

"What caused her to die, do you know?"

"Her salt aura became damaged when she fragmented the star of the sea. In all my time knowing her, not once did I see my mother allow herself to be loved by another. She always poured her heart into the ocean she devoted her life to." She grabbed one of Nyssa's starfish toys and held it up. "If there is anything her starlit corals have taught me, it is to love unconditionally. To light up the darkest places in the sea. That kind of love lasts far longer than any memory." She set the starfish down. "Love is a gift she gave to me by passing on what remains of her Ocean Apothecary."

"Now that she is gone, what are you planning to do?"

"Lachlan wants to move to the mountains. He plans to retire from fishing and go live in some log cabin in the cold," Amy replied, shivering. "It sounds like I might be done exploring the sea."

Henrietta scurried about the table, busying herself with removing items from Amy's silk pouch. She did so quickly, dodging teacups and Damien's watercolor brushes.

Selia glanced at Amy's face, captivated like she had been the first time she set eyes on her star-shaped freckles. "Don't you see? This is just the beginning of what the sea has to share with you. You have so much yet to explore with what remains of your mother's Ocean Apothecary."

Amy grabbed one of the salt crystals Henrietta was trying to snatch. "I feel like I need to apologize for everything I've put you through."

Amy's green eyes locked with her. For a moment, Selia could have sworn that she saw her mother's face reflecting in their emerald depths. "Amy, you and your mother gave me the best gift—to know who I am. I'm not just some moon daughter of Celaeno—I'm part of something much bigger and deeper than I ever could have imagined."

Amy's mouth quirked. "You don't hate me for everything I made you go through?"

"Hate you? No!" Selia stammered. "Because I met you, I was able to learn about all of the individuals from my past that cared for me so that I could have a *future*—so I could start a family. I want you to be part of it."

"How?" Amy asked.

Selia's gaze dropped to a massive ring on Amy's left ring finger. "Wait a minute, are you *engaged*?"

Amy beamed. "I am. Lachlan proposed to me!"

"Congratulations!" Selia said, eying the gem shaped like a sea star glistening on the ring. "It matches your freckles. He must be crazy about you to go as far as to replicate that detail."

Amy flushed, darkening her freckles. "We have nothing planned as of yet. It only happened a few days ago."

"Well, Damien and I are planning a wedding, the one we never technically had before starting a family together."

Amy shrugged. "I have absolutely no idea where to start when it comes to planning a wedding."

"Wait, I know! Why don't we have one together? Why not plan the big day for *both* of us?"

Amy's eyes went wide. "You would want to do that?"

"Of course! You haven't met Damien's family yet. They're absolutely bonkers for big celebrations. You should have stuck around for the Winter Solstice gathering."

"Where is Balfour? Isn't he your daughter's guard dragon?"

Selia's heart both warmed and stung. "He's here, in spirit. I can still hear him rumbling on the distant thunderstorms every once in a while. And he always puts Nyssa down for a nap when I need it most."

"Speaking of storm dragons. Poseidon had always shown interest in my mother when they were in Atlantis. I always wondered if they would end up together one day. A king is nothing without his queen," she shrugged, glancing over at Lachlan in the kitchen. "Someone said that to me at one time. I can't remember who. If only the two would have bonded with one another, maybe none of this would have happened."

A rock clattered onto the table as Henrietta continued removing items from the bag.

Selia grabbed the fossil she instantly recognized. She held it in her hand, swearing that she could still hear Opal's tiny bubbling voice echoing in her mind. "Salt trancing is one thing. But do you have any idea just how magical ocean trancing can be?"

"Not in the slightest," Amy replied, her face brimming with newfound whimsy.

Selia handed her the fossil. "I'm glad that your mother and Poseidon never bonded with one another. That would mean that you and I never would have become friends."

Amy's eyes went wide. "Do you really feel that way about me?"

"I do. How about you?"

Amy glanced down at the fossil. "It wasn't until I was buried deep in that temple that I realized just how lucky I was to have met you and Damien."

Damien's laughter sounded from the kitchen.

Selia glanced over her shoulder, admiring her handsome Scottish husband. She turned back Amy. "I know that we don't technically need men to create a family. But I will say this. There are very good men in this world, ones who would give anything to be with those they love. Had I not stumbled upon your hermit crab and tripped on the beaches at the Celtic Sea, I never would have met him."

Amy's mouth quirked into a smile. Her nose and cheeks flushed, darkening her freckles. "I haven't even met your baby. How can you possibly want me to be part of your family so soon?"

"You mean babies," Selia corrected.

Amy's mouth dropped open. "You're pregnant? *Again*?"

Selia set her hands onto her stomach. "We are. Nyssa is going to have a little sister soon!"

Henrietta darted into the bag and tugged out another item.

"Oh, finally. It looks like she's ready to hand over the message to you," Amy said as Henrietta tugged a scroll out of her bag.

The elated little crab scuttled about, dancing around a scroll that had been pinched to the point it was barely a scroll any longer.

Selia grabbed the scroll and unrolled it, finding a handwritten message.

Blind Moon,

The only reason I am writing this is because of the sacrifice a dragon from the Western trident made for you. One does not easily step into the Great Storm.

I was the one who struck your storm dragon. I have long tried to protect Celaeno's coral remains after Bellerophon abandoned them. After the power I saw unfold between you two, I admit that I severely regret it. When I witnessed the bond between you unfold in the Temple of the Three Origins, I knew that Bellerophon would die for your family—an act of great honor. His choice was what ultimately made me change my mind about Mestor and his brothers. Bellerophon's bond with you is something that will live on, even though he's returned to the Great Storm with our father.

In apology for my actions, I am giving you information on the sea nymph you have long tried to reconnect with. You are right about my identity. However, Naunet no longer lives in the Orient, although that is where we both met. She and I live in Rome. She has long spoken about you to me, and I will do everything in my power to reunite you when the time is right. I cannot do so lightly. Erebéus

has long tried to resurrect his bond with her, which
could endanger her life.

I've included Naunet's new name in this message.
I hope that mother and Celaeno's moon daughter will
be able to reunite one day.

From the Trident of the East,
Ryu Ren Kai
The Lotus Dragon King

Selia's eyes scanned the message again as her mind tried to make sense of the words.

"Dr. Valerie Rivera," Selia said aloud. "Works at an aquatics lab in Rome, Italy." Tears came to her eyes, blurring Kai's words. "Mom, I finally found you…"

EPILOGUE

Valerie

December 1st
Rome, Italy

Cold sweat trickled down my neck as I pressed my eye to the eyepiece of my microscope. The lab was swelteringly hot for entering the winter months, even for the Mediterranean. The windows were open, allowing the voices of people to drift inside.

A mother calling to her daughter broke my focus.

"Selia."

I glanced up from my microscope, jarred by the sound. The name was long gone, buried somewhere in my subconscious. I'd given her the name after I'd found her in the Nile.

Selia, the Blind Moon, my moon daughter.

Knock, knock, knock.

"Not now," I said as my lab intern peeked through the door.

"Dr. Rivera, you have a message from a cardiologist. He wants to speak with you about your, specialty."

"It will have to wait," I said, catching the hesitation before he said *specialty*. While I had worked at this lab for over a decade, my colleagues spread rumors about my personal life like wildfire. They all thought I made money on the side as a prostitute...

I glared at him. "Didn't you hear me?"

My intern closed the door, leaving me to resume my research. It was probably another complaint as to why my antivenin samples were late. I hadn't been producing the quantity the lab needed to put out, due to my recent discovery. I'd been spending too much time on my own personal research, and not enough on what my career working in the medical field demanded of me.

But that was my past life. The midwife of the sea had no purpose in the modern world of science. What work I'd abandoned in Gaia's Codex thousands of years ago, I had started to pick up, again. What was I kidding. I'd been filling journals with my observations of the ancestral salts since the High Renaissance.

By day, I worked in a medical lab in the heart of Rome. Since the awakening period of the arts and sciences, I'd worked as an alchemist, a coroner, and even clairvoyant hypnotist. Today, I was the world's top leading specialist in synthesizing antivenin. While the marine specimens I sampled venom from were in my mind, harmless, that didn't mean that humans were immune to their toxins. I'd seen what one toxic fae being could do to the sea. Over three thousand years ago, I'd witnessed how a simple imbalance in the Abyss could wipe out an entire salt ancestry.

My salt ancestry of Celaeno, the *Dark One*.

My personal research, however, dove into the realm of the afterlife and reincarnation cycles of three separate species. I studied the life cycles of sea nymphs like myself, storm dragons, and their god-like ancestors, the great architects—one of whom still existed today.

He and I were once bonded together. Now, he was an ex of sorts, Someone I relied on goddesses like Hecate to keep away. But recently, I'd felt the prickle of his gaze upon me from the shadows he embodied.

I felt at times that he was watching me.

All the more reason to dive into my research and maintain a healthy distance from him.

I grabbed a petri dish from the microscope I'd been fiddling with all morning. The lens was blurry, and no matter how much I tried to adjust it, I couldn't get it to focus.

Finally, the sharp edges of the dark crystals I'd sampled earlier that morning in the Mediterranean Sea came to light. They shimmered like little stars, ones I had memories of finding in the Nile.

"Celaeno's ancestral salts," I stammered, pulling way. "Why are they *resurfacing*?"

I glanced up at the clock, and that shadow I'd seen drifting in the corner of my lab disappeared, for now.

Panic struck my body. It was only a matter of time before the god of shadows attempted to resurrect his bond with me.

AUTHOR'S NOTE

You, amazing reader, have made it this far. You've met the end of my first fantasy series, books that forced my neurospicy brain wide open and helped me to explore the world of urban fantasy in a way I had not imagined when I first started writing it.

Writing, like the sea, is vastly different once you dive in. It is not the same as it appears once you plunge beneath the surface. I've learned to push myself, and when to pull back. The art of when to keep going and when to slow down will forever be a delicate balancing act.

As I wrote the Ocean Apothecary series, another spin-off series bloomed alongside it, and I knew that Selia, Damien, and Amy's stories would help me set the stage for the historical worldbuilding that dates back to Atlantis. While this series door might close, another has opened.

I started writing Naunet's stories prior to Selia's. And I knew they were too dark for me yet to explore. Hence, Selia's heartfelt character emerged, along with the sweet romance between herself and a quirky Scottish watercolor artist. This is the beginning of something very big. I'm so glad you have come this far with me.

I've learned so much about myself through these characters. Their voices living in my head for years. The concept I wanted to explore stemmed from my background in ecology, where observing relationships between living and non-living things always creates a story. My question was simple: what would happen if a keystone species (like blue minca) disappeared from the sea? What if minca's absence threw off some invisible balance within an ecosystem humans were not aware of? And what would happen if fae, dragons, and sea nymphs were involved? How would it impact their ability to reproduce, and therefore, survive?

How could they restore that balance without compromising their own means of survival?

Being that the earth is a living, breathing, changing entity, our work protecting and exploring her is never quite done. So I'm leaving this message of hope at the end, hope that my readers will continue to explore the characters after this series has ended, as their stories continue on.

I hope these books give you hope for reconnecting with our pasts. Hope of finding lost loved ones. To discover and reconnect with places in ourselves we've forgotten.

This is the end. Or is it? *Henrietta scuttles away and dives into the sea*

With much love,
Amanda

ACKNOWLEDGEMENTS

Writing is not only a self journey. The written word is a work of art that pieces together thousands of little interactions, combining layers of self-doubt and dreaming. My hope is that the result is something my readers will enjoy and connect with.

I could not have created this book without the help of many others. I wanted to acknowledge a few prominent influences in my life that continue to encourage me on this writing journey.

My mom and brother who have always supported my random creative endeavors, whether it be panting, drawing, or writing.

My father who is no longer with us, but still encourages me to write in spirit.

My husband Bill, for supporting me on this journey and for making me laugh with your feedback on my first drafts.

My critique group, who has put up with my stories for the past seven years. Carly, Debbie, and Ed, you've helped me to craft my character's voices as well as find my own author voice.

My alpha and beta readers and street team. Your early feedback makes writing that much more enjoyable.

My editor, Sarah, for helping me see the underlying story I'm trying to share.

My readers, because you are what brings the written word to life.

My taiko group, Sun Mountain Taiko, for drumming with me and driving the rhythm behind my stories.

My local library, where I work in the family and children's department. To my fellow library staff who provide energy and enthusiasm for reading, art, and the community. Your energy is contagious!

The park where I work, providing me with the opportunity to connect others with nature. I'm so blessed to have the Colorado outdoors in my backyard.

STAY IN TOUCH

Visit Amanda's website at www.amandacaseybooks.com to follow along with her writing adventures and become the first to know when she will release her next book!